On autopilot, Vicki reached up to grasp the necklace that had become her touchstone.

When her fingertips found an empty spot on her chest, she felt the empty spot in her heart. She had to find the necklace. It was the last gift Alison had given her.

She approached the counter. "I'm Ms. Hanson, Bell Hanson's mom. I was told I needed to fill out paperwork, but I could swear that I—"

"Yes. Have a seat and someone will be right with you."

Vicki took a chair and told herself it was nothing. *You are safe now.*

The office noise buzzed around her. Needing a distraction, to relax, she looked at the latest breaking news on her phone. But there was no relaxing. Not when two uniformed cops walked in.

She held her breath as the officers moved to the counter. *It's nothing. It's nothing. It's nothing.*

The woman at the front desk got up to greet them. They spoke in hushed voices, then the receptionist looked up and motioned at Vicki.

The officers started toward her. She didn't move, just sat frozen, her heart hitting against her breastbone. A voice inside her screamed, *Run!*

PRAISE FOR
CHRISTIE CRAIG

DON'T BREATHE A WORD

"Craig delivers a top-notch, breakneck romantic thriller."
—Lori Wilde, *New York Times* bestselling author

"Didn't want to put it down. DON'T BREATHE A WORD is a roller coaster ride with riveting suspense, relentless emotion, and characters that will steal your heart."
—Darynda Jones, *New York Times* bestselling author

"Christie Craig is an auto-buy author for me and I loved DON'T BREATHE A WORD. It was twisty and gritty and real and made time fly!"
—Joss Wood, award-winning author

DON'T CLOSE YOUR EYES

"Craig delivers pulse-pounding suspense."
—Lori Wilde, *New York Times* bestselling author

"Romantic suspense fans will mark this as a series to watch." —*Publishers Weekly*

"Nonstop suspense. Craig grabs you and never lets go."
—Kathleen Brooks,
New York Times bestselling author

TEXAS HOLD 'EM

"Fans of fast-paced thrillers and Craig's other books will feel at home."
—*Publishers Weekly*

BLAME IT ON TEXAS

"Complete with genuine characters that have heart, this story will keep you laughing as you turn the pages. A truly fun read!"
—*RT Book Reviews*

"An excellent contemporary romance that will make you swoon!"
—Fresh Fiction

ONLY IN TEXAS

"An entertaining tale with delightful, fully formed characters and an intriguing mystery, along with a nod to dog lovers with a likable pooch."
—*RT Book Reviews*

"A fabulously great read!"
—Night Owl Reviews

ALSO BY CHRISTIE CRAIG

TEXAS JUSTICE SERIES
Don't Close Your Eyes

HOTTER IN TEXAS SERIES
Only in Texas
Blame It on Texas
Texas Hold 'Em

DON'T BREATHE A WORD

A WORD

A Texas Justice Novel

CHRISTIE CRAIG

FOREVER
New York Boston

Copyright © 2019 by Christie Craig
Cover design by Jerry Todd
Cover images by Arcangel
Cover copyright © 2019 by Hachette Book Group, Inc.
Hot Target copyright © 2018 by April Schwartz

Forever
Hachette Book Group
1290 Avenue of the Americas, New York, NY 10104
read-forever.com
twitter.com/readforeverpub

First Edition: November 2019

Forever is an imprint of Grand Central Publishing. The Forever name and logo are trademarks of Hachette Book Group, Inc.

The publisher is not responsible for websites (or their content) that are not owned by the publisher.

The Hachette Speakers Bureau provides a wide range of authors for speaking events. To find out more, go to www.hachettespeakersbureau.com or call (866) 376-6591.

ISBN: 978-1-5387-1162-0 (mass market), 978-1-5387-1164-4 (ebook)

Printed in the United States of America

OPM

10 9 8 7 6 5 4 3 2 1

To women everywhere who struggle to find a sense of self, to find the strength to stand up to those who try to push them down

Women are like tea bags. You never know how strong they are until you put them in hot water.

—Often attributed to
Eleanor Roosevelt

PROLOGUE

Juan held the camera and filmed his wife as she spoke. Angie had come up with this idea of making videos for their unborn daughter so that when she grew up she would know how wanted and loved she was at the start.

"I love you, baby girl, and I love your daddy." Angie spoke to the camera. "This is me and you before you were born. See?" She pulled up her shirt and showed the basketball-sized bump from her seven months of pregnancy. She grinned up at him. Her love for their baby was so bright that sometimes it hurt to look at her. "We're so happy to be having you."

Juan stared at his wife of two years. Love shone from her blue eyes, and a smile of pure happiness added a glow to her expression. A halo of blond hair rested on her shoulders. She was indeed an angel. His angel.

He wasn't sure what he'd done to deserve her, but if

fate ever realized it'd screwed up and tried to take her back, he was prepared to fight. And fight dirty. He was keeping her. She made the bad things in his past feel small. She made the bad things he saw every day feel less horrible.

She waved him forward. "Now put the camera on the stand and come be in the video."

"I'll ruin it."

She made her cute face and gave him a come-here wiggle with her index finger. "Don't be shy."

He did as she said, because telling her no was impossible.

She wrapped her arm around his waist. "This is your daddy. Juan, say something to your daughter." She playfully bumped him with her hip.

"I'm camera shy," he said, but it was a lie. The truth? This whole parenting thing made him nervous. It wasn't that he didn't love the idea of having a child. It just didn't feel real. Sure, he'd placed his hand on his wife's middle and felt the baby move, he'd seen the fuzzy sonogram video that showed the child was a girl, but it still didn't feel . . . true.

And that worried the hell out of him, too. He saw what Angie felt for their unborn baby. As hard as he tried, he couldn't tap into those emotions.

Ricky, his older brother and a father of two, assured him it'd change when he held his daughter in his arms. He hoped like hell Ricky was right. He hoped losing his parents the way he had hadn't somehow damaged him and prevented him from being the kind of dad a kid deserved.

"Juan." She touched his arm. "Say something."

"Okay." Pause. "I think you're going to be the luck-iest little girl in the world. Your mama makes everyone she loves feel special, like they have everything they'll ever need. She's smart and so beautiful. And I'm sure you'll grow up to be just like her."

"Right," Angie said. "Like you aren't easy on the eyes." Angie looked into the camera. "Your dad's friends call him Pretty Boy. He even did TV commercials while he was going through school."

"Don't tell her that." He'd only done it to pay tuition.

Angie laughed. "But I don't love him just because he's a hottie. The day I met him he was getting a kitten off the roof of my apartment building for an elderly neighbor. He was kind to the kitten. He was kind to the neighbor, who was being a pain in the butt. And as a cop, he still helps people every day. It's why I fell in love with him then, and why I love him even more now."

Juan leaned down and kissed her.

The kiss lingered. "Okay." Angie pulled back. "Let's cut off the video."

"And then what?" He waggled his brows.

She stopped taping, pushed a few buttons to send the video to the cloud, then shot him a sexy smile. "If you get the tools and put the crib together, you might get lucky."

"You want to tape that, too?" he teased.

She swatted his ass.

He laughed and went to the garage to get his tools. Their new puppy, Sweetie, followed him out.

He'd just found the wrench when his phone rang.

Anonymous number, it read. He still took the call. "Yeah?"

"You didn't think you'd get away with it, did you?"

The voice, Guzman's voice, yanked the joy right out of his chest. How had the gang leader gotten this number? It could mean only one thing: his cover was blown.

He'd taken one step toward the door, toward Angie, toward everything that mattered in his life, when a massive blast blew him back. The wall of the garage imploded, throwing him over his car.

"Angie? Angie? Angie." Her name fell from his lips like a litany. For one second, he could swear he heard her call his name. Felt her sweet touch to his face. He got to his feet. The taste of his blood thickened his tongue. His ears rang.

Disoriented, he fought his way out of the collapsed garage. Pieces of his roof were scattered over the lawn. Fire claimed what was left of his house.

"Angie!" he screamed, and ran inside.

CHAPTER ONE

Three years later

I love you, baby girl, and I love your daddy."

Sweetie's barks woke Juan up. He must've fallen asleep watching the video again...Crawling out of the recliner, he gave the television screen and everything he'd lost another glance. He walked to the back door. All seven pounds of the dog stood in attack mode.

"What? A firefly up to no good?"

Sweetie growled.

"Fine, go save the world." He opened the door. The white toy poodle, in desperate need of a haircut, raced out. He should take better care of her. Angie would've. Hell, if Angie were alive, the dog would have painted nails and pink bows.

She'd have done the same for their daughter. If they hadn't died.

Leaving the door open, he turned to reclaim his recliner, but Sweetie's growl had him retracing his steps. Thick summer heat brushed over his bare chest. Moving under the covered patio, he focused on Sweetie. Front paws on the wooden fence, she barked as if something, or someone, was behind it.

He started to call her, but swallowed the words when a figure lunged up and over the fence. Not landing in his backyard, but in his neighbor's. The house had been vacant until a couple of weeks ago. Yesterday, he'd heard a kid talking to Sweetie through the fence.

In full cop mode, he ran back through the door, grabbed his gun, and hauled ass outside again.

He bolted over the fence, his bare feet landing in his neighbor's yard with a thud. Blinking to adjust to the darkness, he saw someone at the back door as if trying to break in.

"Anniston PD." Juan's dead-serious tone echoed in the night, joined by Sweetie's barking. "Don't move. Hands over your head. Now!"

The guy, measuring over six feet, turned. Light-colored eyes stared through a ski mask.

Holding his gun in a firm grip, Juan moved in. "On the ground. Do it!"

The man's hands shot high, and he started to get down on one knee. But before his second knee hit the concrete patio, the asswipe grabbed hold of a rusty three-legged charcoal grill and flung it.

The metal slammed against Juan's head. Burnt coals and ash that smelled like dead hamburgers rained down on him. The smell he could handle, the gritty blindness not so much.

Blinking, trying to rid the black dust from his eyes, he saw the perp haul himself over the side fence. Partially blind, pissed, and maybe stupid, he stuck his gun in his pants and gave chase.

He had one leg over the wooden slats when something—no, someone—yanked him back. He landed hard on his ass.

Two perps? How had he missed that?

He rolled once and stood. A kick to his right eye socket took him down again. He gazed up, but could make out only a blurred figure looming over him. A figure holding a baseball bat.

Juan reached for his gun, but saw the bat swing. He caught it, yanked it from his assailant, threw the weapon away, then continued for his Glock but was flattened by a kick to his gut. Pain spasmed through his stomach. Charcoal-flavored ash caught in his throat. Unable to breathe, he watched as his gun was pulled from the waistband of his jeans.

Since he'd lost Angie and his daughter, dying had been one of the multiple-choice options on his what's-next test, but the idea of being taken out by some lowlife home invader, and with his own gun, put a fire back in his belly.

He grabbed an arm. The perp struggled. The gun dropped. Juan, giving everything he had, tossed the asshole off of him. The perp was small. Light. Shit. Was this a kid? When the guy hit the ground, a moan filled the dark air.

Fighting the urge to rub his eyes, Juan lunged to his feet to find his gun. A big mistake. A kick slammed into his ribs, stealing his breath.

Still standing, he body-slammed the guy, landing on top of him.

Then *bam*, Juan had to retract that thought. No, not a guy. A woman.

"Stop!" he spit out. "I'm police."

Her squirming stopped. He shot up on his knees. She scooted a foot away from him.

"That's good." His words came out breathless. "Just calm down."

Forced air filled his lungs. She shifted, and before he could stop it, her right foot slammed into his nuts. "Damn! Shit!"

She stood, then quickly dropped down on all fours and ran her hands over the ground—no doubt looking for his gun.

He tried to stand, but he puked instead. Okay, so maybe he was about to join Angie after all.

He fell back on his butt, blinked, and spit out the bitter taste of charcoal. The woman, a few feet from him, stood, a gun—*his gun*—aimed right at him. A splash of silver moon shifted from behind a cloud, and his vision cleared a bit. She wore a nightshirt. White with black script that read ANGEL AT REST.

He'd hate to see her when she wasn't at rest. What was she doing wearing pajamas to break into…Crap. She wasn't the perp. She was his neighbor. She must've thought *he* was the burglar.

The taste of blood brought on another realization.

He'd just gotten his ass kicked by a resting angel who, standing on her tiptoes, didn't reach his shoulders.

He held his hands up. "I'm police."

"I don't care if you're the pope."

"So you don't trust the pope or the police?"

"Not if they're breaking into my house."

"I wasn't...The guy who tried to break in jumped the fence. I came to help you. I live next door."

"Then why did you attack me?" Her tone came armed with snark.

"Whoa. You attacked me." His throbbing balls were all the proof he needed.

"What's on your face? Why did you run?"

"I didn't...I wasn't. I was chasing the guy breaking into your back door." He ran a hand over his face, flinching when he touched his swollen eye. "And I'm covered in ash from that grill that the asswipe slung at me."

"Riiight." Her grip tightened on the gun. "You think I don't know why you're here?"

"Obviously, you don't. I'm your neighbor, and I work for APD. You don't want to shoot me. Call the police—"

"I already have."

"Good." Then he flinched at the thought of his police buddies seeing him beaten up by a tiny angel.

"Move and I swear I'll shoot you."

A wave of nausea hit. He pushed it back. "I'm not moving. But I'd appreciate it if you'd take your finger off the trigger. It doesn't take much pressure to—"

"You think I don't know how to use this?"

"Okay. You're right. I've underestimated you already. But I don't deserve to be shot."

"Then shut up and don't move."

"I'm not." But it became a lie when his throbbing balls insisted he readjust his crotch.

"You're moving!"

"My balls hurt, okay?" he growled.

Neither of them said another word for several minutes. The only noise in the night was Sweetie whimpering on the other side of the fence. "Where did you learn to fight like that?" Was she an officer herself? Ex-military?

The scratchy sound of her back door opening had her bunching up the nightshirt to hide the gun. As the material rose, his still-watery gaze got a nice view of her outer thigh.

"Au— Mom?" a young voice called.

"Go back inside." The woman looked away from him. "I'll be there in a minute."

Juan considered pouncing to retrieve his weapon, but the child spoke again.

"What are y-you doing?" The fear in the voice gut-punched him.

"Go inside, honey. Now!" Her voice grew stern. Sweetie's bark echoed again. The door closed.

"I'm really the police." Juan softened his voice. "Go inside and check on her."

"Not happening." Sirens and tires screeching sounded in the dark.

"Let them know we're back here before they break the door down and scare your kid," he snapped.

"Get up!" She motioned with his gun. "Walk to the side gate. Now!"

He got to his feet, his balls pulsing with pain. His eyes stung. "Put the gun down or they'll shoot us both."

He moved forward, pushed the gate open. "All's clear," Juan yelled. "APD, Detective Acosta here. All clear!"

Two officers rushed around the corner. Juan recognized Billy Johnston, a fellow poker player, followed by Officer Smith.

Billy yelled out, "Gun!"

Shit. The little ballbuster hadn't listened to his advice.

"Drop the weapon," Smith ordered.

Freaking great. Juan might die tonight after all. "Don't shoot!" Juan yelled. "She thinks I'm the bad guy."

One hand held out to the cops, he scowled at her over his shoulder. "Drop the gun before you get us killed!"

She did, but cut him a look that was equally lethal. Billy and Smith rushed forward. Juan moved in front of his neighbor, stopping them from taking her down. "It's okay. It was a misunderstanding."

He looked back at her. "Go see about your daughter."

Smith stepped in front of her.

"Let her go," Juan said. "She's got a scared kid inside."

Smith backed off, but followed her into the house.

After explaining about seeing the man jump over the fence and getting attacked by his neighbor, then being ribbed by Billy, Juan went inside his neighbor's house.

While his fellow officers stood, he pulled out a kitchen chair. The house was almost like his. His neighbor, a frown on her lips and fear in her eyes, stepped out of the bedroom. Oddly, she appeared more concerned now than when she'd been held at gunpoint.

As she spoke with Smith, Juan studied her. Jeans and a pink T-shirt now hugged her petite, well-toned body. Dark auburn hair framed her pretty face.

Smith's six-foot-four frame could be intimidating, but she faced the officer with a kind of bravado hard not to admire. "As you know, all of this was a misunderstanding."

"Your name, ma'am?" Smith asked, holding a clipboard.

"Nikki Hanson. It's late, so if we could just call it a night…"

"Ma'am, you called us. And we have to make a report."

Juan ran a hand over his sore lip. It was clear his neighbor wanted them gone. But was it the late hour, or something more?

Her gaze met his. She flinched, walked into the adjoining kitchen, and grabbed a damp towel.

"Your head's bleeding." She stepped back. As he pressed the towel to his wound, he noticed she had blood on her elbow, but before he could point it out, she turned back to Smith. "Do I need to sign something?"

"Yes. But I have some questions first. Can you tell me exactly what happened?"

"I heard a noise. I called 911 and ran outside. When I did, I saw"—she looked toward Juan—"him, and—"

Her eyes widened. He knew why, too. With some of the charcoal wiped away, she'd gotten her first look at his face. At his scar. "And I thought he was breaking in." She glanced away, a hint of embarrassment spotting her cheeks. He was used to the reaction. From women especially. Oh, the irony. He'd once been dubbed Pretty Boy, and now women couldn't look at him. "And we fought and then you got here."

Was he grateful she'd left out the part where she'd kicked him in the balls? Hell, it didn't matter. It would've been nice if she'd believed he was police, but he couldn't blame her. Not when he was barefoot, shirtless, and badgeless.

"I see." Smith scribbled down information. "Is there anyone you know who would've tried to break in? An ex-husband? Boyfriend?"

He wasn't sure if anyone else noticed, but her lips tightened. Her eyes flinched. She blinked. Once. Twice. Three times. "No. I'm new in town. Just moved from Colorado."

You think I don't know why you're here? Her words played in his head. "What about someone from outside of town?" he asked.

She faced him. "No."

She didn't flinch that time, not from the sight of his scar or from a possible lie. He still didn't believe her.

"Mama?" The young voice echoed from down the hall.

Conversation stopped. The little girl, wearing a pink nightgown, entered the room. She was four, maybe five, with dark brown hair, brown eyes, and light olive skin. He winced. She looked . . . she looked how he expected his daughter would've looked. His next breath swelled in his chest.

"I'll be right there." Nikki faced Smith and Billy again. "I'm sorry to rush, but my daughter has her first day of school tomorrow. And she's not going back to sleep until you're gone."

Frowning, Smith looked over his papers. "Right."

Juan stood. He offered a quick nod to Nikki as he walked out.

Billy and Smith followed.

The second they cleared the door, Billy grinned. "I can't believe you got beat up by a girl."

"Stop."

Billy coughed to disguise a laugh, then asked, "Do you need stitches?"

"No. It's just a scratch."

"That's a lot of blood for a scratch."

"Head wounds bleed a lot."

Billy frowned back at the neighbor's front door. "Did she seem skittish to you? Almost as if she didn't want us here."

So I'm not the only one thinking something is off. "She's probably worried about the kid." His own words of defense surprised him.

On the way to the car, Smith stopped to take a call. He spoke for a few seconds, then turned around. "Officer Lewis caught a guy in Glenloch subdivision breaking into a house. He had a ski mask on. We're pretty sure it's the same perp. Lewis knows him. Says he's homeless. Usually only breaks into empty houses. We'll need you to ID him to make sure he's our man."

"Yeah, she only just moved in, so he probably thought this place was still empty, too." Juan looked at his neighbor's house. "You going to tell her you got the guy?"

"Why don't you? I gotta assist Lewis with this arrest. I think she liked you better anyway."

Juan frowned.

"I'll swing by when we head back to the station and let you ID him," Smith said.

Juan watched him and Billy drive off before walking back to his neighbor's porch and pushing the doorbell.

He heard Nikki on the other side of the door, and said, "It's Juan. Detective Acosta."

"Yeah?" Her voice lacked the earlier edge. She opened the door.

He met her eyes... brown, or were they?... "I wanted to let you know that they caught the intruder. He was breaking into an empty house a few miles down the road."

Her shoulders dropped and a soft breath sounded on her lips. "Are you sure it's him?"

Her tone, filled with both relief and disbelief, notched up his suspicion. "Who did you think it was?" he asked.

"No one."

"You said something about knowing why I was here."

"I... I was scared, and when I'm scared I ramble."

"Look, Nikki, if you're worried about—"

"I'm not." Her answer came quick and with a sharp edge. Not very convincing.

"The guy the cops caught was trying to break into an

empty home and was wearing a ski mask, just like the guy I saw here. I thought you'd want to know."

She cupped her hands together. "Thank you."

The gratitude sounded sincere. He stood there until he realized he didn't have anything else to say. While still suspicious, he offered her a nod in lieu of goodbye, then turned to go.

"I'm sorry." Her soft-spoken apology had him turning back around and burying his hands in his pockets.

Their eyes met. "Me too." He motioned to her arm. "For your elbow. You should probably wash it."

She stared at her arm as if she hadn't known she'd been hurt.

"I will." Their eyes met again. She closed the door while he stood there.

What was his neighbor hiding?

And who was she hiding from?

CHAPTER TWO

Her head was swimming after dodging all of the cops' questions. Her neighbor had asked if she was worried.

Worried? No, she was petrified. But she had to fake it. Her whole life was about faking it. Most of her résumé was fake. She'd never lived in Colorado. Even her name was fake. Her real name was Vicki. At least "Nikki" was close enough to avoid too many slip-ups. But the biggest lie of all? She was faking being Bell's mom.

"Why were the police here?" Bell asked.

Vicki pulled the sheet up to Bell's chest, forcing a smile. Not that she didn't feel a hell of a lot better knowing the man trying to break in was a common criminal.

"I told you. The neighbor lost his dog and was

looking for it in our backyard. I thought he was a bad man and called the cops. I didn't know he was the police." It was a lie, but the truth would only scare her niece. And she'd been scared for way too long.

"You don't like police," Bell said.

Vicki flinched. She'd never said that, but her niece was way too smart. "Not all police are bad, sweetheart. Look, it's late. And you have school."

"I don't want to go."

"It's going to be great. You'll make new friends. You can wear your new pink tennis shoes and your new princess shirt." Her words felt as hollow as her chest.

A watery sheen filled Bell's big brown eyes. "I want to stay home with you."

"It's only one day, and we'll have the weekend." Because of a busted water pipe in the school, the first day of school had been delayed. Thankfully, her job didn't start until tomorrow.

Bell reached up. Her small hand gripped Vicki's fingers.

"I want to go back to Arizona."

Staying in Phoenix hadn't been an option. Not after seeing the same car parked in front of their house two nights in a row. Vicki hadn't seen the face of the man sitting in the vehicle, but she hadn't needed to see it to be afraid. Especially when the manager of Bell's daycare said a Los Angeles police officer had come in with a photo of a younger girl who looked like Bell and asked if they'd seen a missing child.

"You can't stay home, and I have to work." She'd

been lucky to get a job. Luckier that it was at a gym and she'd be working in the field she was trained in. She'd made a terrible waitress.

She kissed Bell's tiny palm. "I hate first days, too. How about we be brave? I'll do my first day at my job, and you'll do your first day at school, and afterwards we'll go out for ice cream."

"What if I forget my name?" Her bottom lip trembled, and Vicki's breath caught in her chest. Teaching a five-year-old to lie was sure to send Vicki straight to hell. But she'd make it her permanent address and sign over her soul to the landlord to protect Bell.

Vicki brushed a strand of Bell's dark hair off her cheek. "You won't forget because we've practiced it a trillion times. What's your name?"

"Bell Hanson." They'd chosen Bell because her real first name was Belinda and because she loved Belle in the movie *Beauty and the Beast*.

"And who am I?" Vicki asked.

"My mama. Nikki Hanson."

"See?" Vicki said, sounding confident, yet feeling none of it.

But she'd do this. Out of love. Out of guilt.

She pressed a gentle kiss to Bell's forehead. "Love you."

Bell offered a teary, sleepy nod. "Can you read to me?"

"Sure." Vicki pulled a Dr. Seuss book from the shelf.

"No," Bell said. "*Charlotte's Web*. Read the next to the last chapter."

Vicki's chest felt like a sponge, soaking up Bell's grief only to add to her own. The professional advice she'd found online was to gently encourage a child to move away from the subject of death, but to never push, because it might help them cope. "We've read that book. Let's read a different one?"

"No, I want to hear about Charlotte dying."

Relenting, Vicki opened up to the requested chapter and started to read.

She finally recited the last line of the chapter. "'No one was with Charlotte when she died.'"

She swallowed to keep her words from shaking, but she couldn't stop her heart from breaking. Aching for a black spider who'd lost her life, aching for a little girl who missed her mom. Aching because no matter what she'd read in self-help books, Vicki felt inadequate to help Bell.

She didn't know how to be a mother. Not like her sister, Alison, had.

She and Alison used to joke that God had forgotten to give Vicki the maternal gene. She'd wanted to focus on her career, on being a personal trainer to California's rich and famous. She'd wanted time to run marathons, train for her second Ironman competition. And, maybe, she just didn't know how to be a mother because their own mom had failed so miserably.

And yet, here she was in Anniston, Texas, trying to do right by her niece. For Bell, she'd walked away from everything. Her life in L.A. Her career. Dan Jefferies. Her first and only real relationship.

Bell shifted under the sheet. Her nightgown slipped off her shoulder. Vicki lifted the soft cotton over the cigar-sized scars and remembered her neighbor's face.

"Do you think Mama and Charlotte are together?" Bell asked in a drowsy voice.

"Uh-huh." Swallowing the lump of grief, Vicki reminded herself that the articles said Bell's obsession with death was normal. But nothing about this felt normal. Not Bell's fixation on death. Not the hit-and-run accident that left Alison to die alone on the side of the road. And especially not running and hiding from a man who was supposed to be dead.

* * *

The knock on Juan's door came ten minutes after he'd gone into the house. Officer Smith had the suspect in the car. Same dark clothes. Same body shape. When the cop pulled out the ski mask, navy blue with orange rings around the eyes and mouth, Juan confirmed it was the same guy who'd been trying to break into his neighbor's house.

Juan watched the patrol car drive off, and then his gaze shifted next door. *Nikki Hanson, what kind of trouble are you in?*

Not that she couldn't handle trouble. She'd handled him just fine. He passed a hand over his sore ribs.

Moving back inside, he looked at his recliner and the television waiting to replay the DVD.

He should go to bed. But he felt too keyed up to sleep.

He looked at his laptop and the file folder on the table beside his chair. He'd told Mark and Connor, the other two officers working with him in the Cold

Case Unit, that he'd do Internet searches into the missing person case they'd started yesterday.

He hadn't. Lately, work no longer gave him the sense of accomplishment it once had. Was it his upcoming anniversary? Was the grief always going to keep bearing down on him?

He picked up the folder and flipped it open. He'd chosen the Noel case himself after he realized it had loose ties to Guzman's gang, the one responsible for killing his wife and daughter. He'd thought stirring up those demons might give him a sense of purpose.

It wasn't working.

Sweetie ran to the back door, yapping in the same warning tone as she had earlier.

"Seriously?" he asked her.

He went to the window and pulled the curtain aside.

Between the fence slats he spotted a globe of light, a flashlight, shifting in his neighbor's backyard. Was he wrong about the perp he'd identified?

He grabbed his gun and badge, and he and his bruised ribs went back outside. The moon hung low, but the light got swallowed up by the inky darkness.

Moving silently to the fence, he peered through. His adrenaline notched down when he saw Nikki, flashlight in hand, walking in tight circles.

Gone were the jeans. She wore another nightshirt. Not the angel one. This one was black, shorter. Clingy. The material hugged her hourglass curves.

"It's got to be here." Her whispered words flowed over the fence.

"You looking for something?"

She yelped, swung around, and glared at the fence. "What are you doing?" Accusation hung in the hot air.

"I . . ." Why did he suddenly feel like a pervert? "I saw the flashlight and wanted to check on you."

"Checking on me isn't your job."

Her allegation stung.

"You're right." He swung around. He shouldn't be checking on her or checking her out. And that's what he'd been doing.

He only got one step in before she spoke again. "Sorry. You scared me."

He hesitated but didn't turn around.

"I lost my necklace."

The softness of her voice brought him back to the fence. He inched in and heard her catch her breath the moment her gaze met his between the slats. Her scent, a soft feminine aroma, filled his air.

He tried to look away but couldn't. He didn't know if he felt trapped or tempted. Or both.

His gaze lowered to her mouth. Full, lush, curvy to match her body.

Definitely both.

"I must have lost it when . . . when we struggled."

Lured closer, he leaned in. "You want some help looking for it?"

He had no fucking idea why he made the offer. Then he did. He knew exactly why he'd done it. And that was wrong. It'd only been three years. Three years of not wanting, not needing to be with a woman. Didn't Angie deserve more time?

"No." She backed up fast, nearly tripped, as if, like him, she'd felt the need to rewind what'd just happened between them.

"I'll find it tomorrow." She took off.

Relief spread through him. He wasn't ready.

"Night." He watched her reach down and pick up a baseball bat. No doubt her weapon of choice.

He scooped up Sweetie, went inside, and reclaimed his recliner. *You think I don't know why you're here?*

Putting his dog on the floor, he grabbed his computer and Googled the name Nikki Hanson.

* * *

"What the hell are you doing here? My family's here. Damn it!"

"Calm down," Pablo Valado said. With a gallon jug in one hand and a Glock in the other, he continued to pour himself a glass of milk from Detective Sam Milbourn's fridge. "Sam, Sam, Sam. If you'd answered my call yesterday, I wouldn't have to be here, drinking your milk. Oh, and you really need to get a better alarm system."

Sam, Pablo's onetime partner, looked over his shoulder toward the hall as if he was afraid his wife or daughter might walk out. And he should be afraid. Seeing a dead man would scare them.

"What the fuck?" Sam hissed.

"That's what I'm asking you." He lifted the glass of milk, downed a long gulp, then wiped his mouth with the back of his forearm. "You had her in Phoenix, and you let her get away. I've been patient. It's been two weeks and you haven't given me shit."

"I can't help it if she disappeared."

"Yes, you can." He spoke in a soft voice, but he knew Sam heard his outrage. He tapped the barrel of the gun against the glass, the sharp cracking sound echoing in the dark kitchen. "I want that bitch found."

"Why? You don't even care about your daughter. Why can't you just let her go?"

"She's fucking got more than my daughter."

Sam shook his head. "If she had your money, she wouldn't have been working as a damn waitress."

"Alison was the only one who knew I hid things at the cabin. Besides, it wasn't just the money. She took his book with the information. It had everything. Rex's contacts to buyers and sellers all across the states. Going out on his own was going to be twice as hard if he didn't have that.

"Then maybe Alison took it, but she didn't tell her sister. If Vicki had proof you were dirty, she'd already—"

"You're an idiot. Proving me dirty doesn't do her a bit of good because they think I'm dead."

"But again, why isn't she using the money?"

"I don't fucking know. When I have my hand around her throat, I'll ask her!" He clanked the gun to the glass again. "You're going to find her. Screw it up again, and I'll screw you."

Sam squared off. "What good would killing me do?"

"I never said I'd kill you, Sam. I said I'd screw you. Not literally. You aren't my type. But what would your wife think if I sent her the video of you and that whore you met once a week for seven months? Or what would the sergeant think if he knew what really happened to the drugs in the Holt case?"

Sam closed his hand into a fist. "You were lead on that case, not me."

"But you sure as hell took the fifty thousand to look the other way. Besides, it's not my ass on the line. I'm dead, remember? And it's all her fault. If Vicki hadn't talked Alison into leaving me, she wouldn't have taken my money. I wouldn't have had to kill her. Then I wouldn't have had to fake my own fucking death." Not that they could've proved he did it. He'd been careful. But when it was all said and done, he'd realized he hadn't thought it through. If a DA started digging into his past, they could easily unearth stuff, even a few bodies, that he needed to keep hidden.

Sam scraped a hand through his thinning brown hair. A nervous habit. As he glanced again at the hall that led to where his wife and kid slept, Pablo saw fear flash in his light green eyes. Good. Scared people worked harder.

"She must've changed her name again and left Phoenix." Sam's words came out too fast.

"Have you even put out a BOLO with her picture saying she's wanted for kidnapping?"

"I can't list it as a kidnapping. I've posted that she was involved with a missing child in a guardianship battle. Which is a civil case, not—"

"What about Dan Jefferies? The boyfriend. And the Willis woman who worked for her?"

"I haven't spoken with Marisol Willis yet. I talked to Dan again. He swears he hasn't heard anything. I believe him."

Pablo stood. "He swears? And you just believe him? What did you do, ask him nicely?"

"I told him there was a guardianship case. And if we found out he knew something, we—"

"We'd what? Scold him? When the hell did you go soft?"

"I'm not…I'm risking my job by even looking for them. Your sister didn't file for guardianship until after Vicki left town. If that gets out, I'm out of a job."

"You've got a lot more to lose than a job. Give me everything you got on Dan and the Willis woman. I'll go see them."

"You can't—"

"I can and I will. Your job is to find Vicki. And find out who's helping her. Someone has to be. Getting a new identity isn't something just anyone knows how to do."

"Yeah, it's my job. Why don't you leave town? I'll let you know the moment I have something."

"Oh, you'd like that, wouldn't you?" In truth, Pablo would like nothing more than to get the hell out of Los Angeles. But he couldn't do that without his money. And just getting by now was fucking hard. Rex, the man he'd worked for the last six years, barely called Pablo for jobs.

Sam glared. "I looked the other way when you stole money. I helped you disappear. But I didn't offer to do your dirty work afterwards."

"You'll do whatever the hell I ask you to do, and don't try to fuck with me, Sam. Think of your wife. Your kid. Because I'm dead, no one will suspect me. And considering you helped me become dead, you can't say a damn thing."

* * *

At six a.m., Juan poured himself a second cup of coffee. Standing over the sink, he looked out his kitchen window and into Nikki Hanson's kitchen window.

Lack of sleep wasn't going to help his normal pissy mood, especially considering today was his mandatory monthly shrink visit.

Yeah, he should've remembered that before he stayed up until almost four researching his new neighbor. Actually, it wasn't the research. It was the rehashing and reliving the all-too-brief moment on top of her, when their bodies lined up in all the right places.

The actual research took all of ten minutes. He ran her through the DMV. She'd received a new Texas driver's license after she'd surrendered her Colorado license. He knew she was twenty-nine, and was born October 20. Her middle name was Virginia. And she was an organ donor.

But it was what he didn't find that made him suspicious as hell. No Facebook page. No Twitter. No Instagram. No Snapchat. No Pinterest. She didn't have any social media.

That bothered him. *She* bothered him. The niggling suspicion that she'd lied about who might've been breaking into her house bothered him. But mostly, his reaction to her bothered him.

He stared out his window and into hers. Just as he took a sip of coffee, she appeared, and he ducked, not wanting to get caught staring. Sweetie's gotta-pee whimper had him moving to the back door to let her out. Then, to avoid the temptation of staring into her kitchen window more, he sprawled out in his backyard lawn chair. Yapping, Sweetie bolted to the fence.

"Come here, Sweetie," a young voice called.

Little fingers wiggled between the wooden slats. Juan's heart lurched, remembering the daughter he'd lost. Angie had gotten the poodle because she said every kid needed a dog.

The whoosh of the neighbor's back door opening sounded. "Did you look for it?" Nikki's voice rose above the fence.

He looked at his own back door, feeling as if he was eavesdropping, but he didn't stand up for fear he'd be seen.

"Not yet. I'm petting Sweetie," the girl answered. She must have heard him call his dog by name before.

"Be careful. She might bite."

"No. She likes me." Laughter spilled out. "She's licking my fingers."

"Come help me look for my necklace," Nikki said. "We only have a few minutes before we have to get to school."

"Can't I go to work with you, pleeease?" The hand disappeared from the fence.

"No, hon. You have to go to school."

"I don't know anyone. I don't like strangers."

"You'll make friends. You did in Phoenix. You were nervous to go to school there, too, remember?"

Phoenix? Hadn't she said last night that they'd moved from Colorado? And last week he'd seen her car parked in the driveway with a Colorado license plate.

"But I'm scared," the girl said.

"Oh, baby. Come here." Nikki's voice softened. "It's okay, sweetheart, I promise to keep you safe. But to do that, I have to work."

Safe from what? Was this just childhood paranoia or...more?

His gut said more.

* * *

The closer they got to the school's entrance, the tighter Bell held Vicki's hand. Vicki felt that grip like it was around her heart. Why did life have to be so freaking hard?

When she glanced down at Bell, her big almond-shaped brown eyes held a teary sheen. Vicki knelt. "It's going to be okay. You'll have a good day. You are so smart. Everyone's going to love you. And I'll be right here this afternoon to pick you up. You know that, don't you?"

Bell shook her head ever so slightly and tried to blink away the tears. It broke Vicki's heart. The girl had already been so brave, considering what her father had done to her.

Sticking out her chin, Bell said, "I just...miss Mama."

It took everything Vicki had not to succumb to tears, not to snatch her niece up and run. But then what? They had to eat. They had to live. She could go to a shelter, but Pablo was too smart. He'd look there first.

"Oh, sweetheart." Vicki, sucking in air, drew on her last resolve. "We are going to get through this day. We will. And this afternoon we're going to eat the biggest ice cream cone we can find."

Bell nodded. Then she reached up and touched her upper arm where she carried the scars. Scars Pablo had caused.

Vicki brushed the child's cheeks with her fingertips. "Do you remember where we moved from?"

She nodded. "Colorado. I can't say Phoenix or California."

"Right." Vicki pressed a kiss on her forehead and stood up.

She led Bell into the gym, where all the kindergartners were to meet. Stepping in, she forced herself to smile and moved Bell to a table where a woman sat checking in the students.

"Hi. This is Bell Hanson reporting to kindergarten."

"Great. I'm Ms. Kelly." The lady smiled and looked down at the paper. "I don't see your name..." She flipped the page. "Oh, here. And you're in my class, Bell. I'm so lucky."

Bell offered a weak smile.

The woman handed Bell a red sticker. "Can you put this on your T-shirt and go stand with the red team? They're all your classmates."

Bell looked at Vicki as if to plead one last time.

"Go on," Vicki said. "You'll be okay."

Bell walked over to the red-stickered kids, giving Vicki a scared glance back.

"Uh, Ms. Hanson?"

Vicki looked back. "Yes."

"There's a note here that says they need you to stop by the office. Something about paperwork."

"Oh." Fear twisted in her stomach. Her contact from the Abused Women and Children Organization, AWACO, had assured Vicki the paperwork was sufficient and that they wouldn't be questioned. That they'd be safe. Vicki gave Bell another glance.

"She'll be fine." Ms. Kelly offered a reassuring smile. "It's probably best you leave quickly. The longer you stay, the harder the first day is on her."

And me. Vicki waved at Bell, then walked out, fighting the feeling that she was abandoning her niece.

Paperwork? She moved down the hall, seeing the office door and feeling as if an unknown monster waited behind it. When you were on the run, when your life was a lie, it always felt that way. As if around any corner, hidden in any shadow, lurked someone who could see through your façade. Or someone there to hurt you. Someone like Pablo.

She got to the door, wiped her damp palms on the sides of her workout pants, and then looked back down the hall toward the gym. Should she have brought Bell with her, in case...? She pushed the door open.

There were at least four other moms and one dad in the waiting room. On autopilot, she reached up to grasp the necklace that had become her touchstone.

When her fingertips found an empty spot on her chest, she felt the empty spot in her heart. She had to find the necklace. It was the last gift Alison had given her.

She approached the counter. "I'm Ms. Hanson, Bell Hanson's mom. I was told I needed to fill out paperwork, but I could swear that I—"

"Yes. Have a seat and someone will be right with you."

Vicki took a chair and told herself it was nothing. *You are safe now.* Wasn't that what Joanne Butler from AWACO told her just last week?

Not that it helped. The last time Vicki had felt safe was when Pablo, accused of killing her sister, had been pronounced dead. But when she saw that dead man running away from her L.A. condo less than a month later and found her place ransacked...well, nothing felt safe. That same afternoon, she got a phone call from an anonymous number. But there was nothing anonymous about the voice or the threat. "Give me what's mine, or I'm coming for you!"

She'd still been reeling from that call when she got another one. This one from Estella, Pablo's sister, threatening to file a guardianship suit for her niece. It'd be over her dead body that Vicki gave up Bell, but since Pablo had no problem with that scenario, running felt like Vicki's only option.

The office noise buzzed around her. Needing a distraction, to relax, she looked at the latest breaking news on her phone. But there was no relaxing. Not when two uniformed cops walked in.

She held her breath as the officers moved to the counter. *It's nothing. It's nothing. It's nothing.*

The woman at the front desk got up to greet them. They spoke in hushed voices, then the receptionist looked up and motioned at Vicki.

The officers started toward her. A voice inside her screamed, *Run!* She didn't move, just sat frozen, her pulse pumping fear through her veins, making her limbs feel heavy.

CHAPTER THREE

The officers stopped two feet in front of Vicki. Her chest cavity shrank, her lungs refused air, her head spun. How could she prove to them she had guardianship of her niece when members of the Los Angeles Police Department had said otherwise? They'd believe the police, crooked or not, before they believed her.

No! No one was taking Bell.

She'd run. She'd fight.

"Mrs. Evans?" The middle-aged dark-haired officer didn't appear intimidating, but Vicki felt intimidated just the same.

"No, that's me," said the woman sitting two seats down from Vicki.

Air whooshed out of her lungs. Her spine gave, her shoulders dropped.

The officers turned toward the woman. "You reported an accident in the parking lot?"

"Ms. Hanson?" the desk clerk called.

Vicki stood. Knees trembling, she moved to the counter.

The clerk handed Vicki a clipboard. "You forgot to give us an emergency contact, a family member or friend. If you could fill that out, we'll be done."

"Sure." Vicki moved back and sank down in a chair. She stared at the line with a big X. Still feeling gut punched, she took another emotional blow. She had no one she could list. No one she could count on. This feeling, the empty ache swelling inside her was what it felt like to be completely alone.

Without another option, she scribbled down a fake name and number.

* * *

"How do you think you're doing?"

"Great." Juan leaned back in the chair and swore he wouldn't lose it this time. It seemed every time he lost it, he got another month added to his mandatory visits. He'd been coming to therapy since he'd shot and killed Guzman and gotten transferred to the Cold Case Unit, and sixteen months was enough.

"Try again," Dr. Murdock said.

Juan clenched his jaw. The slight motion tightened the scar that stretched across the right side of his face. "Every time I come in here you ask me the same thing. You never like my answer."

Murdock leaned in, placed his forearms on his desk, laced his fingers, and somehow appeared to dissect Juan's soul. "Then try telling the truth."

The muscle beneath Juan's right eye twitched. "I tried that once and you didn't like it."

"It wasn't the answer I didn't like. It was the hole you left in the wall."

"Then maybe you should try a different question." Juan stared at the man's gray eyes.

Murdock's right brow lifted. "Is your temper always so close to the surface?"

"No. You bring out the best in me."

"And what does that tell you?" Murdock unlaced his fingers, found a pen, and rolled it between his palms.

"That I should stop seeing you," Juan said matter-of-factly.

"I think it says you're afraid. Afraid to open up. Afraid to talk."

Juan gritted his teeth. "What is it about shrinks? You always want to talk things to death."

Murdock's posture stiffened. "Talking can help you accept what is."

"You think I haven't accepted this? I don't have a fucking choice but to accept it." He ran a hand down his face, across the leathered skin on his right cheek. *I'm alive and they are dead.* He gripped the arms of the chair until his hands ached.

"Do you still blame yourself?"

"No." It was what Murdock needed to hear, so he said it, but in truth the answer was: *Every day. Every fucking day.*

Angie had wanted him to stop working undercover. But he'd asked for another month. He'd told himself it was to get Guzman—a gang leader and one of Texas's largest drug suppliers—off the street. He'd been so close to grabbing his ass as well as the big fish, the elusive California supplier known only as Rex. But deep down, Juan knew the truth: He'd loved the thrill of catching bad guys.

For a fucking thrill, he'd gotten his wife and baby girl killed.

"You know, when you were promoted to the Cold Case Unit—"

"'Promoted'? Don't try to pretty it up. Everyone knows the Cold Case Unit was meant to be the exit door." And shooting the man responsible for Angie's and his child's murder was what landed him here.

Murdock adjusted in his chair. "True, but you guys changed that. The three of you have solved cases no one else could. I think it's given you new purpose."

Juan couldn't deny that. "It did." He shrugged.

"Did?" Curiosity rang in the one-word question. "Not anymore?"

"I don't know. Aren't you the expert here? Supposed to explain this stuff to me?"

The silence that filled the space made Juan regret his question. Murdock tapped his fingers on the desk. "It's normal, you know."

"What's normal?"

"Experiencing setbacks. You feed off the anger, the need for revenge, for so long. Now that you are trying to move on, even making progress, it's normal to question if letting it go is what's right."

He wanted to call bullshit on Murdock's therapy-speech, but it rang of truth. Hadn't Juan chosen the new case with Guzman ties to rekindle that anger he'd tried to leave behind?

"Do you still play the video of your wife?"

Why had he told Murdock about that?

"Some," Juan said, hoping the answer would end this conversation more quickly.

"Do you still dream about her?"

Another thing Juan regretted telling Murdock. But you couldn't come in here once a month for over a year and not give anything.

"Not as much." It killed him, too. As hard as it was to wake up reaching for her soft body across the bed, he longed for those seconds when he didn't know she was gone.

Murdock studied him as if Juan were a frog he was about to dissect. "You've had so much to work through in your life, between the issue with your parents, and—"

"Stop. Stop right there. That happened almost twenty years ago. Leave it in the past. I have." Hell, he figured Murdock knew about the murder-suicide that had left him orphaned at fifteen. The city dug up stuff on your ass when they hired you. But it was history, had never affected his work, and was none of their damn business.

"Okay." The doctor hesitated as if trying to find a new way to torture him. "Your black eye and busted lip, is that your temper coming out again?"

"No."

"How'd you get them?"

Juan considered his answer, then decided to throw the man a curveball—the truth. "I got beat up by a woman."

Murdock's posture hardened. "I can't help you if you aren't honest with me."

"It's not a lie," Juan said.

"And why would a woman beat you up?"

"She thought I was breaking into her house. But I'd actually run off the guy who was."

"Okay." Murdock believed him. The fact that the shrink could read him so well made Juan frown. "Are you getting out more like I suggested?"

"I still do poker with the guys a couple times a month, and I work."

"How often do you work cases out in the field? It seems you're always here in the office, chasing leads on the Internet."

"I'm good at it. Besides, I do the legwork when I have to." Sure, if he had a choice, he'd stay in, save the world from having to see his scar. Save himself from being reminded he deserved them.

"Have you started exercising yet?"

"I'm running some. I'm thinking of joining a gym." His voice tightened. He hated having to answer to anyone.

"You said that last month." Murdock's tone held only slight accusation, but it was enough to touch a few of Juan's nerves.

"I said I'm going to." He ran four fingers over his cheek.

Murdock leaned in a bit. "Does the scar bother you?"

"It bothers others." Juan shifted in the chair, feeling more and more uncomfortable.

"You know, you can't control how people react, but you can control how you react to their reaction." Murdock's expression showed empathy, his tone concern. "If you accept it, other people will, too. Do you turn away when people look at you? The more you're aware of it, the more they'll be."

"I told you I've accepted it." The tension in Juan's shoulders leaked into his voice.

Murdock nodded. "Acceptance brings change. Or sometimes change brings acceptance. Just go through the motions of enjoying life. Get out more. You might find yourself actually living again."

"I'm fine." Juan sat back in the chair, his jaw locked.

"Are you? Aren't you lonely, Juan? Don't you feel the need for companionship?"

"No." And until last night, until he'd met his neighbor, it wouldn't have been a lie.

* * *

Vicki, feeling like a stretched rubber band about to snap, got home and went straight to the backyard. Sweetie yapped next door. She ignored her. The necklace was here somewhere, and she was going to find it.

Tears threatened as Vicki dropped to her knees where she and her neighbor had fought. Not having anyone to put on Bell's emergency contact list had gut-punched her. Sure, she'd known she was a one-man band raising a child, but today, staring at the paper made it real.

What if something happened to her? Who'd take care of Bell?

Vicki had walked away from everyone she knew. She hadn't even told Misty, her best friend, she was leaving.

Dan was another matter. She'd felt she owed him an explanation. She'd called him only twice since she'd left. Once when she'd arrived in Phoenix and once, two weeks ago, when she got to Texas. The last call had ended too quickly. That hurt. She suspected he had company. Someone who'd taken her place.

She couldn't blame him. She didn't. But it brought home a cold, hard reality.

Even the person she'd once held closest, counted on the most, was gone. Not that the relationship would have lasted. Raising her niece would have come between them. Like her, Dan was a career-minded person. He chose not to have a family so he could pursue his passions.

Breathing in, hoping to dislodge the mass of ugly emotion in her chest, Vicki stood and walked the entire area where she and her neighbor had struggled. Up. Down. Over. Where was the necklace? Pulling her phone out of her pocket, she checked the time. She needed to leave for work.

As she turned back to her house, something brushed up against her leg. She looked down at the white poodle. "You must be Sweetie. How did you get over here?"

The dog stood on her hind legs and danced. She looked like a little stuffed animal in need of a haircut. No wonder Bell was smitten.

Yet as adorable as the canine was, Vicki frowned. "I don't suppose you'll just go back the way you came, huh?"

The dog continued dancing, begging to be held.

"Great. Now what?" Was her neighbor at home or did he leave the dog out all day? The thought of seeing him again after... after what?

Why was it that the moment they'd shared together at the fence felt more embarrassing than the struggle they'd had? Why had his offer to help her look for the necklace felt like something more than just him being neighborly? Why had she let herself forget for even one second that he was a police officer and she didn't trust the police?

Remembering the time, she scooped up the animal, turning her head to keep from being doggy-French-kissed. She hurried through her house and grabbed her purse and keys, hoping to drop off the poodle and then go teach a Pilates class.

* * *

Juan had gotten home from his shrink visit intent on going to the gym. He'd dressed in his workout clothes, psyched himself up to go sweat, to face the stares from those who found his scar disturbing. Instead, he'd let Sweetie out, sat down at the table, and started reading his latest case file. He studied the image of Abby Noel, the pretty blond-haired, blue-eyed mother of one. Only twenty-four at the time.

What were the chances of her being alive after going

missing five years ago? Especially when her boyfriend, Cheng Liu, a drug dealer with Columbian ties, had been found murdered the same day she disappeared.

It was believed Liu had been trying to get Guzman to drop his California drug supplier and work with Liu's Colombian ties. Rumor said Guzman's supplier had ordered a hit on Liu for infringing on his business.

The objective behind Juan's yearlong undercover work hadn't been to get just Guzman, but also the California supplier. An objective Juan had failed to accomplish. One that had become insignificant to him after Angie and his daughter had been murdered.

Juan's gaze drifted back to the picture. Abby Noel deserved justice. Finding the body, finding her killer, would do that.

Today, Connor was taking a trip down to the prison to talk to some thugs who'd been part of Guzman's gang at the time of Liu's murder. Since the detectives believed Abby's disappearance was tied to her boyfriend's murder, looking into that case might help this one.

Mark, his other partner, was talking to all possible witnesses at the grocery store where Abby Noel's abandoned car had been found. Then he was going to drop in on Noel's parents. If Mark wasn't successful connecting with the Noels, Juan would have to go there this evening. Just like he'd told Murdock, when he had to go out to do his job, he did.

Juan looked back at the file. He read the report about Cindy Bates, Abby Noel's best friend and the last person to have seen her alive. Bates had worked with Noel at the Black Diamond, a gentleman's club, and said she'd been with Noel all night. If he wanted to get to the bottom of this, Juan needed more details. Luckily, the officer writing the report had noted Bates's phone number.

Juan grabbed his cell and dialed. A recording stated that the number was no longer in service.

Flipping the page, he studied Noel's phone records. The woman's cell and purse had been found in her car. Her last call, at two a.m., had been to the number he'd just dialed.

If Noel had been with her best friend all night, why was she calling Bates's phone at two in the morning? How the hell had the detective missed this? He checked to see who'd done the interview. It'd been a different detective from who was leading the case but still inexcusable.

Either way, Cindy Bates had lied. Yup, he needed to find her.

He grabbed his laptop and typed in her name. His search engine was offering up some links when his doorbell rang. He'd lived here a year, but this was probably only the third time anyone had come to his door. Certain it was some solicitor selling magazines, he ignored it.

A knock followed—a rather insistent knock. Seriously? If he had to run someone off his porch, he wasn't going to be happy. And neither would they.

Then he heard a bark. He bolted up. One quick glance out the back window told him Sweetie wasn't in his yard. He rushed to the door.

Without even looking out the peephole, he yanked it

open. His breath caught. Wearing workout clothes that clung to her curves and a frown that clung to her lips, Nikki Hanson held out Sweetie.

"I'm assuming she belongs to you."

Feeling his scar pull across his cheek from his scowl, he turned his head away and tamed his expression. "Uh, yes. I just let her out in the backyard." He took the animal from her hands. The brief contact of their fingers caused a spark of something sweet and unwanted that shot right to his gut. And if the startled look on her face was any indication, he wasn't the only one who'd felt it burn.

She took a quick step back. "Well, she must have found a way into my yard."

"Sorry, I'll fix it."

She went to turn away, but he spoke up again. "Thank you."

She offered a slight nod and swung left to leave.

"Nikki?" Her name slipped off his lips before he knew what he wanted to say.

She turned around. Their eyes met. Held.

"Last night, you said . . . you knew who you thought sent me, as if . . . as if you knew who might be out to hurt you."

She shook her head, a little too hard. A little too fast. Her hair, hanging a couple of inches below her chin, flowed around her heart-shaped face. And damn if he didn't note how pretty that face was. A small, slightly turned-up nose. Full lips, almond-shaped eyes that were brown or perhaps dark hazel. And suddenly, he needed to know which. Brown or hazel. He took a step outside his door. Then another. He lifted his gaze. Hazel. They were hazel.

She took a step back. "No. I meant...I thought you were trying to steal something."

She glanced down. A sure sign of a lie.

He should drop it. Let her walk away. It was what he wanted, what she wanted, but... "It seemed like more."

"No." She took another step back, as if his question had crowded her.

"Nikki, if you're afraid of something, I could—"

"I said it's nothing." This time she left, hotfooting it to her Toyota Camry. He stood there petting Sweetie and watched her climb into her car. Watched as her Colorado license plate, not Arizona, disappeared down the street.

Yup. She was hiding something.

CHAPTER FOUR

Vicki finished teaching her Pilates class, then hurried to pick up Bell. She got there early and waited at the front door of the school—all smiles and good times. A happy face for Bell when deep down Vicki felt none of it.

The school preferred parents use the pickup line in the parking lot, but she'd told Bell she'd be waiting here. If she wasn't right where she said she'd be, Bell might panic. After losing her mother, Bell had a few abandonment issues. Hell, after losing her sister, Vicki had a few abandonment issues herself.

The door swept open and a flurry of excited and noisy kids rushed out with their teacher. Vicki prayed Bell would emerge happier than when she'd dropped her off.

She saw Bell grinning, and the heavy feeling in her

chest rose. If this was all she accomplished in life, keeping her niece happy and safe, it'd be enough.

Bell's big brown eyes found Vicki's and she came running, dragging another girl by the hand.

"Mom," Bell said, with only a slight hesitation. "This is Suzie. My new friend."

Vicki knelt down. "Hi, Suzie."

The girl grinned, and then screamed, "Daddy!" at the same time a shadow fell over Vicki. She stood up.

"I missed you, Daddy." Suzie, all arms and legs, leaped up in her father's arms.

"Missed you, too." He kissed his daughter's brow, but his gaze found Vicki.

"Hi," the man said. "I'm Cal Phillips."

"I'm Bell's mom. Nikki Hanson."

Suzie touched her father's face. "Can Bell come over and play sometime, Daddy? Please, please, please!"

"Can I?" Bell chimed in.

No way was Vicki sending Bell to a stranger's house. "Maybe Suzie can come see us sometime."

"That'd be good," the man said. "Suzie and I just moved here over the summer. It'd be nice if we could get the kids together."

"Yeah." Vicki's smile lessened, wondering if his "Suzie and I" comment was an "I'm divorced" hint. He lowered his daughter to the ground and Vicki saw his gaze shift to her left hand.

"Well, we should run," Vicki said.

"Nice meeting you," Cal replied.

"See you Monday," Suzie called out to Bell and the father-and-daughter pair, holding hands, walked away.

"So, good day?" Vicki asked Bell. But the girl wasn't listening. She stood silent in the after-school buzz, watching Suzie and her dad.

Kneeling down, Vicki smiled. "Don't I get a hug?"

Bell wrapped her arms around Vicki and hung on a second longer and tighter than normal. When the child let go, Vicki stood with tears in her eyes and took her niece's small hand. "So, good day, right?"

"The first part was sad, but then I met Suzie. She was sad, too, but we both got happy."

"I'm glad you made a friend." Vicki started walking to the car.

"Did you make friends?" Bell asked.

"Yeah, I met a lot of nice people at the gym." But friends? No. Getting close to people could be danger-ous. Joanne had even warned her about it. And just like that, Vicki recalled the second part of that warning: Steer clear of the police. While AWACO attempted to stay within the boundaries of the law, they often skirted into the gray areas, like creating new identities to help keep women safe.

She needed to remember that when dealing with her neighbor.

"Can Suzie come over sometime?" Bell asked.

"Sure." The desire to remind Bell that she couldn't tell anyone their secrets hit, but she put it on hold, not wanting to spoil the child's mood. "You ready for ice cream?"

Ten minutes later, they sat at an ice cream shop where Bell asked for two scoops of rainbow sherbet and Vicki indulged in one scoop of chocolate. Bell talked nonstop about Suzie, about a boy in class who stuck his tongue out at her, and about her teacher being surprised Bell could read.

After a few minutes, Bell stared down at her ice cream and her smile faded a notch. "Why are some daddies good and some bad?"

The sweet taste of chocolate on Vicki's tongue turned bitter. "Daddies are just men. Some men are good and some...aren't."

"Like dogs?" Bell asked.

"Huh?" Vicki asked.

"Men are like dogs. Some are nice and some aren't."

Vicki held back her smile, but answered, "Yeah, men are kind of like dogs."

* * *

Juan looked up from the computer screen when Mark returned from doing some legwork on the Noel case.

"Get anything?" Juan asked.

"Nothing, but I managed not to get beaten up," Mark answered with a smirk.

His two partners' eyes met and then they both looked at him with shit-eating grins.

"Give it up, would you?" Juan said.

"We just don't get it." Connor chuckled. "Billy said she wasn't even five feet tall."

"I told you, the asshole breaking into the house threw a grill at me. I had soot in my eyes." *And she fought like a ninja and she was taller than five feet.* Mentally he measured her up. Five four, maybe. He envisioned her face and the surprise in her eyes when their hands had touched this morning. Then he recalled her back-off expression when he'd asked about being afraid of someone.

He almost confided in his partners about his suspicions, but considering his proof was only an offhand remark and the name drop of Phoenix, he didn't have much. Well, other than his gut.

"Did you speak to Noel's parents?" Juan asked. Mark busied himself shutting down his computer, getting ready to leave. Since Annie moved in with him and he'd started playing in a band, Mark left at five o'clock every day. When Juan had teased him about it, Mark had told him he'd found out there was more to life than work. He suggested Juan give it a try.

Juan hadn't had a comeback. It hurt remembering when he'd had more than his work but didn't value it nearly enough. When the love of his work cost him everything.

"Went by twice," Mark offered.

Juan straightened the files on his desk. He couldn't complain about Mark's schedule. He was one of the best detectives Juan had ever met. Juan was even glad Mark had found a life, one that included a woman.

"I think they both work," Mark continued. "You should try them tonight. Also, Cindy Bates is no longer at the address you sent. She moved shortly after her friend went missing. Neighbors said the owner of her rental has moved back and is living there now. I got his name in my car, I'll text it to you. You might want to run by there, too."

"I will." Juan only dreaded it a little.

Mark turned to Connor. "How did the prison inter-
views go?"

"I got nothing, but a couple sure seemed interested
in why I was asking. Which makes me think they know
something. One has a parole hearing coming up. I told
him we'd put in a good word for him if he talked, but he
didn't budge."

"Why am I not surprised?" Mark stood up. "Oh."
He looked back at Juan. "I got the DNA back on the
Jacobs case we talked about last month. I want to start
running down a few of the old witnesses."

"We going to run with both cases?" Connor asked.

"Yeah, I think it's doable, don't you?"

"Yeah." Connor and Juan nodded. Juan knew the
evidence in the Noel case was light. Either one of the
few leads would open a door or they'd come against a
wall. Not that they came to a lot of walls.

In the sixteen months he'd worked here, they'd
solved five cases, and only reshelved two. Their success
had caused a stir in the media, and they'd been dubbed
the Three Musketeers.

While validating their worthiness to the department
felt good, Juan could have done without the press.

Mark stood. "Hopefully by Monday I'll get you the
Jacobs info so you can work your Internet magic."

"Sounds good," Juan said.

"Oh." Mark looked back. "We're still on for poker at
your place Sunday, right?"

"Sure." Not that he'd recalled until now.

"Good. My pockets are getting empty." Mark
walked out.

Juan refocused on the Noel file.

"So this neighbor who beat you up, was she pretty?" Connor asked. "Billy said she was hot. Is she single?"

Juan glanced up. "Is every woman a conquest to you?"

"Yeah." Connor smiled. "Why? You calling dibs?"

"I'm calling bullshit. You can't go sniffing around my neighbor to get lucky. Besides, she has a kid."

"Oh," he said.

"Right. Probably not your type." Eager to move the subject off his neighbor, he added, "You mostly date engaged or married women."

"No. For the tenth time, I didn't know she was engaged. And if by married you mean Becky Summers, she was separated."

Juan closed his file. "Yeah, but her husband just lived in her garage."

Connor frowned. "Why is it you remember more about my dating life than I do?"

Juan laughed. "You just don't remember because you only go into relationships you know have expiration dates."

"And I think you remember because you're living vicariously through me."

"Yeah. I want to be stranded in my underwear, hiding in bushes, calling you to come rescue me at two in the morning."

"Hey." Connor held up a hand. "Up until then, that night was memorable."

Juan chuckled. "All I know is I'll never forget it."

"And you don't plan on letting me, either, right?"

Juan laughed. That was the thing about Connor.

While he went through women like cheap toothpicks, the ones he dated didn't seem to want or expect anything different from him.

Juan's phone dinged with a text.

"What? Your neighbor wanting round two?"

"No. It's Mark with the name of Bates's landlord."

"You want me to go there?" Connor leaned his big frame back in his desk chair and set it to squeaking. The man was six four and still looked like the football player he'd been in college.

As tempting as it was for Juan to say yes, the address was on the same side of town as Noel's parents. "Nah, I got it."

"Okay." Connor sounded surprised.

And deep down, Juan supposed he was as well. For the first time, he wondered if perhaps Murdock's pressure for him to get out more was finally taking effect.

* * *

Juan showed up at the Noels' doorstep at six-thirty. The lights were on. He just hoped he wasn't interrupting dinner. He'd gone by Cindy Bates's former address, but Rodger Henley, the owner, hadn't been home. Juan left his card and a note asking Rodger to call him about one of his past renters.

He knocked. A few moments later, the door swung open. A girl, with a big toothy grin and pigtails, smiled up at him. But as soon as her stare reached his face, that grin vanished. Her eyes widened, no doubt at seeing his scar. Automatically he turned his face to hide the scar.

"Who is it?" called a voice behind the girl.

An older man appeared in the doorway. She turned and wrapped her arms around his thighs. "He's scary." Her muffled words hit Juan in the gut.

"Run along to your grandma," the man said.

"I'm sorry." Juan turned so the man would understand why his granddaughter had been so frightened.

"No," he said quickly. "I'm sorry. Kids."

"I understand," Juan assured him. And he did. "My name is Juan Acosta. I'm with the Anniston PD, the Cold Case Unit."

The man's eyes took on the same frightened glint as the child's. Only this time, Juan knew it wasn't from his scar. "You found Abby?"

"No, sir. But we're looking into the case. And we'd like to ask you a few questions. I tried to call."

"Oh. Come on in." He led Juan into the living room, where the child waited with an older woman. "Lacy, go play on your swing set for a few minutes, okay?"

As soon as the back door clicked shut, the woman got tears in her eyes. "You found her?"

"No," her husband assured her. "But he's looking into the investigation."

She wiped a tear from her cheek and waved a hand to the sofa. "Please sit down."

Right when Juan got settled, she spoke again. "I've seen you and your partners on the news. I called several times."

"We got your calls. That's what brought the case to our attention." Along with the ties to Guzman.

She sat up straighter. "I know my husband will argue

with me, but I believe she's still alive. I think a mother would know that."

Mr. Noel let out a sad sound. "It's been five years, Brenda. And even you say nothing could have kept her from Lacy."

The woman put a hand over her lips and more tears filled her eyes. "It's hard. I see her sometimes. In a crowd."

Mr. Noel looked at Juan. "We need closure. We need to bury our daughter."

Juan nodded. "I understand." And he did. He often went to Angie's grave just to say he was sorry. "I've gone over the files, but it always helps to speak to the families again."

Mr. Noel frowned. "Abby had so much going for her. When she got into drugs, she made mistakes. A lot of them. But she didn't deserve whatever happened to her."

"She has so much talent. She can sing. Has the voice of an angel. She's so good at art. People have said terrible things about her, but she's a good girl." Mrs. Noel shot up and grabbed a couple of framed photos from the fireplace mantel and handed them to Juan.

One showed a young woman with a baby. Abby and her daughter. The other was of a younger Abby wearing a cheerleader outfit. Her long blond hair hung down past her shoulders. Her blue eyes showed so much life. Hope for the future. One that drugs ended. She held out her hand, showing something. He studied the photo. It was a rabbit's foot.

"Was there anyone who you felt wanted to hurt her? Anyone you now look back and are suspicious about?"

"Not any more than before," the father said. "She had a new boyfriend, a guy named Cheng Liu. Cops claimed he was a drug dealer. He was found murdered. We just assumed Abby's disappearance had to do with that."

"What about her friend Cindy Bates?" Juan asked.

"I don't think she'd hurt Abby," her mom said. "They were close. Abby called Cindy her twin friend. Kind of looked alike and said they were both interested in music, art, and writing. To this day Cindy sends Abby's daughter, Lacy, birthday cards with poems and a five-dollar bill."

Really? "How long were they friends?" Juan asked.

"Not long," her father said. "She worked with Abby at the Black Diamond. We never even met her."

"Did she spend time with Abby's daughter?"

"It's possible. Lacy lived with us," her mom said. "But Abby would come get her and take her places sometimes."

Mr. Noel spoke up. "Personally, I have always found it odd that she keeps sending cards. And her poems are weird."

"Weird like how?" Juan asked.

"It's just poetry," Mrs. Noel said. "Abby used to write, too."

"Did you keep any of the cards?"

"Yes, I saved them all. One came just last week for Lacy's birthday." She walked out to get it.

"We need closure," Mr. Noel repeated. "Someone needs to pay for hurting my daughter."

Juan nodded. Mrs. Noel returned with an envelope.

Could he get so lucky that there'd be a return address? "The others are here somewhere. I thought they were in the kitchen drawer, but I don't see them. I'll call you when I find them."

Ten minutes later, Juan stood to leave. He placed the frames back on the mantel and took a few seconds to scan the other photos. All were of either Abby or Abby with family.

Mrs. Noel walked up. She touched the photo of Abby in her cheerleading outfit, holding out the rabbit's foot. "She made the cheerleading team that day. She said it was her lucky rabbit's foot. She took that thing everywhere after that. Her grandmother gave it to her before she died."

"And it sure as hell didn't bring her much luck," Mr. Noel said.

Mrs. Noel frowned. "You don't know that. She could be alive."

When Juan walked out, he left with even more questions swirling around his head. There was no return address on the envelope, but Mr. Bates had been right. The poetry was odd.

You lost your mother way too soon
I lost my friend and the pain still looms
I hear her voice
She still sings
Under the sun
Under the moon
Where the flowers are still in bloom

Juan couldn't help but wonder what compelled Bates to continue to send money, birthday cards, and poems to a child so many years after her mother's disappearance.

The obvious answer was guilt. Bates either participated in Noel's death, or knew something.

He was betting on the latter.

* * *

The lights were low, except for on the stage. The tables closest to the entertainment were crowded with men drunk on whiskey and near-naked women. Music, sultry but too loud, seemed forced into the room. With the sound came filtered cold air that smelled like sweat, smoke, alcohol, and hormones.

Juan moved to the table farthest away from the stage. He wasn't here to watch.

It had been five years since the officer noted that Bates was employed here. But since the postmark on the card sent to the Noels was from Anniston, and since there was only one strip joint in town, she might not have found other work.

To this day Juan recalled the talk Christina, his sister-in-law, had given him when she'd found out he and some friends had used fake IDs to get into this very place. "You are too young, and bad things happen there!"

It wasn't until years later that Juan learned Christina's sister had worked here and some coworkers had gotten her hooked on drugs. She'd died somewhere in here, in a back room.

A waitress with hair the color of cherry cotton

candy, wearing little on the bottom and even less on top, spotted him and started swaying seductively his way. As she moved her hips, she balanced an empty tray on her fingertips.

"Hi, I'm Star. What can I get you, pretty boy?" She stopped in front of him, her belly button ring winking in the light.

The use of his old nickname stung more than her flinch when she spotted his scar. But her recovery came quick. A recovery that included her leaning in. The shift offered Juan a better view of her breasts. "I've always thought scars are sexy."

His only answer was a quick nod.

She inched up. "What would you like to drink?"

He pulled out his wallet and dropped three twenties on the table.

She frowned. "I don't do dances."

"I don't want a dance. Just a few answers."

"I serve drinks. I don't do answers."

He added another twenty.

"You're a cop?" It was more of a question than an accusation.

From his pocket, he pulled out the picture of Cindy he'd printed from the DMV files. "Does Cindy still work here?"

Her eyes shifted to the picture, and then to the money on the table. "That's all you want to know?"

"And where I might find her."

"Why don't you just talk to the manager?"

"I'm going to, but I figured her peers knew her better than he did."

She lifted a well-defined brow and looked around to see if anyone was watching. "You got a few more bills in that wallet?"

He pulled one more out.

She brought the tray down and pulled a pen from behind her ear, as if taking his drink order. "Is she in trouble?"

"Not really. I just need to speak to her."

She hesitated. "Cindy left last week. Management fired her because she was losing it." She twirled the pen in tight circles by her temple. "And she lives in . . ." She picked up his money. "West Mount Apartments on Simon Street. Or she did. I gave her a lift home one night when her car broke down. And you didn't hear that from me."

"Got it," he said. "Was she close friends with anyone here?"

She leaned in one more time. "No, she was a loner."

He handed her his card. "If you see Cindy, tell her to call me. Or you call me."

She smiled. "What if I called you for reasons not involving Cindy?"

"I'm just looking for her," he said.

Offering a slight nod, more amused than disappointed, she walked away.

He watched her leave, disturbed by what he felt. Or what he didn't feel. Why was he ten times more tempted by a neighbor dressed in a loose nightshirt than a woman in tight shorts and a top with her breasts on display?

Pushing his drink away, he stood to go have a chat with Black Diamond's manager.

CHAPTER FIVE

Vicki put Bell to bed at nine. Determined to find her necklace, she went back outside with her flashlight. After an hour of crawling around in the grass, she gave up, grabbed a bottle of wine, a glass, a bowl of Cheetos—it was the closest thing to cheese she had—and went back outside to crash on a lawn chair.

Three glasses and two handfuls of Cheetos in, she still lay there reclined on the lawn chair. She stared up at the stars and moon, trying to convince herself it was PMS, not self-pity, she felt at spending a Friday night drinking wine alone. How could she complain when she was alive and Alison wasn't? How, when Alison's death had been her fault?

How, when she'd been the one to introduce her sister to Pablo?

She reached to touch the necklace that wasn't there,

and sighed. She counted to ten before mentally giving herself a swift kick in the butt for feeling so sorry for herself. Then she refilled her glass.

Tomorrow she'd have a wine headache, but tonight she wanted to forget. She pulled the goblet to her lips.

Closing her eyes, she wondered how mosquito-bitten she'd get if she just slept here. The temperature was cooler than it'd been for the past week, and a soft breeze made it comfortable. It almost felt like California weather. Definitely a fluke for Texas.

The sound of a door opening next door had her glancing at the fence. Then came the barking. So her neighbor was home.

Without wanting to, she recalled him shirtless, re-called that brief second when their hands touched this morning. Recalled a spark of unwanted attraction that had unwillingly traveled up her arm and straight to her heart. A spark that reminded her that she was a woman. And he was a man.

Oddly, the scar on the side of his face didn't distract from his tall, dark, and dangerous appeal. In fact, the scar added to it.

The barking and scratching along the fence contin-ued. Should she go inside? But why let her neighbor or his dog ruin what was left of her wine-and-Cheetos evening? Then she remembered the dog sneaking into her yard. Surely, he'd fixed the—

A wet doggy tongue slid across the bottom of her foot.

"Crap!" she muttered.

Then a synonym of that word echoed from the other side of the fence. "Shit! Sweetie!"

Hearing him call the dog, she felt a smile curl her lips. For some reason, she didn't think he'd named the poodle. In fact, she wondered what girlfriend had abandoned the dog at his place. He looked more like the black Lab or pit bull type.

"Come here, girl. Damn it. Where are you?"

The dog jumped up on the lounge and barked. Vicki bit down on her lip, debating. Then, "I've got her. Again."

"I'm sorry. Again. I forgot about the fence. Had to work. I'm fixing it tomorrow. I'll come around."

She was still trying to get Sweetie off her lap without spilling her wine when he showed up. Standing over her, wearing a pair of dark jeans and a white button-down shirt, Juan looked devilishly handsome. She noted he stood slightly to the side, as if hiding his scar.

Was the move subconscious? Probably not.

Sweetie jumped off the lounge chair. Feeling awkward, Vicki went to stand, but as she got one foot on the ground, her second came down on the dog. Trying not to hurt the poodle, she reared back and watched in horror as her wine splattered against Juan's white shirt.

"Crap," she said again, then without meaning to, she laughed.

He looked down at his shirt, and instead of the scowl she expected, he smiled.

"Sorry." She worked on taming her own smile.

"Not a big deal." His grin reached his eyes and butterflies took flight in her stomach.

Sweetie stood on her hind legs and begged to be picked up. He scooped her up.

"Bad dog, Sweetie."

Hearing him say the dog's name unleashed her smile again. "You didn't name her, did you?"

"No," he said.

"A girlfriend?"

A pause hung in the air. Pulsed like it was important. "My wife."

"Divorced?" she asked, unable to shut up. Yeah, when she drank she got chatty. Dan had pointed that out several times.

"No. She died."

"Sorry." When she drank she also got a little too emotional, and she felt his loss filling her chest. Or maybe it was her own loss she was feeling.

She pulled her glass closer.

"Me too." As the dog reached up to lick his face, he lifted his chin. "You?"

"Me?"

"Divorced?" he asked.

I need to stop this. Need to shut up. "Yes. Yes, I'm divorced." Was it her, or did that sound like a lie?

His gaze stayed on her eyes. Why was he looking at her like that? Finally, his attention shifted to the ground beside her lawn chair, where she had set her flashlight and wine bottle.

"Still looking for your necklace?"

"Yeah." Was it getting hotter?

"I have a metal detector that might help you find it."

"Really?"

"Let me get it." Before she could stop him, he'd left. Or had she not wanted to stop him? Or was she just halfway drunk?

Or am I just lonely?

Was there an all-of-the-above box to check?

Sober up! Before...

Before what? He came through her gate with the metal detector, minus the dog, and walked directly toward her. "It should work."

He moved in. Close enough that his nearness became her only thought, but not in a bad way. He smelled like her wine and fresh night air. He turned the detector on and smiled. It hummed and she felt the hum create a purr of sweetness low in her abdomen.

"You got anything metal to test it?"

"Wine opener." She pointed beside the lounge. He moved the detector over the opener. It beeped.

"Good to go. Let's see if we can find it." He walked past her to the spot where they'd struggled. His white shirt stretched across his wide shoulders. His jeans hugged his backside like the material had memorized his shape.

He took a few steps forward and then back, waving the detector side to side. She stared at his— The detector's beep sounded and she brought her eyes up.

"You found it?" She hurried over. They both knelt and reached for the grass. Their hands met. Both jerked back and looked up. Their eyes met.

She looked away first. His hands shifted back across the grass.

"It's not your necklace." He held up a nail.

She stood. "Can I try?"

He passed her the detector. She handed him her wineglass.

He brought the glass to his nose. "Cabernet?"

"Yes. Feel free to finish it. I've...I've had enough." And the fact that she'd just offered him a drink proved it. "There's a little left in the bottle."

"I think I will." He snatched up the bottle and emptied it into her glass. She started moving the detector back and forth. When she looked up, he had her glass to his lips. Probably where her own lips had touched.

There should be nothing sensual about someone using her glass. And yet there was. Maybe it was the moonlight. Maybe it was the late hour.

She continued waving the detector over the grass, hoping not to miss an inch. But she wasn't thinking about her necklace. Her thoughts went to Juan without that white shirt. While her eyes stayed downcast, she felt his warm gaze on her skin.

"You know I'm a cop, but I don't know what you do."

She bit down on her lip and felt the blades of warm grass between her toes. "I teach fitness classes."

"What type of fitness?"

"Yoga, Zumba, Pilates."

"Kickboxing?"

She looked up. Even through the darkness she saw his smile. He touched his bruised eye.

She grinned. "No. Don't teach that."

"Maybe you should." Humor laced his tone.

"I did say I was sorry, didn't I?"

"Yes, you did."

"Good." She looked back at the ground.

He moved in, stood close. "Do you teach at your own studio?"

"No. I got a job at a gym close by."

"Which one?"

She hesitated, not liking the questions. "You going to take a Pilates class?"

He chuckled. "No. My sister-in-law works at Finally Fit across town."

"That's where I work, but the one here on Main." Thank goodness it wasn't the same one. She didn't need another connection with this man.

"Small world," he said.

"Yeah."

"What brought you to Anniston?"

The question came off as casual, but considering it would require a lie to answer, it felt complicated and intrusive.

"Just needed a change." The night seemed warmer. The air thicker.

"Where did you live in Colorado?"

A drop of sweat slid down between her breasts. The closer she let him to her, the more questions he'd ask. The more lies she'd have to tell. She had to nip this in the bud now.

"Boulder." It was where Nikki Hanson, a year younger than her, was from. Where the real Nikki had lived before she moved to South America when she was nineteen and was killed in an automobile accident. Normally, AWACO legally changed someone's name, but because Pablo had worked for the police, they were afraid he'd still have contacts. They'd given her the name of someone whose death had gone unreported. Someone who was as close to invisible as possible.

Vicki's palms felt sweaty holding the detector, and she cut it off. "You know, it's getting late." Moving closer, she held the detector out to him.

"Keep it," Juan said. "You can search more tomorrow."

She should say no, but she really wanted her necklace. "Thanks."

He held up the glass, still half-full.

"Take it with you," she insisted.

"Thanks. I'll return this when you return the metal detector."

"Deal." Her gaze shifted to his chest again. "You should soak your shirt. If it doesn't come out, I'll pay for it."

"Not necessary." He took one step backward, his eyes on her. "Goodnight, Nikki. Sleep well." The way he said her name, the way the words slipped off his lips, made it feel intimate, like a pillow-talk kind of tone.

"Goodnight." She swallowed a sigh of desire.

When he left, she took the detector inside, set it by the door, dropped down on the sofa, and indulged in a few more minutes of self-pity.

* * *

Juan got back to his house and downed the wine in one gulp. Then he ran a rough palm over his face. When his hand hit the numb area of his right cheek, he realized that not once had Nikki's gaze gone to his scar. And not once while he'd been standing in front of her had he thought about it.

His pulse raced at the base of his neck. His blood stirred down south in ways it hadn't in years. What was it about that woman that made him want things he hadn't wanted since he lost Angie? If she'd looked like Angie or even had some similar characteristics, he could blame it on that. But that wasn't the case.

There was nothing about Nikki's jean shorts and blue T-shirt that screamed *Come and get me, boy*. She hadn't even had on any makeup. Not that she needed it. The most erotic thing about her was her bare feet, her light pink painted toenails.

Yet when he looked at her not-so-short shorts, not-so-tight T-shirt, and pink toenails, all he thought about was sex. Him removing her clothes. Her removing his. Their limbs tangled up in the sheets. Him on top of her. Her on top of him.

Shit! Was it the roll on the ground they'd had last night? The first pair of breasts he'd felt under him that flipped a switch? It didn't make any frigging sense.

And he was a "sense" kind of guy. He liked his ducks in a row. And right now his ducks were running amok.

Why did he feel certain she'd lied about being divorced? Was she running from a husband?

He fought the temptation to call his sister-in-law and ask for a copy of Nikki's employment application. Christina not only managed the south-side gym, she helped oversee the gym on his side of town, too. But that request would require an explanation. And could result in Nikki losing her job.

He couldn't do that.

Because everything pointed to the fact that Nikki Hanson was afraid or hiding from something. Or someone. Was that the connection he felt? Empathy? He knew what it was like to run from something. Even if that something was a memory. Make that *memories*. Juan had plenty of demons to run from, and not just the ones from the night his wife and child died. There was the loss of his mother many years before that.

He'd thought he'd spend his whole life living with the pain and regret of not having been home earlier to save his mother's life. But Angie changed that. She'd pulled him out of those shadows and given him a future that was beautiful and hopeful. Then, because of his mistake, he'd lost her, too.

He walked to his laptop and put Nikki's name and Boulder, Colorado, in the NCIC, National Crime Information Center. There were two hits. One was a fifty-year-old woman, and the other was the right age. He clicked on the second and waited for the information to download. It wasn't worth the wait. Nikki V. Hanson had nothing on her record. Other than her old driver's license number, he got zilch.

He grabbed his credit card and paid for the public record search. More times than not, private searches gave more than the official police searches. When it finally handed over the information, he realized he'd wasted forty dollars. Other than an old address, it gave him nothing. No family, no employment history. No marriage or divorce records, either. Hell, he didn't even know if Hanson was her married or maiden name.

He did another search of the social media pages and got zilch again. What was he missing? Then it occurred to him, there was one he hadn't checked: Myspace. While it had fallen out of favor years ago, he'd recently read about someone finding a fugitive through an old Myspace account.

He found two twelve-year-old accounts on a Nikki Hanson. He clicked on the age-appropriate one. She was from Boulder. Hope spiked when he saw her middle initial was V. And her profile wasn't restricted.

He'd found her. But there was only one blurry image of her dancing with her hair swinging around her face. He leaned in and stared at the blue-eyed teenager on the screen. It wasn't his neighbor. Or was it? If he ignored the hair and eye color, because those could be changed with dye and contacts, it could be her. But was the shape of the chin the same? Perhaps it was the angle of the photo that made it appear different.

What were the chances that there was another girl about the same age, with the same name, same middle initial, who lived in the same town? Slim. And yet...

He searched through her friends and found three from Colorado, then switched over to Facebook to track them down. Unfortunately, the names were common. He sent messages to eight possible matches. One of them should be able to tell him more about Nikki V. Hanson. Somehow, some way, he was going to get to the truth.

* * *

Eight hours. Eight fucking hours Pablo waited, parked in his rented Chevy Malibu, in front of Dan Jefferies's house. Where the hell was the guy? Jefferies worked as an engineer for an oil company. Which meant regular hours.

At three a.m., Pablo's patience snapped. His stomach growled from hunger. Thirst made his mouth dry. And he had to piss.

Putting gloves on, he got out of his car. His footsteps sounded too loud in the silence of the night. He crept to the back of the house, wrapped his hoodie around his fist, and broke a window.

Shattering glass echoed. He glanced around, afraid the neighbor's lights would flicker on. They didn't. The idiot didn't have an alarm.

Ten minutes later, he sat at the kitchen table, eating a bowl of Cheerios. When he'd worked for LAPD, there'd been a serial killer who broke in, killed his victims, and helped himself to whatever was in the fridge. For some reason, that bothered the public and his fellow officers, but Pablo kind of admired the guy. Pablo didn't want to see the food go to waste.

He kept his Glock resting right beside his Cheerios just in case the bastard returned. When Pablo finished eating, he rummaged around looking for any connection this guy might still have to Vicki. A stack of mail was on the table in the entryway. He thumbed through it. Nothing but bills and junk mail. But holy hell he wanted Vicki found. He wanted his money found. He wanted a new life, instead of living in the damn shadows.

He wanted Vicki dead, right after he fucked her.

He'd had a hard-on for her the first time he'd met her. They'd gotten to talking after both attending an interest group for triathlon training. But she'd made it clear from the start she wasn't interested.

He wasn't used to being rejected. But he hadn't given up. Instead, he convinced her they could just be training buddies, certain he'd win her over. That never happened. Then she'd introduced him to her sister.

He'd decided if he couldn't have Vicki, he'd have Alison. But she turned out to be a poor substitute. Then the bitch had gotten pregnant and he was stuck. He'd married her. A huge fucking mistake. She kept her nose all up in his business. Yeah, he worked for LAPD, but his real money came from his side jobs. The badge was the reason Rex Esparza had hired him. It afforded Pablo the things he deserved. Things he'd provided to Alison and the little brat, but neither had appreciated the extras.

Then she'd started getting mouthy, talking back to him, asking questions about where he got his money. He'd had to teach her a lesson, because how else was she going to learn? The last time, Vicki got involved.

If not for her, Alison wouldn't have left. She wouldn't have stolen his money or the logbook. If not for Vicki, he wouldn't have had to kill Alison and then fake his own death to get out of going to prison. He hoped like hell Vicki knew it was her fault that her sister died. When he found her, he'd make sure she knew.

But damn it, where was Dan? He rummaged through

drawers and cabinets. He found a framed photograph of Dan and Vicki taken in what looked like Hawaii. He recalled her telling him they'd gone. Did the image being hidden away mean they were no longer together? Did it mean Dan wouldn't know where she was?

He wouldn't believe that, not until he got Dan alone and demanded answers. Unlike Sam, Pablo knew how to make people talk.

Furious that tonight had been a waste, he grabbed his phone and dialed Sam's number. It rang, rang, and rang.

"Do you not know what time it is?" Sam bit out when he finally answered.

"It's time for me to get answers. I'm here at Jefferies's house. Where the hell is he?"

"You're what? Fuck, Pablo, I already spoke to him. He might recognize you. He could go to the police. They might believe him. Then they'll start looking into my calls with him."

"If he recognizes me, I'll take care of it."

"You're crazy. This could lead back to me. Then who are you going to get to help you? Leave Jefferies alone!"

"Did you talk to the bitch's clients to see if any of them had heard from her?"

"I don't know where Jefferies is and none of Vicki's clients knew she was leaving. They were pissed."

"Someone knows where she is, and I'm losing patience. Find her or I swear, that sweet little wife of yours is going to know that I'm not happy!"

There was a pause, then, "I'm trying." He could hear the fear in Sam's voice. Good. He should be afraid.

"Look, I checked with a contact I have at the underground railroad for abused women," Sam continued. "There's two of them here in L.A. Someone's supposed to call me back."

"She wasn't abused," Pablo snapped.

"Yeah, but she saw you at her place. She knows you're alive, and if she convinced the organization that you're still alive, maybe they helped her. Like you said, someone had to have helped her disappear. I'm working this. So back off."

"I'm not backing off, Sam. Find her."

CHAPTER SIX

The next morning, Juan, with a cup of coffee in his hand and a phone to his ear, stared at his computer screen.

"You coming to dinner?" his brother asked.

"I said I was, didn't I?"

"Just checking," Ricky said.

"I'll be there. See you then." Juan hung up. He hadn't gotten any replies to his Facebook messages about knowing a Nikki Hanson.

After downing the cream-laced brew and taking care of Sweetie, he took off to go buy wood and supplies to fix the rotten fence boards and even picked up a couple of gifts for his nephews for tonight. When he pulled back into his driveway, his gaze shifted to the house next door.

Was she up yet? Was she cuddled up on the sofa

watching Saturday-morning cartoons, as he envisioned Angie would have done? As his mother had done with him and his brother?

Yeah, his mom had loved him and Ricky to a fault. But she'd had one flaw: choosing their father. A father who loved his whiskey, women, and song more than he'd loved his wife and kids. But she believed a woman should stand by her husband, no matter what. Even after she finally wised up and forced him to leave, she hadn't filed for divorce. Till death do us part, she'd vowed. And his dad made sure that's the way it had ended.

Raking a hand through his hair, Juan pushed away the past, reached for his purchases, and went inside.

Thirty minutes later, on his knees in the grass, working to remove one of the rotten fence boards, he heard his neighbor's back door open and close.

He listened. Was Nikki in her backyard? Sweetie, whining and barking at his own back door, drowned out any other noise. He continued working. But when he pulled off the board, a face appeared where the slat had been. He got his first up-close look at the girl. A sweet, young, brown-eyed-cherub kind of face. Her eyes were large, her nose slightly turned up, her mouth a bow.

"Hi," she said, dimples dancing in her cheeks.

Then her eyes widened, her dimples vanished, and he knew she'd seen his scar.

"Hi," he offered, thinking she'd run off.

She didn't. The child remained frozen, squatted at the fence, staring wide-eyed through the slats of wood.

"Sorry." He started to get up when she spoke again.

"You got burned." The words came out almost a whisper.

Surprised by her accurate assessment, he swallowed. "Yeah."

Another beat of silence followed, and then, "Are you Sweetie's dad?"

"Yeah."

"I like her," she said.

"I think she likes you, too."

She gave him a toothy grin.

"Is that her barking?" the child asked.

"Yeah. I think she hears you."

Her grin widened. "I'm Bell."

"Hi, Bell. I'm Juan. I saw you—"

"I know. The other night. Can I play with your dog? With Sweetie?"

Juan almost said *sure*, but caught himself. "Uh, if your mom says it's okay."

"I'll go ask." She popped up.

He waited, listened, and hoped Nikki would come out. But when the door reopened, only light footsteps came running to the fence. He saw Bell's pink tennis shoes before she crouched down.

"She said I could for a little. We're going grocery shopping soon."

"Okay." Did this mean Nikki trusted him? Or was she standing at the back window listening and watching? "I'll get Sweetie."

He passed the dog through the open slat of the fence. While he worked, he listened to the child play with Sweetie.

"Is she a puppy?" Bell asked, stopping by the fence again.

"No, she's three."

"Is she a poodle?"

"Yeah."

"I think she needs a haircut," Bell said. "They are supposed to be puffy on top of their heads and tails."

"Yeah, I was thinking that, too."

"My mom could probably cut it. She cuts my hair."

He chuckled. "I think I need to take her to the doggy salon."

"They could put bows in her hair." The child laughed. "I've seen pictures of poodles with bows."

"Yeah, they could." He remembered Angie had kept the dog in bows.

"Sweetie likes marshmallows," she said.

"She does?" Juan asked.

"Yeah, I save her some from my Lucky Charms in the mornings. I hope that's okay."

"Yeah, a few won't hurt her." He sawed the board to fit in one of the slots.

When the roar of the saw ended, Bell asked, "Is she trained to shake hands?"

"Yeah." He remembered Angie working with the dog to sit, stand, and roll over. Sweetie would even dance for a treat.

The girl started giving the dog commands. Her laughter snuck through the fence and into Juan's mood.

"You're a policeman, aren't you?" Bell asked, her pink shoes appearing at the fence.

"Yes."

"Mom said you are a good policeman."

"She did?" He was tempted to ask the child a few questions, but it felt wrong.

"Yes."

"Bell." Nikki called her daughter. Had she been listening to their conversation? "We need to go now. Pass him back the dog. And say thank you?"

"Okay," Bell said.

Juan waited to see if Nikki would speak to him. She didn't.

The child reappeared at the fence with Sweetie in tow. "Here you go."

"Say thank you," Nikki repeated.

"Thanks for letting me play with her." Bell did as told.

"You're welcome," he said.

"Can I do it again sometime?" Her tone was pleading.

"Sure." His smile appeared effortlessly.

She gave Sweetie a hug, then a gentle push through the missing slat in the fence. He took her. "Have a good day," he said.

"You, too," her young voice chimed, and then she was gone. He heard their back door close. For some reason the silence that followed seemed to mean something. Something sad. Like an echo of the emptiness in his life.

He sat there on the grass, holding the puppy that was supposed to have been for his daughter and fighting a shitload of regrets.

* * *

Around three, Juan pulled into West Mount Apartments, where the waitress at Black Diamond had told him Bates lived. Before he left, he'd gotten four replies from the Facebook messages he'd sent out to possible friends of Nikki V. Hanson. None of them was from Boulder and all claimed they'd never friended anyone by the name of Hanson on Myspace. Four down and four to go. All he needed was one.

He drove around until he spotted the apartment manager's office.

Cool air welcomed him as he entered the office. A woman stood from a desk.

Her "Hello" came with a smile.

He waited for the flinch when she got a good look at his scarred face. She didn't disappoint. But she recovered quickly. People in business usually did.

"I hope you're apartment shopping. We have some nice units."

"Sorry." He showed her his badge and handed her his card. "I was hoping you might tell me if Cindy Bates lives here?"

"I know that name." She frowned slightly. "But let's make sure I'm right." She moved back to her computer. A few taps into her keyboard and her frown deepened. "Yeah, I thought it was her. She lives here, but not for long."

"Meaning?" he asked.

"We handed her an eviction notice last month. She has to be out next week. The other manager tried to speak to her yesterday about some complaint, but she either wasn't home or wasn't answering her door."

"What's her apartment number?"

"Two twenty-three. It's on the south side. If you talk to her, can you remind her she needs to be out by next week?"

Juan didn't answer. Delivering eviction notices wasn't the best way to win over a witness.

By the time he made it up to her apartment, sweat had collected on his brow. He knocked. No answer. He tried again and even announced himself as police.

Nothing. He knocked on the neighbor's door, and a woman with a baby on her hip eased it open. "Yes?"

"Hi, I'm looking for your neighbor, Cindy Bates. Was wondering if you've spoken to her lately."

"No. But I want to." Her tone carried hints of anger. "She stopped my husband and asked if he wanted a private lap dance in her apartment. Said the money was going to orphans."

"Sorry." So Bates might be worse off than he thought. "When was the last time you saw her or heard anything from her apartment?"

She stared hard at the badge. "Yesterday. Her music was up too loud."

"Thanks." He left her a card and asked her to call if she heard anything from the apartment.

He'd just settled in his car when his phone rang. He didn't recognize the number.

"Juan Acosta."

"Yes. My name is Mrs. Henley. You left your card in my mailbox?"

Henley? He remembered. Yeah, the name of the landlord who owned the house Cindy Bates had rented.

"Yes, I was hoping to get a forwarding address of a renter who'd leased your house several years back, but I've since found the address."

"You're talking about that stripper, right?"

"Yes," he said.

"Well, my husband's not here, but you might want to talk to him."

"I appreciate that," Juan said. "But like I said, I found out where she lives."

"Okay, but she's weird. She showed up here a few days ago. Kind of freaked my husband out."

"What happened?"

"I don't know. He just said it was weird."

"Really?" Juan considered. "Can you give me his number?"

"I could, but he's fishing. No reception on the lake."

"Can I stop by this evening?"

"Sure. He should be home around six."

When Juan hung up, he realized he'd be seeing more people today than he had in the last six months. That proved Murdock was wrong when he'd called Juan a borderline recluse.

None of it was easy. He still felt mighty uncomfortable, but he was beginning to believe that maybe one day his life would be almost normal.

Almost.

* * *

Pablo waited until four in the morning, hoping Dan would return home. Finally, he went back to his North Hollywood apartment and snagged a few hours of sleep. He hated this part of Los Angeles. But he couldn't live anywhere near where he'd lived before. He couldn't risk running into an old acquaintance. Not that it'd be easy to recognize him. He'd grown his hair out, put on weight, and even removed tattoos.

Slamming his coffee cup on the table, he grabbed his phone and found Dan Jefferies's number. It rang once, twice, three times.

Finally, the phone clicked. "Hello?" The voice sounded like he'd just woken up.

"Mr. Jefferies?" Pablo said, barely cutting the edge off his tone.

"Who's this?"

"Detective Sam Milbourn. I need to ask you a few more questions about Vicki Trever."

"I already told you I don't know where she is."

Was that a lie Pablo heard in those words? "You haven't heard from her at all?"

"I'm in Denmark and it's nighttime here. So if you don't mind—"

The avoidance was Pablo's answer. "Look, Mr. Jefferies, this isn't a game."

"Hell. I haven't heard from her." This time the lie was even clearer.

"When will you be back in town?" Pablo closed his fist.

"Uh . . . Next Thursday, but like I said—"

"The one coming up or the next?"

"The next, but . . ."

Fuck! "Well, look to hear from me then."

"But I don't know anything. It'll be a waste of your time."

"Then it's my time to waste," Pablo said. "Get some rest, Mr. Jefferies." *You are going to need it.* He hung up and kicked the kitchen chair clear across the room.

Staring at the upside-down chair, he recalled the other contact he had. Marisol Willis. She'd worked for Vicki. Looked like he'd have to pay Marisol a visit.

CHAPTER SEVEN

Vicki lay on the sofa, Bell pressed up against her, as they watched cartoons. Bell was big on cuddling. Vicki wasn't sure if it was normal or if losing her mother had brought it about. Not that it mattered. If letting the child lie close to her brought her comfort, Vicki was for it. She wasn't above admitting it brought her a little comfort, too.

Her niece turned to Vicki. "I love you," Bell said.

Vicki hugged her closer. "I love you, too." Their noses almost touched.

"Eskimo kisses." Bell brushed her nose against Vicki's. Vicki was transported back to when her mom used to do that with her and Alison. Or at least she'd done it during her sober times. Funny how little things got passed down.

Bell reached up and touched her own face, and her smile faded. "I like our neighbor, Juan."

"Okay, but you should call him Mr. Acosta." The mention of her hot neighbor sent a wave of flutters to Vicki's stomach. After staying awake half the night, unable to stop thinking about how good the couple of brief touches had been, she felt more than a little wary. Wary of letting him close, wary of how much she wished she didn't have to keep him at bay.

Why did he have to be a cop?

"Do you like him?" Bell asked.

"He seems nice. But... you know we have to be careful. Not tell people our secrets."

Her niece frowned. "Because they might take me away from you?"

Vicki nodded. She couldn't tell Bell the truth. That her father was still alive. Knowing that would terrorize the child. So Vicki had explained that her father's sister, Estella, was trying to take her away from Vicki. And it wasn't a lie. Even worse was that Los Angeles police were saying Vicki had broken the law by leaving. And that *was* a lie. Joanne, from AWACO, confirmed that Estella hadn't appealed to courts until after Vicki had left. But to prove that, she'd have to go back. And risk that Pablo wouldn't be waiting. That wasn't a risk she'd take.

Bell blinked up at her. "Did you know he has a scar on his face?"

Vicki swallowed the quick emotion that formed in her throat. She tucked a strand of dark hair off her niece's cheek. "Yeah, I saw."

Knowing the conversation might move to Bell's own scars, Vicki sought the right words, but the cartoon came back on and the child rolled over. "I like this cartoon," Bell said.

"Me too." Vicki gave her niece a squeeze.

In a few minutes, Bell turned around. "Sorry your toenails don't look like flags."

Vicki lifted her bare feet and smiled. They'd spent thirty minutes painting each other's toenails. Bell got smiley faces. Having colored an American flag at school, Bell had wanted to paint stars and stripes. "I love them."

Ten minutes later, a chirp sounded from the kitchen. It took Vicki a second to realize it was her cell phone. Since she'd had it, it had rung only once, when she'd received the call that she'd gotten the job at the gym.

Leaving Bell to her cartoon, she hotfooted it into the kitchen. By the time she reached the phone, panic tightened her stomach. Taking a deep breath, she picked up the phone. "Hello?"

"Nikki?" The voice was deep, unsure, and unfamiliar.

"Who is this?" she asked.

"It's Cal."

She didn't know a Cal, did she? Fear quickened her breath and she got that fight-or-flight feeling. And while she knew how to fight, with Bell, flight was the only way.

"Cal Phillips, Suzie's dad. Our kids are in the same class."

Relief spilled over her. "Oh, yes. Suzie's dad. Of course. How . . . how did you get this number?"

"Bell gave it to Suzie."

Bell suddenly appeared in the kitchen doorway. "Please, can she come over? Please, please, please."

Mr. Phillips continued, "Suzie has been pestering me since we got home from school yesterday to call and see if they could play."

Vicki had a whole lot of reservations, but the pleading on Bell's face convinced her.

"How about if Suzie comes over tomorrow?" Vicki asked.

* * *

"Tío!"

Juan heard his nephews, ages eight and six, call him the second he walked through his brother's door.

"Hey, guys! Got you something." He moved in, juggled the wine and flowers, and handed Tomás the bag with the gifts.

"Cool!" they both called and ran back outside, no doubt to fill up the water guns he'd bought them.

Juan saw his brother, Ricky, standing at the grill in the backyard and was heading that way when his sister-in-law called to him from the kitchen.

As he'd parked in front of the house, he'd noted the other cars in the driveway. He'd thought this was a family dinner. Considering he'd just admitted to being a socialite, he decided to endure.

He moved inside and spotted Christina and her brother's wife, Linda, sitting at the kitchen table, along with another woman he didn't recognize.

"Look at you," Christina said, motioning to the wine and flowers. "You didn't have to— Oh, Dios. What happened to your face?"

She shot up from her chair. While she was only eight years his senior, that hadn't stopped her from taking on the maternal role. He'd been fifteen when he went to live with Ricky and Christina. "It's nothing."

Frowning, she took the flowers and the bottle of cabernet from his hands. "I'm glad Ricky isn't a cop."

"Yeah," Juan said, letting her believe his black eye was work-related. No way in hell was he volunteering that a woman had beaten him up.

She looked at the bottle. "I haven't heard of this wine."

"I tried it last night. It was good." When he'd gone to find a bottle for tonight, he saw the wine Nikki'd had the night before on the shelf. He'd bought a couple of bottles for himself as well, but he couldn't deny that he hoped to share them with Nikki.

Remembering the connection his sister-in-law had with his neighbor had him wishing he could get a peek at Nikki's job application. But no matter how many times he tried to figure out a way to ask without risking Nikki's employment, he couldn't.

"Thank you, but you didn't have to bring anything."

"Hey, you serve me home cooking, it's worth it."

She grinned. "Well, I must admit your brother is doing most of the cooking tonight. All I did was make the rice and beans. He's grilling the steaks and corn."

"But no one's rice and beans are like yours."

Christina looked at the other two guests. "See why I love this guy?" His sister-in-law set the bottle on the table and looked back at him. "Juan, you know Linda, and this is Karina, Linda's friend. She just moved here from New Mexico."

Juan nodded. "Welcome to Texas."

"Thank you. I've heard so much about you. It's nice to finally meet you." Karina's smile and tone were just a bit too flirty.

Shit! Was his sister-in-law trying to set him up?

"Yeah," Juan said. "I'm going to...hang out with the guys." He walked out, hoping when he got in the backyard, he'd find a Mr. Karina.

He didn't. And the guilty looks his brother and Christina's brother, Leo, shot him were pure apology. He walked up to them and frowned.

"Shit! What happened to your face?" Ricky asked as he turned a steak.

"It's nothing," he said.

"Well, I'd hate to see the other guy," Leo said.

"Yeah." Juan looked back at his brother. "Tell me Karina being here isn't some kind of setup."

"I'm sorry." Ricky held up a hand. "I wanted to warn you, but I like sleeping in my own bed."

Leo chuckled. "And she's hot."

Linda called out to her husband, who went to see what he'd been summoned for.

Juan stood there, frowning at Ricky. His brother's expression darkened. "Just play nice."

"I'm not an asshole," Juan said. "But it's not going to work. First, I don't like being played, and second, I'm..." He was going to say not ready, but after meeting his neighbor, he couldn't say that with honesty. "I don't like being played."

"Christina worries about you. I worry about you. It's been over three years."

"I know how long it's been. And if the time comes—"

"When," his brother said. "*When* the time comes. Look, we loved Angie, too. But you've got to start living, brother."

Juan exhaled. "When the time comes, it'll be with someone I choose."

"But Karina *is* hot and—"

"She probably is, but I didn't notice, so you know what that means?"

"It means you gotta open your eyes."

"My eyes are plenty open," he said before he realized what that told his brother.

"Really? So you've met someone."

Juan's frown tightened. "I've noticed someone."

"But you haven't met her?" Ricky lifted a confused brow. "What are you, back to *Playboy* magazine? Or is she one of those online pay-per-minute—"

Juan shut him down with a scowl. "I've met her. But it's not…It'll happen when and if it's right." Saying that aloud had his chest feeling suddenly hollow. Was he really considering this? Was it possible when he still loved Angie so much that he didn't feel whole without her?

"Who is she?" Ricky asked.

Christina walked out onto the patio. "Your brother brought me wine and flowers."

Ricky pointed the spatula at him. "Why do you always have to make me look bad?"

"You shouldn't make it so easy," he said.

Christina looped her arm with Juan's. "What do you think of Karina?"

"He's already met someone," Ricky spoke up.

"Who?" Christina's grip tightened. "When are we going to meet her?"

"It's not...We're not..." Shit. How could he make sense of something he didn't understand himself?

* * *

"It's going to hurt. No medicine." Tears filled Bell's eyes as Vicki studied her niece's scratched knee.

"Honey, we need to get the germs out. It's just peroxide. Not alcohol. It's the kind that bubbles up." Vicki had Bell sitting on the side of the tub, blood running down her knee.

Bell had seen another little girl about her age playing across the street, and in hopes of making a friend, she'd begged to go outside and ride her bike. Unfortunately, the other girl had gone inside and after only the first trek down the sidewalk, Bell had hit a rock and fallen off the bike.

Vicki swiped Bell's bangs off her brow. "I promise it won't sting."

"Pinky promise?" Bell's voice shook and she lifted her hand.

Linking her smallest finger with Bell's, Vicki was yanked back to her own childhood. To all the pinky promises she'd made with Alison. Two years older than Alison, Vicki had taken her role of big sister seriously.

"Come on, Alison. Get out." Vicki opened their bedroom window.

"I hate hiding in the shed," Alison pleaded. *"There's spiders in there."*

"They're good spiders. They won't bite. And if I see a bad one, I'll kill it."

"Promise?" Alison asked. *"Pinky promise?"*

Vicki locked her pinky with Alison's. Then, carrying a blanket and pillow, they crawled out and crept across the backyard to the shed where their dead father's old lawnmower and tools were.

Vicki, only nine, was scared of spiders, too. But she knew that she could step on a spider. She couldn't protect Alison from the drunk two-legged monster her mom had brought home. And the last time he'd been there, Vicki had woken up to him standing in their bedroom.

She didn't really understand what the man had been doing, his hand in his pants, but she was smart enough to know it wasn't good.

Pulling out of the past, she poured the peroxide on Bell's knee. "Now, that wasn't so bad, was it?" Vicki asked.

"Not too bad." Bell looked down at her knee. "I wish that little girl would have stayed outside."

"I know. But it's getting dark."

Bell frowned. "I wish I had a sister like you had my mom. Mama said you two were best friends."

"Yeah, we were."

"Do you miss her as much as I do?" Bell asked, and got tears in her eyes again.

"Yeah. I do."

* * *

Two hours later, Juan left his brother's. As he drove to the Henley place, he conceded that everyone was right. Karina was pretty. And nice. To her credit, when she got a good look at the right side of his face, she didn't flinch. Obviously, she'd been warned.

But as pretty and nice as she was, he simply wasn't interested. And for the rest of the party, instead of working on being a good conversationalist, he found himself thinking about the woman who had interested him. He even snuck away to check and see if he'd gotten any more messages from the Myspace connections.

It was almost eight when Juan arrived at the Henley house. He wasn't sure if speaking to Mr. Henley, Cindy Bates's former landlord, would give him any more information to help find her, but he needed to exhaust all leads. His gut said Cindy held the clue to what happened to Abby Noel.

He knocked on the Henleys' door. A boy around the age of eight opened it.

"Hi. Is your mom or dad home?"

"Yeah." The boy stared up at Juan. At his scar.

"Who is it?" a woman asked.

The boy didn't answer.

The woman appeared at the door.

"I'm Detective Acosta. I spoke to you earlier."

"Yeah." She met his gaze, then did the normal cut of the eyes away.

"What happened to your face?" the boy blurted out.

"Tommy!" the mom scolded.

Juan said, "I was in an accident."

"Did it hurt?"

"Tommy!" the woman reprimanded the boy again.

Juan gave the woman a smile. "It's okay. I have a nephew his age." He looked at Tommy. "Hurt like the devil."

"My husband is cleaning fish in the backyard. Come on back."

Juan followed her into the backyard.

"Hon, the cop is here."

The man turned away from a table where he was cleaning his catch.

"I'm Detective Juan Acosta."

"Yeah, my wife told me she found the note and card and called you. I'm glad. The chick freaked me out."

"When did she show up?"

"Two days ago. Tommy saw her from the living room window just sitting on the swing." He motioned to the yard. "I came out and she was...acting really strange."

"Did she say anything?"

"I asked what she wanted and she told me that she used to live here, and I told her I knew that because I was the one who rented the house to her." He poked at another fish with his knife. "She just sat there swinging like she had all day. I told her she was going to have to leave. She got upset and said I didn't appreciate all she'd done for the place. Said I owed her five hundred dollars."

"What did you tell her?"

"I reminded her that it was five years ago and I'd given her deposit back. And told her I never asked her to do any of the upgrades."

"Did she do a lot of work?"

"She painted, added a cabinet in the bathroom, and did some landscaping. And yeah, she was the one who bought the swing. But she left it here. I mean, if she'd insisted that she wanted it back, then I'd have let her take the swing, but I'm telling you, I don't think she was all there. She looked like she'd been crying."

Juan glanced at the swing. It wasn't that expensive. Not that it didn't look nice beneath the big magnolia tree in the front corner of the garden.

"She didn't say anything else?"

"No."

"Well, if she shows up again, make sure you call me." Juan handed the man another card.

None of this added up. Why was Cindy Bates acting so strangely, and could it all be connected to Abby Noel's disappearance?

* * *

When Juan pulled into his driveway later that night, he noticed a light on in Nikki's living room. The thought of taking her glass and a new bottle of wine over to her house crossed his mind, but his gut said it'd be pushing it. So did his heart.

Still, when Sweetie darted out the door, he stepped outside, stood there listening, hoping he'd hear Nikki in her backyard. No such luck.

So he left the dog to her business and checked again to see if he'd gotten anything new from any of the possible Myspace connections. He hadn't.

The Noel file rested beside his computer. He hadn't gotten shit on her, either. His gut still said that Bates held the secret to solving the Noel case. He pulled out the emergency contact number he'd squeezed out of the manager of the Black Diamond. At this hour, he questioned if he should wait until the morning.

Remembering Henley saying how strangely Bates had behaved, he decided the late-night intrusion might be merited.

The call went straight to voice mail. He left his name, said he was a detective trying to reach Cindy Bates. It was tempting to add something about his concern for Bates's well-being, but that felt like a bit too much.

He hung up, put the beer he'd bought for Sunday's poker party in the fridge, and then dropped into his chair. That's when he realized Sweetie hadn't come scratching on the door. He walked into the backyard. He called once. Twice.

"Shit!" he said. She had to have found another way into Nikki's yard. He considered jumping the fence, but based on what happened last time he'd entered without an invite, he took off back into his house.

He grabbed Nikki's glass and one of the bottles of wine he'd purchased and headed next door.

CHAPTER EIGHT

Vicki was on the couch, deep in the world of her romance novel, when her doorbell chimed. Seeing it was after eleven, she went straight to panic. Who could it be?

She grabbed her phone from the coffee table, punched in 911, but didn't hit dial. One step closer to her front door and she heard the bark coming from her back patio. Panic fading, she peered out the front window and saw Juan standing on her porch.

As she opened the door, a line from the novel tiptoed across her mind: *She found herself wishing she'd met this man at a different time. A different place—like in Alabama, when her life wasn't one big question mark.*

Vicki had never lived in Alabama, but replace it with California and...

"I'm so sorry. I hope I didn't wake up Bell," he said

the second she opened the door, and then he handed her a bottle of wine and her glass. "Sweetie got out again."

Her gaze spilled over his wide chest. Another line from the book whispered across her memory. *"I'm actually really good at sex."* She'd bet Juan was better than good.

Sweetie's bark at her back door pulled her mind to the present. She stepped back. He stepped in. "I thought you fixed the fence."

"I did. But there must be another hole. I was going to jump the fence, but after last time, that didn't seem like a good idea." He offered another apologetic shrug and soft grin. One that came off sexy. "I do learn from my mistakes."

Rattled by her sensual mood, she looked at the bottle of wine, surprised it was the same one she'd been drinking last night. "And this?"

"An apology gift? I saw it at the store today and bought a couple of bottles."

"That's sweet, but you didn't have to do that." She held the bottle out to him. He didn't take it back. Sweetie barked again. Vicki went to let her in.

The dog bounced through the door, cocked her head and looked at Juan, then ran to Vicki. Vicki set the wine down on the coffee table and picked up the dancing poodle. "So you're a little escape artist."

"I think you've stolen my dog," Juan said.

"I'm sure it's Bell," Vicki said. "She feeds her marshmallows."

"Yeah, but I'm betting she likes women more than

men." He motioned to the metal detector leaning against the wall beside the back door. "Did you find your necklace?"

"No. I was going to look some more tomorrow, but you can take back the detector if you need it."

"No. I was...going to suggest we try again. I'm completely free. Now."

Now? The word *no* sat on the tip of her tongue. All she had to do was...

"We could open the bottle, grab another glass, and try to find the necklace. One glass," he said, as if he could read her reservations.

Logic said this wasn't wise. But everything else said yes. Yes to finding her necklace. Yes to not spending the rest of the evening alone. "I..." She looked at the clock on the wall.

"It's Saturday night. And since I'm the reason you lost the necklace, it's only fair that I help you find it." His gaze stayed on her face.

"One glass," she said.

He smiled. "Why don't you pour, and I'll start looking for the necklace?"

She offered the smallest of nods, watched him pick up the metal detector and walk outside.

Still snuggling his dog, she stood there a good thirty seconds. The dog tilted her muzzle back and licked her across the cheek. "Okay, a glass of wine. A little conversation. No harm done, right?"

* * *

Seeing Nikki walk out with two glasses and a flashlight under her arm had him recalling what he'd told his brother. *I've met her. But it's not... It'll happen when and if it's right.* He hadn't decided if it was right, but there was something about her that made him feel alive again.

Did she feel it, too? Maybe. She'd agreed to let him help her find the necklace. Not that he hadn't seen her hesitancy. In fact, when she'd first opened that door, he could swear he saw fear in her eyes. He supposed a doorbell late at night could put any woman on alert, but again his instinct said it was more.

Sweetie darted out behind her. "Tomorrow I'll find out where she snuck through."

Nikki nodded. He moved in and set the metal detector against the lawn chair she'd been using last night.

He took a glass from her, brought it to his lips, and took a slow sip. "You know, there are forty-dollar bottles that don't carry this much character. It's fruit forward. A slow finish. Chocolate and blueberry, or maybe raspberry, but with just enough toasted oak that it adds to the flavor and doesn't overpower it. And it has great fingers, too." He twirled the glass and looked at it.

"Wow. You know your wine," she said.

"No. I'm a complete fake. Just repeating what my sister-in-law said about it tonight. I have no idea what 'slow finish' or 'fruit forward' mean. I have no idea how wine can have fingers. And when I think about toasted oak, I think of toasted oats and Cheerios."

Nikki laughed.

He let himself savor the sound before speaking. "I had dinner at my brother's tonight. My sister-in-law,

Christina, is a complete wine snob. One of her life missions is to find a great cheap wine. I think you might have helped her accomplish that. When I left, she was sending my brother out to pick up a case."

"The same sister-in-law who works at Finally Fit?"

"Yup."

She nodded. "Well, I'd never tried the wine until last night. But I'd heard about the winery, so I picked up a bottle. She's right. It's good."

"So you're a wine connoisseur?" he asked.

"Maybe a bit more than you are. But not by much."

He stared at the wine. "Well, I think I should probably go pick up some more bottles. She belongs to a wine club and every store in town is liable to sell out once she tells her friends about it."

She smiled and silence fell. "So you have a brother?"

"Yeah. You? You have siblings?"

Her gaze immediately shot to the left as if she needed to think about the question. And it wasn't a think-about-it kind of question. He sipped his wine and stared at her over the rim of the glass. *What all are you hiding, Nikki? And why?*

"No. Only child." She reached for the metal detector and moved into the yard. He picked up the flashlight and followed her, shining light on the ground as she waved the detector over the grass.

"You have other siblings?" she asked, almost to fill the silence.

"Nope. Just one brother." Sweetie curled up on the lounge chair as if to nap.

"Older? Younger?"

"Older, by eight years," he said.

"You close?"

"Yeah. We're it when it comes to family."

She stopped and looked up. "He have kids?"

"Yeah. Two boys. Eight and six. Full of life, mischief, armpit sounds, and pet lizards and snakes. They give Christina a run for her money."

"Sounds like a good evening," she said.

"It was okay," he said, realizing his tone had given more away than he'd meant to.

"Just okay?" The metal detector hummed.

He ran a hand over his chin. "It turned out to be more of a dinner party than just the family."

"And you aren't the dinner-party type?" She took another step.

He waved the light across the grass, considering his answer, but when only the truth came to mind, he went with it. "Normally I don't mind, but let's say Christina's trying to put a little pressure on me to...broaden my horizons."

Nikki looked up, questions in her eyes.

"She had someone there for me to meet."

"Oh." She looked away. "And don't tell me, 'she had a good personality.'"

He grinned. "No, she was...pretty. And nice."

"But?" She focused on the ground again. When he didn't answer, she asked, "How long ago did your wife die?"

"Three years," he said.

Her eyes met his again. "Your sister-in-law is right. You need to...'broaden your horizons.'"

"I think I'm getting there." He held her gaze. Something said she knew exactly what he meant. Which explained why she immediately went back to moving the metal detector.

It was a full thirty seconds later when her question spilled out into the night. "How did your wife die?"

The answer ran around his head and bumped into his heart. He wanted some more info from her tonight, but he was giving more than he got.

"I'm sorry," she said. "That's none of my—"

"No," he said, realizing if he gave a little, she might, too. "I was working undercover and the bad guys found out. A bomb was put under our house."

He heard her intake of air. Shock. Empathy. Funny how just a gasp could tell so much. "My god. I'm sorry."

"Me too."

They walked the grass in silence, as if too much had been said too quickly. Each taking slow, easy steps, eyes to the ground. He focused the light close to where she waved the metal detector. She took a step and the light hit her bare feet. Expecting to see her sexy pink-painted toenails, he stopped, a little surprised.

Her toes looked . . . red, white, and gray and it wasn't just the nails that were painted but the ends of her toes as well.

She wiggled her toes as if noticing they were in the limelight, then glanced up, grinning. "Bell and I gave each other pedicures. She got smiley faces. I got . . ."

He grinned. "Armadillo road kill?"

Her laughter spilled into the night air, then looking

down, she curled her toes in the grass. "Be nice. It was supposed to be stars and stripes like the American flag. We didn't have blue, so she used gray. But her creative vision didn't quite pan out."

He laughed again, but it came with a somber thought. Angie would have done that. She'd have let their little girl paint her toenails, her whole damn foot, and worn it proudly. "That's…"

She looked up. "What?" she asked with humor, but her smile faded, probably because his had.

"Nothing, just…you're an amazing mom."

It wasn't the first smile he'd gotten from her, but it may have been the first real one. For sure the most beautiful.

"Thank you. I work hard at it, but it…I mean, it's not that hard because she's the amazing one." Pride echoed in her eyes and tone.

"She seems smart," he said.

"She is. Today I told her she could pick out a half gallon of ice cream. She stood in the freezer section for ten minutes reading all the different flavors. When she hit one she couldn't read, she asked me what it was. Neapolitan. She was blown away that it had three flavors in it and picked it. On the way home, she asked me what the ice cream had to do with horses. I said it didn't, but when we got home we Googled it. How did she know that there was an extinct horse that was called a Neapolitan?"

Love and pride sounded in Nikki's voice and his admiration of the woman standing in front of him grew. "Maybe *Sesame Street*?"

"Probably. She's like a sponge."

"Or maybe she takes after her mom," he said.

"No." Her smile faded a notch. "She's way smarter than...I ever was." She sipped her wine.

They went back to necklace hunting, moving around in the late-night silence. After a couple of minutes, the quietness felt empty. "What made you want to become a cop?" she asked.

Not only was she good at asking questions, but the ones she chose hit hard and heavy. Telling himself he didn't want to put a damper on the evening, he offered a vague answer. "A need for justice."

They took a few more steps. He chanced throwing the question back. "Why did you go into fitness?"

She lifted her head, pulled her glass from her mouth, and her eyes met his. A drop of wine lingered on her bottom lip and he wanted to taste it, taste her lips.

"A need for justice," she answered.

He lifted a brow.

Her tongue dipped out and caught the drop of her wine. "My mom had a bad habit of choosing men who thought their fists could solve problems. I wasn't going to let it happen to me."

It was what he thought to be the most honest answer she'd given him to date. And he wondered if one of those men was behind whatever it was he suspected she was hiding. More than anything, even more than he wanted to kiss her, he wanted her trust. *What's going on, Nikki? What are you afraid of?* He ached to ask, but sensed he'd lose the little ground he'd gained.

Instead, he spoke another truth. "And you think you're not smart?"

She looked up, and they shared another honest gaze. He went back to wanting to kiss her, and damn if he didn't think she was thinking the same thing.

But right then his phone, stuck in his back pocket, rang. "Excuse me," he said.

It was an Anniston area code. However, he didn't recognize the number. He took one step back for privacy. "Hello?"

"Detective Acosta?"

"Yes," he answered.

"I'm Candace Brown. You gave me your card. I'm Cindy Bates's neighbor."

"Yes," he said.

"I know it's late. But you said to call if something happened and there's something happening over there right now. Fighting."

"How bad does it sound?"

"Bad," she answered.

"Okay, I'll call it in. I'm on my way." The sooner he got to Cindy Bates, maybe the sooner he could find out what happened to Abby Noel.

He hung up and met Nikki's gaze again.

"Work?" she asked.

"Yeah. Sorry to bail on you. I gotta go. But... thanks." He collected his dog from the lounge chair. He looked back at Nikki. "I had a great time."

"It... was just a glass of wine. And you brought the wine."

He smiled. "Not because of the wine, because of the company."

* * *

Juan called for a car to meet him at Bates's apartment. He arrived before the backup team, so he patted his gun in his shoulder holster and took off up the stairs to Bates's place.

He'd no more than reached the second-floor landing when Bates's door swung open. A man the size of a large bear stepped out. Light flooded out behind him. Then Juan noticed blood running down the man's face and on his knuckles.

Juan froze. "Stop right there. Anniston P—" He hadn't finished announcing himself when all three hundred pounds of man charged him.

The man bulldozed into him, and Juan lost his footing. While he worked to save himself, the man flew down the steps. Juan broke his fall by grabbing onto a metal slat of the railing. Unfortunately, the sharp edge ripped into his right palm. The pain offered a shot of adrenaline.

He blasted down the stairs after the perp. The man hauled ass across the parking lot, Juan hauling ass right behind him. The night was quiet and the sound of their feet slapping the pavement echoed in the darkness.

"Stop! Police!" Juan yelled.

The man moved faster. Feeling the burn in his palm, Juan pushed himself. A car up ahead beeped as if the man had unlocked it.

"I said stop!" Juan growled, gaining on the asswipe. Pushing his legs faster, harder, he caught the guy's shirt. The man twisted, hit the ground, rolled. But he didn't stay down. He popped up with a knife and a murderous glint in his eyes.

"Drop it." Juan raised his Glock. Finger on the trigger, he meant business. "Never bring a knife to a gun fight," he spit out, the barrel of the weapon slick against his bloody palm.

The knife's six-inch blade clanked on the pavement. Without being told, the man held up his hands. Obviously, he was familiar with the routine.

"What did I do?" he asked, his breathing labored.

"You mean besides attacking an officer?" Juan said. "You tell me. Why did you run?"

Right then a patrol car raced into the parking lot, sirens blaring and lights flashing. The man at the end of his gun looked around as if tempted to run. "Don't do it, buddy."

When the officer got out of the car, Juan recognized it was Billy. They exchanged nods.

"I didn't know you were a cop," the perp said to Juan. "And I didn't do shit. She attacked me." He lowered one hand to his head. "Look at me."

Yeah, his condition worried Juan, because if this asshole looked that bad, what did Bates look like? Juan moved in and kicked the knife away. It didn't appear to be bloody. For that, Juan was grateful.

CHAPTER NINE

As soon as the handcuffs were on the perp, Juan said, "I'm going to check the apartment."

"She's the one who attacked me!" The bozo started bitching again. Ignoring him, Juan ran back to the apartments and bolted up the stairs. Heart beating to an adrenaline tune, he felt the blood oozing from his palm.

He approached the door with caution. "Police." He knocked, and the door, left ajar, swung open. "Ms. Bates?"

No answer came. Only a dead silence.

Afraid she was unconscious or worse, he moved in. Gun held tight, he looked left, then right.

"Police," he repeated, mentally preparing himself for what he might find. As a cop, especially before he worked in the Cold Case Unit, he'd faced a lot of ugly.

You'd think he'd have gotten used to it, but it was a bitch every time.

He took a quick look into the kitchen. No Bates. But blood smeared the white tile, showcasing some footprints. His next intake of air smelled coppery. What was the chance all that blood was from the perp in handcuffs? Slim.

He moved into the short hallway. Hands still tight on the gun, he pushed the bathroom door open with his foot. Nothing there, but more blood where it appeared someone had tried to wash up in the sink.

His mind wandered to Nikki, who'd taken up fitness to keep this kind of shit from happening. Yet she was running. Had someone hurt her like this? Had she bled at the hands of some asshole before she learned to fight?

Pushing thoughts of his neighbor away, he turned to the door of the only other room in the apartment.

"Police." He gave the partially closed door a nudge. Shoulders tight, he swept his gaze over the room, expecting to find a battered and bruised woman, hopefully still breathing.

No woman, breathing or otherwise.

Clothes were piled on the bed. An open suitcase lay there as if someone was packing. A trail of blood on the beige carpet led to the closet.

"Shit." Gut knotted, he jerked open the door. Nothing.

Where the hell was Cindy Bates?

He moved out of the bedroom. Then out of the apartment. When his feet hit the landing, he heard a car squealing off on the opposite side of the building.

Juan moved to the railing to get a better view. Through the distance and darkness, he could call it a small red or burgundy car. An old Saturn, maybe? And his gut said the person driving like a bat out of hell across the parking lot was Cindy Bates.

He closed his fist against the sting in his palm. When he looked down, he saw the blood ooze between his fingers. Then he noted the blood splatter on the concrete landing.

Not all his. And he was pretty damn sure the rest wasn't all from the asshole in handcuffs. How badly was Cindy Bates injured?

Pissed he'd lost her, Juan shot back down the stairs to where Billy waited with their perp.

"And?" Billy asked.

"I think she just drove off." He looked at the man sitting on the concrete. "How bad was she hurt?"

"I told you she came at me."

"I didn't ask you that. How bad was she hurt?"

"I don't know. I'm not a doctor. I had to defend myself."

"Right." Juan moved in. "You got ID on you?"

He didn't answer.

"You search him yet?" Juan asked Billy.

"Was just about to do that," Billy said. "I called for paramedics."

"Stand up," Juan insisted, and then motioned for Billy to do the search.

Billy looked down at Juan's hand. "You okay?"

"Yeah," Juan said, but he'd yet to look and see how bad it was.

Twenty minutes later, the paramedics had arrived and decided that the perp, J. T. Cote, didn't need medical treatment, but Juan did. J.T. had two previous convictions for drug possession with intent to distribute, as well as an arrest warrant. He wasn't going home tonight.

"Where's your girlfriend?" Billy asked J.T. as he was putting him in the back of his car.

"She's not my girlfriend!" J.T. insisted. "Look, she stole from me. I came to collect and she attacked me."

"What did she steal?" Juan asked.

When J.T. didn't answer, Juan guessed. "Drugs?"

The man still didn't answer, but from the grim line of his mouth, Juan figured he was right.

* * *

"This is not your week."

Juan looked up from his palm being stitched to Connor walking into the ER. "What the hell you doing here?"

"Billy ratted you out. I ran into him at the pub by my place. He said you came here to get sewn up."

"Don't move," the doctor said.

"Sorry," Juan growled.

Connor looked down at Juan's palm. "Does that hurt?"

"No. It feels great." Juan glared at his partner. "Didn't you have a girl at the bar lined up to go home with you? Why'd you come here?"

"I had two, but I sacrificed for you. You owe me."

"I'd think so." The young doctor grinned.

"Right," Juan said.

The doctor did his last pass with the needle, knotted it, and stepped back. "Fifteen stitches. You're lucky you didn't cut a tendon. The nurse will be in to discuss follow-up care."

When the doctor stepped out, Connor asked, "So what happened?"

"Didn't Billy fill you in?"

"Only a little. He was meeting a girl there."

Juan explained how he'd found Cindy Bates's address and had given the neighbor his card. He went on about getting the neighbor's call and what had happened.

"And you don't know how badly she's hurt?" Connor asked.

"No. But there was a trail of blood leading to where her car was parked."

Connor ran a hand over his chin. "If she was hurt, why would she run?"

"Drugs, maybe. Or something more."

"You really think she knows something about Noel's disappearance?"

"Yeah, I do." He told him about discovering that Noel's phone had made calls to Bates during the time Bates claimed they were together. "And get this. She sends birthday cards to Abby's kid every year."

"So you think she does it out of guilt? You think she just knows something or is more involved than that?"

Juan pushed off of the hospital bed and stood up. "That I don't know. I got an emergency contact number from the Black Diamond. Her sister. I called and left a message, but haven't heard back."

"And you don't have names of any friends she might go to?"

"No. Everyone claims she was a loner. A waitress from the Black Diamond said Bates had been falling off the edge lately. She was fired last week."

"Do you know what she's driving?" Connor asked.

"Yeah. A burgundy Saturn. I ran her through the system. Her license is expired. She got a ticket last week. I put her name out as a person of inquiry, told them not to detain her, but contact us if found. She's also being evicted from her apartment, so if we don't get to her before she moves out, I'm afraid we'll lose her."

"Okay. Maybe we should have the patrol do drive-bys."

"Already set that up. But I'm doubting she'll go back there tonight. I'm pretty sure she ran because she saw Billy's lights in the parking lot. I figured I'd drive over tomorrow morning."

"Give me the address. I'll run by on my way home just to make sure."

"It's late, you sure you want to do that?"

"I barely sleep," Connor said. Juan lifted a brow at the confession. He knew that, like him, Connor had demons that kept him up at night. Three years ago, right about the same time Juan's life went to hell, so had Connor's. A drug raid gone bad. It had been ruled a good shoot, but the perp had been a kid. That was tough.

The nurse came in, bandaged Juan's wound, gave

him his walking papers, then handed Connor her phone number.

"Seriously?" Juan asked when the nurse left. "How do you do that?"

Connor smiled. "I was talking to her before I checked on you."

"You didn't come here for me. You came to hit on the nurses?" Juan shook his head.

Connor laughed and they walked out of the ER together.

"I'll see you tomorrow for poker," Connor said.

Before his friend stepped away, Juan's phone rang. His first thought was Cindy Bates's sister, but it was an Anniston number.

"Bad news?" Connor asked.

"Don't know." Juan answered the call. "Acosta."

"Hi, it's Star. You said for me to call you if I saw Cindy." The soft feminine voice hit a few familiar notes, but not enough for him to know who it was. "When I was leaving the club, she was parked by my car. She offered to sell me some drugs. She obviously had sold some already because she had a wad of money on her."

Juan remembered the waitress at the Black Diamond. "Is she still there?"

"No, I warned her that she could get into a lot of trouble doing what she was doing. She told me the money was for a good cause—some orphaned kid or something. And she looked bad, like someone beat her up. I told her she needed to go to the hospital, but I could tell she wasn't going. Then I told her a hot cop had come by asking about her. She ran off."

"How long ago was that?"

"Thirty minutes."

Juan frowned. Cindy could be anywhere by now. "Thanks. Call me again if you hear from her, maybe quicker next time."

He hung up and explained the call to Connor.

"You talk about me getting a nurse's number when you got strippers calling you?"

"That's work-related," Juan said.

"Right," Connor answered.

Twenty minutes later, Juan pulled into his driveway. He hit the garage door opener, but didn't pull in right away. Instead, he sat there in his running car, staring at the house next door, thinking about Nikki.

Remembering . . . her smile, her laughter, and the way his blood hummed when he was close to her.

Her house was dark—it was after two in the morning, she was sleeping. A slow, seductive image formed in his mind. Nikki in her nightshirt, her hair scattered on a soft pillow. Him in bed with her, running his hand under that nightshirt, removing it. Him tasting her lips, tasting all the secret parts of her body. Him aching to bury himself inside her.

He raked a hand through his hair. It was going to be a long, hard night.

* * *

The sound of pounding on his door woke Pablo up. He rolled out of bed and looked at the clock. Two a.m. He knew who it was. Sam. It made sense, he worked

Homicide. Pablo knew the body would be found sooner or later.

He went and took a piss, then started for the door. On the way out of the bathroom, he saw his face, the scratch marks down his cheek. He frowned. Marisol Willis, Vicki's ex-employee, had gotten him good. The bitch had paid for it, though. His plan had been to just ask a few questions. Unfortunately, she'd recognized him. How was he to know Vicki's employee would have recognized him? Even then, he hadn't planned on making her suffer. He could have snuffed her out real quick-like, but no, she'd gone and made it hard on herself.

A damn shame, too. Because he hadn't gotten anything useful. Not that she didn't try. One mention of visiting her kids' bedroom and the mother sang like a canary about how Vicki had seen him running from her condo the day he'd searched her place for his money. How she'd gone to the police about him being alive. But he'd known that. Sam had told him.

The knocking started again when he made the living room. He picked up his gun from the coffee table before moving to the door. Sam was gonna be pissed. Not that he'd try anything. Sam was a coward. Pablo wasn't sure he'd ever used a weapon on the job.

"Stop," Pablo said right as he turned the lock.

"You did it, didn't you?" Sam barged in.

Pablo shut the door. "Keep your voice down. The walls are thin."

"You bastard!" Sam seethed.

"And it's your fault," Pablo said. "If you'd found Vicki, or better yet, not fucking lost her two weeks ago, Marisol Willis would still be alive. This is on you, buddy!" He pointed his gun at Sam. "And don't forget it."

"What kind of animal are you?"

"The kind who wants justice. The kind who isn't a coward. The kind who gets the job done. That said, I have to give you credit. You were right. She didn't know where Vicki is."

Sam's face paled, went green like he might just throw up. "She didn't do anything. She was innocent. And you killed her."

"Not that innocent." He turned his cheek and with his gun motioned to the scratches. "Believe me when I tell you that she regretted laying her hands on me."

"You're sick." Sam cupped his hand over his mouth.

"I'm sick of waiting, but I've already told you that. Have you heard anything from the group that's hiding abused women?"

"I left a number. They're supposed to call me."

"Call you? Fuck that. Find them."

"It doesn't work that way, damn it. They don't trust cops. I was told they'd have to look into me before I'd hear from them."

"I don't have time! I'm running out of money and patience."

Sam just stared at him. "I can't believe you killed that woman. I told you I'd—"

"Stop whining. It could have been worse. I could have killed the kids. I chose not to. So give me some credit. But not too much credit. Because if you let me down, people you love will pay."

For one second Pablo thought Sam might have grown a pair, because his hand reached in his coat as if to pull out his gun. Pablo slammed him against his living room wall, lifted his gun, and pressed it in the man's right eye socket.

"Don't do it, buddy. Even if I have to kill you, I'll still go after your wife. So you'd better find Vicki Trever or more people are going to die."

CHAPTER TEN

Bell's shattering scream jolted Vicki from a deep sleep. Out of bed in a fraction of a second, she bolted through her room, panic zipping through her like lightning chasing darkness in a black sky. The thought searing through her mind as she cut into the child's bedroom was *Why didn't I grab the baseball bat from the closet?* But instinct said to get to Bell. Instinct said this was just another dream.

Bell stood in the middle of the room, her tiny fists drawn to her chest, her eyes closed, screaming.

She was alone. The only person hurting her right now was in her head.

Every nightmare Bell had, every time Vicki was yanked from sleep in the middle of the night, Vicki hated Pablo more. Hate usually led to anger, but sometimes it took her someplace else. It took her to fear.

Fear Pablo would find them. Fear she wasn't big enough, strong enough to stop a madman. That even her baseball bat wasn't enough. Fear she'd failed to keep the last pinky promise she'd given her sister before they'd unplugged her from life support. A promise that Vicki would protect Bell.

"Sweetheart!" Vicki pulled her niece into a soft hug. "It's okay. It's just a bad dream."

Sobs—deep, soul-hurting sobs—shook the child as she gripped handfuls of Vicki's nightshirt in her fists.

"It's okay," Vicki whispered, rubbing her hand down the child's head, gently cupping her shoulders and pulling her against her. Bell buried her tear-dampened face into Vicki's nightshirt.

"It's okay," Vicki repeated. But it wasn't. Damn it to hell and back. It wasn't okay. A child should never have lived through what Bell had.

"It was just a dream," Vicki continued. "I'm here. We're okay."

"He was hurting us again!" Bell said, then reburied her face into Vicki's side.

Pain, raw and deep, rose in Vicki's chest. She fought to push it away, fought not to let the child feel her rage.

"It was just a nightmare, baby." Vicki scooped her up and carried her to bed. She dropped down on the mattress and pulled Bell's tense body close. "I'm here. Everything is okay."

The room remained silent for several minutes. Vicki continued to run her hand gently over Bell's back.

"I wish I'd had a good daddy like Suzie." Her niece's voice shook.

"You've got me," Vicki said. "And I love you to the moon and back."

"You aren't going to die like Mama, are you?" Her shoulders started shaking again.

"No, I'm here. Right here with you."

A few sleepy moments passed before Bell spoke again. "Why are some people so mean?"

"I don't know, sweetheart," Vicki said. "But let's think about good things. Look at your toes. They're smiling at you."

Bell didn't look down, but instead wrapped her little arms around Vicki's neck and hung on. "Can you sleep here with me for a while, please?"

"Yeah."

Vicki lay there, running her hand over Bell's tiny shoulders, staring at the ceiling. She felt her niece's small body relax when sleep claimed her, but Vicki couldn't sleep. Getting up, she checked the locks in the house.

Then she moved back into her bedroom, opened the closet, and stared at the baseball bat. It was one of the few things Vicki had brought with her. It had belonged to her dad. But it wasn't his connection to the object that held appeal.

It had saved her mother's life.

She'd been thirteen. Alison, eleven.

The memory played like a bad horror movie in her mind. *Get in the closet*, she'd yelled at Alison.

But he's hurting her.

I know, I'm going to help, but you stay in the closet! They'd lost the house by then, lost the shed that they'd hid in when things got bad. If they hadn't lived in a second-story apartment, she'd have made Alison climb out the window. The closet was all she had. But when she'd pushed Alison through the door and told her to hide behind the lower rack of clothes, she'd spotted the one thing she had of her father's, his baseball bat. She'd grabbed it, shut her sister inside, and gone to help her mom fend off her crazy-ass boyfriend.

When she got into the living room, Andrew had her mother down on the floor. Her mom was kicking, her arms flailing at her sides, but she wasn't screaming anymore. That was because Andrew had his hands around her throat. He was killing her.

Vicki screamed for him to let her mom go. When he didn't, she did what she had to do. She swung. Swung hard. The sound that bat made hitting his head still haunted her sometimes. But she didn't regret it. She couldn't.

There wasn't a doubt that Andrew would have killed her mom. She knew the police wouldn't have arrived in time. As it was, they burst in the door a couple of minutes later. Her mom was still on the floor, gasping for air. Andrew was still unconscious, blood oozing from his temple.

Vicki was standing there in shock, still holding the bat. She thought he was dead. Thought she'd killed him. She still couldn't find it in herself to be sorry.

The police had to pry the bat from her hands. Not that they blamed her. They blamed her mom. So did Vicki. Andrew was the sixth piece-of-shit man her mom had taken up with since her father's death.

Andrew woke up before the ambulance got there. They took him and her mom to the hospital. That was the first time Vicki and her sister had been in temporary foster care. Mom went into rehab for two weeks. She stayed clean after that for about a year. It had been a good year, too. But it didn't last.

Closing her eyes, Vicki tried to push the bad out of her head and think about something, anything good. Nothing came to mind. Instead, fear stayed in the pit of her chest. She picked up the bat and carried it with her back into Bell's bedroom. If only she'd had that bat when Pablo had been hurting Alison and Bell. If only she hadn't introduced Alison to him. If only Vicki had fought harder to stay in Alison's life when Pablo started isolating Alison and Bell. If only Vicki had been closer, she'd have known about the abuse. If only Alison were still alive. *If only*...

She reached up for the missing necklace.

Vicki set the bat beside the nightstand and crawled into bed with Bell. An hour later, she still lay there, listening to her niece sleep, listening to her breathe, and still feeling afraid.

Right before slumber claimed her, one good thing whispered across her mind. Her neighbor, sharing wine and conversation, and, for a short while, making her feel less alone. He'd tried to protect her when someone was breaking in. If Pablo found them...? Just knowing Juan was next door made her feel...safer.

Was there any way to hold on to that, without letting him get so close that her secrets were exposed?

* * *

Sweetie's gotta-potty whine woke Juan up at seven the next morning. "Female bladders," he muttered, and pushed out of bed. The first thing he realized was that his hand was throbbing. The second thing he realized was that his hand wasn't the only body part throbbing. The fantasies he'd indulged in last night had lingering effects.

Ignoring both body parts, eyes half-shut, he moved through the living room. He went to open the back door only to remember Sweetie had escaped again last night into Nikki's yard. Wearing only his boxers, he snagged the leash, then shoeless, shirtless, and still sporting a stiffy, he walked into his backyard.

The sun, only peeking up past the eastern horizon, spit out a few golden rays. The cool night air hung on in the dusty morning and dew clung to the grass.

"Do your business," he said, yawning.

Sweetie squatted, peed, and he'd started to lead the animal back inside when the sound of a door opening next door reached his ears. Sweetie barked.

Glancing down at his still-present early-morning problem, he turned his back to the fence. He scooped the poodle up and headed back inside to his bedroom. But suddenly energized by the thought of seeing Nikki, he yanked on his jeans, pulled on a T-shirt, stopped in the kitchen to pour himself a cup of coffee, and hurried back outside, alone.

He moved to the fence and peered through the slats, making sure it was Nikki and not Bell. It was. She lay stretched on the lounge chair, wearing jean shorts and a T-shirt. She had a book in her hands and a cup of steaming coffee sitting on the small plastic patio table.

She opened the book and her gaze lowered. A light chuckle escaped her lips, which lifted with a smile as if she'd read something funny.

Warmth flooded his chest.

When he started feeling like a Peeping Tom, he said, "Good morning."

She jerked as if he'd startled her. Her arm hit the plastic table beside her, flipping it over. Her cup fell to the ground, spilling its precious liquid. Frowning, she dropped the book in her lap and glanced over to the fence.

"Sorry," he said. "I thought you heard Sweetie a second ago."

"I did, I just didn't know you were…out."

"Since she got in your backyard again, I can't just—"

"Yeah, I forgot," she said.

"I thought I could let her out and maybe you could call her and I could see where she's escaping from."

"Oh…sure," she said.

"Is now good?" Damn if some of last night's fantasies didn't send a thrill down low in his abdomen.

"Yeah." There was hesitancy in her tone.

"How do you take your coffee?"

"What?"

"Coffee. I just made a fresh pot. Good stuff. I special-order it." He glanced at her mug lying on the ground. "Looks like I owe you one now."

When she didn't answer right away, he said, "Cream? Sugar?"

It took two more long seconds for her to accept. "Just cream." Her tone still leery.

He rushed inside, ran to the bathroom, rinsed his mouth out with mouthwash, and ran a hand through his hair. He caught a quick glimpse of himself in the mirror. For a second, he didn't recognize the man staring back. A man with hope. A man who felt alive.

* * *

Juan returned to the backyard with Sweetie and Vicki called the dog. The little escape artist barked and mere seconds later she ducked under some fencing and raced at Vicki. Almost immediately, Vicki heard her gate open and glanced back. Juan, walking toward her, wore a navy T-shirt just snug enough to showcase his hard chest, flat stomach, and tight muscles.

Holding two cups of coffee, he smiled and kept coming. His gait was slow. Sexy. Steam rose from the cups, but she wasn't sure which was hotter, the coffee or the man. He looked a little morning mussed, still slightly sleepy as if he'd just rolled out of bed.

She missed waking up with someone. Missed sleeping with someone. Not just the sex but the company. That first early-morning look at someone when nothing is between you and him but a smile, the sheets, and the promise of a new day.

She and Dan had stayed at each other's home at least three times a week. Knowing that someone had taken her place stung. But not as much as it should have. Maybe it would've changed into something deeper. As crazy as it felt, she mourned not so much what they had, but what she'd hoped it would become. Her relationship with Dan had been comfortable, because they'd known each other so well.

But Juan was different. She barely knew this guy. And yet somehow she did. She knew he'd lost a wife he loved. She'd seen the remnants of grief in his eyes. She knew his heart was big enough, soft enough to love a fluffy and frilly dog. And she knew he bolted over her fence that first night to protect her for no reason other than that it was the right thing to do.

"Hope it has enough cream." His hand brushed hers as she pulled away.

"I'm sure it's fine," she said, again feeling the tingle of his touch. "So you saw where she got through?"

"Yeah. She's turning into a regular little escape artist." He walked over to the fence with Sweetie at his heels, prancing as if proud of her accomplishment.

"You are a bad dog," he told her, but the scolding came with a scratch behind her ears.

"Seriously, she wasn't doing this until you guys moved in. I'll fill it." He felt around on the ground. "I might have to come over here and fill it on this side as well."

He stood up, and she was aware of how small she felt beside him. Most of the time, she disliked that feeling. But Juan's size didn't intimidate her. He made her feel feminine. Aware of all the differences between a man and a woman.

"Sure. Just let me know."

"Oh, I will." He smiled as if teasing her about their first meeting. "I'm a quick learner."

She remembered the novel she'd been reading. The shared smiles, whispered secrets, soft kisses, and... *Stop*.

She'd thought reading about romance would have satisfied her craving for intimacy, but instead it just made her hungrier. Maybe she should go back to boring biographies.

She sipped the coffee and moaned. "This is good."

"I'm not much of a wine connoisseur, but I know good coffee."

"You used real cream, didn't you?"

"Of course. That's the way I drink it. But don't kid yourself. It's the coffee that's special." His gaze fell on her.

When he lifted his cup to his lips, she noticed the bandage on his hand. "What happened?"

He looked down. "Just work."

"Tell me you didn't get shot?"

He grinned. "No."

"Stabbed?"

"Not nearly as exciting. There was a scuffle is all."

"Stitches?" She made a face as if she felt his pain.

"A few."

"What kind of police are you?" A little voice inside her said asking questions could lead to being asked questions, but with the butterflies in her stomach fluttering, talking calmed her nerves.

"Detective. I work in the Cold Case Unit."

She lifted a brow. "You're one of the Three Musketeers?"

His forehead wrinkled. "You've heard of us?"

"When I first moved here there was some news coverage on the case you guys had just solved."

"Yeah." He sounded sheepish.

"You say that like it's a bad thing."

He brought his mug up for another sip before speaking. "We're trying to do our job. The press gets in the way most of the time."

"Did you catch the man last night? Did you solve the case?" She was worried she sounded overly inquisitive, but she was genuinely interested in hearing more about his work. And maybe if she kept asking him questions, he wouldn't have time to ask her any.

"We caught the guy, but no. The case is still open. We just picked up a piece of the puzzle and are still trying to figure out if it fits."

"So being a cop is about putting puzzles together?"

"Yeah. In some ways."

Did he see her as a puzzle? She sure as hell hoped not. She sipped the coffee again. The dark roast flavor lingered on her tongue. It was better than the fancy coffee that she used to buy when money wasn't an issue. One of the luxuries she'd given up when she walked away from her life. "So what kind of coffee is this?"

He smiled. "I order it online. Grind the beans myself."

"You have good taste."

"I know what I like." Innuendo flavored his tone.

He was flirting. She tried hard not to enjoy it, not

to let the perceived compliment slide like a warm touch over soft places. But it did feel that way.

She held the cup closer, trying to rein in the conversation and her emotions. "There was just a story on the news about specialty coffees. One about a coffee bean that's processed after being digested by some Asian catlike creature."

He lifted a brow and stared at her over the rim of his cup. "You mean kopi luwak? The beans are fed to an Asian palm civet. And yes, it does kind of look like a cat."

"This isn't...?"

His brow stayed raised.

"Seriously?" She handed him his cup back.

He laughed. The sound, pure tease, came out deep, masculine, hypnotic, and rusty. Why did she think it had been a while since he'd laughed? His dark eyes brightened with humor. "No. It's Four Barrel. But I saw the same show. I would never drink anything that came out of the rear end of a catlike creature." His smile tightened his eyes. "I'm definitely more of a dog person."

She laughed and realized she hadn't laughed like this in a long time, either. It felt good.

Right then a light hiss filled the air. Before she realized what it was, the sprinkler system sprayed her from behind, the cold spritz hitting her legs. Releasing a squeal, she jumped out of the way. As she danced to the right she saw him catch the spray directly in his face.

He darted to the side. They collided. The coffee in

her cup splashed out and just like the wine from a couple of nights ago, it found its way to his shirt.

She bit down on her lip and tried not to laugh. But as she lifted her eyes, the sound escaped.

Coffee dripped from a dark strip of hair hanging down his brow.

"First wine and now coffee. Sorry."

It wasn't until she breathed and felt her breasts against his chest that she realized how close they stood. It wasn't until she saw his lips that she realized how badly she wanted to be kissed. It wasn't until he dipped his head that she realized it was actually going to happen.

She knew this could only lead to trouble, but found herself leaning into him anyway. His lips tasted like the coffee, and his tongue, warm from the brew, swept across her bottom lip. For one second, two, maybe even three she kissed him right back. She wanted it.

Then reality hit. She jerked away. Touched her lips, which felt damp, slightly swollen. "No. I can't...I'm not..."

"I'm sorry." He took a step back. "I just...You...I thought..."

"Yeah," she said. "I did, I'm not saying you...But no. I can't."

"Why?" he asked. "God knows I have my own reservations, but..."

Neither of them could complete a sentence.

"I..." She searched for an answer, one that didn't give anything away but would make her feelings clear. "I'm not ready to broaden my horizons."

* * *

Juan, regret churning in his gut, walked back inside his house and set Sweetie down. The dog turned and looked at him and whined as if reading the frustration billowing from him.

One step forward, three steps back. Or maybe it was like ten steps back. Shit! Why had he kissed her? Was it too soon? Sure, he hadn't had much practice lately, but he certainly could tell when a woman was kissing him back. She was as into it as he was. So why did she push him away? Maybe deep down he'd been hoping she'd do just that. Maybe he wasn't ready, either.

He sat down at his kitchen table. The thought hit that he needed to get the house ready for the poker game. But seeing his laptop in front of him, he booted up his Facebook page and saw he had two messages.

Both were from Nikki Hanson's Myspace page connections. The first was short and succinct. And startling.

He went to the other. It held the same emotional punch.

Yes, they knew her. Yes, they went to school with her. Yes, it was sad/terrible/unthinkable how she...*died*.

Nikki V. Hanson was dead. Or a Nikki Hanson who was born the same year, lived and grew up in the same town, was...dead.

Coincidence? He didn't think so.

Who the hell had he just kissed?

CHAPTER ELEVEN

Needing to burn off his frustration, Juan grabbed some tools and stole dirt from the middle of his backyard to fill the hole by his fence. One shovel of dirt. Two. Three.

He yanked off his shirt and worked up a sweat.

Done filling the hole, yet still feeling irate, he went to mow the front yard. He still had four hours before the guys showed up to play Texas Hold 'Em.

He was pushing the mower over the last strip of grass, sweat pouring off of him, when movement caught his eye. He looked up. And there, standing on his lawn, was Bell. Bell holding Sweetie.

She must have found another escape hole. Reaching down, he cut off the mower and moved toward the little girl.

He reached for the squirming poodle in her hands. "Thank you."

The little girl didn't say anything, just stared at him.

"She must have gotten in your yard again," he offered.

She turned to go, then turned back around.

"It's not your fault," she said.

"What?" he asked.

"It's not your fault," she repeated in a voice full of tenderness, yet somehow haunted.

"What's not my fault?"

She pulled up her shirtsleeve, exposing...Juan's breath locked in his chest. The child's words from earlier replayed in his head. *You got burned.*

Now he understood why Bell would know the type of scar.

He counted four, no, *five* round nickel-sized burn scars on the child's upper arm. "That's what my mama used to tell me to make me feel better."

Every muscle in his body knotted, including his heart. Someone had hurt her. Intentionally. Those were cigarette or cigar burns. He held his rage in, but his hold on Sweetie unintentionally tightened. She whimpered and he softened his grip.

His next words came out without thought, but with purpose. Someone had to pay. "Who did that to you, Bell?"

She yanked her sleeve back down. Something akin to guilt filled her eyes, as if she'd said something she shouldn't. She swung around and ran back through the side fence to her backyard.

Sweetie barked as if she wanted to give chase. He considered going after the child himself.

The only thing that kept his feet planted in his front yard was the fact that the scars weren't red or raw. They weren't recent. They had healed, like his. Healed on the outside. But on the inside?

As rage built up in his chest, questions built up in his head. He shot inside and dropped Sweetie down.

Was this what Nikki was hiding from? Was she running from a husband or a boyfriend who'd done this to her child? Or had she...?

No, he remembered Nikki's painted toenails. The love in her voice when she talked about her daughter. He'd bet his right arm that Nikki wasn't hurting Bell.

Then the child's words echoed in his head. *That's what my mama used to tell me to make me feel better.*

Why did the term "used to" make him feel as if she was no longer with her mama? Was this another thing Nikki had lied about? Being Bell's mom?

Or was he reading into something that wasn't there?

His phone rang. He picked it up and checked the number. It was a Houston area code.

"Detective Acosta," he answered.

"Yes, my name is Kathy Jones. You called me about my sister? I'm sorry I missed your call last night. Is Cindy in trouble again?" Ms. Jones asked.

Juan explained his need to speak to her sister about a missing persons case, then, keeping it vague, he told her he suspected her sister was injured. "I was hoping you might be able to tell me where she is?"

"I can't. She cut herself out of my life years ago. Believe me, my brother and I have tried to help her, but she...won't even talk to us. When she stopped communicating with us, we even drove up there. Went to the strip club where she worked. The owner said she'd quit."

"Well, she started back. She was working there until a week ago."

"It's sad, but we tried."

"When's the last time you saw her?"

"Almost five years ago. She texted me for a while. I'd call her and she wouldn't answer. I left messages. Told her our brother and I agreed to help her out if she moved up here, got into a rehab. She texted back and said she was fine."

"Before she dropped out of your life, did she ever mention a woman named Abby Noel? A friend of hers who went missing?"

"No, not that I remember. When did she go missing?"

"Five years ago."

"Do you think Cindy has something to do with her friend going missing?" Shock played in her voice. "Oh, God, you don't think she killed her, do you?"

"We're not sure if or how your sister is involved, but we think she might know something that could help us," Juan said. "Do you know of any friends here? Anyone Cindy would go to if she needed a place to stay?"

"No." Her shock faded to concern. "Do you know if she's still doing drugs?"

"I don't know that for sure. I was told by her apartment manager she's being evicted. She lost her job a week ago, too."

"I wish I could do something, but...how can I help

someone who doesn't want help? Someone who won't even tell me what's going on?"

"I don't know." His thoughts shot straight to his neighbor.

When she hung up, his phone dinged with another call. He looked at the number. It was Cindy Bates's old landlord.

"It's going too far," Mr. Henley said first thing.

"What's going too far?"

"She was here again. I think she slept on the damn swing. I let my dog out and he started barking. When I looked, the gate was open and there was a blanket on the swing. I don't get it. Why the hell is she doing this after all this time?"

"I don't know," Juan said. "How long ago did she leave?"

"Twenty minutes ago. I should have called you right away, but I was so pissed I wasn't thinking. How can I stop this? She's a nut job and I don't want her around my family. Can I get a restraining order or something?"

Juan heard the rising tension in the man's voice. "I don't think you've got enough for that yet, but—"

"What the hell good is calling the police if you don't do anything?"

"Look, believe me, we're looking for her. Put a better lock on your gate. And next time call me right away. Meanwhile, I'll get a patrol cop to come by and you can make a report."

When Juan hung up, he remembered he'd planned to drive by Cindy's apartment this morning. Glancing at his phone, he realized he had enough time before the poker game to make a quick trip to the apartment complex.

He remembered Bates's sister's words. *How can I help someone who doesn't want help? Someone who won't even tell me what's going on?*

Maybe you don't stop asking. He had questions for Nikki. Questions he wasn't sure he had the right to ask, but was going to ask anyway.

* * *

"What does...sal...u...ta...tions mean?" Bell asked.

"It means 'hello' or 'greetings.'" Vicki, standing beside the sofa, found Bell's matching Cinderella sock among the clean clothes and put the two together. Bell sat on the floor with her *Charlotte's Web* book in her hands, thumbing through it, finding words she didn't know, trying to pass time until her friend Suzie arrived.

Vicki's mind shot back to Juan's kiss, while she stared at the pile of laundry. She could have stopped it. She should have stopped it. Why hadn't she stopped it?

Because I didn't want to!

Her mind kept taking her back to how he'd tasted. To the way his lips slid across hers, so hot, so gentle. To the way his tongue tempted her own to play.

"Aunt— I mean, Mom. Do you think Wilbur and Charlotte were in love?"

Vicki looked at her niece. "I think they loved each other."

"Like boy-girl love?"

"I think they were just friends." Vicki reached for her

red bra, which she'd accidentally put in the dryer instead of just hanging up to dry, due to her brain fog.

"Because they didn't kiss?" Bell asked.

"Huh?" Vicki asked.

"Is the reason you don't think they were in love because they didn't kiss?"

"Sort of," she said, unsure how to answer.

"When people kiss, do they love each other and then get married?"

Vicki hesitated. Was it just a coincidence that both she and her niece were thinking about kissing? "Sometimes . . . and sometimes they just like each other a lot."

"I want you to get married. So I can have a daddy. But I want you to marry a good one. Like Suzie's father."

"Uh, well . . . Right now I'm happy with just you and me."

"Is Juan a good one?"

Coincidence? Or not? "You should call him Mr. Acosta."

"Okay. Is he a good one?"

"Why would you ask that?"

She glanced down at the book. "Because you kissed him."

Vicki almost gasped. "You . . . saw that?"

Bell nodded. "I heard Sweetie bark and looked out my window and you two were kissing."

Vicki exhaled, her brain working double time trying to decide what to say. "It was a mistake."

"Why?"

Why indeed. "Remember I told you that we can't get too close to anyone, that we can't tell our secrets?"

"Did you tell him a secret when you kissed him?"

"No, but..."

"But you were really close to him?" Her big brown eyes widened. "Like this." She pressed her palms together.

"Yeah." Vicki could still feel his hard body pressed against hers. "Mr. Acosta and I are just neighbors and there's not going to be any more kissing."

"But he's one of the good ones, right?"

"Yes, I think he's good."

Bell blinked. "Do you think his scar makes him ugly?"

Emotion filled Vicki's chest. "No, sweetheart. He's a very nice-looking man. A scar doesn't make people ugly."

Bell bit down on her bottom lip. "I don't like people to see my scars. I feel bad that his is on his face. He can't hide it with a shirt like I can. And when people see it, I know they stare. It's hard not to. And I think it hurts him."

What the hell could Vicki say to that? She knew Bell's scars hurt her, too, and every time she thought of the bastard who'd done that to her, Vicki's blood boiled.

"I'm sure Juan wishes he didn't have the scar on his face, too, but it doesn't stop him from being a very attractive man. A scar is just a mark, it doesn't tell people who you are."

Vicki moved across the room, knelt down, and hugged her niece.

Bell's little arms hung on to Vicki's neck so tightly she felt the squeeze in her chest. "I love you," she whispered in Bell's dark brown hair.

"I love you, too," Bell said.

Vicki went back to sorting laundry. All the while trying to sort out emotions.

The doorbell rang. She jolted.

"Is that Suzie?" Bell jumped up.

Vicki caught her arm. "It's too early to be Suzie. I'll answer it."

Fear filled her niece's eyes, and she hated herself for letting her own emotion show. Would there ever be a day when a doorbell or phone ringing wouldn't take them right to panic? Stiffening her backbone, she went to the side window to see who was at the door.

A quick check had air catching in her throat, but not from fear.

Taking a deep I-can-do-this breath, she looked back at Bell standing only a few feet behind her. "It's Mr. Acosta. I'm going to step outside to talk to him. I'll be right back in."

Her niece's eyes rounded in what looked like concern. Then, she ran back into the living room.

Vicki, unprepared to face Juan but sensing he wasn't going away, opened the door.

As he stood there, a summer breeze brought his scent of men's soap and shampoo to her nose. His already dark hair appeared darker, as if still damp. His brown eyes met hers.

"Can we talk?" he asked.

She stepped out and closed the door. "Look, there's not a whole lot to say. It was a mistake."

"I don't..." He paused and ran his hand through his hair. "I'm not here about the kiss," he said.

"Then what?" she asked.

"Bell's scars. Who did that to her?"

His words ran laps around her head. "How do you know—?"

"She showed them to me to make me feel better about mine. And if you're half the mother I think you are, you won't get upset with her. But . . . I can't see those scars and not worry—"

His words, the accusation she thought she heard, had her spine lifting and locking. "If you think I did that—!"

"No. I told you, I think you're a great mom. But I think you're afraid of the person who did. I'm a detective. I'm picking up all kinds of vibes that you're scared. You can trust me."

He had no idea how badly she wished she could. But Joanne from AWACO had warned her to stay clear of the police.

"Was it her father?"

"Please, just—"

"That's who you thought sent me the other night, wasn't it? Talk to me."

She couldn't. "There's nothing to talk about."

"Is the divorce not final? Does he have rights to Bell? Is that why you're running?"

"I'm not . . ."

"I get it, you don't trust me, but—"

"I don't trust anyone!" she snapped, and instantly wished she could draw her words back in. But maybe a little of the truth would satisfy him.

"I understand when you come face-to-face with evil,

it makes it hard to trust anyone. I've been there. I've faced a few monsters myself. Like the one who killed my wife and baby. But I'd never do anything to hurt you or Bell. I want to help."

"Okay, Bell's father hurt her, and now I have a big problem trusting people. But we don't need help. And the kiss was a mistake. Can't we just be neighbors?"

His mouth thinned. "Did he get locked up for doing that?"

"Yes." And he had, for a few days.

"Is he still locked up? Is he looking for you?"

She shook her head. "Please. I don't want to talk about this."

He stared at her, as if finally hearing her. He held his palms up. "I'm sorry," he said. "I get it. I just...If you need anything, please call me."

She almost said *I won't*, but what if she did? "Thank you." She turned around and went back inside. Her pulse fluttered in a frantic pace at the base of her neck. His words replayed in her head and slammed into her heart. "*I've faced a few monsters myself. Like the one who killed my wife and baby.*" He'd lost a child, too.

Then she saw Bell, standing in the entryway with tears in her eyes. How much had she heard?

"Are you mad because I showed him my scars?"

"No." She pulled her niece close. "We just have to be careful."

CHAPTER TWELVE

Thirty minutes later, still running the conversation with Nikki through his mind, Juan pulled out of his garage to do a drive-by of Cindy Bates's apartment. When he backed out, he noticed a red Porsche parked in Nikki's driveway. The license plate was Californian.

What if...this was Bell's father? What if right now she needed help? He stopped his car. A man, a tall, slick-haired blond guy wearing a Hawaiian shirt and khaki shorts, walked out of her front door. Nikki followed. They stopped at the edge of her porch. Juan studied Nikki, whose smile appeared fake, forced, and fragile. But she didn't look afraid.

Who was he? Someone she worked with? A boy-friend?

The man laughed, and as he spoke he touched her arm. Juan saw her fake smile fade. Saw her take a small step back. She waved back to the front door as if trying to escape the guy. Juan tensed, waiting to see if the man pushed. He didn't. He nodded and walked to his car.

So, not a boyfriend but a wannabe.

Nikki, still standing on the porch, shifted her gaze to his car. To him sitting behind the wheel. To him watching her. She turned and went back inside. Confronting her about Bell's scars had been a mistake.

Juan backed out of his drive, hoping he might find Cindy Bates at home. When he pulled into the apartment parking lot, a cop car with its lights on sat running in front of her building.

What were the chances it wasn't about Cindy?

None, he realized when he walked up the same steps he'd chased the guy down last night and saw two cops. He recognized both from the precinct as they stood by the broken window into Bates's apartment. But he wasn't sure they'd recognize him.

"Hey." He showed his badge.

Juan explained about the fight last night. They shared that a neighbor had spotted the broken window and the front door ajar at Cindy Bates's apartment.

"Are you sure this wasn't done last night?" Officer Danes asked.

"Yeah. This is new."

"Do you think the guy you collared came back?"

"No. He was arrested and is being held," Juan said.

"So someone else broke into her apartment?" Officer Hall asked.

"Looks that way," Juan concluded. "I guess the guy could have used his one call to phone someone to break in. Maybe the drugs were still here. Have you gone inside?"

"Just to make sure no one was in there."

Juan walked through the door, and the two officers followed.

Last night he'd been riding an adrenaline high and had left to get his stitches before really checking out the place.

"What are you looking at this Bates girl for?"

"She's a possible witness on a cold case," Juan said.

"So was last night and this break-in a coincidence, or do you think the two cases are connected?"

Juan considered it. "More than likely has to do with the drugs."

Other than what looked like a mess created by last night's scuffle, the place was spotless. Normally, someone strung out on drugs wasn't a neatnik.

Paintings in cheap frames hung on the walls. Real paintings, not prints. And the artwork was excellent. He remembered Mrs. Noel saying that Cindy and Abby both liked art. One painting was of a tire swing with a little girl in it. The other was a beach scene with a child holding a seashell.

He walked into the bedroom. In the corner was an easel with a half-painted picture of a young girl on a carousel horse. Bates liked painting kids.

For some reason there was something slightly familiar about that painting. Like he'd seen it before. Did Bates copy famous paintings?

He went to the bedside table and opened a drawer. There was a journal. More poems. He read one.

Oh, my lie. Oh, my sin. Oh, my friend.
I know my place. Where you stay. Beneath the
*   birds, and where the angels sing.*
On a prayer. On a wing. But no, I still sing. I still
*   swing.*
You live in the mirror and I see your face.
As intricate as lace.
I sit here, while you rest there in my place
I cry tears for you. I cry tears for me.
I cry tears for who I used to be.
And the angel I can no longer see.

Juan wasn't a poet, but even he could see that Bates's real talent was with a paintbrush and not a pen.

He headed to the bathroom. The only things in the medicine cabinet were condoms. He realized something that felt off. Bates didn't have one prescription. Which was odd. Drug addicts usually had several pain prescriptions that they'd convinced doctors to give them.

In the cabinet drawers, he found a bottle of hair dye, a brush, and some makeup.

Stepping out into the living room, he saw the cops were back on the balcony. Spotting a frame facedown on the carpet, he picked it up. In it was a photograph of two young women with a baby. He recognized the blonde as Abby Noel. The redhead had to be Cindy Bates. The baby was probably Abby's daughter, Lacy.

The frame had the word *Sisters* written across the bottom. They did look enough alike to be sisters.

He stared at the baby Abby held. Was there really a

bond between Cindy and Lacy? Enough to send birthday cards every year. Or were those cards just a way for Cindy to nurse her own guilt?

He looked back at the photo, at Cindy's face. "You know who killed Abby Noel, don't you?"

* * *

Sweetie barked. Juan pushed his cards aside and pulled away from his dining room table. "Don't deal me in on this one. I gotta take her out," Juan said.

"Why don't you just let her out?" Billy asked.

"I can't. She keeps getting into the neighbor's yard." He got up from the table.

"The neighbor who gave you the black eye?" Billy asked, pointing to the left and grinning.

"Yeah." Juan frowned. The guys were having way too much fun at his expense over his incident with Nikki.

"How many times have you seen her since she kicked your ass?" Connor asked.

The guys all laughed. Juan ignored the question, grabbed the leash, and went to walk Sweetie in the backyard. She tugged her way to the fence, sniffing as if trying to sense whether anyone was on the other side. Obviously there wasn't anyone in Nikki's backyard because Sweetie then tugged him in another direction and did her business.

He was letting the dog inside when he heard Nikki's back door open and then the voices. Giving the dog a nudge through the door, he lingered on the patio.

"I like your mom," a little voice said.

"I do, too," Bell answered.

So Bell had a friend over. Could the man leaving earlier have been...?

"My dad said your mom was pretty," the other kid said.

"She is pretty," Bell said.

"She's not as pretty as my mom was," the child spoke again. "What are we looking for?"

"My mom's necklace. She lost it somewhere out here. She's really sad. It was special. A gift from my..."

"Your dad?" the little girl asked.

"No. Her sister."

Her sister? But Nikki had told him she didn't have siblings. More lies? But why?

"Do you miss your dad?" Bell's friend asked.

"No," Bell said a little too harshly.

"Why not?" the child asked.

"He wasn't a good dad like yours."

Juan's gut tightened.

"What did he do?" the child asked.

Juan held his breath and listened.

"Mean stuff." The two words came out with caution and caused Juan to tighten his fists.

Silence followed Bell's reply, and then she asked, "Does your dad ever do mean things?"

"No. He loves me a lot."

"Do you miss your mom?" Bell asked.

"Yeah. I still cry sometimes. I hate cancer. That's what took her away. And sometimes I'm afraid I'll get it." Another pause happened. "How did your dad die?"

Die? Juan waited for Bell to correct her.

"His boat exploded."

Juan ran a hand over his mouth and recalled not believing Nikki when she told him she was divorced.

"It blew him up, too?" Bell's friend asked.

"Yeah," Bell answered. Then, "Have you ever read *Charlotte's Web*?"

"I can't read yet. Is it a good book?"

"Yeah," Bell answered. "You should get your dad to read it to you. Mom reads it to me almost every night. Charlotte's a big black spider and she dies. She dies all alone."

"That's sad. I don't think that's a good book."

"Yeah, but first she saves Wilbur. He's a pig. He's sad when Charlotte dies, but then he meets Charlotte's children. And he gets happy again."

"I'm not happy yet," the little girl said.

"Me either," said Bell.

"It's hot out here," the friend said. "Let's go back inside and play in your room. But you don't have a lot of toys. You need to come to my house and play."

"I used to have a lot," Bell added on a sad note.

"What happened to them?"

"We had to move."

"Why didn't you bring them with you?"

"We were in a hurry."

Why were you in a hurry, Bell? Juan heard the door open, then close. Shit. Perhaps he should be embarrassed at eavesdropping on kids, but damn it, he wasn't. Why all the secrecy? Why the lies?

How could he get Nikki to trust him enough to tell him the truth?

* * *

After a few more hands of poker, the guys started saying their goodbyes and heading for the door. Everyone left except Connor and Mark. Juan started gathering cards and poker chips. He'd already filled them in on the phone calls from Bates's old landlord and her sister and about her apartment being broken into, but he suspected they'd hung out to talk about the case. Which would have been fine if his mind weren't focused on the conversation he'd overheard between Bell and her friend.

"I wouldn't be surprised if Bates has already skipped town," Connor said, snagging a couple of beer bottles and tossing them in the trash.

Juan stood up and slid the cards back into their poker box. "That's what I thought, but there was still a lot of her stuff in her apartment." Juan heard voices outside the front window and turned to peer out. Nikki and Bell stood in their driveway with the man in the Hawaiian shirt and another girl about Bell's age.

The man was all smiles, his attention on Nikki. Not that Juan blamed the guy. She had on jeans that did wonders for all the dips and curves beneath, and a red tank top that hugged her breasts. Again, not overtly sexy, just girl-next-door gorgeous. He remembered Bell's friend saying, *My dad said your mom was pretty.*

"Juan?"

"Yeah?" Juan turned from the window, knowing he'd tuned out.

"Did you want to keep Annie's potato salad? If so,

give me another bowl. She swore if I didn't bring her bowl back she'd put me on the couch. I've lost two of her bowls at our poker games already."

"See, that's why I don't want to live with a woman." Connor laughed. "She'll take away sex for a damn bowl."

Mark chuckled. "It was an idle threat. She likes my body too much." His gaze went back to Juan. "You want it or not?"

Laughter, kid laughter, sounded outside and he turned back to the window. Connor moved up next to him and pulled back the blinds. "What's got your attention? Oh. So that's her, huh?"

"The kickass neighbor?" Mark, carrying the bowl of potato salad, moved in beside Juan and opened the blinds to see out.

"Who's the guy in the Porsche?" Connor's tone hit a nerve. "You got competition?"

"Stop." Juan pushed away from the window and motioned for them to do the same.

Mark cut him a grin. "You really got a thing for her?"

"It's not like that," Juan lied.

"Then what's it like?" Mark glanced down at the potato salad.

"Yeah, what's it like?" Connor held open the blinds again and leaned in.

Juan tucked his hands in his jean pockets. "Something's up with her."

"What do you mean?" Mark's eyebrows rose in curiosity.

He confided in his two partners about the lies he'd caught her in.

"Did you run her through the system?"

"Yeah. She's got nothing." He went on to tell them about hearing Bell say she wanted to go back to Arizona, about Bell's scars and finding no social media page, and even about discovering a Nikki V. Hanson who was dead.

"If she's lying about her name, she could be running from the police." Mark's tone came out all cop.

Juan felt suddenly protective. "But it could be the wrong Nikki Hanson."

"Could be." Mark shrugged.

"You think she did that to her kid?" Connor's expression darkened.

"No," Juan answered. "She comes off like a great mom."

"You know abusers can be normal people." Mark pulled the potato salad spoon out of the bowl and ate a bite.

Juan exhaled, accepting that he didn't really know Nikki well enough to defend her, but… "I know, but I'm telling you it's not that."

Mark moved into the kitchen with the potato salad. Juan followed. "Seriously, I don't think she's done anything. I think she's scared."

"Of her ex?" Connor, who'd followed, pulled a chair from the kitchen table.

"I was thinking that, but…" He told them about confronting Nikki about her ex and her telling him he was wrong, then what he'd heard Bell say about her dad dying in an explosion.

"Well, that's not good." Mark leaned against the counter.

"I know, but maybe the kid just got it wrong. Maybe Nikki told the kid her father was dead. I mean, I couldn't blame her, considering what he did to the girl."

"There's a lot of maybes there." Mark dropped the spoon into the sink. "I need a—"

"Here." Juan went to the cabinet, pulled out a bowl, and handed it to Mark. Then he went back to the table.

"Not having a presence on social media is suspicious." Mark emptied the salad into the plastic bowl.

"I know," Juan admitted.

"You're not thinking she's part of the witness protection program, are you?" Connor asked.

"No." Juan had considered it and ruled it out. "The feds do a better job. They would have deleted the Myspace account. My gut says she's in trouble and just doesn't trust anyone."

"Or doesn't trust you because you're a cop?" Connor leaned back in the chair. "She could be the one who caused the explosion on her husband's boat."

"No," Juan insisted, though the unwelcome thought had crossed his mind.

"Well," Mark said, "truth is she really hasn't done anything wrong. It's not against the law to lie to your neighbor."

"I know," Juan said. "But—"

"But you aren't going to stop looking into it." Mark cut him a worried glance.

"I'm telling you, I think she's running from someone."

"She's a damsel in distress and you want to save her."
Connor chuckled.

"No," Juan said, but thought *Maybe*. Because he'd
let his very own damsel down. But damn it, he knew
that was only part of it. Was he honestly ready to start
caring for someone else?

"I get it. Follow your gut," Mark said.

Juan raked a hand through his hair. "I shouldn't
have asked her about her kid's scars." *Or kissed her.* "I
think that made her nervous."

"Just be careful," Mark said. "But hey, I know a
cop, Ian Crowder, in Boulder. I'll give you his number.
Maybe he can look around and find something out."

"Yeah," Juan said. "Thanks. I'll call him."

* * *

"I said slow down!" the bitch under Pablo hissed when
he ripped her top off her. "I don't want—"

"I brought you up here to screw you, not romance
you." Pablo pushed her down on his bed.

Right then Pablo's apartment doorbell rang. A
second later, his phone did the same.

"Shit!" he muttered. Couldn't a guy get a little ass
without being interrupted?

The only people who called him were Rex, needing a
job done, or Sam. He hoped it was Rex. His cash was
getting low.

Then again, if Sam had news on Vicki, he'd take that
because that could lead him to his nest egg.

The second he lifted on his elbow to check the

number, the bitch bolted off the bed. He spotted Rex's number on the screen. "Just get the hell out of here," he told her.

"You said you had some rock."

"I do, but you gotta earn it." He grabbed his phone. The junkie stood there, her arm covering her breasts as if she was debating if staying was worth some rock.

"Leave." He took the call as she snatched her shirt off the floor and tore out of the bedroom. "Yeah," he answered.

"Open your damn door!" Rex's graveled tone hinted at trouble. Someone had pissed him off. Taking care of the idiots who got on Rex's bad side was mostly what lined Pablo's pockets these days. That and accompanying his guys on some of the larger drops.

Pablo popped up and started for the living room.

When he walked in, the chick stood at his opened door holding her shirt over her breasts, staring at an unhappy Rex and his brother, Antonio.

"Nice tits," Antonio said.

The girl glared back at Pablo, then bolted between the two men.

"What's up?" Pablo asked, not liking the sharp-eyed way the boss looked at him. First thing he thought was that Rex had finally caught on to the money Pablo skimmed off the top of his drug profits. Not that he'd been able to do it lately. When he'd been a cop, the jobs had been different and opportunities loomed at every turn.

Rex's frown deepened and his brother shut the door. "I got a call."

Shit. Why the fuck had Pablo left his gun in the bedroom? "From?"

"A buddy whose brother is doing ten years in a Texas pen. Cops are looking into one of my old problems that was handled by you."

"Which old problem?"

"A Colombian runner, a Chinese guy, who tried to take over my route in Texas. Five years ago."

"I remember. His name was Cheng something. I took care of him myself. There's nothing that could lead back to you."

"He had a girlfriend, Abby Noel," Rex bit out. "I think her body was disposed of and never found."

"Then they got shit. No body, no case."

"Not so. Word is that police are asking around at the strip joint for a friend of Noel's because they think she knows something about the murder. Would you stake your life that she doesn't? Because if this comes back—"

"I only took care of the Asian guy. You sent someone else with me."

"You were in charge."

The anger in Rex's voice had Pablo's shoulders knotting. "Fine. You want me to clean up the mess one of your other guys made? I'll do it."

"What I want is for people to stop fucking up! I've managed to stay off the police radar and I want to keep it that way."

"I'll fix it," Pablo said.

"No. I've already sent someone. But you are dangerously close to outliving your usefulness around here.

First, you aren't employed by LAPD anymore. Second, half my guys don't want to work with you. They say you walk around with crazy eyes, thinking only of the bitch who snagged your kid."

"I'm working on that."

"Work faster and get your shit together. Meantime, I have a package and a car I need you and Antonio to pick up in San Diego."

"When?"

"Now. Is that a problem?"

"Whatever you need." The words left a bad taste in his mouth and the urge to slam his fist into Rex's smirk hit so hard he had to take a step back.

"It's parked at the bus station in San Diego. I expect you to be back here by midnight."

"What are we bringing in?"

"A hundred pounds of powder. Don't screw this up."

"I won't." Pablo hated the tone he had to use. Hated being questioned. Hated how it reminded him of the line he'd had to toe with his father.

But for now, Pablo would pick up Rex's package. He needed the funds. Next, he'd get Dan to tell him where Vicki was. Then, with his nest egg back in his own damn hand, Pablo was going to teach Rex a lesson—just like he had with his father.

CHAPTER THIRTEEN

Y ou look sad today," Bell said as Vicki secured a backpack onto her niece's shoulders.

Starting her second full week of school, Bell actually looked forward to attending school. Vicki had driven Bell to school that Monday morning but parked instead of dropping her off at the front entrance, as parents were supposed to do. Last Friday there had been a male teacher opening the car doors and helping the children out, and she'd seen how Bell had reacted.

What Vicki couldn't understand was why Bell didn't seem to be afraid of Juan. Was it the fact that both of them had scars? Bell had asked yesterday if she could go over to his house to play with Sweetie. Vicki had taken her out for ice cream instead.

"Me? Sad? No." She kissed the child's forehead, forced a smile, and again debated whether she'd been right or wrong in not telling her niece what the day was. That it was her mother's birthday. "I've got you, don't I?"

"Yeah," Bell said. "You'll be right here when I come out?" She'd asked this every day.

"You bet I will."

"Pinky promise?" Bell held out her hand.

"Pinky promise." They locked fingers.

She stayed until Bell walked into the school, linking hands with the kindergarten coordinator. Then Suzie moved in and the two girls hugged each other. Seeing the smile on her niece's face made the sweetness of the moment turn bitter. Alison should have been here to see this.

With two hours to kill, Vicki drove back to her house, and as she was passing a florist, a memory hit.

"It's her birthday!" Alison said, anger in her tone.

"I know. It's just that I have a client that I have to see today. Why can't we go tomorrow and take them?"

"Because it's her birthday today. Anyone walking in the graveyard will see that's it's her birthday and she doesn't have flowers. She was our mom. She deserves flowers on her grave."

For what? Vicki had wanted to ask her sister. Yeah, when their mom was clean and sober, she'd been a decent mom. Problem was, most of her life hadn't been spent clean or sober. But Vicki couldn't say that to Alison. For everything Vicki held her mom responsible for, Alison forgave her. Every birthday and Mother's Day, Alison insisted they go to the grave.

Vicki actually took most of the blame for her sister's

blindness to their mother's ways. Vicki had shielded her from so much of the ugliness.

Vicki pulled up into her driveway. But she didn't get out.

Unlike her mother, Alison did deserve flowers on her birthday. She pulled out her phone and searched for a florist in the next town over. When she found one that was about forty-five minutes away, she backed out of the driveway and headed to the freeway.

* * *

Monday afternoon, irritated that a week had passed and they were still hitting dead ends on the Noel case, Juan, Connor, and Mark sat at their desks and pulled out the file to do one of their brainstorming sessions. Unfortunately, Juan's head hurt and his brain didn't feel up to storming.

"Here's a question," Connor said. "Are we spending too much time looking for Cindy Bates to find answers on the case? Or—"

"Tell me another lead and I'll follow it." The irritation Juan felt at life in general rang in his voice.

Connor leaned back in his chair and lifted his feet to his desk. "As I was going to say: or . . . is this all we really have?"

"You think we're chasing our asses on this case?" Juan asked, his tone getting tighter. "Fine. If we don't solve it, I'll take the hit."

"Nobody's taking a hit," Mark said. "We work the case and look for any leads that pop up."

Juan gripped the armrest of his chair. "Sorry, I'm in a pissy mood."

"No more than usual," Connor added with a touch of humor.

Juan shot him the finger, but smiled. Before he could offer a comeback, his cell rang. He studied the screen. It was a Colorado number.

"Acosta," he answered, and gestured at his partners to give him a few minutes.

"Hey, it's Ian Crowder."

"Hi, Ian. Did you find anything?" Juan cut Mark a quick look. Mark's friend in Colorado had been more than eager to help when Juan had called him last week.

"More interesting is what I didn't find. There's no death certificate on Nikki Virginia Hanson."

Juan's mind chewed on that information. So Nikki could be telling the truth.

"However, I did come across an old address and I stopped by there on my way home last night. The Hansons don't live there anymore, but I talked to a neighbor. She was older than dirt and her memory wasn't spot-on, so she can't tell me how far back, but she swears she ran into Nikki somewhere. Could be as much as ten years ago. She said Nikki was hanging out with a Hispanic man."

Juan ran a hand over his face. That man was probably Bell's father.

"This woman is like ninety. So I'm not sure how much stock we can put into what she says."

"Yeah, but it kind of fits," Juan said. He'd been

wrong. Nikki hadn't lied to him. And he felt bad for doubting her. Felt bad for even calling Ian to look into it.

"Then it helps?" Ian asked.

"Yes, thank you."

When Juan hung up, Mark turned and looked at him. "Did he find anything on your neighbor?"

"There's no death record. Looks like she's telling the truth. And I've been acting like some stalker trying to prove things that don't exist." He picked up a pen and poked a notepad out of frustration.

"I wouldn't kick yourself. You had reasons to be suspicious. Just the kid saying her father is dead, after her mom said she was divorced, would cause me to question things." Mark folded his arms behind his head.

"She's five years old. I shouldn't have taken that seriously."

"True. I'd still be careful. When your gut says something's off..."

"Yeah. Well, right now my gut says I screwed up."

"So unscrew it," Connor added. "Ask her out on a date."

Juan shot Connor his second one-finger salute. But Connor's advice was sounding less like betrayal to Angie and more like moving on. Was he ready?

* * *

Pablo paced around the cemetery parking lot, waiting for Sam to get there. The California sun beat down on the pavement. He'd called his ex-partner every day to see if he'd heard anything from that women's program. And every day the man said no. Sam was walking on thin ice.

Finally, Pablo saw Sam pull in and his patience almost snapped watching the pisser take his time getting out of his car. Even after he shut his car door, he looked around before walking over.

"What fucking took you so long?"

"I was working a case." He looked around. "What are you doing here?" Sam asked in a disapproving tone. "If someone saw you—"

"Someone left flowers on Alison's grave," Pablo said.

"What?"

"On Alison's grave. There're flowers. I remembered it was her birthday and I recalled that every birthday, Alison and Vicki would have flowers delivered to their mother's grave. So on the off chance I decided to check and I was right. I knew that bitch would mess up sooner or later!"

"Wait. You think Vicki put them here?"

"No, I doubt she's that stupid. She probably had them sent here. Go get those flowers. I'm pretty sure there's a card. Find out how they got here. And go straight there. Find out where they were ordered from. We'll know where she's living then."

"I'll look into it." Sam held a hand at his brow to block the glare, then gazed out at the gravestones.

"Do more than look into it. Find her. This shouldn't take so damn long! Go. I'm serious, I want to hear back from you today on this!"

* * *

Monday evening, Vicki was back on the front porch watching Bell ride up and down the sidewalk on her bike. She'd tried to convince Bell to stay in or to play in the backyard, but she'd finally given in to the little girl's pleas and relented, dragging chairs, glasses, and a pitcher of lemonade outside for them. Reaching down for her glass, Vicki's side pinched. Since work yesterday she'd occasionally felt a light pain. Probably a slightly pulled muscle.

Thankfully, Bell still had training wheels, so Vicki could just sit and watch and maybe even enjoy the sunset. Her gaze shifted next door. She'd been in the kitchen when she'd heard Juan's car pull in. She hadn't seen him in over a week, since he'd knocked on her door wanting to talk about Bell's scars. But she'd thought about him. Thought about him losing his wife and his baby. She ached for his loss and she longed to see him, to tell him how sorry she was.

She knew that it was for the best to keep her distance, but every morning and evening she was tempted to step outside, hoping Sweetie would accidentally find her way into their backyard again.

A jogger coming down the sidewalk toward Bell caught her eyes. Worried Bell might run into him, she held her hand over her eyes to block the lowering sun. Her gaze focused on the shirtless man. She stood up to call for Bell to pull to the side, but no sooner than her feet hit the porch, she realized it was Juan.

He stopped and spoke to Bell. Then his gaze shifted to the house, to her.

Smiling, he came right toward her. The rays of golden sunlight made the sweat on his shirtless body glisten. A soft want-that breath left her lips.

"Hey," he said.

"Hi." She forced a smile.

"I've been hoping to talk to you. I'm sorry for reacting like I did about Bell. I overstepped my boundaries."

She hadn't been prepared for an apology—hadn't been prepared to see so much of his skin. Unable to come up with a suitable answer, she just nodded. He dropped down in the chair she'd brought out for Bell.

"And I'm sorry I..." He looked back to make sure Bell was still on the sidewalk. "...kissed you."

Still unable to force words out, she nodded again.

"I'd really like to be neighbors. Friends. You know, like you suggested."

She couldn't find a reason to say no. Well, she could, starting with that her whole life was a lie and he was a cop with questions. If that wasn't enough of a reason, there was her reaction to his present state of undress. But obviously, she needed a reason that didn't make her sound like she was hiding something or ready to jump his bones.

"Okay," she finally managed. "Neighbors."

He looked down at the pitcher of lemonade. "I'd kill for something to drink."

"Help yourself."

He poured himself a glass. She turned and watched Bell pedaling down the sidewalk, anything not to gawk at his bare chest, which still had little droplets of sweat slipping down past his nipples following his abs to get soaked up by the elastic band of his shorts.

"You ever jog?" he asked.

"Yeah, but..." She forced her gaze up, keeping her eyes on his face. "Now I mostly get my exercise at work."

Bell suddenly appeared in front of them. "Can I play with Sweetie?"

"I don't mind. You'll have to keep her on a leash." He looked at Nikki. "If it's okay with your mom?"

"Sure. But not too long. You have to get ready for school tomorrow."

"I'll be right back." He set his glass down.

She couldn't help watching him walk away. Heaven help her, he had the body of a god.

"I like him," Bell said.

Me too. But she reminded herself what she'd told Bell earlier. They had to be careful.

Right then, Juan turned around. She lifted her eyes quickly, but she was pretty certain he knew she'd been checking out his ass. Their gazes met.

His heart-melting smile made her feel like a teenager again, waking up those hot-boy butterflies. This didn't feel careful. This felt good. Dangerously good.

* * *

Sweetie, dancing on her hind legs, met Juan at the door. He picked the happy dog up, sharing her excitement. "She was checking out my ass," he said, feeling hopeful, feeling enthusiastic, feeling something he hadn't in a long time.

"You want to go play with Bell?" he asked the dog. He'd been so damn tempted to knock on her door this past week, but he'd been afraid even that might scare her off. Hell, he'd even considered digging up the holes he'd filled in so Sweetie could get in her backyard again.

Realizing how sweaty he was, he ran into the bathroom, started the shower, stripped, and stepped under it, not waiting for it to get hot. Thirty seconds later, he jumped out, snagged a T-shirt and a pair of jeans. Dressed, he hurried back into the kitchen, opened a bottle of wine, and grabbed Sweetie's leash.

The dog looked up, her entire body wagging. For one second, he questioned what he was about to do. Take a step? But wasn't he tired of questioning it?

He started out, then, realizing he was hungry, grabbed last night's leftover pizza from the fridge. He juggled things around, wine bottle under an arm, wineglasses in one hand, and pizza box and leash in the other.

Nikki looked at him as he cut across to her yard. "What are you doing?"

"I haven't had dinner."

Bell came running over. "Sweetie!" His dog pulled on the leash to get to the child.

Bell picked up the dog and giggled as Sweetie licked her cheeks. He handed Bell the leash. "Can I have some pizza?" the girl asked.

"That's why I brought it out. It's cold. Do you like cold pizza?"

"I like pizza any way," Bell said.

"You had dinner," Nikki said.

Bell made a face. "But it's pizza. You don't have to be hungry to eat pizza."

"Fine," Nikki relented.

Juan set the wine and glasses on the driveway, opened the box, and held it out.

Bell looked into the box as if weighing her selection. "Does it have pepperoni on it?"

"Of course. It's not pizza without pepperoni, right?"

"Right," Bell said.

The kid took the slice of pizza, then looked at her mom. "Can I walk Sweetie down the street?"

"Just down a few houses. Don't go in the road."

Juan sat down and moved the open pizza box to Nikki. "Cold pizza?"

"I ate dinner."

"But it's pizza." He tried to imitate Bell's expression.

Laughing, she took a slice. He put the box down and poured them each some wine. "Here."

She accepted the goblet with four inches of her recommended Cabernet. "Thank you."

"You're welcome." He stretched out his legs and when he accidentally brushed against her, he shifted the chair back.

"Coffee, wine, pizza, and a puppy," she said. "You're a full-service neighbor."

Smiling, even though her words sounded part complaint, he looked over the rim of his glass at her watching her daughter. "I try. How old is Bell?"

"Five." She sipped the wine.

"She seems very well adjusted. I mean, considering...
you know." He pulled out a slice of pizza for himself and
took a bite.

"She is, for the most part." She pulled off a piece of
pepperoni and ate it.

He hesitated, not sure what was off-limits. "How
long have you been divorced?"

Nipping at her lip, she looked away. "A couple of
years."

From those actions, he suspected it was a lie. He
could almost feel her guard inching up. He searched for
another subject. "She looks like you." He took another
bite of his pizza.

Nikki turned to him. "You think so?"

"Yeah. I mean, she has darker features, but I see it in
the nose, the mouth." He continued to look at Nikki.
"The shape of the eyes, too."

"I see it sometimes," she said.

"Is she half Hispanic?"

The question appeared to startle her. She offered a
weak "Yes."

A few seconds later, he said, "I look at her and think...
that's probably what my daughter would have looked
like."

She stared down at her pizza. "How old was your
daughter when... when she died?"

It was his turn to be put in the hot seat, but he'd been
the one to bring this up. "She wasn't born yet. My wife
was seven months pregnant when it happened."

Damn if her eyes didn't get moist. "I'm sorry."

He felt her sincerity echo inside him. "Me too."

She looked up at the sky turning shades of pink and orange. "Life sucks sometimes, doesn't it?"

"Yeah." *But it's sucked a lot less since I met you.*

She glanced over with a sad smile. "Then there's wine, pizza, and sunsets."

"And puppies," he offered. He clinked his glass with hers. "Here's to neighbors."

They both brought their glasses to their lips. He remembered their kiss. And damn if he didn't want to do it again. As well as several other things.

"This is nice," she said. "Thank you."

"You're welcome." A question pulled at his mind. He knew it was risky, but decided to go for it. "It wasn't a bad kiss, was it?"

She looked away.

"I know it's not going to happen again, I just...I don't know, I thought it was great. And maybe my ego feels a little dinged. It's been a while since..." He reached down and picked up another slice of pizza. "Since I wanted to kiss anyone. Maybe I just need to know it didn't suck before I try it again. On someone else, of course."

She faced him. "I don't for one minute think your ego got dinged."

He sent her a questioning gaze. "Why not? Guys have egos."

"Some guys do, just not you." She glanced up the street to check on Bell.

"Why not me?" He leaned forward to see her face and twirled the glass in his hands.

She looked over and rolled her eyes. "You have"—

she waved her hand up and down—"too much going for you to be insecure."

Surprised by her words, he laughed. Then he reached down for the wine and refilled their glasses. "Are you saying you find me attractive?"

He could swear her cheeks reddened. "Just neighbors, remember?"

"Okay, I'll stop. But for the record, it's mutual." He turned his glass. "So, I'm just wondering why—"

"I thought you were going to stop," she said.

"I am." He paused. "Eventually."

She stared at the street, but from her profile, he saw her frown.

He went for another truth. "Actually, I think these days all most women see when they look at me is my scar."

She turned to him. "Then they're idiots. And I'm serious."

He soaked up her compliment.

She frowned. "Your scar is this big." She held up her fingers about two inches apart. "There's over six feet of perfection. Your scar isn't...that bad. And I'm not just saying that."

Something warm filled his chest. "I believe you. I saw you checking out my ass. My unscarred ass."

Her face reddened again, but she laughed.

He could get used to the sound of her laughter. "Thank you, by the way."

She pulled in her smile. "You're welcome, I guess."

They sat in silence for a few minutes, eating cold pizza and drinking wine. He considered the lie he thought she'd told about the divorce. Had she left without ending the marriage?

Then he recalled something she'd said earlier about getting into fitness because her mother had a fondness for men who used their fists.

Why was it hard for him to believe that she'd married someone who could do what he did to her daughter? Oh, he knew how it went. Female children of abusers married abusers and male children turned into abusers. But he and his brother hadn't followed that pattern, and for some reason he found it difficult to believe she would have.

He looked at her. "How long were you married?"

She frowned. "It's a perfect sunset and I have a glass of wine in my hands. Can we not talk about that?"

He stretched his legs out in front of the lawn chair. "Okay, let me get this clear. We can't talk about us being attracted to each other..."

She lifted an eyebrow at him.

He grinned. "Or about your ex. You pick the topic of conversation."

"Tell me about your work," she offered.

He debated what to tell her as Bell walked up. "Can Sweetie go inside with me and play in my room?"

"I don't mind," Juan said.

Nikki shifted in her seat. "It might be time to call it—"

"Please," Bell said. "I want to play ball with her."

"Okay, but only for a few minutes." Nikki gave in.

A mosquito buzzed past Juan's glass. "Why don't we take the party inside?"

Nikki's nod wasn't particularly joyful, but she wasn't pushing him away, and he took that as a win.

Moving inside, Juan set the wine and what was left of the pizza on the coffee table. When Nikki dropped on the sofa, he sat beside her. Not too close. But close enough that the thought of getting closer hung in the air like a dangling carrot. And when he reached for another slice of pizza, his knee touched hers. She didn't flinch. Another win.

He started the conversation comparing their pizza preferences. Black olives or no black olives. Anchovies or no anchovies. Thin crust versus pan. Pizza-wise, they were compatible.

He told her the different pizza restaurants that delivered to their subdivision. Every now and then they'd hear Bell laughing and Sweetie barking.

"She's having fun. Thank you," Nikki said.

From there, he told her funny stories about being a cop. Yeah, he had a hell of a lot of sad stories he could share, but he didn't want to spoil the mood.

"Seriously, he held up the store with a potato peeler?" she asked, laughing.

"I swear," he said. "The media dubbed him the Tater Robber. Then there was the woman who came home, went to pee, and spotted a man standing in her shower behind her frosted shower curtain. She begged him for her life for about two minutes. He never said a word, just stood there. She finally got the nerve to make a break for it. She called 911. We tried to talk the man out for a good ten minutes. He wouldn't say a word. Finally, we charged in with guns drawn. Behind the curtain we found her husband's wetsuit hanging on the showerhead. In her defense, from behind the curtain, the wetsuit did look like a man."

"That would've freaked me out." She laughed again and damn if she wasn't beautiful. After a moment she said, "I'm sure not every case is funny."

"They're not. Which makes it more important to laugh at those that are."

"Have you ever been shot?"

"Yeah."

"Where?"

Juan pointed to his left side, where he had a small scar.

"Who shot you?"

"Another cop," he said.

"Seriously?"

"Yeah. Not his fault, I was undercover. A bust gone bad. A drug dealer started shooting. The cops fired back. I was just unlucky enough to catch one."

She looked down at his right hand, which no longer sported a bandage. "How did you really hurt your hand?"

He opened his palm. It was practically healed. "I had a scuffle with a guy, grabbed the underside of a banister, cut it on some sharp piece of metal."

"Why were you chasing him?"

"He was at a female witness's house. When I said I was a cop, he took off. I discovered he'd beaten up the witness I was looking for."

She frowned. "Is she okay?"

"Enough to run away while I was catching the asswipe who beat her up."

"You didn't catch her?"

"No."

"Why did she run away? What did she witness?"

"Possibly a murder. Her friend went missing five years ago. And the friend's boyfriend was murdered. His body was found. But not his girlfriend's. When going over the file, I found some inconsistencies in what this witness told the cops back then. As for why she ran, we think it might be connected to stolen drugs."

"But you don't think she's the one who killed her friend or the boyfriend?"

"I don't think so. Supposedly, they were close friends. The witness even sends birthday cards and money to her friend's little girl."

"Who's taking care of the child?"

"The missing girl's parents."

"Do they think their daughter's dead?"

"The father does. The mother can't accept it, but realistically, I think she knows the truth. But without a body there's no closure. We hope to find her and get justice."

"And that's what you do? Offer justice? You said that's why you're a cop."

"Yeah."

Their gaze met and held. He was close enough to see the specks of gold and green in her eyes.

"That's all so sad."

"Which is why I preferred to tell you about the Tater Robber."

"Yeah." She looked down at her hands, then back up at him. "Did you get justice? For your wife and daughter?"

"Yeah." He remembered all too clearly firing the bullet that took Guzman's life.

"Is he in jail?" she asked.

"No." He didn't say he was dead, or that he'd killed him, but he sensed she understood.

"Did it help?"

The question seemed personal, and he suspected she was needing a little justice herself. No doubt from her ex who'd hurt Bell. He understood, and maybe for that reason he told a truth he'd never said aloud.

"Not really. The need for revenge consumed me. It took almost two years, but I finally caught up with him. He pulled a gun on me first. But it was what I wanted. Afterwards, when I saw him lying there dead, no pain, no regrets, I realized the man would've suffered more if they locked his ass away for the rest of his life. The feeling, the ache I carried around that I thought would go away, didn't."

He inhaled, then said another truth. The thing he told himself when he thought about killing Guzman. "On the flip side, he needed to be stopped before he hurt other people."

"I'm glad you got it. The justice." She looked up at the wall clock. "Oh goodness. It's ten." She stood up. "Bell has school tomorrow." She walked into the hall and peered into Bell's bedroom. Glancing back, she smiled. "They're both asleep."

He walked up behind her to peek in. She went to turn and came right against him. Her warm hands lifted to his chest. Shock widened her eyes, but she didn't jump back. They stood there, so close, and it felt like time stopped.

Her touch sent a current of pleasure down south.

Not thinking, just feeling, he lowered his head. His lips hovered only an inch from hers.

Her tongue swept across her lips, leaving a sheen of moisture that he ached to taste.

"You should..." She didn't finish.

"What?" He lifted his hand to her face. Traced a finger up her chin, and swept a lock of her hair off her cheek. "What should I do, Nikki? What do you *want* me to do?"

She swallowed. "Sometimes we don't get what we want."

"And sometimes we should go for it." Was that what he was doing? But damn, he didn't want to think about that now. He just wanted...He wanted.

"Maybe you're right." Then she lifted up on her tiptoes and kissed him.

CHAPTER FOURTEEN

Her taste flooded his senses so fast it had him craving more. He went in deep. He went in fast, afraid it'd end too quickly.

His tongue slipped between her lips. She shifted closer. He slipped his hand down to her waist. It fit in that sweet feminine curve as if the shape had been made for him. He brought her closer against him. She slid one warm palm under his T-shirt. When her fingers brushed against his abdomen he got so hard he felt his zipper.

How long had it been since he'd been touched?

He didn't remember moving her to the sofa, but suddenly they were there. He sat down, and she came with him, straddling his lap. Her weight rested right where he needed it. Or almost. He lifted his hips and she pressed closer. She yanked his shirt up as if requesting he remove it, and he caught the bottom hem and tugged it off, pulling his lips from hers only long enough to get it over his head.

As her hands moved across his chest, his nipples tightened and the sweet ache went lower. He let himself fall to the side and she came with him, now on top of him. Their bodies met in some tender places. And they moved in that age-old rhythm of two people wanting and needing more.

He slipped his hands up the back of her shirt, touching soft bare skin. Then he shifted around to hold her silk-covered breasts in his hands. Her nipples pebbled against the fabric. He rubbed over the tight nubs and she moaned.

Her hand eased down his chest, down past his navel, and over the bulge in his jeans. A moan of sheer pleasure escaped his lips and he flipped her over. He unsnapped her shorts and slid his hand inside, dipping under the elastic of her panties, down past her soft mound, and then lower until he found the moisture he craved.

She rotated her hips, taking his finger deeper, and he let her control the movement. And what sweet movement it was. A slow up-and-down that came with her soft tight breaths.

And then Sweetie barked. Not from the bedroom, but right at his ear.

Nikki ended the kiss, turned her head, and gasped, "Bell?"

Glancing up, he saw Bell wasn't there. Nikki blinked. Regret filled her gaze.

He pulled his hand from inside her panties and she scrambled to get up. With two hands she pushed her hair back high on her forehead and held it there. Her eyes found his. "I'm sorry. I shouldn't have..."

He had to reach into his jeans to adjust things before sitting up. "Why not?"

She shook her head. Her eyes filled with tears. "Please go."

"I'd rather talk. Whatever is—"

"No. I don't know what I was thinking. No, I wasn't thinking. I can't..."

"Are you still married?"

She shook her head. "No."

The honesty in that one word sent relief through him. But the look in her eyes yanked it away before he could savor it. "Please go."

"Nikki, if we could talk..."

"That's what we were supposed to be doing and this happened."

"Then maybe it's not wrong." Was he trying to convince himself or her? "Maybe—"

"I'm not ready. I've got Bell, and that's all I need to worry about right now."

Just like that he realized he wasn't ready, either. He didn't even have a condom. He hadn't thought to buy them because...he hadn't planned on having sex.

An image of his wife, round with his child, filled his mind, and guilt tossed cold water on what was left of his need tightening his lower body.

He stood, scooped up his dog, and walked out without saying another word.

* * *

Pablo parked in front of Rex's house. The boss had called an hour ago and said he wanted to see him. Pablo'd rather have a tooth pulled, but until he got his money back, he was at the asshole's mercy. Before he got out of his car, his phone rang.

It was Sam. "Tell me you have something."

"I do. The flowers were ordered from a place in Texas. I called that florist and the store manager said the customer paid in cash. So there's no record. No name, no credit card. And the employee who worked that day is out on a family emergency. She won't be back for three days."

"Where's the florist at?"

Sam hesitated.

"Where?" Pablo snapped.

"A small town in Texas called Red Clay."

"They have to be from Vicki," Pablo said. "She's there!"

"We don't know that."

"Yeah, we do," Pablo said. "Go there. Take photos of the bitch and my kid. Check in with all the schools to see if they have a student fitting my daughter's description."

"Are you forgetting, I have a job?" Sam's voice lacked respect.

"Get off. Claim it's an emergency. I want you there by morning."

"You think I can just take off now?"

"That's exactly what I think. And it's exactly what you are going to do."

Sam must have heard the fury in his voice. "I'll call, but then what? You can't just go there and kill her. It'll fall on me."

"If you love your family, it's a chance you're going to have to take."

* * *

Tuesday morning Vicki sat at her kitchen table. She'd barely slept. Her side had hurt the first part of the night, and all she could think about was how Juan probably considered her a tease. How could he not?

But dear Lord, if Sweetie hadn't entered the room, she'd have had sex with him right there on the couch. Right where Bell could have walked in at any moment. What kind of a parent was she?

And if only that were the worst of her wrongdoing. Hadn't her plan been to remain polite but distant? Be the neighbor who could wave at him, say good day, goodnight, and pretend his kiss hadn't mattered at all?

Where had things gone so haywire?

The answer bounced back.

Right after sitting down beside him, when he made her feel...normal. Made her feel as if she were just any other woman and he were just any other man. A man whose story intrigued her, whose flirting warmed her, whose sense of humor teased her. A man whose heart seemed so broken and his pain so familiar that she ached to be the one to help him heal.

But the closer she got to Juan, the more questions he'd ask, and the more likely it became that he'd discover her secret. While it almost seemed impossible for someone who seldom trusted anyone, she wanted to trust him.

But Joanne had made it clear. A cop would be obligated to turn her in as soon as he learned about the report about the guardianship case. It didn't matter that the claim wasn't true.

Maybe she needed to consider how soon she could find a new place to live. She still had twenty thousand dollars from her life savings. But she'd already gone through twenty thousand. AWACO had helped her with new identities, and even helped find affordable housing, but after that she and Bell were on their own.

How did anyone live on minimum wage?

She rose to refill her coffee and the pain in her side pinched again. Standing, she waited for the discomfort to pass. She couldn't afford to be down and out. She had two Zumba, a Pilates, and two yoga classes today.

Refilling her cup, adding milk, she sipped the coffee and remembered that Juan's coffee had tasted better. Then she remembered how awesome it had felt to have his hands moving over her, inside her.

Yup, she was going to have to move.

Picking up her phone, needing a distraction from the ache building low in her abdomen and the loneliness building in her life, she hit the news app.

A selection of links came up. Ten Things to Make Yourself Sexier. Nope. The next piece about Russian spies held no appeal. Scowling, she found a link to the *Los Angeles Times*. Feeling wistful for L.A., she swiped the screen that opened up a list of articles.

Mother of Twins Killed While Babies Were in
House: Willis Murder Remains Unsolved. Not wanting
to go there, she moved to the next link, but then the
words *Willis* and *twins* struck a chord. It couldn't be.

Vicki opened the link. A gasp left her lips when she
saw a picture of her one-time employee.

"No!" She read the short piece, stating the police
had yet to make an arrest in the nine-day-old murder
that had left residents in the North Hollywood neighborhood terrified for their own safety. Marisol, who'd
helped answer emails and set up client appointments,
hadn't worked for Vicki very long, but even so, she'd
thought of her as a friend.

She couldn't be dead. What kind of a monster
could...

A gut-punching possibility hit.

What if Pablo did this? What if Marisol was killed—
if her little girls were going to be without a mother—
because of Vicki?

Slammed with grief and guilt, even the air tasted bitter.

Vicki insides started shaking. There was only one
person she could reach out to for more information.
She needed to speak with Joanne.

Vicki pushed in the number. Right before she hit
dial, she realized the time. It was five in the morning
in California. But remembering Marisol's picture, Vicki
hit the call button.

It rang once. Twice. Three times. Finally a voice
answered. A sleepy voice. "Hello?"

"Joanne? It's me, Nikki Hanson...Vicki Trever."
Saying her real name gave her pause.

"What's wrong?" Joanne's tone went straight from sleepy to concerned.

"Marisol Willis was killed."

"Who?"

"Marisol Willis. She worked for me. I just saw it online. She was murdered last week. You don't think...Am I the reason she was murdered?"

Vicki held her breath, waiting for Joanne to assure her it wasn't.

The line remained silent. No assurances. "Did she know where you are? About AWACO?"

"No."

"Does *anyone* know where you are?"

"I haven't told a soul."

"Then relax. I'll look into it today. I'll call you as soon as I know something."

"But what if—"

"Relax."

"Relax? A woman, a mother was killed. And it might be my fault."

"You don't know that. Let me make a few calls."

"But..."

"Listen to me. We have someone with the program who works homicide for the LAPD. I'll see if he can tell us anything."

Joanne hung up. Vicki set the phone down, her heart breaking for Marisol. She'd been a good person. A great mother. She didn't deserve to die.

Then Joanne's question echoed in her mind. *Does* anyone *know where you are?*

She hadn't told Dan where she was, but he knew

about AWACO, and she'd called him. From her phone. An area code would tell him she was living in Texas. Maybe even in Anniston.

Fear rose in her throat. Dan would never tell. She trusted him. Or she'd been closer to trusting him than any other man.

But...if Pablo did kill Marisol, would he go after Dan? Or could Dan already be...

She grabbed the phone and dialed Dan's number.

It went straight to voice mail. "Hi, I'm in Denmark. Leave a message, and if it's important I'll get back with you later."

He wasn't even in the States. He had to be safe. But what about when he got home?

The line beeped. *Leave a message? Don't leave a message?* "Dan, it's me. I just wanted to say that you should be careful if anyone's asking questions about me. You know what I mean. Remember Marisol Willis, my employee? Something terrible happened. Just be careful."

Hanging up, Vicki felt nauseous. Breathing deeply, she walked into her niece's bedroom, the pain in her side reaching for her ribs. Leaning against the doorjamb, she saw Bell sleeping peacefully. The urge to grab her and run hit hard. But where would she go?

Her phone rang on the kitchen table. She shot back and checked the number before answering. It was Joanne.

"Hello?"

"You don't have to worry. I just spoke to my contact.

Police are pretty sure it was her ex who killed her. She'd just taken out a restraining order against him. They just don't have enough evidence to arrest him yet. So relax. This doesn't appear to be about you."

Vicki sank into a kitchen chair. It should make her feel better, but Marisol was still dead.

"Are you doing okay?"

"Yeah." The truth leaked out. "It's hard."

"I know. But you're alive."

And Marisol isn't. Neither was Alison. A lump of emotion filled her chest. "I'm going to get a new phone. I'll call you with a new number."

"Why?" Joanne's question was loaded.

Vicki wanted to lie, but Joanne was the only person who was helping her. She owed her the truth. "I called Dan to warn him."

The line went silent. "Your boyfriend?" Disappointment echoed in Joanne's voice.

"Ex-boyfriend. But yes."

"You told him where you were?"

"No, but I called him on my phone. I know I shouldn't have, but...I'm sorry. It's hard. I'm...alone."

"I know. You're right, you shouldn't have, but I get how hard this is. And you're right to get a new phone. Don't use this one again in case they get a trace. Text me your new number." She paused. "And Nikki, we have someone relooking into Pablo's death."

"And?"

"Right now we have nothing that proves he's alive. But..."

"But what?" Vicki asked.

"His old partner, Sam Milbourn, has been asking questions at one of the women's shelters here. Someone shared with him a little about the organization."

"They know. They know I'm with the program."

"No, they don't know."

"Pablo sent him. He must have figured it out."

"We don't know that. He said he was looking into becoming a volunteer to help out women and children. Maybe after seeing what Pablo did to Alison, he wants to help."

"No, he's lying. You can't tell him anything. He's helping Pablo."

"I'd never tell him anything. I haven't—"

"Even though he's a cop?"

"Our priority is your and Bell's safety."

"And what if he gets a warrant? What if—"

"Calm down. It wouldn't be the first time we've skirted the law. And I've got my guy looking into Milbourn. If he's dirty, this might be the lead we need to catch Pablo."

* * *

Juan pulled into a drugstore parking lot on his way back to the office after letting Sweetie out at lunch. He'd spent most of the morning trying to forget about how good those few minutes with Nikki on the sofa had been. How close he'd come to stripping off her clothes and burying himself inside her. Without a condom. The question now was if he was going to buy some. It felt both so damn right and so damn wrong.

And considering how Nikki had tossed him out, needing them felt unlikely.

And yet...

He sat a good five minutes in the car before getting out and buying a twelve-pack of condoms.

Shoving them into the glove compartment, he told himself that just because he bought them didn't mean he'd use them. He told himself even if he had sex, it didn't mean anyone would take Angie's place. No one could.

He'd just settled in at his desk when Mark came back from lunch and dropped in his chair. "You okay?" Mark asked.

"Yeah. Why?" Juan could hear the edge in his own voice.

"I don't know. You might have seemed pissed off this morning." Mark spoke in his don't-want-to-step-on-your-toes tone.

"I'm fine." Juan rolled his shoulders.

"This about the neighbor?"

"No," Juan lied, and his shoulders jerked back.

Mark continued to stare. "You really like her, don't you?"

"I think she's scared." The omission of just how much he liked her dropped to the pit of his stomach. "But yeah, I like her."

"Have you...asked her out or anything?"

"I don't think she's open to dating."

"So you've asked, tried to—"

"Yeah."

Mark studied him. "You still think she's hiding something?"

"Yeah. But I don't think she's a criminal."

"I'm happy that you're...you know, moving on. It's time, don't you think?"

"Is it?" Juan ran a hand over his right cheek. When his palm scrubbed the scar, he barely felt it, but that little bit of numbness was all it took for the guilt to come flooding back. "Maybe I like her because I know she's not available." He stared down at his palm—still red where the stitches had been, but the cut had healed. Funny how the body could heal itself so damn quickly, but not the heart.

"Either way, it's good to see that you're...waking up. And given what she went through with Bell's father, maybe she just needs a little more time."

"Yeah." Maybe he did, too. But he couldn't stop thinking about last night. Or the condoms in his glove compartment.

While it was hard to admit, he knew it wasn't all about the sex. He hadn't enjoyed just the sofa time of their evening. Flirting with her had felt electric. Entertaining her with his stories and hearing her laugh had been cathartic. Sharing things had...felt right. Then there was his need to protect her.

And when he wasn't thinking about her, his mind went to Bell. To her scars. To her words. *It's not your fault.* He closed his eyes. He remembered Angie asking him to quit working undercover a month before the explosion. Probably before his cover had been blown. *It kind of is my fault, Bell. It kind of is.*

"Hey." Connor walked in.

"Where have you been?"

Connor dropped at his desk. "I paid another visit to the perp who beat up Bates."

"Did a week plus in jail help him recall anything?" Mark's chair squeaked when he leaned back.

"Nothing." Frustration leaked out in Connor's tone.

Footsteps sounded in the hall. Juan looked up. The station's clerk, Mildred, stood in the doorway, a hand on her hip. "Someone's here to see you." Her eyes were on him.

"Who?" he asked.

"She wouldn't give me her name, but she has your card. And she has pink—"

"It's me," a voice echoed from the hall, and Juan saw a quick glimpse of pink hair behind Mildred.

Mildred swung around. "I told you to wait."

"Yeah," said Star, the waitress from the Black Diamond. "I never was good at minding."

"Well, your mama should have taught you better." Mildred turned around and stared at Juan as if their guest's rude behavior were his fault.

"It's okay," he told Mildred. "Let her in."

"Fine." Mildred huffed as she walked away.

Wearing a pair of black shorts that showcased a nice pair of legs and a bright blue shirt cut low enough to catch a man's eye, Star sashayed into the room. She didn't wear nearly as much makeup as she'd worn while waitressing, and Juan noted how young she looked. Hell, was she old enough to serve drinks?

She bypassed Mark's desk and headed right to Juan. She stopped a foot from where he sat.

"What brings you here, Star?" Juan asked.

"Do I need a reason?" Humor sounded in her voice.

"I'm afraid you do."

"You still want information on Cindy?" she asked.

"Yes."

"Well, why don't you buy me lunch and I'll tell you what I know."

"I've already eaten. Why—"

"But I haven't." She slipped one hand on her hip.

He hesitated. Did Star really have something? "Okay. There's a Whataburger across the street. I'll buy you lunch."

She lifted one brow. "What I got is worth more than a burger."

"Really?"

Connor cleared his throat to hide his laugh.

Star nodded at the man, then smiled.

"Okay, I'll make it a meal deal." Juan stood up.

Connor coughed again. Star cut him a seductive smile. "Is he always this cheap?"

Connor leaned an elbow on his desk. "I'll bet you can get a cookie out of him, too."

"I like cookies." She turned to Juan.

He grabbed his gun out of a drawer and headed for the door. "Let's go."

"Bring me back a chocolate shake," Connor said.

Juan glared back at him. Connor coughed again.

In less than five minutes, Star had ordered herself a lunch deal, a cookie, and a shake. They got their drinks and had just settled in a booth when he finally spoke. "What do you have for me?"

She looked up at him through long lashes. "You don't waste any time, do you?"

He frowned. "No games, okay?"

"I'm not playing games." Her soft Southern accent told him she wasn't Texan. Alabama, maybe? He wondered if she was a runaway.

"Then talk. Or do you want money?"

Her frown deepened. "No. I just…I thought we could be friends or something."

He inhaled. "I'm honored, but you're a witness on a case."

"Did you miss the 'friends' part?"

He put the straw in his drink. "I didn't miss the 'or something' part."

She grinned.

A young man brought out her food. Juan watched his so-called witness unwrap her burger. She popped a fry into her mouth. Then she picked up another one and pointed it at him. "Why do I get the feeling you're a decent one?"

"A decent what?" he asked.

"Guy. Cop. Person."

"I try. But seriously, I don't have time to chat." He started to stand.

She motioned for him to sit back down. "But seriously," she mimicked him, "I have something on Cindy."

Frustrated, he fell back into the booth. "Then talk."

"I went in to pick up my paycheck this morning. There was a guy there chatting with Mr. Grimes, aka the Grinch, my boss." She ate a fry. "And he was asking questions about Cindy. He wanted to know where she was. Said something like…'She hasn't been at her apartment.' It sounded like Grinch had given him her address earlier."

Juan sat up straighter. "Do you know who he was?"

"I didn't, but after he left I heard Grinch talking to Bo, one of the bouncers. Grinch was nervous, told Bo that the guy worked for some drug dealer from Los Angeles. He said he recognized him from years ago when something went down." She smiled as if pleased with herself. "I thought that was something you should know."

Juan took in the info and turned it over in his mind. *Was this who broke into Bates's apartment? Could this relate back to the Liu killing?*

"What did this guy look like?"

"Big guy. At least six three. Dark hair and light eyes. Had a tattoo, a spiderweb, on the right side of his neck, looked like a prison tattoo. And he walks like a linebacker, ready to plow into someone."

"That's a good description." Normally people couldn't even remember what hair color a perp had.

"I got something better." She held out her hand. "His license plate. He was driving a cream-colored Corolla."

Juan pulled out his phone and took a photograph of her palm, then he looked up. "You're right. You deserved more than a burger. We're probably going to need you to give our artist a description of the guy. But I'll call you." He reached for his wallet and pulled out a couple of twenties.

"No." She held up her hand. "Keep your money."

She picked up another fry. "I might need something from you sometime."

Juan placed the money on the table. "Need what?"

"I don't mean anything illegal."

"Then what do you mean?" He leaned back in the booth.

She bypassed his question. "You talking to Grinch about Cindy has gotten rumors flying."

"What kind of rumors?"

"Someone said all of this is connected to an old murder case."

"Who said that?"

"It was hearsay. I can't even tell you who said it." She paused. "Is it true?"

"I can't say. I should be going."

"Wait," she said. "Another reason I came was I wanted to be sure you didn't get the wrong idea about Cindy."

"What wrong idea?"

"I think I sounded judgmental when I told you about her selling drugs."

"What do you mean?" he asked.

"It's just...she's one of the nicer ones. Yeah, she's been acting strange lately. But I don't think she uses. She told me she got clean a while back. I believed her."

"Okay." He pushed the money across the table. "Take it. I have to get back to work."

She handed him the milkshake she hadn't touched yet. "Tell your hot partner it's from me. And I'd appreciate it if you didn't mention me to Grinch if you speak to him again."

Juan took the milkshake and returned to the office.

"That was quick," Connor said.

Juan set the shake on the guy's desk.

"I didn't think you'd get it."

"I didn't. She did."

"Did she really have something?" Connor asked.

"Yeah." He told them everything.

"You think this guy is tied to Noel and Liu's cases?" Mark asked.

"I think it's worth finding out," Juan said. "Can one of you run this license plate and check to see if a big linebacker with a spiderweb tattoo was questioned in the Liu or Noel cases? I'm going to have a talk with Star's boss again." Juan pulled out his phone, snagged a pen and paper, and scribbled down the license number.

"You want to do the Internet check and I'll go talk to the guy?" Connor offered.

"No, I'll do it," Juan said.

"Okay." Connor shot Mark a look that seemed to mean something.

"What?" Juan asked.

"Nothing," Connor said. "Just…normally you'd prefer to stay put."

"Yeah, well, things change." Juan pushed away from his desk.

"Yeah." Connor leaned back in his chair. "We're noticing."

Juan walked out and the truth of his statement came with a punch in the gut. He was changing. *Acceptance brings change. Or sometimes change brings acceptance.* Murdock's words set off a tiny alarm in his gut.

CHAPTER FIFTEEN

That was good, guys. You did great," Vicki said to her Pilates class of fourteen women. She forced a smile on her lips. But in truth, she felt winded, cold, hot. Oh, hell, she felt sick. And it wasn't from just the news of Marisol.

She couldn't miss work. Couldn't *afford* to miss work. Yet the slow drum of a headache played right behind her eyes, and though she'd skipped lunch, she felt queasy.

Thankfully, this was her last class. She glanced at the clock on the wall. She had thirty minutes to get to the school to pick up Bell. Thankfully, she'd used her lunchtime to grab a new phone and some Tylenol. She was pretty sure she had Pepto-Bismol at home.

"See you next time." As everyone started leaving, she used a towel to mop the sweat off her brow. When she looked up, one of the class attendees, a dark-haired woman, walked toward her.

"I love how you lead a class." She offered Vicki her hand.

"Thank you." Vicki pushed herself into PR mode. "I teach it on Wednesday and Friday, too."

"I know," the woman said. "I'm Christina Acosta. I manage Finally Fit on the south side of town and also help out around here. I thought I could use a workout. And I'm impressed. If Lucy isn't careful, I'm going to try to steal you to work at my location."

In spite of the woman's compliment, Vicki's warning bells rocked, rattled, and rang. Had Juan told his sister-in-law about her? How Vicki had mistaken him for a burglar, beaten him up, been willing to kiss him like a hormonal teen, then sent him packing? *Crap.* "Yes, you're Juan's sister-in-law."

Christina's eyes widened. "You know Juan?"

Okay, this was really awkward now. "We're neighbors. He mentioned you worked at the other gym."

"Oh, okay. He didn't mention you. I mean, I'm sure he would have if the subject would've come up. I've barely seen him lately."

The awkwardness reached a new level. So not good when you were dealing with someone who had the power to put you on the unemployment line.

The thought of losing this job and having to go back to waitressing had Vicki putting on a good front. "It's a pleasure to meet you."

"Yes." Christina looked as if she was still reeling from the fact that Vicki knew Juan. "So...neighbors?"

"Yes."

Christina smiled. "He's a great guy."

Vicki nodded again.

Right then the receptionist stuck her head in the door. "You have a phone call, Nikki."

Vicki clutched the towel. "Did they say who it was?"

"No. Just that it was urgent."

* * *

"Always happy to have a police officer stop in, but weren't you just here asking the same questions?" Mr. Grimes, or as Star called him, Grinch, asked.

"Yeah." Juan's tone should have given the guy the first warning that this wasn't a friendly visit, but Grimes continued to look too chipper. "I stumbled across something else."

"What?" the man asked, leaning against the bar.

Juan wasn't about to rat out Star by throwing her name into the mix. "Cindy's place was broken into. And we arrested someone who claimed they bought drugs from her and the sale supposedly went down here. You know how bad that looks for a place like yours. Cops could get all up in your business."

"I told you I fired her. Whatever she was doing around here is on her, not me."

"I know, but there was a car with out-of-state plates hanging around the night her apartment was tossed." That, of course, was a lie, but this bozo didn't know that. "Seems like somebody's looking for her, and you'd be the first person they'd go to."

"Yeah, but I'm not in the business of passing out info on my ex-employees."

"You gave it to me. And I'm not taking it personal, but I don't even think you like me." Juan looked around. "I'll bet cops swarming this place pretty much shuts it down for a while, doesn't it?"

The Grinch's expression matched his nickname. "Fine, a guy came looking for Cindy the other night. He wanted her address."

"And you gave it to him." Juan frowned.

"He wasn't the type to take no for an answer, if you know what I mean."

"What's his name?"

"I don't know. I didn't exactly ask to see his ID."

Juan just stared at him.

"I'm serious. I don't know."

"Have you seen him in here before?"

When he hesitated, Juan jumped in. "You can make this easy for yourself. Or—"

"Okay. Yes, I've seen him in here before."

"When?"

"It's been a while."

Juan rubbed his hand over his scar. "Months? Years?"

When the guy flinched, hope flared in Juan's gut. Damn it if he might not just find out what happened to Abby Noel but solve the Liu case as well.

He'd missed this. Missed actually doing the legwork in lieu of staying in the slow lane and doing Internet searches.

"How long?" Juan repeated.

"Four or five years, I'd guess."

"Was he here the same time Abby Noel went missing?"

"Maybe. But I really don't know much. I'd just started here. She went missing the same week. I barely knew the chick."

"Yeah, but her boyfriend, who I heard hung out here as well, got murdered. And when someone gets murdered, people have a tendency to remember things."

The man ran a hand over the bar as if debating.

"So if the cops showed up here at around eleven, how much coke would we find on your employees?"

Frowning, Grinch pushed away from the bar. "Fine. He was here about the same time the dancer went missing. And I remember him mentioning he was from L.A. But I don't know if he had anything to do with the murder or the chick disappearing."

"Luckily, I consider that my job. But I'll need you to come down to the station and see if you can give us a good description."

"Not in a million years. Absolutely not. I won't get involved."

* * *

Vicki couldn't drive fast enough to the school. According to the nurse who'd called her at the gym, Bell was running a fever and throwing up. Vicki kept telling herself that kids got sick, that this wasn't anything to panic about, but not once since she'd had Bell had she run a fever. And what if it was something really bad? What if she had to go to the hospital?

They didn't have insurance. Other than a fake vaccination record and birth certificate, she had zero paperwork on her niece. They'd want the name of a pediatrician in Colorado. She could find one, but what if they requested records? What if they saw Bell's scars and started asking questions?

It wasn't until Vicki parked at the school and was hit by another wave of nausea that she remembered her own illness. They probably had the same thing. Which meant it was just a virus. Which meant she didn't have to panic. Knowing that didn't help. The thought of Bell sick had Vicki's stomach knotting and feeling worse.

She rushed into the school and asked where the nurse's office was. Pointed in the right direction, she took off.

Pushing inside the room, Vicki spotted a nurse. "Hello, I'm Nikki Hanson, Bell Hanson's mom."

"Yes." The middle-aged woman with bright red hair introduced herself. "Poor girl. She's resting now, but she's thrown up several times."

The nurse led Vicki to the back, where Bell lay on a cot with a bucket in her hands.

When Bell saw Vicki, the child started to cry. "Oh, baby." Vicki rushed in.

Bell buried her head on Vicki's shoulder. Vicki looked at the nurse. "Should I take her to a doctor?"

"I don't think that's necessary. I've had three kids in here with this today. I think it's a stomach virus." The nurse gave Vicki some easy care instructions and they headed to the car.

Bell curled up in her car seat. "My stomach hurts."

"I'm sorry, hon." Vicki pulled out of the parking lot. "When we get home I'll give you something that might make your tummy feel better."

"No medicine!" she cried, and then came the sound of Bell throwing up. Thankfully the nurse had given them a plastic bag, just in case.

"Oh, honey," Vicki said. "I'm driving as fast as I can."

* * *

"How did you get him to come in?" Mark asked as he and Connor walked back into their office.

Juan looked up. He'd left them down with Mr. Grinch and the sketch artist to come back and make a few phone calls. "Are you kidding? An upstanding, caring citizen like him? He jumped at the chance to help."

Connor and Mark both laughed and settled at their desks.

Juan added, "Let's just say I pointed out the pros and cons of not pissing me off."

"One day you'll have to fill me in on those," Connor said.

"When you piss me off, I will," Juan said. "Did you get anything on the license plate?"

Connor looked back at him. "Yeah, but nothing that's going to help. It was stolen yesterday on the north side of town from an apartment parking lot."

"North, huh? So if our perp is from Los Angeles like Mr. Grinch thinks, then maybe he flew in and needed a ride," Juan mused aloud.

"Good thought," Mark said.

Connor leaned back in his chair and put his feet up beside his Steelers coffee mug. "When we get the drawing, I'll see if we can't get our hands on some airport security film of flights coming in from California."

Juan stared down at the Noel file again. "I can't help but think it's because we opened the case that they're coming after her now."

"Do you want me to go back to the Black Diamond tonight and ask around?" Connor readjusted his feet. "Maybe another employee might have a clue where she is."

"Star said Cindy was pretty much a loner, but I guess it wouldn't hurt to try." Juan let go of a frustrated sigh. "If this person looking for Cindy is really tied to the Liu case, they're going to want to shut her up permanently."

"We don't know that for sure," Mark said.

Juan frowned. "We kind of do. Remember, Star said people were whispering it was about an old murder."

Mark nodded. "Did she tell you who said it?"

"In our second conversation, she said another waitress heard one of the customers say it. And I just hung up with that waitress and she said it was a new customer—a guy with average build, average height, and light brown hair. It could be half the population. She can't even remember what night she heard it. I told her to call me if she remembered anything."

"You think she might be lying?" Mark asked.

"It didn't sound like it," Juan admitted, wishing it had. They could really use a break here.

Mark pushed back from his desk a bit. "Give me her contact info and I'll go question her in person."

"It wouldn't be on us if someone was tipped off that we're looking into the case," Connor said, "but it would suck if something happened to her."

"Hey." Mildred moved into the room and over to Juan's desk. "Mrs. Noel dropped these off when you were out. Said they were birthday cards you wanted to see."

"Yeah." He took the brown manila envelope, but his gut said they weren't going to help. "Thanks."

Mildred left.

Mark spoke up. "Birthday cards?"

"Yeah, remember I told you that Bates sends cards to Abby Noel's kid?"

"That's decent of her," Connor said. "Most addicts aren't nearly that conscientious."

"I know," Juan said. "I assume it's out of guilt, but Star said she was a nice person. That she even got clean."

"But she stole those drugs." Mark exhaled.

"And there's that," Juan said.

Mark seemed to consider all the information. "We don't have enough to get permission to assign someone to watch Cindy's apartment, do we?"

"No, but patrols are doing drive-bys."

"Then we might have to stake it out ourselves," Mark said. "Annie's going out to dinner with her friend. Why don't I go park at Bates's apartment and see if she stops by."

"Okay," Juan said. "Call me when you're ready to leave and I'll take a shift after you."

Mark turned in his chair and it squeaked. "Okay, we're doing this, but just to play the devil's advocate, we all know we could be wasting our time. This might not have anything to do with the Liu murder. Plus, she could have already left town. And we could be wrong and she may not know shit about Noel's disappearance."

"Yeah," Juan answered. "Or we could be solving not just one case, but two. What are the chances that a woman's boyfriend is murdered and she goes missing the next day and it's not connected?"

"Very slim." Mark's words came out in almost a growl. "But . . . it's just nothing is cut-and-dried about this case."

"I'm going to grab the Liu file and go through it again." Connor dropped his feet off his desk. "And when the sketch is finished I'll make a few calls to see if we need a warrant to snag some film from the airport. I'll take a shift at Bates's apartment tomorrow."

Juan nodded. "I'll see Mr. Grimes out and then I'll start going through mug shots looking for anyone who might fit the sketch."

"We're going to solve this one." Mark got up and pulled his gun out of his drawer.

Juan hoped Mark was right. For the Noels. And for Cindy Bates.

* * *

Juan spent the rest of the afternoon on the computer looking at mug shots, hoping to find a dark-haired, six-foot-plus guy with a spider prison tattoo. He hadn't found anyone in their database. Considering the guy was from Los Angeles, he called the LAPD, offered to send them the sketch to see if someone there could look into their database and call him if they found anything. They were happy to help but couldn't promise a speedy turnaround.

He headed home and was almost there when his phone rang. Checking the screen, he saw his sister-in-law's name.

"Hi, Christina," he said.

"I like her," his sister-in-law said.

"Who?" he asked.

"Your girlfriend."

"Girlfriend?"

"Okay, call her your neighbor."

Air caught in his throat. "You met Nikki?"

"*Sí*, and I like her. But I'm going to hate her tomorrow when my muscles are sore from taking her Pilates class. Why didn't you tell me you knew her?"

"It didn't come up." What exactly had Nikki told his sister-in-law?

"I hope her daughter's okay?"

"Huh?"

"The school called earlier and said her little girl was really sick."

"With what?"

"I don't know, but Nikki hurried out. I heard something about a high fever. Can you let her know we have someone to cover her classes if she can't make it tomorrow?"

"Yeah. I will."

He hung up. A sense of urgency he shouldn't feel pulled at him. How many times had she insisted she could take care of herself? So why did he feel the need to charge in to help?

He parked in his garage, put Sweetie on her leash, and walked over next door.

He waited a good sixty seconds after ringing her bell, and was about to leave when he heard footsteps approaching the door. She greeted him with a frown and she looked pale, with dark circles underlining her eyes.

"Hey. Christina called and said Bell was sick." Sweetie started yanking the leash to go inside.

"It's a virus. She'll be fine. Thank you." She started to shut the door.

"You don't look well, either. Can I do anything?"

"No." She looked ready to bolt. "I think I got it, too. But—"

"I need to run to the store." It was a lie, but a good one. "You need anything? Soup? Medicine?"

Interest flashed in her eyes.

"You're really going?" Desperation sounded in her voice.

"Yes."

She hesitated.

"I'm going. What do you need?"

"Pepto-Bismol and maybe some soup. Kid's Tylenol. And a thermometer," she added.

"What kind of soup?"

"Chicken." Suddenly covering her mouth with her hand, she swung the door half-closed. He heard a gagging sound.

He took a step closer. Sweetie barked as she tried to get inside. "You okay?"

"Yeah. Sorry."

"I'm good at holding hair back." As his words slipped off his tongue, he remembered Angie's three months of morning sickness. The thought thumped him in his chest. A pang of grief followed at the memory of what she said every time she threw up: *It'll be worth it when I see my baby smile.* She'd been robbed. And so had he. And yet here he was, offering to hold a different woman's hair. It felt wrong, and yet somehow not so wrong.

She was his neighbor and he wanted to help her.

But he couldn't deny that wasn't all he wanted.

CHAPTER SIXTEEN

Vicki had made Bell and herself a pallet on the hall floor in front of the bathroom. Once she'd gotten home, she'd discovered she had only one dose of Pepto left. She gave that to Bell.

Wrapping her arms around her niece, who still complained of a stomachache, she tried to comfort her while fighting wave after wave of nausea.

She'd barely managed to clean up the entryway floor.

I'm good at holding hair back.

Juan's words echoed in her head. Was there really a guy out there who'd do that? After she'd pushed him away again last night, the fact that he'd offered to go to the store shocked the hell out of her. The fact that she'd accepted both shocked and scared her.

"I don't feel good," Bell cried.

"I know, sweetheart." Vicki rested her hand on the child's forehead. Bell felt hot, but with Vicki feverish herself, it made it hard to be sure.

"Do you want some more ice chips?" Vicki asked.

"No."

The doorbell rang. Knowing it was probably Juan, she forced herself off the floor. "I'll be right back." She stopped by the sofa where she'd dropped her purse and pulled out a couple of twenties.

Answering the door, she looked up at Juan with bags in both his hands and concern in his expression.

"Hey. Let me bring this in." He went to sidestep her. She shifted in front of him.

"No. I can take it." She noticed how full the bags looked. "What all did you get?"

"Just a few extra things." He walked around her and dropped the bags on her table. He unloaded a few of his purchases. "My mom always got us ginger ale and Popsicles when we were sick. I thought Bell might like that." He pulled out the box. "I'll put these in the freezer."

Vicki blinked. Her head hurt, her stomach hurt, her side throbbed. And seeing Juan so eager to help made her heart hurt. "Thank you."

"Can I have a Popsicle now?" Bell's voice came behind her.

Vicki turned. "Sure."

Juan opened the box. "You want red, white, or blue?"

"Red," Bell answered, offering an appreciative look that wasn't a smile but was close.

Juan opened the Popsicle, bunching the paper at the

bottom, and handed it to Bell. "Hope it makes you feel better."

The tenderness in his voice had a knot tightening in Vicki's throat.

"Thank you." Bell looked up at him with big brown eyes.

"Yes. Thank you," Vicki echoed.

"You want one?" he asked her.

"No, thanks."

He walked to the table and pulled out the other items from the bags. "I wasn't sure what kind of chicken soup, so—"

"How much was it?" she asked.

"We can deal with that later."

She held out the twenties. "Will this cover it?"

"I left the receipt in the car. Pay me later."

Bell curled up on the sofa. Vicki looked from her niece to Juan. "You should—"

"Can I heat up some soup?" He moved into the kitchen with the Popsicles and she heard her freezer open and close.

When he walked out, she stepped away. "I'm sure this is contagious. You should go."

"I never catch stuff like this," he said.

"I don't think you should chance it."

He frowned as if trying to think of a reason to stay. And God help her, but part of her wanted him to stay. To help care for Bell. When had she started trusting him?

"We just need to rest."

His eyebrows lifted as if her sendoff caused a visceral

reaction. Then she felt it, too. Regret. Remorse. She felt like a real bitch.

"Christina said if you need to miss tomorrow, they have someone who could cover your classes."

"Thanks. I'll call her."

When that stretch of silence grew awkward, he started for the door. She followed him.

Opening the door, he turned. Met her gaze. "If you need—"

"I won't."

"At least take my card. Call me if anything changes." He retrieved a card from his wallet and put it in her palm.

The second his hand touched hers, emotion swelled in her chest.

"I'll come check on you," he said.

"Not necessary."

His mouth thinned in disappointment. Her heart felt the same pull.

He ran a hand over his chin, looking frustrated. "Then give me your number so I can call and check in."

"We'll be fine."

Noting his frown, she realized how badly she was treating him. "I'm sorry," she said before she could stop herself. "I'm sorry for mistaking you for a burglar. I'm sorry that I'm coming off like a bitch."

"You're not coming off like a bitch. You're coming off—"

"I'm sorry that I'm not in a place to accept... everything you're offering. It's not you. It's me. And I'm sorry."

He shrugged. "I'm just being a neighbor. You're sick and your kid's sick and I just want to help."

"You have. And it's too much already." Realizing she still had the money in her hands, she held it out. "Let me know how much I owe you."

He left without taking it.

Vicki rested her head against the door and tears of frustration filled her eyes. How could it be that she'd completed the Ironman competition, yet all it took was a stomach virus and a sick kid to make her want to scream uncle?

* * *

Juan had barely gotten off Nikki's porch when his phone rang. "Yeah," he answered without checking the number.

"She's back again."

His mind raced as he tried to recognize the voice. "Who?"

"That Bates woman. I just got home and she's sitting on my porch swing. My husband said to call you."

He realized it was Mrs. Henley's voice, the owner of the house Cindy Bates had rented. "Okay, don't go in the backyard. Don't look out the window. I'm on my way." It would take him fifteen minutes, so he called to get a unit there as quickly as possible and gave them a description of Bates's car.

When he pulled up to the Henleys' place there was a cop car in the driveway. An officer stood on the porch speaking to Mrs. Henley. He didn't see a burgundy

Saturn parked out front, but he still jumped out and headed to the door.

Mrs. Henley looked at him. "The dog barking scared her away right after I got off the phone with you. I went out and tried to stall her. She asked me for money. Said we owed it to her and that it was for an orphan fund. I told her to let me get my purse, but I was so nervous, I think she knew I was just trying to stall her. When I came back out, she was gone."

"Shit!"

The patrol cop looked at Juan. "I've called in to be on the lookout for her car."

Mrs. Henley crossed her arms. "Why does she keep coming here?"

"I told your husband to secure your back gate. Did he?"

"He said he was going to do it this weekend."

"Maybe you should get him to do it sooner," Juan recommended.

"Who did that to her face?" The empathy was clear in her voice.

"We have the guy locked up," Juan said.

The woman frowned. "She left a notebook on the swing if you want to see it."

Juan followed Mrs. Henley into the backyard. He picked up the artist notebook. Written in neat handwriting was poetry. He read the first two lines.

I'm ready to join you, my friend.
My heart just will not mend.

The next page had the same poem he'd read in her journal at her apartment. The one about a mirror and a face. The next page had some detailed sketches of a birdbath with a couple of birds perched on the side. Another page had different kinds of statuary. An angel, a concrete stand with a moon and a sun. Like in the paintings at her place, talent shone in the work. He looked around and saw she'd been sketching items from the garden area.

"Seriously, I'll look at how much the swing costs and I'll give it to her. I'll even pay for the birdbath and all."

"So she did all this?" He looked at the corner garden.

"Yeah. I'll pay for them, too."

"I don't think it's all about the money. I think this place feels like home."

"Well, it's not her home anymore."

"I know. Did she appear to be on drugs?"

"She was nervous, but not like she was high on anything. Do you think she's dangerous?"

"I don't know her well enough to say. But I would keep your guard up and make your husband put a lock on the gate."

Juan left with the notebook. The first line of the poem echoed in his head. *I'm ready to join you, my friend.* Was Bates thinking of killing herself?

* * *

At almost midnight Tuesday night, Vicki and Bell lay on opposite ends of the sofa. The television had played on a kid channel all day, although Bell mostly slept.

Vicki had stayed awake on mama duty and watched over Bell, who'd had a temperature on and off, but now her own sickness was taking its toll.

Her niece wouldn't eat any solid food, but she drank the ginger ale and ate Popsicles. Vicki's appreciation for Juan kept going up, while her willpower kept going down. She'd fought the urge to call and say thank you a dozen times.

Rolling over, she felt the throbbing in her side worsen. She hissed as the pain radiated across her stomach. This had to be more than a stomach virus. It had to be the flu.

Chills, stomach pain, body pain. She couldn't remember ever being this sick. Surely this thing couldn't last much longer.

Bell moved up on the sofa and stretched out beside Vicki. Just the soft pressure of the child against Vicki's side made her moan. She wanted to ask her niece to move away, but how wrong was that? So she rested her arm around the child.

"You're hot," Bell said a few minutes later and woke Vicki up.

"Yeah," she answered.

"Do you need a Popsicle?" Bell asked. "It made me feel better."

"No, hon. I'll be fine. But it's late." Obviously after napping all day Bell wasn't very sleepy now. "You know what? I might fall asleep. Can you be good and watch TV? And if you get to feeling bad, wake me up. Okay?"

"Can I play games on your phone?"

"No, baby." She needed to set the alarm so she'd

wake up to give Bell more medicine in case her fever came back. "Just watch TV now."

"What about your old phone? I found it in the garbage."

"No. It's broken." She forced herself to sit up. When she did, the blanket slipped off her legs, and goose bumps crawled up her calves. Her head swam and she clung to the edge of the sofa. She managed to reach the phone to set it.

"Are we going to sleep on the sofa?" Bell asked.

"You want to?" Vicki fell back on the cushions and pulled the blanket back over her.

"It would be like a sleepover party." Bell sounded chipper.

"Yeah." Vicki forced a smile.

"I'm kind of hungry," Bell said.

"You want some soup?" But did Vicki have the energy to get it?

"Yes."

With Bell on the mend, Vicki could hope she wasn't far behind. She pushed up again. Her arms trembled. Her head pounded. Damn, she was so cold. She perched on the edge of the sofa for several seconds, garnering her strength so she could walk. Then as she pushed up, her knees nearly buckled. She caught herself on the arm of the sofa.

She made it to the kitchen, but had to hold on to the counter to keep standing. Wasn't there some rule that mothers couldn't get sick at the same time as their kids? She supposed it didn't translate to pretend moms.

Shaking, Vicki opened the Chicken and Stars soup

and poured it into a bowl. The smell almost turned her stomach. She stuck it in the microwave. When another wave of cold hit her, her entire body shivered. Her fever must have gone up again. While the microwave hummed, she found the liquid Tylenol and took a big swallow. The sweet taste curled her tongue and for a second she didn't think she was going to keep it down.

She stood there, hanging on to the counter for dear life. When the appliance dinged, she somehow managed to get the soup out. Some of it spilled out of the bowl as she moved back to the sofa. But she didn't care.

"It might be hot. Be careful." She placed the bowl on the coffee table and literally fell back on the couch.

Bell slid off the sofa to the floor and looked at her soup. Vicki realized she'd forgotten a spoon. A knot of desperation swelled in her chest.

"Can you get yourself a spoon?" she asked Bell, who looked up at her as if worried.

"You don't look good," Bell said.

"I'll be better tomorrow." She watched Bell get up to get her spoon. Vicki pulled the blanket over her and tried not to think about the jackhammer going off in her head.

CHAPTER SEVENTEEN

Pablo parked a few houses down from Dan Jefferies's place. It was eleven p.m., and most of the neighbors had their lights out.

Vicki's boyfriend wasn't due back for two more days, but Pablo couldn't help but think he'd missed something that could lead him to Vicki. She'd dated the man for years. And Pablo kept thinking about what Sam said about Vicki not having his money.

When Alison left, she'd packed a lot of shit in boxes. What were the odds that Vicki didn't know Alison had taken his money? When he'd tossed Vicki's condo before she ran away from L.A., he hadn't found Alison's things. What would she have done with those boxes? Could she have stored them at Jefferies's place? In his attic maybe?

Plus, he'd seen a few things he could sell for some extra bucks.

He fucking couldn't believe he was down to hocking

stolen goods. But Rex had screwed him again. When he'd paid for the last job, he'd only given Pablo half of what he used to pay him.

When Pablo confronted his ass, he'd said, *You just aren't as valuable as you used to be now you don't work on LAPD.* First the man degraded him—talked to him like one of his peons. Now Rex was cheating him out of his money. Hadn't the latter been the last straw with his own old man? He'd found Pablo's stash of cash and taken it. And what Pablo had done to him as a result hadn't been pretty.

The sound of a motor filled the late night. He looked up. A car drove down the street. Its headlights flashed across Pablo's car. *Dan coming home early?*

Eyes on the rearview mirror, he saw the car pass Jefferies's house. Pablo's frustration coiled up in his gut like a snake.

Reaching for his phone, he dialed Sam's number. When the call connected, Pablo jumped right in. "Why haven't you answered your phone today?"

"Service sucks here."

"Tell me you got something!"

"If I had, I'd have found a way to get in touch with you," Sam Milbourn answered, his tone sounding like he was already asleep.

"What the hell have you done all day?"

"I went to nine schools in a thirty-five-mile radius and showed your daughter's picture. No one claims to have seen her."

"What about gyms? The woman's addicted to working out."

"I'm going to them tomorrow. But there's only six in this area."

"What about the bordering towns? She's not completely stupid. She probably wouldn't send flowers from her own town."

"The six includes the three closest towns."

"Then go farther out. Do both schools and gyms. There's a new town around every corner. I know because I've been down in that area before doing work for Rex." *Rex, who fucking forgot everything I did for him.*

"You do realize how big Texas is, don't you?"

"I don't care." Pablo slammed his palm on the steering wheel. "She has to be around there. You keep looking until you find her."

"I'm trying," Sam bit out.

Was he? Why did Pablo not believe the man? His tone? The fact the man fought him at every turn when it came to searching for the bitch?

"Try harder!" Pablo hung up and got out of his car.

Dressed in all black clothes, gloves, and a hat to keep his hair hidden, he moved through the darkness to the side gate. He'd rigged it when he was here last time so he could open it without any trouble.

Five minutes later, he stood in the house, tossing drawers and stacking anything that looked of value. He came across a metal box in the bottom dresser drawer. Nothing but photographs. He started to toss it down, but he saw a picture of Vicki with Alison, his daughter, and Dan Jefferies. So Jefferies had met Alison.

He stared at Vicki's face. "Where the fuck is my money? Goddamn it, I'm going to enjoy killing you!"

He threw the box across the room, and something flew out and skidded across the wood floor. He looked down. It was a key. He picked it up. It was small, like a padlock key. On it was a piece of tape with the words *Unit 106* written on it.

Jefferies had a storage unit. Could Vicki or Alison have hidden his money there? Where the hell was this place?

He remembered the mail stacked on the table. Shooting out of the bedroom, he flipped through the envelopes until he came across a bill from Full Service Storage.

The address was on the bill.

* * *

At almost one a.m., Juan leaned his head back on the headrest in his car and stared out at Cindy Bates's apartment door. Rolling down the window an inch, he waited for another breeze. The night seemed almost as quiet as it was hot. But damn, he wished she'd come home and he could get her in protective custody before she ended up on a slab at the morgue.

Mark had called him around eleven and said he'd be heading home, so Juan came straight here. It wasn't as if he'd been sleeping.

He was still too keyed up. Still pissed at Nikki for being so damn stubborn. The woman looked like she could barely stand up, but refused to let him help her. All he'd done since he got back home from the Henleys' was fret about her. Why wouldn't she give him her number so he could just call and check in?

He kept hearing her words. *I'm sorry. I'm sorry for mistaking you for a burglar. I'm sorry that I'm coming off like a bitch. I'm sorry that I'm not in a place to accept... everything you're offering. It's not you. It's me. And I'm sorry.*

She'd never come off as a bitch. She'd come off as scared. Not weak scared, but tough scared. He recalled his mom bringing feral kittens home hoping to tame them enough to be adopted out. They'd look at him as if they wanted to play, wanted to curl up in his lap or sleep on his chest, but when he got close to them, fear took over and their claws came out.

"You need to be more patient," his mom would tell him. "Let them come to you." She'd click her tongue and say, "*Mijo*, patience is not your virtue." Then she'd put a soft hand on each of his cheeks, and say, "But caring is."

His mom had been wrong. Caring was his curse. The more he cared, the more he hurt. He'd cared about his mom. About not being there to protect her. He'd cared about Angie. About not being able to save her. When Angie first got pregnant, he'd worried he didn't care enough, and then he'd lost his chance to care.

Part of him knew this was why he'd spent the last three years hiding from the world. He didn't want to care about anyone else.

So why did he feel as if the tide had turned these last few weeks? Was it just time? Had his lonely existence finally taken its toll? Or was there something about Nikki that caused the change?

Was it even fair for him to want to win her over when

he doubted his heart would really be free? He wasn't sure he could love again. Never like he'd loved Angie.

Headlights spilled into the parking lot and drew him out of his reverie. He turned to see if he could make out the type of car. Distance and darkness hampered his vision. Then the vehicle drove to the back of the lot, and when it passed under a light, he got a glimpse of burgundy. Cindy?

His pulse raced as he watched the car park. He reached for the door handle, then hesitated. Wanting her to get far enough from her car that if she saw him, she couldn't jump back in her vehicle and take off.

Shouldering back in the seat, he couldn't see her yet, but he heard a car door open, then close. Footsteps clicked on the pavement. He stayed in his car, waiting. He had her. Damn, this felt good.

Then he heard another car door opening. "Cindy?" A male voice called her name.

"Who...?" Jumping out of his car, Juan spotted her standing between the rows of cars. Then he heard the pops. One. Two. Three shots rang out.

"Get down!" Gun drawn, he rushed toward her, darting between the rows of cars. Bates hit the ground. Was she responding to his order, or had she taken a bullet?

He got close enough to see she lay facedown on the pavement, not moving. His gut said she'd been shot. Knowing the shooter was still there, Juan gripped his Glock, his pulse thrumming in his ears.

A car revved its engine. He ran out between the rows of cars. "Police!" A cream-colored Corolla hurtled toward him.

He dove between two cars. His shoulder slammed against the pavement. He rolled on his stomach and shot at the tires. The pop of return fire had his blood pumping, fizzing. He got to his feet. Shot two more times.

The car swerved, hit a Toyota, then careened out of the parking lot. "Damn!"

Grabbing his phone from his pocket, he rushed to Bates, still facedown on the pavement. "Don't be dead. Please don't be dead." As he neared, he saw the dark pool of blood around her shoulder. He called for backup and an ambulance.

When he dropped down on his knees beside her, she moved. He gently turned her over. Blood ran down her temple. Had she taken a bullet to the head? Then he saw another wound right in the V of her shirt. Her eyes opened. Desperate blue eyes met his. She tried to talk, but couldn't. Blood spilled out of her chest.

He yanked off his shirt and pressed it against the wound in her chest, hoping to stop the bleeding. Her red hair lay spread around her head. Blood continued to ooze down her cheek. "I have help coming. Hang in there."

* * *

"Sorry, I need to get out of here." Juan stood the second he saw Connor walk into the ER waiting room. Juan had called Connor as soon as he'd gotten to the hospital.

"Have you heard anything?" Connor asked.

"They say they're taking her to surgery, but haven't

yet. She took one bullet to the chest, another in the head. They don't know if she'll pull through. They already called Homicide in and they took over the scene. Sorry, I need to—"

Connor rested his hand on Juan's shoulder. "You okay?"

"No. I need to get out of here." He tore down the hall to the ER exit. Connor's footsteps followed.

"Why don't I take you out for a drink?" Connor asked.

"No. I'm going home."

Connor moved in front of him. "Slow down."

Juan slammed his palm on the hospital wall. "That's just it. If I hadn't slowed down. If I'd gotten out of the fucking car when I first saw Bates, I could have stopped this."

"This isn't on you."

"Why the fuck do people keep saying that?" He exhaled. "She begged me to get out of undercover. If I'd gotten out when—" Realizing what he'd said, he shut his mouth.

Connor just stared.

"I called Bates's sister. But I don't think she's coming. I got a BOLO out on the shooter's car. But right now...I need to go." Everything was taking him back. The blood. The smell. The sound of the hospital. He'd made them bring Angie here. It didn't matter that they'd said it was too late. Too late for her and his baby. It didn't matter. He wanted a miracle.

He hadn't gotten one.

* * *

It was after two in the morning when Juan got home. He stood in the middle of his living room, his gut a knot, his chest jammed with emotions he didn't want to feel. Rushing into the kitchen, he reached in the fridge for a beer. Then, realizing that wouldn't cut it, he found the scotch his brother had given him for Christmas.

He poured himself four fingers. Craving numbness, he gulped half of it in one swallow. It burned all the way down to his stomach. He moved into the living room, turned on the DVD player, and started the video.

Angie appeared on the screen. "I love you, baby girl, and I love your daddy."

Tears filled Juan's eyes. He hadn't watched the video since...since he met his neighbor. And before that he'd watched it most every night.

He dropped into his recliner and brought the cold glass to his lips. The sharp sting of scotch filled his nose. He was about to take another gulp when his cell phone rang from the kitchen.

Probably Connor checking on him. He didn't want to be checked on. So he ignored the ring and watched his wife press her hands to her round abdomen. Watched everything he'd lost.

His doorbell rang. Had Connor followed him home?

Bolting up, Juan shot across the floor to his door, ready to give his partner hell. He looked out his dining room window. He couldn't see the porch, but he could see the street. Connor's car wasn't there.

The doorbell rang again.

Suddenly leery, he pulled out his gun. When he did,

he saw he had blood on his jeans. Cindy Bates's blood. He moved to the door and looked out the peephole.

The fish-eye view was empty. No one was there.

Had he imagined the ring? He was about to walk away when it rang again.

He swung around, gun out, and jerked open the door. Bell stood there in a pink nightgown, her toenails painted with smiley faces. Her teary eyes widened in fear.

He holstered his gun. "Bell, what are you doing here?"

Her bottom lip trembled. "My mama's sick. Her alarm is going off on her phone, but I can't get her to wake up. Can you help her?"

"Yeah." His own pain forgotten, he grabbed the girl's hand and led her next door.

"Where is she?" he asked, walking inside.

"On the sofa."

He hurried over. Nikki lay there huddled beneath a blanket. "Nikki?" He called her name and knelt down.

She didn't move. Fearing the worst, he touched the side of her neck. A flutter of her pulse whispered across his fingers, but her skin felt so hot it almost burned. *Shit!*

He debated calling an ambulance, but he knew he could get her to the hospital faster. Looking at Bell, in her nightgown and barefoot, he said, "We're going to take your mom to the doctor. Can you get your shoes on?"

She nodded, but didn't move.

"Hurry."

Tears ran down the child's cheeks. "She's not going to die, is she?"

"No," he said, not knowing if it was true but saying it anyway.

She moved to the other side of the room and slipped on some flip-flops.

He needed his car keys. "I'll be right back."

In record time, he had pulled into Nikki's driveway.

Rushing inside, he picked her up. She stirred a little.

"Nikki." He pulled her against him. "It's Juan. I'm taking you to the hospital."

She muttered something. Something about Bell.

"I got Bell," he assured her, then realized he'd need her driver's license and insurance stuff. He looked at the child, who stood frozen looking up at him. "Do you know where your mom's purse is?"

She nodded.

"Can you get it?"

She went into the kitchen and came back with it.

"Let's go."

Bell followed.

He put Nikki in the backseat, opened his passenger door, picked up Bell, and placed her in the seat.

"I need my car seat," she said as he reached around her to buckle the seat belt.

"It's okay. I'm going to drive real safe."

"But Mama says it's the law."

He didn't have time. Nikki might not have time. "I know, but I'm the police, so I can do this. Okay?"

He drove fast, but mindful that he had a child in his front seat and a very sick woman in the back.

He heard Bell crying and glanced down at her. "It's okay. We're taking her to see a doctor."

"Why isn't she awake?"

"I don't know." He touched the girl's shoulder. "Are you feeling better?"

She nodded and wiped her palms over her wet cheeks.

Three minutes later, he pulled up at the emergency doors. He cut off his engine and exited the car. He got Bell out, then yanked open his back door and picked up the still-unconscious Nikki.

"Follow me," he told Bell, and rushed through the doors.

"I need help," he called out to the officer sitting behind a desk at the front. The man picked up a phone. Ten seconds later the door to the back room opened and a nurse rushed out with a stretcher.

"What's wrong with her?" the nurse asked.

"I don't know," Juan said. "She's burning up. She was throwing up earlier."

Juan felt a bump against his leg. He looked down to find Bell, still crying, standing beside him. "It's okay." After placing Nikki on the stretcher, he reached down and picked up the sobbing child.

She rested her face on his shoulder and continued to cry.

The nurse looked at them. "You need to register her."

"Yeah," Juan said. "I need to park my car and get her purse."

The nurse pushed Nikki into the back.

"Don't take her away," Bell cried.

"It's okay," he said. "They're going to make her feel better." And with everything he had, he prayed that wasn't a lie.

* * *

"Insurance card?" the woman sitting behind the registration desk asked. They'd waited ten minutes before someone motioned him to come up to the desk. Bell sat in a chair beside him, looking small, hurt, and exhausted.

"I don't see one." He fumbled through her wallet. "Here's her driver's license."

The woman picked up the card but appeared surprised. "Aren't you her husband?"

"No."

"Boyfriend?"

"No."

"But you kissed her," Bell said. "I saw you. Doesn't that make you her boyfriend?"

Juan's surprised gaze shifted to Bell. But for the life of him, he didn't know what to say. The silence grew long and the kid waited for an answer. "Well, I guess, sort of."

When he looked back at the woman, she was smiling. He frowned. She pulled in the expression. "Nearest relative?"

"I don't know. I'm her neighbor. She just moved here." He glanced at Bell. "Do you have any family?"

She shook her head extra hard. "No." He couldn't say for sure, but something said that was a lie.

He looked back at the hospital employee. "Sorry."

"I guess you wouldn't know any medical history either, then?"

"No."

"Okay," she said as if this were his fault. "I guess I'll have to have the patient fill this out when she regains consciousness."

"That'd be best," Juan said.

A nurse walked up. "The doctor would like to speak to you."

"Is something..." He stopped before saying *wrong.* "Sure." He stood up. "I have her daughter. Is that okay?" He hoped she understood what he meant.

"It's fine."

Bell scooted off the chair and reached for his hand. It felt so tiny in his. So fragile that he wanted to pick her up and hold her close.

They were led into a room.

"The doctor will be right in." The nurse left.

"You want to sit down?" He motioned Bell to a chair.

She yawned, claimed the chair, and pulled her knees up. Only the tips of her flip-flops and her smiley-faced toes peered out from under her pink nightgown.

"You tired?" he asked.

She nodded.

A man wearing a white coat appeared at the door. "I'm Dr. Hernandez."

"Can we talk out there?" Juan gave a slight nod to Bell. "I'll be right out the door."

The doctor stepped back into the hallway.

"Please tell me she's okay," Juan said in a quiet voice.

"We don't know yet. She has a temperature of a hundred and five. We're trying to get that down. We've started her on some broad-spectrum antibiotics. I was told she was throwing up."

"Yes, she thought it was a virus. Her little girl had one."

"Is her daughter okay?"

"She seems okay." He suddenly felt gut-punched. "But you should check her, too."

"I'll have the nurse assess her. How long has the patient been like this?"

"I don't know. I saw her around six this evening. She was throwing up then. I know she worked today, so I don't think she was too sick." He filled the doctor in on everything he knew.

The man nodded. "She's semiconscious, but still out of it. Did she have diarrhea? Was she drinking fluids?"

"I don't know. I'm sorry. I brought them ginger ale."

"We've pulled some blood to see if there's an infection going on. It's not back yet. I don't think this is just a virus. I mean, the fever could be due to dehydration. But I'm worried about septic shock."

"What is that?" Juan asked.

"It means an infection has gotten into her blood."

"How serious is it?" Juan asked.

"Serious," the doctor said. "I'm not saying it's gone that far yet. We've taken a culture, but—"

"I want to go see my mama," Bell cried. Both the doctor and Juan turned to see her standing at the door, listening. "Now!"

"You'll be able to see her soon." The doctor touched her forehead. "Were you sick earlier?"

She nodded. "The nurse said it was a stomach virus."

"You went to the doctor?" the man asked.

"No. A nurse at school."

The man smiled at her. "Was your mama sick with it, too?"

Bell nodded.

The doctor looked at Juan. "Maybe I'm wrong and this is just a virus."

"Is she going to be okay?" Bell asked.

The doctor touched her shoulder. "We're trying to make her better now."

"You have to make her better!" Sobbing, Bell turned around and buried her face against Juan's leg. "She can't die!"

Juan picked Bell up again. She wrapped her arms around his neck and continued sobbing.

The doctor sent Juan a look of apology. "You can hang out in the waiting room. I'll let you know as soon as I learn something. The kid looks fine. I wouldn't worry about her."

Juan, with a crying Bell, sat down on one of the love seats in the ER lobby. He tried comforting her, but she pushed his hand away. "I want my mama," she wept over and over again.

A couple of people in the waiting room stared at him as if it was his job to console her, and he was failing miserably.

And he was. He didn't know what to do. Bell's sobs yanked at his heart. He kept whispering to her that it was going to be okay. After a good ten minutes, her sobs quieted, though tears still slipped down her cheeks. She started rubbing her eyes. She looked exhausted. He knew how she felt. She finally closed her eyes. But even in her sleep, she whimpered.

When that stopped, he felt a wave of relief, but it immediately vanished when he realized a bigger problem. What was he going to do with Bell tonight? And tomorrow?

Closing his eyes, he leaned his head back against the wall. His thoughts went to his daughter and Angie, then to seeing Bates lying in a puddle of blood. Logically, he knew he'd played no part in her getting shot. Emotionally, he felt it was on him. Had Bates gone into surgery?

When he'd moved his car, he'd seen Connor's truck. So Connor was still here. Juan should call him, check in, apologize for running out. But he'd have to get his phone out of his jeans pocket, and with Bell's head on his leg, that might wake her. He looked down at the child again. His chest knotted.

"Juan?"

He looked up. As if he'd summoned him, Connor walked over.

"What are you...?" Connor's gaze fell to Bell.

"My neighbor. I had to bring her in."

"What's wrong with her?"

"Could be flu. But they're worried she might have a serious blood infection."

"Is she going to be okay?"

"They don't know yet. How's Cindy?" Juan asked.

Connor took the chair beside him. "She pulled through the surgery, but it's still touch-and-go. They said the bullet to the head didn't do much damage. It was the one in the chest that was the problem."

"Did her sister show up?"

"No."

"Did we get anything on the suspect's car?"

"Not yet." He glanced at Bell. "So that's your... neighbor's kid?" Connor asked.

"Yeah."

"Does she have family here?"

"I don't think so." Juan ran a hand over his chin.

Connor's eyes widened. "What are you going to do?"

"I don't know. I...don't know how to care for a kid."

Connor looked at Bell, then back up at him. "Not for nothing, but you seem to be doing a pretty good job."

"Looks can be deceiving. She cried herself to sleep," he said quietly.

"You could call Child Protective Services."

Juan flinched. "Her mom's sick, not abandoning her."

Connor's phone rang. He shot up and walked a few feet away to answer it. Connor talked for a few minutes, then eased over to Juan. "They found the car. But our suspect is gone."

"Shit!" Juan said.

A woman sitting across from him shot him a look that said a man with a kid in his lap shouldn't talk like that, and she was right.

"I'm going to go make sure they check it for prints."

Juan nodded.

"Call me if you need anything." Connor left.

Ten minutes later, the doctor walked out the door of the ER and came right toward him.

And from his expression, he didn't have good news.

* * *

Pablo had gone through every box, every old suitcase and plastic container in Dan Jefferies's storage unit. Not only wasn't his money here, there wasn't even anything that appeared to belong to Vicki or Alison. He picked up a box and shook the contents. Not even a goddamned thing worth selling.

Why the hell would Jefferies rent a storage unit to store a bunch of shit? Looking around, he decided that maybe coming here hadn't been a waste of time after all. If Jefferies recognized him, the man would have to die. And that storage unit could be a convenient place to dispose of the body.

He dropped down in a chair and raked all ten fingers through his hair. Then, pulling his phone out to check the time, he saw he'd missed a text from Rex.

It read: Need you and Antonio to do a pickup. Come see me..

"Why? So you can cheat me out of more money? Fuck you!"

Then again, if it was a pickup, he'd be carrying cash to pay for the purchase. Maybe he'd do this job after all. Maybe it was time for him to shit or get off the pot.

He needed money now. Why not just take it? Fuck Rex.

CHAPTER EIGHTEEN

Vicki woke up hearing voices, distant but close. Low but loud. Clear but garbled. She was here but not. A beeping echoed in the background. She concentrated on the annoying noise. Then in some distant part of her brain, she remembered she was supposed to wake up to check on Bell. Bell had a fever. They'd both been sick. Vicki needed to make sure Bell didn't need more medicine.

Vicki tried to blink away the confusion, to wipe clean the blurry feeling messing with her mind.

"Ms. Hanson?"

She nodded. She finally was able to focus. A man stood over her. Dark eyes, dark hair. Pablo? Panic filled her and she fought to sit up.

"No. Relax." Hands came down on her shoulders and held her back.

She blinked again. Her vision focused. Not Pablo. The smells in the room invaded her senses. The sterile scent took her straight to Alison. To her being hooked up on life support. To Alison being unplugged because there was no brain activity. To her sister being dead. Murdered. To Vicki's last promise she'd made to her comatose sister. To take care of her daughter. She reached up for her necklace. It wasn't there.

"I'm Dr. Hernandez. You need—"

"My . . . my daughter?" she said. "Where is she?"

"She's okay," the man said. "You're in the hospital. You're—"

"Where's my daughter?" she asked again, pushing the doctor's hands away.

"Your neighbor has your daughter. Let's worry about you right—"

"I need to see her!" Vicki tried again to push up on her elbow.

"Right now we need—"

"You aren't doing anything to me until I see my daughter."

He looked as if he was going to argue, but then he spoke to someone else in the room. "Get her neighbor."

Frowning, the doctor added, "We've got to get you ready for a procedure called extracorporeal shock wave lithotripsy. You have a kidney stone that has caused a blockage and a severe infection. It's gotten in your blood. It's critical that it be done ASAP so you don't lose a kidney or worse."

She nodded. The pain in her side peaked. Swallowing a moan, she closed her eyes. Footsteps sounded. She opened her eyes. Juan stood in the doorway, holding a sleeping Bell. Her niece's head rested on his shoulder.

"You've got three minutes." The doctor walked out.

"Is she okay?" Vicki asked.

"She was worried. But she fell asleep."

Tears filled Vicki's eyes. "How . . . how did I get here?"

"When Bell couldn't wake you up, she got afraid and came to my house. I brought you here."

"She must have been so scared." Vicki reached out and Juan moved closer. She ran her hand down Bell's back. "I know this is a lot to ask, but can you please take care of her while I'm in here?"

He hesitated.

Desperation swelled in her chest. "She likes you. She trusts you. Please. I'm begging you."

"Isn't there someone else?"

"No. She's a good kid. You've seen her scars. She's had a tough life. Please do this for me. For her."

Concern pulled at his brows. "I don't know how to—"

"Please."

A nurse and an anesthesiologist walked in. "We're going to have to get you sedated now."

"One minute." Vicki looked at Juan.

The nurse shook her head. "Sorry."

The anesthesiologist walked over and pushed a needle into Vicki's IV.

"Please." Vicki looked at Juan.

"I got her," he said.

"Thank you." A realization hit. If something happened to her . . . what would happen to Bell? Her world started spinning. "Don't let anyone take her. He'll hurt her..." She tried to push out the words, but they wouldn't come.

"You're going to have to leave," the nurse said to Juan.

Black spots started going off like fireworks in her vision. The last thing she saw was Juan looking down at her. He ran a hand over her cheek. Tender. Caring. She should have told him about... She should have trusted him.

* * *

It was six a.m. when Juan got back to his place. He put Bell, still sleeping, on his sofa and collected a blanket. As he covered her up, she turned on her side and put her tiny hands under her cheek. She looked like a little angel. And for the next few days, he was going to be responsible for that angel. That scared the hell out of him.

The idea that he might have to tell the little girl her mother wasn't coming home had his gut pumping acid. Sweetie tried to jump on the sofa, but he scolded the excited dog, then picked her up and held her in apology.

He pulled the dog to his chest and scratched behind her ears. The doctor said Nikki's procedure had gone as well as could be expected. The kidney stone had been broken up. Juan had waited, wanting to talk to her, but an hour after the procedure, she still hadn't woken up. Her fever had risen again, but they'd upped her dosage of IV antibiotics and hoped it'd come down soon.

Realizing he couldn't do anything for Nikki, he'd left his card in her room and come home.

Juan sat down in his recliner and pressed his face in

his hands. Between watching Cindy Bates bleed out and then seeing Nikki unconscious, he felt the damn Grim Reaper hovering close by. While the cop in him worried about Bates, everything else in him ached for Nikki. And for Bell.

Why hadn't he insisted on going to check on them? If he had, maybe he could have gotten Nikki to the hospital earlier. Maybe...

Exhaustion pulled at his mind. Closing his eyes, he remembered his time together with Nikki. Her laughter. Her kisses. How alive she'd felt in his arms. How alive she'd made him feel.

Staring at the ceiling, he thought he'd fall instantly asleep, but his mind raced. His gaze kept shifting to Bell. How could Nikki have no one to count on? No one to call to care for her kid? No family? No friends? It didn't make sense.

He exhaled and looked at the time. Obviously, he wasn't going to work today. He fought the urge to pick up the phone and call the hospital to see if Nikki's fever had dropped, but it'd only been thirty minutes since he'd left.

She had to pull through.

But what if she didn't? Why hadn't he insisted she tell him who he could call about Bell?

Suddenly remembering his sister-in-law worked with her, he found Christina's number and hit the call button.

"You're up bright and early," his sister-in-law said in lieu of hello.

"Never been to bed," he said as he moved down the hallway to his bedroom.

"That's not good. Is everything okay?"

"No. It's Nikki."

"Your neighbor? Oh, is her little girl okay?"

"Yeah, Bell's fine. It's Nikki." He told her what had happened. There were a lot of "*Dios míos*" on her side of the conversation.

Then he said, "I was hoping maybe she put an emergency number or nearest relative on her job application?"

"You don't think she's going to—"

"No," he said, but the question gut-punched him. "I'm just covering my bases."

"Let me check. I'm at my desk now."

He heard her tapping on the keyboard. Would it be this easy? He walked back down the hall to check on Bell. Still asleep.

"Sorry. She didn't list anyone."

No, it wasn't going to be that easy. And what did that tell him? It said his gut had been right all along. Nikki was running. He couldn't believe she didn't have one person who cared about her or her daughter.

"I don't know why we didn't notice it," Christina said. "Well, I guess I do. She was a quick hire. We were desperate to find someone, and Nikki was up-front about having another interview with Be Fit gym. The manager was afraid she'd go with them. But I have the names and numbers of her last employers. Both are gyms in Colorado. Maybe they'll have an emergency contact."

"Yeah." He moved to the kitchen table, where he had a pen and pad. He wrote down the names, addresses, and phone numbers of the employers.

"Who is taking care of her daughter?" she asked.

Juan looked back at the sofa where Bell slept. "I am," he said in a whisper.

"Oh. Are you okay with that?"

The thought to ask for help tickled his mind, but he recalled how adamant Nikki had been about it being him. He remembered the burns on Bell's arm and shoulder and could only imagine how hard it was for Nikki to trust him. As uncomfortable as the task felt resting on his shoulders, he answered, "Yeah. I'm fine."

When he hung up, he called the hospital and got good news on both sides. Bates hadn't regained consciousness, but she was still hanging in there. Nikki's fever was coming down. She was slowly waking up.

An hour passed and, still unable to sleep, he decided to give the gyms a call. The first number went straight to an out-of-service message. The next one did the same.

He moved to the kitchen table, got on his laptop, and typed in the names of the gyms. Both were out of business. Was that a coincidence?

Damn it, Nikki. What are you hiding?

He glanced back at Bell. Sweetie had jumped up on the sofa and was curled up beside her.

"Don't wake her up," he told the poodle. Then he dropped down in his chair.

It felt like he'd barely fallen asleep when his phone rang. Jarred awake, he grabbed his phone. It read: Westside Hospital.

He went to swipe to take the call, but first his eyes shifted to Bell. The sofa was empty.

"Bell?" he called out.

No answer. He dropped the phone and bolted up. "Bell?" He saw the front door slightly ajar.

The phone continued to ring. He hauled his butt outside.

"Bell?" Juan stood in his front yard, fear became a mass in his chest. He'd lost her. Damn it, he'd lost her.

"Bell?" he yelled as loud as he could.

He heard barking. Sweetie's bark. Hope flared.

Following the sound, he shot across Nikki's yard. Her front door was open, and Sweetie stood in the entryway.

"Bell?" he yelled.

The child came running around the corner. "Where's my mom?"

Juan drew in air. His lungs latched on to the oxygen and held it until his chest felt ready to explode. "Don't ever do that again! You don't leave the house without telling me. Understand?"

Even before the girl's bottom lip started trembling, he regretted his tone. But damn it, she'd scared him.

Realizing he wasn't the only one scared, he knelt down. "I'm sorry I yelled. I was really worried when I couldn't find you."

She nodded. "Where's my mom?"

"Your mom's in the hospital. We took her there last night."

"Why didn't she come home with us?"

"She's sick and had to sleep there. So I brought you back with me."

"Why? Why did you leave her there all alone?" Tears filled her young eyes.

"Your mom was sleeping and they don't let kids stay in the hospital if they aren't sick."

"Why not?" Her bottom lip trembled.

"Because they don't want kids to get sick. Why don't we go back to my place?" He reached for her hand. She backed up.

Considering what her father had done, he didn't blame her. "Bell, you came to me to help your mom last night. I helped her. You can trust me, okay? Sweetie trusts me." He knelt down and held his hand out to his dog. She came running over. "See?"

Bell nodded. "I want to go get my mama. I don't like hospitals. People die there."

"Actually, hospitals are where they go to get better."

"Not everyone gets better. People die there. I know it." She inhaled a shaky breath. "I want to see her now."

He couldn't help but wonder who it was that Bell knew who'd died. Her father? But according to Nikki he was alive.

"I'll have to find out if she can have visitors. If she can, we'll go. But I need to feed you breakfast and you need to put on some clothes. Can you get dressed?" When she nodded he said, "Okay, go do that."

She took off. Juan, still feeling panic fizzing in his blood, took in a deep breath.

A few minutes later, he was walking back to his place, Bell running ahead with his dog. Looking down, he saw Sweetie's ball in the grass. When he reached to pick it up, he spotted something glinting in the sun.

He reached over and found the silver chain. It was Nikki's necklace.

On the chain were two charms. One was a heart locket. The other had some kind of inscribed emblem. She hadn't lost the necklace during their scuffle after all. Maybe it had been when she'd come out front to speak with the officers.

He brought the necklace closer.

You did it, Nikki. September 2015.

On closer inspection he realized it didn't read *Nikki*, but *Vicki*. Then he recognized the emblem as an Ironman triathlon symbol.

Was Nikki not even his neighbor's name?

CHAPTER NINETEEN

Bell looked back at him. Juan dropped the necklace in his pocket.

He heard his phone ringing before he got to the door. He ran to pick it up. It was the hospital again.

"Acosta," he answered.

"Where have you been?" It was Nikki and she sounded panicked.

"I was getting Bell some clothes." He took in a breath. Should he tell her he'd found the necklace? Or wait until he looked into it? "How are you feeling?"

"Is that my mama?" Bell asked.

"Better," Nikki said.

Juan nodded at the child.

"I want to talk to her," Bell said.

Juan watched Sweetie run over to the worried girl. "Bell wants to come to see you, but I'm not sure she can go into the ICU."

"They're moving me to a regular room soon. Is she okay?" Nikki asked.

"She's fine. Just concerned about you. Here she is." He handed Bell the phone and listened to see if she was going to rat him out about losing her.

"Are you still sick?" Bell asked.

Juan ran a hand over his forehead. The beginning stages of a headache had started to hum.

"I want to come see you," the child said, then listened. "I am. I just want to be with you." Tears filled her young eyes. She nodded. "Okay. Please don't die!" She started sniffling. "Promise?" Pause. "Okay." She handed the phone back to him. "She wants to talk to you."

He took the phone and then put his hand on Bell's shoulder, hoping to offer some comfort. She must not have been too mad at him because she buried her face in his leg. He continued to run his hand over her neck as she sniffled against him. Each little sound made his insides ache.

"Thank you again so much," Nikki said. "I'm sorry I was upset. I got worried when you didn't answer."

"I get it," he said, still reeling from his own Bell worry. And now he was also worried about who he was really talking to. "Call me when you get moved, and I'll bring Bell."

"Are you...are you okay not going to work?"

"I've got some sick days."

"I don't know how I'm going to repay you."

I do. How about telling me the truth? He couldn't say that to a woman still in the ICU. "Just get better."

"I will knowing she's okay. Thank you."

"You've already said that."

"I know, but I think it merits saying again."

They hung up. Bell looked up at him. "Are we going to see her now?"

"We have to wait until they move her to another room. She's going to call. Then I promise I'll take you to see her."

She studied him as if trying to decide if she believed him. "Pinky promise?" She held out her little hand.

"Yeah." He curled his little finger around hers. "What do you eat for breakfast?"

"Cereal."

"I have Frosted Flakes. You like that?"

She nodded. "Do you have cornflakes, too?"

"What?"

"Mama mixes the good kind with the healthy kind. She says the good stuff has too much sugar, but I like it."

"Well, I don't think it'll kill you this once." He fixed her a bowl and told her he was going to change clothes. He almost got to his room and then turned back around. "Don't leave the house, okay?"

"Okay. Can I give Sweetie a bite of my cereal?"

"Yeah, but just a little."

She stared at him. "I'm sorry I left earlier without telling you. I get scared sometimes."

"You're not scared of me, are you?" He walked closer.

She stood there almost as if considering her answer. "Not too much. Mama says you're a good guy. And she doesn't normally like policemen."

"Why not?" The question slipped out before he realized it.

Bell stiffened. "I don't know."

He touched the necklace in his pocket. "I'll be right back."

In his room, he pulled out the necklace again. The locket had a little catch to open it. Part of him felt like he was invading her privacy. But he was watching Nikki's daughter. If something was going on, he needed to know.

He opened it. There was a tiny photograph on each side of the locket. Two girls. He studied them both. He couldn't tell which one was his neighbor. The girls looked too alike.

He turned the locket over and read the engraving. *Vicki and Alison, Sisters Forever.*

Do you have any siblings? he recalled asking her.

She'd lied. At the time he'd even suspected it. So why did it sting now? Because she trusted him to watch her kid, but not enough to tell him the truth?

He closed the locket and stared at the Ironman emblem. An idea hit. He walked back to the kitchen, where Bell was still eating. "Hey."

She looked up. "You didn't change your clothes."

"You noticed that, huh?" He forced a smile.

She nodded.

"Yeah, I needed to check something on my computer."

She scooped up another bite of cereal. "Can I go outside in the backyard and play ball with Sweetie?"

"Sure," he said, knowing Nikki...Vicki let her do that.

He sat down at the table and typed in Triathlon competition 2015.

Several links came up. He clicked on the one that listed the names of those who'd completed it. He narrowed the directory by country, gender, and age range.

He scrolled through a few pages and saw it. The name Vicki. Vicki Trever.

He went back and clicked on the links with images. He tapped on the table, waiting for them to load.

The page popped up. He scanned the images. One. Then, two.

The third one was a group shot. And there she was.

* * *

The nurse who'd let Vicki use the floor's cell phone walked in. Vicki handed it back to her.

"Did you find your daughter?"

"Yes. Thank you." When Juan hadn't answered his phone, Vicki had panicked. Her heart told her that her niece was fine—that Juan was decent, kind, and he'd never do anything to hurt a child. But trust didn't come easily.

Vicki could hear the advice her mom had given her only a day before she'd died. "Take care of your sister. She's not as strong as you are. She trusts too much. But someday I hope you'll learn to trust. You don't have to be alone in this world."

At the time, Vicki had been furious at her mom's words. How could she have learned to trust when the majority of her childhood had left her unable to trust even her mom? How many nights had Vicki not known if her mom would come home, or stayed awake worrying her mom wouldn't come home alone?

And as much as Vicki had resented her mom, Alison had excused her. To the point that Alison wouldn't let Vicki donate their mom's things to charity. She'd insisted Vicki put them in a storage unit until they could go through them later when the grief had lessened. *Her things hold memories*, her sister had claimed. But Vicki hadn't wanted to remember. Alison never again mentioned her mom's belongings and Vicki preferred to pay for the storage than to face that trip down memory lane.

Take care of your sister… You don't have to be alone… As those parting words played in Vicki's head again, they stung because not only had she failed to take care of her sister, but she realized how alone she really was right now. So maybe her mom had a point.

The beeping sound had Vicki opening her eyes. The nurse looked at her blood pressure reading on the machine. "From one to ten, how is your pain?"

"It's not bad." Vicki lied because she needed to be clearheaded when she saw Bell. The thought of how close she'd come to dying and abandoning her niece kept echoing in her conscience. What if Juan hadn't come to the house? What if she'd died last night? Sooner or later, someone would have discovered their true identity. And Bell would have been sent to live with Pablo's sister. And then Pablo could have gotten to her.

Vicki had thought by not trusting anyone she was protecting her niece. But that no longer felt so true. She needed to trust someone. And no one had come closer to earning her trust than Juan.

But how much could she trust him? Should she tell him everything? What if he didn't believe her? What if…?

* * *

Juan did a Google search on Vicki Trever. The first hit that came up was a website for Vicki Trever, Fitness Trainer. He clicked on it. Her picture appeared on the screen and the website listed her location as Los Angeles, California. The last time it had been updated was ten months ago.

At the bottom of the page, he spotted a list of her qualifications and clients. He read the names, then saw a link that read <u>References</u>. He clicked it.

There was a number. He grabbed his phone and dialed the number.

"Price Jacobs," a man answered.

"Yes, my name's Juan Acosta. I found your name on Vicki Trever's website as a reference."

"Oh, yeah. But I haven't heard from her in months."

"So how well do you know her and would you recommend her as a trainer?"

"You kidding me? She's the best. I broke my leg and I was going to give up running. She worked with me. Got me in even better shape than I was before. I was one of her first clients when she went into business for herself. She even rented my garage apartment for seven months when she was waiting on her condo to get completed.

I'd still be using her, but I got laid off at work last year and had to cut back. Whatever you do, don't spar with her. She's little, but that girl can give you a run for your money."

Yeah, she can. Juan mentally gathered the information. "How dedicated is she to the job?"

"Never seen anyone more dedicated. You know she works with movie stars, don't you? Last I heard, she was working with Bruce Willis. She trains some of the guys with the Lakers and the Chargers. Well, she did before she disappeared. She's top-notch. As for being dedicated, I've seen her work sixteen hours a day."

"That's a lot. So her being a mother didn't interfere with the work?"

"A mother? Vicki doesn't have kids."

Shit! It was worse than he thought.

Price continued, "Well, I guess she could now. That's a shocker. She just . . . was always so career focused. Did she marry that Dan guy she was dating? I mean, seriously, she just up and left."

"I'm not sure," Juan said. "We haven't really talked about personal stuff."

"Well, tell her congratulations. And tell her I'm a little pissed that she left without saying goodbye. In fact, can you give me her number?"

"Yeah, let me text that to you," he said.

"What kind of training are you doing?" Price asked.

"Just getting in shape." Juan managed to end the conversation.

Hanging up, he sat there staring at the computer. Bell wasn't Nikki's daughter. What the hell was going on?

Running a hand over his face, he got online and checked her name to see if he found anything on the criminal history database. There were four Vicki Trevers. Only one in the right age bracket.

He clicked on it.

He read the screen. "Damn." LAPD sought Vicki Trever as a person of interest in a missing child case. Don't approach. Don't contact. Call Detective Sam Milbourn. It listed the officer's phone number.

He stood from the kitchen table and looked outside at Bell. She sat in his lawn chair, tossing the ball to Sweetie.

Had Nikki kidnapped Bell? He remembered Bell's scars. If Nikki had taken the girl, she had to have a damn good reason. Right?

Then something else odd hit. Why wasn't it called a kidnapping? He went back to his computer and typed in Vicki Trever missing child. More often than not the media coverage gave more details than some of the basic police records. Oddly, there wasn't anything. Why? Missing children were a favorite media topic due to the emotional response.

Something didn't add up. There was only one way to get answers. He had to call this Detective Milbourn.

Not that he'd show his cards. Not yet.

CHAPTER TWENTY

Juan dialed the contact number for Detective Milbourn at the LAPD. It rang four times before someone picked it up. "Detective Carson."

"Yes. I was trying to reach Detective Milbourn."

"You got his desk. He's out for a few days. His phone's been ringing off the hook. What can I do for you?"

"This is Detective Acosta, from Anniston PD in Texas. I'm working on a case and I found the name Vicki Trever mentioned. When I did a criminal background check on her, I found Milbourn's information. Can you tell me what that's about?"

"Trever?" Carson said as if he wasn't sure. "It's not ringing any bells."

"It mentioned a missing child." Juan heard the man typing into a computer.

"Oh, yes. I got it now. She left the state with a guardianship case ongoing."

Well, that explained why it wasn't listed as a kidnapping. "Isn't that a civil case? Why is LAPD involved?" Juan asked.

"The child is the daughter of Milbourn's old partner, Officer Pablo Valado. He was killed."

Juan recalled Nikki's dislike of police officers. Was Valado Bell's father?

"Valado's sister filed for guardianship," Detective Carson continued. "And with the case ongoing there's a restraining order restricting Trever from removing the child from the state."

It still sounded more like a civil suit, but maybe the laws were different in California. Juan jotted down the name Pablo Valado and decided to play stupid. "So she's the mother?"

"No. She's the aunt. The child's mother passed away. Do you have her in custody?"

"No." It was time to pull back. "A witness used the name when interviewed, but she later disappeared. This Vicki Trever was the only one in the age range that would fit. To confirm I got the right person, my Vicki Trever is black, in her forties?"

"No. This Vicki is white, late twenties."

"Well it's not her, then. Our witness must have used a fake name. We were afraid of that since she didn't have any ID on her and the address she gave was bogus. Sorry to have bothered you."

Juan hung up. So Nikki, or rather Vicki, was running to keep Bell's other aunt from getting guardianship. Why?

And why had she lied about Bell's father being

alive? Then another question hit. Who was she afraid of?

Armed with this latest information, he did another Google search. He typed in the name Pablo Valado.

* * *

Juan, holding Bell's hand, walked into the hospital entrance looking for Mildred. He spotted her sitting across the room, leafing through a magazine. She stood, waved, and smiled extra big at Bell.

Juan, a headache brewing, guided Bell that way. When he'd called Mildred and asked if she'd spend her lunch hour away from her desk and helping him out by watching a five-year-old at the hospital, he'd had to give a little explanation.

But only the part about her being his neighbor. He didn't want to explain Nikki's brush with the law, not to Mildred or to Mark or Connor. He needed explanations. And the person who needed to explain was Nikki. Only then would he decide if he got his partners involved. He knew not calling in her location immediately could come back to bite him in the ass. He didn't want them bitten for his mistake.

"Hi. Mildred, I want you to meet Bell." The girl's hold on his hand tightened. "Bell, Mildred's the lady I told you about. The one I work with who has a granddaughter your age."

Bell gazed up at him, fear shining in her big brown eyes. "You said I could see my mama first."

"Yes, I did. We'll visit with her for a bit, and then I

need to talk to her and you'll go to the cafeteria with Mildred. Okay?"

"But can I see her again before we leave?"

Juan nodded. The close relationship between Bell and Nikki was telling. Bell clearly felt safe with her. He couldn't believe Nikki would be trying to harm her niece. His gut said there was more to this story. His Google search on Pablo had confirmed the story he overheard Bell telling her friend in her backyard. The child's father had died in a boat explosion that had been ruled an accident. But he also learned that right before Pablo's demise, Bell's mother had been killed in a hit-and-run. Had someone taken them both out? Had Pablo's "accident" been a suicide due to his guilt of possibly being his wife's killer? He searched again to see if the articles named any suspects in Alison Valado's death. None had.

Questions: He had a shitload of them. And he preferred getting those answers from Nikki. Or Vicki, his mind suddenly corrected.

"Aren't you a pretty one," Mildred said. "And Bell is a lovely name."

Bell smiled shyly.

Mildred opened what looked like a beach bag. "I brought puzzles, games, crayons, and a coloring book. When we go to the cafeteria, we're going to have fun."

Bell glanced into the bag with interest. "I like puzzles."

"Me too," Mildred said.

Juan gave Mildred a thank-you nod and motioned for her to follow them.

Nikki had called about thirty minutes after he'd gotten off the phone with Detective Carson to say she'd been moved. Knowing he needed a private conversation, he'd called Mildred to join him at the hospital.

They got off the elevator. Mildred spotted a waiting area and said she'd be there. He and Bell found the room number Nikki had given him.

He knocked on the door and pushed it open when he heard her voice.

Bell barreled into the room. Nikki, sitting in a chair, smiled and held her arms out. "Come here."

Bell ran right into Nikki's arms. "Are you okay?"

"I'm fine."

"Are you coming home now?" Bell asked.

"I think I need to stay at least one more night." She glanced up at Juan with a smile that looked real but apprehensive. Her hair was a little messy. She still had purple circles under her eyes, but she appeared ten times better than she had last night. "Thank you for bringing Bell."

He nodded, wondering how thankful she was going to be once he started grilling her about her lies.

Bell spoke up again. "Juan said you had a stone in your kidney and they broke it up. Did it hurt?"

"No. I was asleep when they did it." Nikki kissed the girl's forehead.

Juan watched them. The love between these two was like a living, breathing thing.

"Have you been good for Juan?" Nikki asked.

Bell looked over at him, almost as if she worried he'd rat her out. Little did the child know he felt the incident made him look worse.

"She's been great."

"I scared him," Bell confessed. "I woke up before he did and went to our house without telling him. He was upset when he found me."

Frowning, Nikki looked at Juan. "I'll bet that scared him."

Juan lifted a brow. "I didn't hear her get up. I should have, but..."

"No. She shouldn't have left." Nikki gave the girl a scolding look.

"I told him I was sorry," Bell said quietly, and hung her head.

Nikki glanced at Bell. "That's good. Don't ever do that again."

"I won't." Bell sat in the chair beside Nikki. "I was scared when I woke up and you weren't there. I thought you were home. I wanted to make sure you were okay, because last night you wouldn't wake up."

"You still shouldn't have left his house." Nikki looked at him. "I'm sorry."

"All's well that ends well." But for the life of him, he didn't know how all of this was going to end.

Bell's little legs started pumping back and forth. "Juan said I was playing hooky today. Do you know what that means?"

Nikki grinned. "You're skipping school."

"Yeah, but he said I'd probably go tomorrow."

"You should," Nikki said.

"Oh, guess what? Sweetie slept with me on Juan's couch."

"She did?" Nikki smiled. "Well, that's fun."

"I know. She keeps giving me kisses. I'll bet I've gotten a million kisses. But she cried when we left. I know she's missing me right now."

"I'm sure she is because I missed you."

Bell grinned. "When you get home I bet she'll want to kiss you, too." The girl looked around the room but kept talking. "Mildred brought puzzles."

Nikki looked at him. "Mildred?"

Before he could explain, Bell did. "She's Juan's friend. She has a granddaughter. So she likes kids. She met us up here because Juan said he needed to talk to you alone." Bell made a face. "I think he might be going to kiss you again."

Juan's mouth dropped open and Nikki's eyes widened.

Bell continued, "But he did tell the lady at the hospital last night that you weren't his girlfriend."

"Uh." Juan pulled his hand out of his pocket and cupped a palm over his mouth for two seconds, squirming a bit under Nikki's questioning gaze. "The...the front desk needed information about your condition and was surprised when I didn't know everything."

Nikki nodded with what looked like understanding.

He reached out to Bell. "Why don't I take you to Mildred so you two can go play in the cafeteria?"

Jumping down from the chair, she twirled around with an abundance of energy. "Okay, but remember you said I could come back here when you're done talking."

"Yep," he said.

Nikki hugged Bell. "I love you."

"I love you more." The child reached up and slipped her hand into Juan's. The feel of her tiny palm spoke of trust and warmth filled his chest.

He just hoped Nikki, or Vicki, would trust him, too... trust him with the truth.

CHAPTER
TWENTY-ONE

Nerves frayed, Vicki waited for Juan to return. What did he want to talk to her about? The worst-case scenario played in her head. He was going to refuse to care for Bell.

She didn't have anyone else to ask. Was there a twenty-four-hour babysitting service? How would Bell feel having a stranger take care of her? How would she feel leaving Bell with a stranger?

Her mind raced. She'd decided to trust him. But she'd been thinking it'd be better to be out of the hospital. To be able to run if he...if he felt duty bound to turn her in. But if he wasn't even willing to care for Bell?

Every time she moved, her side throbbed, but until she knew what Juan was going to say, she couldn't allow herself a dose of the morphine. By God, if she had to, she would run. A knock, his knock, shattered the sterile silence.

"Come in." He took one step into the room and she saw the crease in his brow. The set of his lips. Whatever he was about to say, he wasn't happy.

"Please tell me this isn't about you not being able to watch Bell. It's only for another day or so. I'll pay you for missing work."

His frown tightened. He moved in and sat on the edge of her bed. "It's not that."

"Then what?" she asked.

He reached in his pocket and pulled something out. It dangled in the air.

"My necklace." She touched her chest where the jewelry usually fell. Tears welled in her eyes. "You found it. Thank you."

He handed it to her and she held the piece of jewelry to her heart.

When she looked back at him, he appeared almost angry. "You want to tell me who you really are?"

Her lungs refused her next gulp of air. Her stomach clenched. Had she been wrong in thinking he'd understand?

"I wanted to tell you." She closed her hand on the pendant in her hand. "I actually told you some of it. But I was going to tell you everything when...when I got home."

"Why don't you tell me everything now. Tell me why you took Bell."

"I didn't take..." She swallowed the fear closing her throat, but it swelled bigger in her chest. "I need you to believe me, Juan. You can't—"

"It's hard to believe someone who's been lying." The

edge to his voice cut into what little confidence she had about telling him the truth.

"I know I lied, but I'm trying to protect Bell. You have to promise me—"

He breathed in, his mouth thinning before he spoke. "I can't make any promises until you explain this."

She nodded. "You're right. I'm running." She could hear the desperation in her voice and hated it. All her life she'd fought to be capable, to never be at the mercy of someone else.

"From?" His brown eyes met hers directly.

"Bell's father."

Juan ran his palms down his thighs and squeezed his knees. "The truth." Frustration deepened his voice and made her twice as antsy.

"It is the truth. My real name is Vicki Trever. Bell isn't my daughter. She's my niece. Pablo Valado is her father. He's the one who...burned her with a cigar. At the same time he did that, he beat my sister so badly he almost killed her. She left him, and we filed charges. She got paperwork done that gave me guardianship of Bell if anything happened to her. Then two months later, Alison was killed by a hit-and-run driver."

Juan's eyes tightened. "He's dead. I read the articles."

"His body was never found. That piece of information was only in one of the articles. And I saw him. He ransacked my condo. He even called and threatened me." Tears slipped down her cheeks. She wiped them away.

"You saw him after the boat exploded?"

"Yes."

Juan ran a hand down his face. She knew he was

digesting what she said, probably trying to figure out what he believed.

"Did you tell the cops? Did they look into the call you got?"

"Of course I did. They didn't believe me. The number was listed as anonymous. And they said there was a significant amount of his blood on what was left of the boat. But I think someone helped him. That he staged the accident to get away with murder."

"Did the police look into your sister's death?"

"They claimed it was probably a drunk driver. That there was no proof it was Pablo. They said I needed to go see a psychologist or a grief counselor. Was I grieving? Hell yes I was. But I saw him. He called me and threatened me. And I couldn't get anyone to believe me."

Juan sat there listening and she could tell she hadn't convinced him yet.

"Alison and Bell were all I had. And all of this is my fault. I introduced her to Pablo." Her chest burned with guilt. "When he hurt Bell and Alison that last time, she wanted to go into a program that hides abused women, and I begged her not to because I'd lose her. So she didn't. And now she's dead."

He moved off the bed and came and sat down in the chair beside her. His knees touched hers. "They are accusing you of abducting a child."

"That's a lie, too. I left before Estella ever filed for guardianship. I didn't break any laws."

"Estella is Pablo's sister?"

Vicki nodded. "And she didn't care about Bell. She never came to see her during the two months after Alison left Pablo. She didn't even call until the day I saw Pablo. That's the first time she mentioned she'd fight for guardianship. I'm sure Pablo put her up to it. I was so scared that I went to Joanne that night. She believed me."

"Wait, who's Joanne?"

"Joanne Butler. She's part of the Abused Women and Children Organization. They're the ones who helped me. Gave me paperwork to change my identity. I went to Phoenix first as Cara Black. But a car, the same car, was parked in front of my house two days in a row. Then I found out from Bell's day care that someone was showing pictures of Bell and asking questions."

Juan held out a hand as if to suggest she was talking too fast. "So this program provided you with a license, social security number...?"

She nodded. "In most cases they help women change their names legally. But because Pablo was a cop and we knew he was still alive, they found me the name of someone who had passed away but whose death wasn't filed.

"I wanted to tell you the truth when you asked me about Bell's scars. But AWACO warned me not to go to the police unless we were in immediate danger. Plus Joanne said the LAPD had listed me as being a suspect in a missing child case and I was scared you'd turn me in." She took in a shaky breath. "I'm still scared. Pablo was a dirty cop, working for drug dealers. Can't you see how hard it was to trust another cop?"

"You think I'm dirty?"

"No," she admitted. "But I was scared, Juan. I couldn't risk telling you."

"How do you know Pablo was dirty?"

"Alison told me. She said he made way too much for it to be a police salary and she saw him once hiding what looked like cocaine in an old cabin they had."

Juan sat there. He didn't even seem to blink.

Fear yanked at her sanity. "You still don't believe me, do you?"

It was a yes-or-no question, and he was taking way too long to answer.

"I don't disbelieve you, it's just . . . It's a lot to take in. You're talking dirty cops, murder, and faking a death. That's a lot."

She felt the white walls start to close in. How fast could she find Bell and run? "Please, if you turn us in, Pablo could get Bell."

He frowned. "I'm not going to turn you in. I'm trying to digest this."

Relief spiraled through her. "Thank you." A sob rose in her throat and she covered her mouth.

"I'm sorry," she said, trying to pull herself together. "I've been running nine months, and I've been afraid for so long. And then when an ex-employee of mine was killed I thought it could—"

"What? Who was killed?"

"Marisol Willis, she worked for me. I thought Pablo could have done it. I called Joanne, and she said they suspect Marisol's ex-husband murdered her. But when you get that afraid, it's hard to let it go."

"I'm not going to let anyone hurt you." He put his hand on her shoulder and squeezed. "Does anyone know you're here?"

"Dan. He knows I'm with the program. And when I found out about Marisol, I called him and warned him."

"He's another employee?"

"No. We were dating."

She spotted a slight tic in his jaw. "And he knows you're here in Anniston?"

"No. But I called him, so he'd have my number. My old cell number. It's got a Texas area code."

"Do you have any proof that Pablo is still alive, or even anything on his illegal dealings?"

"No." Then she remembered. "Wait. I do. My sister told me there was a book, someone gave it to her. At first, I thought it was his sister, but then when she threatened to take Bell... All I know is that Alison said it was like a logbook that Pablo kept. She was supposed to threaten to hand it over to the cops if he caused trouble. She gave me a key to a safety deposit box a few days before she was killed. I'm sure it's in there."

"Do you have the key?"

"Yes, it's with our real birth certificates and social security cards. In an old purse in the back of my closet." And just like that, a realization hit, one that caused chills to climb up and down her arms. "You don't think..."

"What?"

"When he called that day, he said he wanted what was his. I just assumed it was Bell. I didn't even think about the book."

"Where's the deposit box?"

"In California."

"Have you ever looked at it?"

"No. I didn't think it'd do me any good. I mean, the

authorities thought he was dead. How was proving him dirty going to protect us? Even now, what good...?"

"It'll at least help encourage the police to look closer at his death."

"But you can't tell the police about me, so how are you going to explain having—"

"Let me figure that out." His face softened, and his tone expressed concern. "Trust me."

She took a deep breath as an emotional ache filled her chest. "I'm trying."

Her door swung open. They both jumped, then saw it was the doctor.

"Hey." The man nodded at Juan. "She looks better now, doesn't she?"

"Yeah," Juan agreed.

"She's lucky. You got her here in time for the antibiotics to work like a charm. This could have turned out different."

Vicki nodded, understanding exactly what he meant. "Can I go home today?"

"Not yet. We want to keep you on IV antibiotics for another twelve hours. I'm sure you still have some pain in your side, and it could hurt for a few days. But you're young and healthy and I'm betting in two days you'll feel like a million bucks. I'll check on you tomorrow."

He smiled and walked out. The silence in the room became too loud. She looked at Juan. "Tell me you believe me when I say Pablo is alive."

He hesitated. "I believe you believe it. And I promise you I'll look into it."

* * *

Juan wrote down all the names and information Vicki had told him about. His mind raced at how to find answers. Logic said he might be getting in over his head. Legally, his badge dictated he let the Los Angeles police know he had Vicki. But he'd never been the biggest fan of logic.

Did he believe her sister's husband had faked his own death? Like he told Vicki, he believed she believed it. But he couldn't deny it sounded more like a movie of the week than reality.

First, he needed to get whatever was in that safety deposit box. But how? It was in Los Angeles, and he was...An idea hit. Jody, an old friend who now worked for the DEA in L.A., could be the perfect person to ask for help, since the case did involve a drug angle.

She'd probably think he was crazy, but he knew her well enough to know she'd look into it if he asked. He also knew he could trust her not to act on any information he gave her on Vicki. Yes, he'd call her as soon as he got home.

Before he went down to collect Bell, he went to the ICU. Why, he wondered, did it feel colder in here? And sadder? "Cindy Bates?" he asked a nurse at the desk.

"Room eight."

He passed several rooms before finding it. The second he walked in, he regretted coming. She lay so still. The only thing moving was her chest, up and down, as the tube taped to her mouth pumped oxygen into her lifeless body. Her head was wrapped with bandages. Her skin looked gray, except for the black eyes and swollen nose.

A dark-haired nurse walked in and stopped short, as if surprised to see him. "Look, Cindy, you have company." She spoke as if the unconscious woman might just answer back.

Even knowing the impossibility of it, he waited and hoped. He finally glanced up. "How is she?" His words came out a mere whisper.

"She's better. Her blood pressure is back to normal. I think she'll be waking up soon." She patted the too-still woman's arm. "Right, Cindy?"

Cindy still didn't respond.

Juan motioned for the nurse to step outside the room. Once there, he asked, "How is she really?"

"Just like I said. Her vitals are better. They're doing another MRI later to see if there's still swelling in the brain. Are you family?"

"No, I'm Detective Acosta. I'm working her case. Is the brain swelling the reason she's unconscious?"

"It could be. Is she in trouble?" the nurse asked.

"No, she's not under arrest or anything. She's a witness. I thought I'd check in on her."

The nurse glanced back through the door at Cindy. "It's sad when they don't have anyone. I didn't realize there were so many people who are completely alone until I became a nurse."

"Yeah." As Juan walked away, he thought about how much he'd been isolating himself since Angie's death. How alone he'd been.

When he got to the lunchroom, Mildred and Bell had company. Mark sat with them.

Juan was instantly hit with the debate whether to tell his partners about Ni— Vicki. But his gut said that before he dragged them into this, he needed more information.

"And here he is," Mark said to Bell.

Scooting off a chair, Bell ran over and hugged him.

"She was getting worried," Mildred said.

Bell looked up. "You talked to my mama a long time. Can I see her now?"

"Sure." He focused on Mildred. "Thank you so much."

Mark stood up, meeting Mildred's gaze. "Can you give me a few minutes with Juan?"

"Sure." Mildred motioned Bell back to the table.

"You get anything on the Bates case?" Juan asked as they stepped a few tables away.

"They're still going over the car the shooter used. I finally got to talk to the waitress who said a customer mentioned the Cheng Liu case being connected to our looking for Bates."

"And?"

"It's like you said. She doesn't remember anything else and I don't think she's lying." Mark frowned. "How's Bates doing?"

"Still unconscious."

"Is everything okay...with you?" Mark asked.

"Yeah. I'll come to work tomorrow after I drop Bell off at school. I'll have to leave early to pick her up. But I'll work at home."

"I wasn't asking because of work. I meant how are

things with your neighbor? Are you okay getting stuck with her kid?"

Stuck? He'd felt incompetent, not stuck. "Yeah, it's fine." Or would be when he got to the bottom of everything.

"Seriously?" Mark asked. "Why did you bring Mildred up—"

"I needed to ask her about any other family. And there isn't any." The lie tasted bitter.

"I guess taking it slow is kind of off the table, huh?" Mark's question rolled over raw nerves.

"What was I supposed to do? Not take her to the hospital?" His question came with ire.

Mark lifted a brow. "I'm just concerned."

"Well, don't be. Last I checked, I'm of age."

Mark held up a hand. "Sorry, didn't mean to intrude."

The apology took Juan down a few notches. "No, I'm sorry. I'm tired. But I got this." He felt Bell watching him. "Let's walk her up to her mom's room and we can talk in the hall."

They moved back to Bell and Mildred. "I got it from here," he told Mildred. "Thanks again."

"Anytime. She's a sweetheart." Mildred hugged Bell. "I hope we can play again soon."

"You could come over to Juan's house," Bell said. "We could play with Sweetie, too."

"That sounds like a great idea." She stood and handed Bell the tote bag. "Why don't you take this and do some more pictures and a few of the puzzles."

"Thank you." Bell looked up at him. "Will you do them with me?"

"Sure." They started for the elevator. Bell kept peeking up at Mark as if nervous. And it made the little action of her slipping her hand into Juan's feel somehow precious. He gave the tiny hand a squeeze as they entered the elevator. "Mark works with me. He's a good guy."

Bell nodded.

Mark smiled down at Bell. "Looks like you and Juan are friends, too."

Bell gazed up at his partner. "Yes. He's my mom's friend, too. Not her boyfriend, even though he kissed her."

"Is that so?" Mark bit back a smile as they stepped out of the elevator. "I'll wait right here." Mark motioned to the family room.

Nikki's door was closed. Juan knocked. No one answered. He eased open the door. The bed was empty. Something about the silent room bothered him.

Walking to the bathroom door, he gave it a tap. "You in there?"

No answer.

Bell looked up through big scared eyes. "Where's my mama?"

"I don't know." His heart knocked around in his chest as if it had come loose.

A nurse walked in. "Where's our patient?"

Juan swallowed when he saw fear filling Bell's eyes. "I was going to ask you that."

CHAPTER
TWENTY-TWO

I'm here." Vicki stepped into the room from the hall, pulling her IV pole. Bell ran and wrapped her arms around Vicki's leg. "I got orders to walk."

Vicki's chest tightened when she saw the tears in her niece's eyes.

"I thought you died!" Bell sniffled.

Vicki lifted her niece's chin. "Do I look like I'm dead?"

"No."

Vicki glanced up at Juan and knew Bell wasn't the only one worried. Did he think she'd bailed and left her niece? Considering she'd lied to him, she couldn't judge him for not trusting her, but it still stung.

"I'm not going anywhere," she said with all sincerity.

"Right." Juan's shoulders relaxed. Was that an apology in his eyes?

She felt her knees give a little and reached out for the bedside table to steady herself.

"Let me help you." He moved in before the nurse and put his hand around her waist. Through the thin hospital gown, she felt the warmth of his palm. The strength in his touch. The need to let someone catch her. Butterflies she didn't think she should feel less than a day after almost dying fluttered inside her.

Now that he knew the truth, they could explore whatever this was between them. Could she take her mother's advice and learn to trust? Or was she destined to hide her heart away for fear that trust and love was the pathway to becoming someone's victim? Hadn't that been the route of both her mom and sister?

* * *

Juan paid the delivery guy and brought the pizza inside. It was two o'clock. Because he hadn't been hungry, he'd forgotten to feed Bell. What kind of babysitter was he? He felt better knowing Mildred had bought her some milk and cookies.

"Pizza's here," Juan said.

"Good." She stared at a phone in her hand.

"What are you doing?" She'd been coloring earlier.

"Playing games. It's my mom's old phone, it only works for games."

"Are you winning?"

"I'm not that good." She made a face.

Juan dished up a slice of pepperoni pizza and took it and a glass of milk to her in the living room, where she sat on the floor. They'd left Nikki, or Vicki, with the promise to come back this afternoon. Funny how he'd already started thinking of her as Vicki.

"Here you go." He set the plate and milk down.

Bell looked up. "Where's the salad?"

"I didn't know you wanted a salad." He frowned.

Bell made a face. "I don't. I hate vegetables. Well, I like peas and corn. But nothing else."

Juan smiled. "I'm not a big fan of vegetables, either."

"Mama makes me eat two bites of vegetables with lunch and dinner. For my bones."

"Let's make a deal. I won't make you eat any right now, but we won't tell her."

"Like me eating all Frosted Flakes and not healthy ones?"

"Yeah."

Bell grinned. Then her smile faded. "I'm still worried about my mom."

Vicki had told Bell that Juan knew the truth about their past. On the ride to the house, she'd told Juan about her mom dying after getting hit by a car.

Before he could respond, she continued, "You know what I'm scared of?"

"What?" His grip on the wheel had tightened, thinking she was going to say her father.

"That I'll forget. I don't want to forget my mama." Through his rearview mirror he'd watched her big brown eyes tear up.

Juan told her he knew how she felt, that he'd lost his mom, too. "You won't forget her. I haven't forgotten mine. You don't forget people you love." He knew that was true.

Bell picked up her pizza. "I know she's just my aunt, but I still want to call her mama."

"You should. She takes care of you like a mom."

"She loves me a lot." Bell took a bite of pizza, then returned to the game on her phone.

The child's confidence in Vicki's affection came off so matter-of-factly, so honest, that it touched him. "I can tell."

"Are you going to finish coloring?" She set down the phone and pointed to the half-colored picture he'd done earlier.

"Well, I need to make an important call. Can you eat and watch TV?" He needed to find out what was in that safety deposit box.

She nodded. "Do you want me to finish coloring your dog?"

"Yeah." His gaze shifted to the breakfast table, where he'd brought in Bates's notebook as well as the poems Mrs. Noel had delivered. His gut said he was missing something. But his gut wasn't being specific.

Hell, his gut was torn between thinking about this case and everything he'd learned about Vicki.

"Do you want me to turn the TV to the kids' channel?" he asked.

She nodded and hugged Sweetie. Juan changed the channel, grabbed his phone to call Jody in L.A., and walked into the extra bedroom he used as an office. Calling her wasn't easy, and not just because of the wild story he had to tell about Vicki. Jody was another friend he'd pulled away from since Angie's death.

She'd sent him a sympathy card when Angie died.

And she'd called and left a message and even emailed several times. He hadn't replied. Didn't want to hear someone else say he needed to move on.

Picking up the phone, he dialed.

"What the heck," Jody said in lieu of hello. "Are you a mind reader? I was about to call you."

"Really?"

"Your name came up on an investigation that's connected to one we're working."

"What investigation?"

"The Liu case. Drug dealer who had some Colombian ties. He was murdered five years ago."

"Yeah, but it happened in Anniston. Why are you working on it?"

"I'm not really working it. We made a drug bust and one of our perps wants to give up Liu's murderer for a deal. Our guy used to live in Texas and was part of Guzman's gang. We did some homework and found out you're working on a Noel case that everyone thinks is connected."

Her words had him sitting straighter. "You got a suspect? That'd be great."

"Not so great. It's iffy."

"Why?"

"He's blaming a cop. A dead cop. But the perp says the cop's not really dead."

Juan's head spun in a slow circle. "You aren't talking about Pablo Valado, are you?"

"How did you know?"

"Shit. This is crazy." He ran a hand down his face.

"What's crazy?"

"I was calling about him."

"What? Are you looking at him for this, too?"

"Uh, can what I tell you stay between us...for now?"

"I don't see why not. What's going on?"

He told her about Vicki and the abused women's organization that was protecting her.

"I know of the organization," she said. "They do good work. They helped the wife of a drug dealer who testified against him last year. It wasn't a big enough case to get her in the witness protection program. But they gave her a fresh start. How does this involve our dead cop?"

He filled her in about the book Vicki's sister said was proof Valado was dirty, then the safety deposit box, and even about the murder of Marisol Willis.

"Damn," Jody said. "That's quite a story."

"I know, but...I believe her." And he did. Any doubt he'd had just got washed away. "Especially with what you just told me."

"It does add validity to her story. I'll look into it."

"Do you know what's in this book?"

"No. Only what I told you."

"She has the safety deposit key?"

"Yeah. I can send it."

"Actually, if I get her to sign something I could probably get a warrant quicker."

"Yeah, send the forms."

"I'll get it to you in a couple of hours. Same email?" she asked.

"Yes."

"So you really were just ignoring me."

"Sorry. I just needed to work on things myself."

"Have you worked through them?" she asked.

"I'm making headway." But he didn't care to talk about that. "Have you looked into the possibility of Valado being alive?"

"Only enough to know we can't rule it out," she said. "The body was never found."

There was another truth Vicki had told him.

"And considering he was a suspect in his wife's death, it's suspicious."

"Seriously? I never read that in my research," Juan replied.

"Yeah, it was buried deep in some files. You know how cops are. They never want to convict one of their own."

"True." Another truth hit. With Valado alive, Vicki and Bell could really be in danger. Juan's shoulder blades drew together. He told himself the man didn't know where they were, but it didn't help.

"I'll look into things on my end," Jody said. "Do you know anything else about the Willis murder?"

"Just what I told you. I haven't had a chance to even look online." The call ended. But having a few minutes, he Googled the name Marisol Willis. When he read that Willis had been tortured and killed while her babies were in the house, he slammed his laptop closed. What kind of monster did that? The answer came quickly. The kind who'd put a lit cigar to his daughter.

Trying to push away the ugliness, he went to check on Bell. Barely in the hall, he heard Angie's voice. "I don't love him just because he's a hottie. The day..."

When he stepped into the living room he saw the

video playing. He drew his shoulder blades together. Bell had the remote in her hands.

He moved in and cut off the TV.

She frowned. "I was trying to change channels."

"Yeah."

"Who was that?" Bell's big brown eyes looked up at him.

"My late wife." He hoped the truth would end the conversation.

"Oh." She picked up a crayon and started coloring, then looked up. "What was she late for?"

An unexpected chuckle slipped off his lips, but he pulled it in. "No. That means...she passed away."

She blinked. "She died?"

"Yeah."

"Do you miss her like I miss my...late mom?"

He nodded.

She pursed her lips as if thinking. "Is that why Vicki, my new mom, isn't your girlfriend?"

Her question kicked him in his gut. "You finished with your pizza?"

She nodded. He moved to the table and picked up her plate.

"My mom does that, too," Bell said.

"Does what?"

She continued to color. "Asks a question instead of answering one."

He hadn't thought he could be put on the spot by a five-year-old. "It's just...a hard question to answer."

Her big brown eyes lifted. "Because you still love your wife?"

An ache swelled in his chest. "Yeah."

"I still love my real mom, but I love Aunt Vicki like a mom, too. Is it different with girlfriend kind of love than it is with mom love?"

He wondered if kindergartners could tell when an adult was squirming. Not seeing any other way out of the conversation, he asked, "You need more milk?"

* * *

After an hour of mulling over what he'd learned, he decided to call Vicki. Knowing he couldn't talk about this with Bell in the room, Juan went back into his office and called her. She'd been shocked Pablo was connected to one of his cases.

Vicki expressed concern about her name being leaked and Pablo finding her. He assured her that Jody wouldn't do that.

"Besides, I'm not going to let him get anywhere close to you."

"Thank you." She hesitated before speaking again. "So you believe me now?"

"Yeah." He almost apologized for doubting her, but could she really blame him when she'd lied to him?

"Is Bell behaving?" Vicki asked.

"Yes. She's a good kid."

"I know." Pride rang in her tone.

"As soon as Jody sends the papers, I'll bring them to you. And I'll bring your phone. Do you need anything else?"

"No. I'm fine."

"You don't want your own pajamas or . . . underwear?"

She was quiet for a second. "I hate to ask you to do that."

"Why? Don't want me going through your panty drawer?" He laughed and then instantly worried he'd crossed a line.

Her chuckle put him at ease.

"I like hearing you laugh." His voice deepened as he remembered the evening on the sofa.

Silence filled the line. "My life's a mess," she said. "I'm sorry I dragged you into it."

"You didn't drag me. And for the record, mine's in chaos, too. Maybe we can help each other sort things out."

"I'm afraid I'm not very good at sorting."

The fact that she had reservations actually made him feel a little better about his own. "Why don't we just see what happens. Enjoy each other's company."

"I'd like that," she said, and somehow he could hear the smile in her voice.

Getting off the phone, he moved to the dining room table and went through the Bates file again. He reread the poem on her sketch pad.

Oh, my lie. Oh, my sin. Oh, my friend.
I know my place. Where you stay. Beneath the birds, and where the angels sing.

Was this about Abby?

Staring at the sketches of statuary, he went for another slice of pizza and knocked the pizza box onto the floor.

"Shit!"

Bell cleared her throat in a scolding manner. Flinching, he glanced back at her. "Sorry."

"You owe me a dollar," Bell said.

"Huh?"

"Anytime Mama says a bad word, she has to give me a dollar. One day I made five dollars."

He bit back a smile, feeling better about letting the word slip. "Deal."

His laptop dinged with an email from Jody. There was an attachment. He just hoped whatever was in that safety deposit box helped implicate Valado, proved he was alive, and took Juan a step closer to making Vicki and Bell safe.

* * *

"What kind of shit is this?" Antonio, Rex's brother, pointed to the radio dial.

Pablo gripped the steering wheel a little tighter. "It's called classical." *It's for smart people.*

"Sounds like elevator music." Antonio changed stations. Antonio was dumber than the tarantulas who parked their asses in the middle of the road and became oily smears.

Pablo frowned. Offing this idiot was going to feel good.

The Sonoran Desert was the hottest fucking place in California. The sun beat down on the car. The glare and the temperature caused his head to throb. The car's air conditioner ran full blast, but he was still sweating.

Pablo loosened another shirt button. He felt antsy,

almost claustrophobic. Killing Antonio and taking the money was sure to bring Rex after his ass. But all along he'd known he'd have to kill Rex—especially after he found his logbook with all of Rex's contacts and attempted to start his own drug business.

"Look, there's another one." Antonio pointed to the tarantula in the road. "I hate those suckers. Pull over. I want to shoot this one."

When Pablo didn't stop, Antonio grabbed the wheel and swerved the car.

"Fuck!" Pablo said. "Don't you know shit like that will blow a tire in this heat?"

"I said pull over!"

"It's a damn spider and it's a hundred and ten degrees out there!" *Just a few more miles and you can hang out with spiders and rats and roaches.*

A glint of anger darkened Antonio's eyes. "Rex is tired of your shit. He told me to watch you. He heard how you hurt your own kid. That's sick, man. So unless you want me to tell Rex to get rid of your ass, stop and let me shoot the damn tarantula!"

Pablo's chest burned with indignation. Maybe he didn't need a few more miles. He swung the car around and brought it to a bone-jerking halt.

Antonio grinned. "Now, wasn't that easy?"

"Go shoot it already." Pablo took in short, tight breaths and rolled down the windows.

Antonio got out of the car.

Hot air like angry bees surrounded Pablo. The sun on the side of his face stung. As soon as Antonio turned his back, Pablo brought out his gun and shot the piece of shit. Antonio landed with a thud on the hot road, sounding like a dead squirrel falling from a tree. Pablo knew that sound. He used to shoot 'em when he was a kid. Shooting squirrels was how he'd blow off steam after one of his dad's beatings. It always calmed him. Especially when he'd pretend it was his old man falling dead.

Pablo rose up off the seat to make sure Antonio wasn't moving. He wasn't. Blood and white matter pooled around his head.

The man's last words echoed in Pablo's mind. *Now, wasn't that easy?*

"Yeah, that was a piece of cake." Pablo rolled up the windows, changed the radio back to classical music, and with a hundred thousand dollars in the trunk, he turned the car around and headed back to L.A.

The money wasn't anywhere near enough, but it would keep him until he found Vicki Trever—found his cash and his book. He smiled. Killing Antonio felt good. But killing Vicki would be more fun.

CHAPTER TWENTY-THREE

Juan and Bell walked into Vicki's hospital room. Vicki, sitting in a chair, looked up. The small room smelled like soap, as if Vicki had just showered.

She smiled. "Hi."

Bell ran over, flapping her dollar bill. "Look. He said the *S*-word."

Vicki cut her eyes at him. "Uh, that's our deal, sweetheart. Juan doesn't have to pay."

"It's fine," Juan said. "Personally, I think it's brilliant. But I hear you lost five dollars in one day."

She half smiled. "Bad day."

Grinning, he placed a plastic bag with a nightshirt and underwear on the bed, then sat on the edge. When he looked down, he saw her toenails still bearing Bell's artwork.

"I hope you like my selection." There was only a

hint of suggestion in his tone. He'd picked the nightshirt she'd worn when she'd kicked his butt, the one that read ANGEL AT REST.

"I'm sure it's fine." Her cheeks reddened. Even wearing a hospital gown and no makeup, she was beautiful.

She moistened her lips. The shine left by the quick swipe of her tongue had him recalling their time on her sofa. His mouth on hers.

"Thank you." She shifted in her chair.

"You don't need to say thank you."

"Oh, yes I do. You're my knight in shining armor."

"Like Lancelot?" Bell asked.

"Yeah," Vicki said.

Bell jumped up in the chair beside her mom. "You know, he kissed the queen in that movie. I saw it on TV."

"Uh, yes, I think he did." Vicki's eyes, carrying a slight smile, met his and held.

This, the feeling, whatever you called it, was more than a sexual pull. It was...the need to see her smile more often. To protect her. To win her trust. It was respect and attraction, all wrapped up in one. And it still scared and exhilarated him at the same time.

He recalled questioning his attraction to Vicki earlier and thinking how different she was from Angie. Now he realized how alike they actually were. Not physically. But where it mattered—on the inside.

Why did it still scare him?

He stood up. "I brought the paperwork Jody sent about the deposit box. As soon as I get back to my place, I'll send it to her. But I want to check on my witness during visiting hours. You guys good for a few minutes?"

"Of course. Is everything okay?"

"Yeah. I won't be long."

He hoped Cindy Bates would be able to give him answers soon, so he could find out more on how the Noel case was linked to Valado.

* * *

Vicki watched Juan leave, feeling as if she couldn't get enough air. He really was her knight in shining armor.

Vicki brushed Bell's hair from her eyes. "I miss you."

"I miss you, too. Don't tell Juan, because it might hurt his feelings, but he can't color very well."

Vicki chuckled, then her chest was gripped with emotion. "He colored with you?"

Bell made a funny face and pointed to the page. "He started coloring the dog blue. I fixed it for him. Boys don't color as good as girls."

"Some do," Vicki said.

"Not him," she said. "He can't even stay in the lines."

"Well, you make sure to be good. When I get home we'll bake him some cookies or make him dinner. A lot of dinners. We owe him big-time."

"He likes pizza," Bell said. "But he's like me. He doesn't like vegetables."

A laugh escaped Vicki's lips. "Sounds like you two are getting along great."

"We are. I like him." She swapped colors and started coloring a tree.

"Me too." Vicki's heart took a nosedive.

"You know what?" Bell asked.

"What?"

"When I look at him, I don't see his scar. I mean, it's there. I can see it, but I don't think about it. I wonder if that's what people would think if they saw my scars."

"I'm sure," Vicki said.

"Oh!" Bell laughed. "Sweetie pooped in the kitchen."

"She did?"

"Yeah, but Juan didn't get mad. He loves Sweetie a lot."

"Yeah. He's a nice guy."

"I know. Too bad he can't be your boyfriend." Bell kicked her feet back and forth.

"You don't think he can be my boyfriend?" Vicki asked.

"No. 'Cause he still loves his wife."

Vicki's breath caught on her tonsils. "He told you that?"

"Yeah. He said it was different than how you can love two mamas."

"Oh." She wished that didn't sting.

"She was pretty, too."

Vicki swallowed. "You saw a picture of her?"

"No. A video. She had a baby in her tummy. And she kissed Juan. A big kiss like in the movies. I was changing channels and I used the wrong remote. It came on the TV. He got sad and turned it off. But he didn't get mad."

"Good," Vicki said. But it didn't feel good. It hurt knowing Juan had lost so much, and maybe would never be ready to love again.

* * *

Juan pushed the double doors of the ICU open. The cold, and maybe hopelessness, in this part of the hospital reminded Juan of the morgue. He spotted room eight and walked in. Cindy Bates lay there. A machine marked her heartbeats. And the tube disappearing into her mouth still forced oxygen into her otherwise lifeless body.

He stood by her bed, recalling how the nurse had talked to Bates earlier. "Hey. It's Detective Acosta. Just wanted to stop in and say I'm working the case. Trying to find out who did this." He hesitated. "By the way, I...saw your paintings. You're good."

"Hello," a voice came from behind him.

Flinching, he turned. The woman in her mid-forties wore a white coat. "I, uh, the nurse spoke to her earlier when I was here. I was..."

She smiled. "You should talk to her. It helps a lot of my patients. I'm Dr. Swain. And you?"

Juan motioned for her to walk outside.

"I'm Detective Acosta."

"Oh. Is she...?"

"Just a witness," he answered. "We're trying to find out who did this."

The doctor nodded. "She's lucky. Her vitals are looking better. The bullet to the head barely penetrated the skull. The one in the chest did considerable damage, but the surgery repaired everything."

"So why is she still unconscious? The nurse said they were doing another MRI."

"Yes. Unfortunately, we don't know why she hasn't

woken up." She frowned. "She has cuts and bruises on her face from what appears to be from an older injury. Do you know who did that?"

"He's in jail."

"Good." Empathy filled her gaze. "She has older needle marks in her arm."

"I heard she got clean," Juan said.

"Yes. Her blood didn't show signs of drug use." She frowned. "My brother was a drug addict. He's been clean ten years and is doing great, but the only way he did it was with the support of our family."

"I've seen people deal with it. It's tough," Juan said.

"Since we haven't seen any other friends or family come by, I'm guessing Cindy probably got clean by herself. That's admirable. Takes gumption. But I guess sometimes a person needs something to live for. I'm not so sure the girl in that bed has a reason."

* * *

"That's sad," Juan told Bell, finishing off chapter twenty-one in *Charlotte's Web*. When they'd gone to her house to get her pajamas, she'd grabbed the book and asked if he'd read it to her.

"The next chapter is better," Bell said. "Wilbur meets Charlotte's babies."

"Then why didn't you want to hear that chapter?" he asked.

She pulled the cover up to her neck. Her eyes looked heavy. "I like this chapter better. 'Cause I like how it makes me feel."

He frowned. "You like feeling sad?"

"No." She pursed her lips as if thinking. "I like knowing that other people feel sad, too. That I'm not the only one."

His chest swelled with the need to fix the brokenness inside of her. But how? "You aren't the only one. But I don't think your mama would want you to be sad."

She bit down on her lip. "But if I'm happy, won't I forget about her?"

Subconsciously, it was what he'd thought, too, after Angie died. "It feels that way, doesn't it? But I don't want to think we have to be sad. Tell me something good about your mama."

She smiled. "She loved potato chips mixed with ice cream. And she could touch her tongue to her nose." Bell's tongue came out, but it didn't reach her nose.

He laughed. "See. You remember happy things, too."

She yawned. "Tell me something good about your wife. Late wife."

He exhaled. "Your mom reminds me of her."

"My aunt mama?"

"Yes."

"Then she was nice," Bell said.

"Yeah."

She petted Sweetie, who was curled up beside her on the sofa, then snuggled deeper into the blankets. She'd begged him to let her sleep here and for him to sleep in the chair, because she didn't want to sleep in a strange room alone. He'd relented.

"I'm sleepy," she said.

"Go to sleep." He stood.

"Juan?" Her sweet little-girl voice barely reached his ears.

He turned. The shoulder of her nightgown hung down and he saw her scars. If he got the chance, Juan would make sure Valado paid for what he'd done to his daughter. He had to swallow to push out the word. "Yeah?"

"I don't like my mama in the hospital, but I like staying here with you and Sweetie."

"I like it, too."

She rolled over.

And so did his heart.

Was this what he would've felt for his daughter?

Juan's phone vibrated in his pocket. He'd turned the ringer down so as not to wake up Bell. He pulled it out. Jody. Hurrying back into his office, he answered, "Yeah."

"We got into the safety deposit box," Jody said.

"And?" he asked.

* * *

Vicki looked at the clock. It was almost nine. Bell had called an hour ago to say goodnight, and Juan had told her he'd call her when he heard from his law enforcement friend in L.A. She wondered if his not calling meant they'd struck out with the safety deposit box.

Impatient, she dialed. It rang four times before he answered. Each ring had her pulse racing faster. If the safety deposit box yielded nothing, would Juan lose faith in her? Reconsider helping her?

"Hey," he said. "Sorry, I was still on the line with Jody."

"Did she get anything?"

"We hit the jackpot. The notebook has names, dates, and they've already matched several of them to drug buys. It might lead us to finally figuring out who Rex is."

"Rex?"

"The man Valado worked for in California. We believe he's a big drug supplier."

She rolled the edge of the hospital sheet. "Does any of this prove Pablo is alive?"

"No. Not yet. But it's a start."

When she didn't say anything, he added, "This is good news, Vicki."

Hearing him use her real name was a shock. "I know, it's just... I want this over with. I'm tired of running. Tired of being afraid he's going to hurt Bell." Tears stung her eyes.

"I'm not going to let that happen."

"I know, and I'm indebted to you." But Bell's little bombshell about Juan claiming he couldn't love again had affected her more than she wanted to believe.

"You're not indebted to me."

"I am. Seriously, I don't know what I would do right now without you."

"I don't want you to think..."

"Think what?" she asked.

"Whatever happens between us should be because it feels right, not out of debt."

"It's pretty clear this thing between us isn't about obligation." She bit down on her lip. "I practically threw myself at you." She closed her eyes and wished she'd kept silent.

"Oh. I forgot about that." His laugh flowed through

the phone. "I'm joking. It's *all* I've thought about. Are you wearing your nightshirt?"

Butterflies fluttered in her stomach. "Yeah."

"You took my breath away when I first saw you in it."

She could hear the smile in his voice. "You mean when I kicked you?" She laughed.

"Then, too. How long did you train for the Ironman triathlon?"

"Only nine months. But I was in shape because of my work."

"That's admirable. What made you do it?"

"I was working as a trainer. I thought it'd be great PR. Before I realized it, it felt like a challenge. But like I said before, being able to protect myself has always been important. I started taking karate when I was sixteen. I had plans to try again for the triathlon, but..."

"But what?"

"Pablo attacked Alison. She stayed in the hospital for a week, then she and Bell moved in with me. He almost killed her."

"Is that when he hurt Bell, too?"

"Yeah. He's a sick bastard." She closed her fist around the sheet. "All the energy I had put into working out, I put into taking him down. I hired a lawyer." Air caught in her throat. "I should have stopped him years before."

"Had he hurt her before?"

"Yeah. I didn't know about most of it. I saw a bruise on her arm right after Bell was born. I lost it. Alison got angry. She claimed she tripped and swore he didn't do it. But I should have known. He followed the pattern of all abusers, treated her like a princess at first. Then he started isolating her from everyone. I still saw her, but not nearly enough. I was starting my business. When I'd call her or when I'd insist on seeing her, she'd tell me she was just busy being a mother. I let her pull away."

"You can't blame yourself."

She swallowed. "I introduced them. Pablo and I had been training for the Ironman. He asked me out, but I wasn't interested. He seemed nice. He was a police officer. I thought . . . " She swallowed.

"You didn't know."

Guilt filled her chest. "I should have. I grew up with abusers. Like my dad. Like my mom's boyfriends."

He didn't speak for several seconds. "Were you abused?"

"A few tried to put their hands on me. One got physical, hit me, but he didn't get anywhere and I wasn't . . . I didn't let him win. I was more worried about protecting Alison. She was two years younger." Vicki inhaled. "What's terrible was even after Alison and Bell came to live with me, I was angry at Alison for allowing Pablo to hurt them when she'd seen our own mom get hurt by men."

"Someone once told me that we either grow up to make the same mistakes as our parents or make different mistakes in an overzealous attempt to not be like them," he said softly.

Vicki considered it. "It's true."

"So you're the overzealous one?" he asked.

"Yeah. No one can hurt you if you don't let them close."

"What about the guy you told me about? Dan? Weren't you serious?"

"Yes and no. We dated for almost three years. But he liked his space. And I guess I did, too. There was never any talk of marriage or..." *Love.* "He didn't want anything more. And I was okay with that." Or she had been until she'd gone to him about disappearing with AWACO. She'd thought he'd at least try to talk her out of it. He hadn't. It wasn't even as if she'd have stayed, but right then she'd realized how little their relationship had meant to him.

"There's nothing wrong with not wanting more."

She closed her eyes. Was he talking about himself, too?

"Not everyone is looking for the same thing," he offered.

"You must think I take all the fun out of dysfunction," she said, trying to lighten the conversation.

"No, I get it. I'm an overzealous person, too. I think that's why I... come off a little strong when I think... when I think a woman is in an abusive situation."

"That's not a bad quality."

"I work at keeping people at arm's length, too."

"Losing your wife and child must have been unbearable."

"It was, but I was a bit of a loner even before that. A lot of that has to do with my parents."

"What happened?"

Silence reigned before he spoke. "Dad was a mean drunk. He never raised his hand to me or my brother, but Mom wasn't so lucky. She finally got the courage to leave him."

"Good for her," Vicki said.

"He couldn't accept it. He killed her. Then killed himself."

She gasped. "I'm sorry."

"Me too." He got quiet. Something told her there was more. She wanted to ask, but instead just waited and hoped he'd share.

"I was late coming home that night. When I got there, Mom was dead on the kitchen floor. I saw my dad kill himself. For the longest time, I beat myself up for not being there to stop him."

"I'm so sorry. But I understand why you became a cop."

"Yeah."

"So maybe we both take the fun out of dysfunction," she said.

He laughed, but it came without humor. "Or maybe we're survivors."

"That sounds better."

The line went silent again. She wasn't ready to say goodbye. "Is Bell asleep?"

"Yeah. She's such a good kid."

"I know," Vicki said. "I'm so afraid I'm going to mess up. I didn't plan on having kids. I don't really know how to be a parent."

"Are you kidding? You're doing an amazing job. She told me today how much you love her."

Vicki's chest grew warm. "She did?"

"Yeah. And I don't think a kid could want or need anything more than to know they're loved."

"Well, she's right. I do love her. I used to think my career was everything. Finishing the Ironman was huge. Now I look at her and realize what's important."

The conversation shifted. He told her about his brother, Christina, and his nephews. And for a little bit she felt like a teenager, holding on to every word a boy said. Lulled by the sound of his voice. Wishing and wanting. Then she remembered, *Too bad he can't be your boyfriend.*

While they were talking, he went online to read about different stages of the Ironman competition. "Damn. No wonder you kicked my butt."

She laughed.

They were about to hang up when he said. "Wait. I just got another email from Jody."

"What does it say?"

He didn't answer right away and then said, "Shit."

"What?" She tightened her hand around the phone.

"I told Jody about Marisol Willis's murder. Asked her to look into it."

"And?"

"Willis's ex-husband has an alibi for her murder. He didn't do it. They found some DNA at the scene. They're checking it. If it's Pablo, they'll have confirmation he's alive and reason for a warrant."

"So she was killed because of me."

"You didn't do this," he said.

She bit down on her lip. "When will they know if it was his DNA?"

"She's asked for them to rush it, but she doesn't know how long it'll take. There's a backlog of testing to be done."

CHAPTER
TWENTY-FOUR

Juan walked Bell to the front of the school. Vicki had called this morning, worried the school would have a problem with him picking up Bell in the afternoon because he wasn't listed on her paperwork. So he'd arrived early.

"Are you coming in?" Bell asked, holding his hand.

"We're going to the office first," he said.

As he moved, he looked around at the people standing in front of the school. Logic said Bell was safe, that Pablo hadn't found her, but damn if he didn't still worry.

He walked to the office counter and explained that he was Vicki's neighbor and would be picking Bell up.

"Oh," the clerk said, frowning. "Her mother needs to put you on the authorized pickup list."

"Yeah, but she's in the hospital. I can give you her

phone number, and if there's something she needs to sign before I pick Bell up, I'll be happy to get it to you."

It took speaking to two other people and one lady calling Vicki before the problem was solved. And he still had to get Vicki's signature on the form granting him permission to pick up Bell that afternoon.

"I'm sorry it took so long," the assistant principal said.

"No, I appreciate you being careful." He wanted to warn them about Valado, but considering that would have to include the fact that Vicki was using an alias, it didn't seem like a good idea. He walked Bell back to the front of the school where kids gathered.

Bell's grip on his hand tightened. "I kind of wish I could play hooky again."

Someone called out Bell's name. Juan looked over and saw a little girl standing beside the Porsche-driving bozo he'd seen on Vicki's porch.

The girl ran over.

"Why were you out yesterday?"

"I played hooky." Bell grinned.

"Who's this?" The girl stared up at Juan and flinched when she saw his face.

"My neighbor. He's not my mom's boyfriend, but he still kissed her. Mama had a stone in her kidney. He's a good guy like your dad. Remember the dog I told you about? She's his."

The girl's father lifted a brow. "Hi, I'm Cal Phillips, Suzie's dad. Is Nikki okay?"

"Yes, she's fine. I'm watching Bell for a few days."

The bell rang. Still holding his hand, Bell looked up at him. "Can I give you a goodbye kiss?"

"Yeah." Juan knelt down. She kissed him on his scar. And damn if his heart didn't drop.

"Mama meets me right here after school." She pointed to the front doors.

"Bell, why don't you come over to our house today?" Cal looked at Juan. "I mean, if it would help."

"Can I?" Bell asked.

"I think I'd better pick you up," Juan said. "Maybe we can ask your mom when she's feeling better."

"Yeah," Cal said. "I'll arrange a playdate with Nikki. Nice to meet you."

Juan could tell the man didn't mean it. And that was just fine.

* * *

"Hey." Juan's voice from her open doorway brought Vicki's gaze up. He wore khaki Dockers and a white button-down shirt. His neat, freshly showered appearance made her feel wrinkled and frumpy.

She was a mess. Fear and guilt buzzed through her veins.

Juan stepped to the bed. She caught hints of men's soap, a spicy scent that had her wanting to be closer. "Is Bell okay? Did she give you any problem?"

"No problem. She ran into her friend." He sat down on the edge of her bed and studied her. "What's wrong?"

Vicki blinked. "What's not wrong? I'm scared. And I

go between hoping it's Pablo's DNA at Marisol's place so we'll have proof, and hoping it's not. Because if it is, then...she died because of me."

He took her hand and gave it a squeeze. "First, nothing has happened to prove he knows where you are. And second, if Pablo is the one who killed Marisol, it's not on you."

"He's a monster. You saw what—"

"Hey." He put two fingers under her chin and lifted her face. "I'm not going to let him hurt you or Bell."

She nodded. He leaned in and kissed her lips. Not a kiss meant to seduce, but one meant to comfort.

"I'll pick her up as soon as school's over."

She nodded.

"What time do you think you'll get released?" he asked.

"They said I have to wait for my doctor. He doesn't do rounds until three or four. But—"

"Great. I'll come here right after I pick her up."

"I can get an Uber. You've already—"

"No."

She noticed a purse under his arm. He saw her gaze lower.

"It's Cindy Bates's. The nurse gave it to me. Patients aren't supposed to have personal items in the ICU. They found it in the ER."

"You went to see her again?" Vicki asked.

"Yeah."

"How is she?"

"The same. She's breathing on her own, but they won't take her off of the ventilator until she wakes up."

"Has her family even called and checked in?" she asked.

"They haven't called me. They could've called the hospital. But she has a phone in here." He motioned to the purse. "I thought I'd see if she has any messages or texts from friends. Maybe she has someone, but they don't know what happened to her."

Vicki realized again what kind of man Juan Acosta was. The kind who cared for someone he didn't even know. The kind who'd jumped the fence to help a neighbor he hadn't met. The kind who took off work to take care of a neighbor's kid. "That's nice of you."

He winked. "See, I'm a nice guy."

"No, you're a freaking saint." She put her hand on his arm.

He smiled. "A saint wouldn't be wondering if you were wearing the lacy white underwear I brought you."

She grinned. "Okay, so you're a saint with a libido."

He kissed her again. This one had a hint of seduction in the delivery. Not that it lasted long or even pushed any hospital limit. It was just there in the soft way his lips touched hers. The way his finger caressed her face. The way he looked at her when he pulled back.

He continued to study her. "You look like you didn't sleep well."

"I didn't."

"Well, why don't you try to get some rest. Let me worry about everything for a while."

* * *

Juan walked into the office. Connor and Mark were both on their computers. Juan had almost called them last night and told them about discovering who his neighbor was and what she was running from, but not wanting to put them in any kind of trouble for not handing over information, he decided to see what Jody got today first.

"Hey," Mark said. "We just got a call from Homicide. They found a print on the car the Bates shooter used."

"We get a name?" Juan dropped into his chair and placed the purse and notebook containing Bates's poems on his desk.

"We're running it through the system now. Hopefully we'll get something."

"Did you see Bates this morning?" Connor asked, studying his computer screen.

"Yeah. Still unconscious. But the ER sent up this." He held out the purse.

Connor chuckled. "I was gonna ask when you started carrying a purse."

Juan frowned. "Bates was wearing it when she got shot. Her phone's in here. I'm hoping to track down a friend by looking through her texts."

Connor pushed away from the computer. "Good idea."

"Yeah," Juan said. "The doctor pointed out that Bates got clean and she can't imagine she did it completely alone. Someone has to care about her."

"I agree." Mark leaned back in his chair until it squeaked, his gaze zeroed in on Juan. "How's your neighbor?"

"Fine. She's coming home today."

"How's the babysitting gig?" Connor piped up.

"It's easier than I thought. I mean, I forgot to feed her lunch yesterday." Juan exhaled. "But I'm learning." He leaned back in his chair, remembering the kiss on his cheek. "She's a good kid."

"Mildred was raving about how smart she is," Mark added.

"Yeah, she is."

"So you're making out with her mom, but you aren't her boyfriend?" Humor punctuated Connor's question.

Juan frowned at Mark, knowing that info had come from him, since Bell had shared it with him at the hospital yesterday.

Mark shrugged. "Sorry. It was funny."

"Right." But Juan didn't want to talk about Vicki yet. He glanced at his phone, wishing Jody would call.

Mark stood up. "You know the Bolton case we talked about looking into next? I made a few calls and thought I'd start doing some legwork since we're on hold on this one. Call me if you need me."

"Yeah," Juan said.

"I'm going to grab lunch." Connor stood. "You want me to bring you something back? A burger? A Hooters waitress?"

"I'm fine." His partners left. Juan stared at his phone again. Five minutes later, realizing he was wasting time, he opened Bates's purse.

Pulling out her phone, he spotted something white and furry at the bottom. He turned the purse over and shook it. A white rabbit's foot rolled out.

Rabbit's foot? Why was this familiar?

It took several seconds, but he remembered. The picture of Abby Noel holding one. Mrs. Noel's words replayed in his head. *She made the cheerleading team that day. She said it was her lucky rabbit's foot. She took that thing everywhere after that.*

Was this Abby's?

Juan picked up Cindy's phone and it came on. The background was a photograph of a girl on a carousel horse. Hadn't he seen it before? Then he remembered where. The half-finished painting at Cindy's apartment.

Even then he'd thought he'd seen the image somewhere before. Where? The answer hit. At the Noels' house, on the mantel.

But why would Bates have a photograph of it on her phone?

Shit! He yanked open the notebook and reread the poem.

Oh, my lie. Oh, my sin. Oh, my friend.
I know my place. Where you stay. Beneath the
birds, and where the angels sing.
On a prayer. On a wing. But no, I still sing. I still
swing.
You live in the mirror and I see your face.

Was she saying...?

He called Mark, then Connor, and told them to meet him at the hospital ASAP.

* * *

When he walked into the ICU waiting room, Mark and Connor were there.

"What's going on?" Connor asked.

Juan motioned for them to step outside, away from the family huddled in the corner. Once out of the room, Juan said, "I don't believe Abby Noel's dead. She's the one in the ICU."

"What?" Mark asked.

"Yeah. Mrs. Noel told me that her daughter called Bates her twin friend. Said they looked alike. I saw a picture of them at the apartment that confirmed it. And there was red hair dye in Bates's apartment. Then there's the mystery as to why Bates was sending Noel's daughter birthday cards. It's because Lacy is *her* daughter."

Mark rubbed his chin. "But Bates and Noel both worked at the Black Diamond. Wouldn't someone there have noticed the switch?"

"I'm betting the turnover in the Black Diamond is fast. Star, the waitress, didn't work there when Noel did. Even Grimes said he'd only been there the week before Noel disappeared."

Mark frowned. "Good point, but—"

"I got more." Confidence sounded in Juan's voice. "When I saw the unfinished painting in Bates's apartment, it felt as if I'd seen it before. I had. At the Noels'. The girl in all her paintings is her daughter. And when I opened Bates's phone, her background is the carousel picture. Only Mrs. Noel's in it, too."

"Maybe Noel sent it to Cindy before she died," Mark said.

"No, Lacy was a baby then. Plus, there're other pictures. Photos of the Noels with the child. Whoever took those pictures has been following the Noels. I don't think a friend would go that far. Also, I found a rabbit's foot in Bates's purse. Another picture at the Noels' was a picture of their daughter with a rabbit's foot. Her grandmother gave it to her."

"Okay, I'm warming up to the idea," Connor said.

"Then there's the poetry. She writes about seeing her friend's face in the mirror."

"But if that's Noel in there"—Mark pointed to the ICU doors—"where's Cindy Bates?"

"Unfortunately, I think I know that, too. I'm betting she's buried in the Henleys' backyard. I think someone killed Bates thinking it was Noel."

Connor didn't look convinced. "Why do you think she's buried there?"

"The poems imply someone's in that garden, and Bates keeps going there, like she's grave sitting."

"Damn," Connor said. "If you're right, you really knocked this one out of the ballpark."

"Shocking isn't it?" Juan said. "I brought a fingerprint scanner. We'll know soon."

"Are Noel's prints in the system?" Connor leaned back on his heels.

"Yeah. I checked. She was arrested a few months before she went missing."

"Then let's do this." They walked into the ICU.

CHAPTER
TWENTY-FIVE

Thirty minutes after the prints came back, Juan parked in front of the Noels' tile store. He walked inside, still unsure how to deliver the news.

"Welcome," a male voice called from the front counter.

Juan and Mr. Noel made eye contact. Noel looked at a woman at a corner desk. "Lola, watch the store for a bit."

Mr. Noel waved Juan forward. "You got our message?"

"What message?" Juan asked as he followed Mr. Noel behind the counter.

"We didn't have your card with us, so my wife called your office."

"Sorry, I've been out."

Mr. Noel stopped in front of an office. "Then why are you here?" He drew in a sharp breath. "You found her?" His expression darkened. "If my daughter suffered, don't tell her mother."

"Let's sit down." Juan motioned him forward and saw Mrs. Noel inside the office, working at a desk.

"I've got it right here. It's crazy." Mrs. Noel pushed an envelope toward him.

"What's crazy?" Juan asked.

She motioned to the envelope. "The money we just got. It came yesterday but I didn't open the envelope until this morning. Five dollars in a birthday card is one thing, but this is ridiculous."

"How much money?" Juan remembered Star, the waitress, saying Bates was selling the drugs to help an orphaned kid.

"Almost twenty thousand."

"That is a lot of money," Juan said.

"But he's not here for that." Mr. Noel's tone signaled confusion. "What's up?"

Juan started. "You were right, Mrs. Noel. Your daughter isn't dead. In fact, I'm sure it was her who sent the money."

Mrs. Noel's face paled. Mr. Noel let out a graveled gulp of air. "Are you...? Don't tell us this if you aren't sure."

"I'm sure. But your daughter is in the hospital. In the ICU."

"My girl's alive?" Mrs. Noel sobbed, then asked, "What's wrong with her?"

"She was shot. Doctors believe she's going to make it, but she's still unconscious."

Mrs. Noel bolted up. "Is she at Westside Hospital?"

"Wait." Mr. Noel motioned for his wife to stop. "Who shot her and where's she been all this time? Is someone after her? Is she safe?"

"We don't know everything. But she's been using Cindy Bates's identity. As for who shot her, we're still trying to figure that out. But we haven't let out to the media where she's hospitalized."

* * *

By noon, Juan was parked in front of the Henleys' house.

Mr. Henley hadn't taken kindly to news that he possibly had a body in his backyard. Not that Juan blamed him.

When Juan got out of his car, he heard barking. The front door to the house opened and Mr. Henley, wearing an attitude, stepped out.

"I sure as hell hope you're wrong," Mr. Henley said through tight lips.

"We all do." Juan rotated his shoulders.

"Where do we think the body is?" Duncan, the owner of the cadaver dogs, bounced on his heels, excited.

"Backyard," Juan said.

While Juan introduced Mark and Connor to Mr. Henley, Duncan opened the van. Two dogs, a German shepherd mix and a large poodle-looking dog, bounced out, but immediately sat and waited for Duncan to put their leashes on.

Sweat rolled down Juan's brow as he watched Duncan lead the dogs into the backyard. If the animals didn't pick up anything, it'd make his assumption come off as half-baked. Part of him still hoped he was wrong. Was it too much to ask that Bates was just off somewhere living her life in the shadows?

Probably.

The dogs, noses to the ground, moved back and forth. As they neared the back corner of the yard, both animals pulled harder on their leashes. At the birdbath, they sat and barked.

"We got a body," Duncan said as if it was a good thing.

"I wondered why the plants always grew better over there." Mr. Henley shivered as if appalled.

"I'll call Stone," Mark said, referring to the medical examiner. "He'll bring a dig team."

"All from a poem." Connor patted Juan on the back. "You did good on this one."

Good? Juan preferred to save victims, not find them dead. But cold cases usually meant discovering cold bodies.

Juan's cell rang. He pulled it out, hoping it was Jody. It wasn't. It was the hospital, not the number he associated with Vicki's room, but the one from the ICU. Shit, it'd be a bitch if Abby Noel died now.

* * *

Mark and Connor waited at the Henleys' for the body to be exhumed. Juan headed to the hospital to talk to Noel, who'd woken from the coma. He had one hour before picking up Bell. He couldn't be late. Not even for this.

Abby and her mom looked up when he entered the room. "Can I have a moment with your daughter?"

"She's still weak," Mrs. Noel said.

"I understand."

The woman left with reluctance. Abby Noel's face was still bruised, her nose swollen. Tears brightened her blue eyes. "How did you figure it out?" Her voice came raspy and raw.

"The pictures on your phone. The paintings. The poetry. And the rabbit's foot."

She brushed tears off her face. "You've been up here before this, haven't you? I recognize your voice."

He nodded and sat in the chair beside her bed.

She blinked. "I didn't kill Cindy."

"Who did?" His tone came out all cop.

"I didn't know him, but I'd seen him at the strip club a few days before it happened. Him and two other guys came looking for my boyfriend, Cheng Liu. Someone said they were from California."

"Did you see him kill her?"

"No." Emotion shook her voice. "Cheng asked me out that night, and Cindy had agreed to work my shift for me. No one could tell us apart if she wore a blond wig. I'd loaned her my car. I was with Cheng when... I saw him get shot."

"What happened?" Juan asked.

"I was waiting in Cheng's car while he went back to his apartment for his phone. An SUV pulled up, I heard shots, saw him fall." Abby shuddered.

"What did you do?"

"I ran into a bar next door to the parking lot. When I

went back to Cindy's house to get my car, I saw the guy leaving her house. I know they thought she was me."

Juan's mind raced to keep up. "So the person who you saw leaving Bates's house is the one who killed Liu?"

"I don't know for sure."

"Did this guy leaving Cindy's place drive the same SUV?" Juan asked.

"No, but I knew he was one of the guys who came to the Black Diamond a few nights before."

Juan gave her a few minutes before asking, "Do you think you could describe that guy?"

She nodded.

"Excellent. I'll bring a sketch artist in." Juan stretched out his legs in the chair. "What happened to you after that?"

"I called the new manager of the Black Diamond, said I was Cindy, and quit. I took her ID and moved to Florida to live with an old boyfriend. I was so afraid that if they knew I was alive, they'd not only kill me but go after Lacy. I pretty much stayed high the whole time I was away. But I thought about Lacy every day and eventually just had to see her again. I swore I'd get clean. I did it for her. But I realized that even clean, I was a screwup. How could I ever deserve to be her mother?"

"You were going to kill yourself."

Crying, she nodded. "But first, I wanted to give her some money, so she could put it toward college and make something of her life." She wiped her eyes and looked up. "I'm going to jail, aren't I?"

"I can't say that right now. Why don't you just concentrate on getting well."

* * *

Vicki stepped out of Bell's bedroom after reading her
a story. She found Juan in the kitchen washing dishes.
"You've outdone yourself."

He dried his hands on a towel and smiled back at her
over his shoulder. "Just being a good neighbor."

He'd picked up Bell from school, then stayed at the
hospital for four hours waiting for Vicki to be released.
After he drove them home, he left to pick up her
medicines, and returned with bags of Chinese food.

During dinner, Juan passed his peas from his fried
rice to Bell's plate while Bell passed him her bamboo
shoots. Sweetie waited under Bell's chair for any little
tidbit she dropped. The entire evening from vegetable
swapping to goodnight kisses was just so Norman
Rockwellish, so family-like, it made Vicki want to cry.

He moved away from the sink and brushed Vicki's
hair off her cheek. "How are you feeling? You need a
pain pill?"

"No. I'm good." And she was. The pain in her side
was gone. She placed her hand on his chest. Warm muscles came against her palm. She could feel the slight
thump of his heart. Her own pulse picked up. Lifting
her eyes, she met his gaze and held it.

"I should...let you get some sleep. I'll be here at
eight to drive Bell to school."

"You don't have to drive her. I think I can—"

"I want to." He leaned in. His lips brushed against hers. Not overtly sexual, but tender. And that made the moment even more powerful. She couldn't help but wonder how she'd lived without this feeling for so long. The feeling that she wasn't alone.

He pulled back. Not wanting to lose the closeness, she leaned her head on his chest. His hands shifted to her waist. They just stood there. Holding on.

He leaned his face down and pressed a soft kiss into the top of her head.

She closed her eyes and breathed in his scent. "This feels good."

"Real good." His whispered words stirred wisps of hair at her temple. "But I should...go."

Looking up, she lifted to her tiptoes. His mouth lowered and the kiss felt like a promise. It wasn't until she watched him walk away—still feeling his lips on hers, the hum of his pulse against her ear—that she realized the promise he offered might not be the one she really wanted. *Too bad he can't be your boyfriend. 'Cause he still loves his wife.*

She'd never been a forever-or-nothing girl. She'd learned to appreciate the here and now, to live in the moment, but she had a feeling her moments with Juan wouldn't be enough. While this man, almost too good to be true, offered her protection and affection, he might not ever be able to offer her his heart.

Somehow she was going to have to remember that. Especially now that it wasn't just her heart, but Bell's, that could be broken.

* * *

With Antonio dead and Rex's money burning a hole in his trunk, Pablo couldn't return to his apartment. Rex would have all his men searching, offering a fifty-thousand-dollar bonus to the man who put a bullet in Pablo's head. Not that he'd find him. Pablo had tossed his phone so he couldn't be tracked and bought another one. The car had been left parked on a street of a bad neighborhood, keys on the dash. By now the vehicle was torn apart and sold as parts.

And since today was the day Jefferies had said he'd be home, Pablo had hunkered down at Jefferies's last night and helped himself to the man's scotch.

He'd slept late and passed time by watching the last season of *Breaking Bad*, which he'd never seen. Then he went through Jefferies's things again and found another picture of Vicki. She was sitting in bed, the sheet pulled up to her chest, her shoulders bare. Had they just fucked? Staring at the image, Pablo imagined screwing her. Why not let her experience what a real man felt like just before she died.

He wondered how long it'd take her to tell him where his money and book were. How much pain would he have to inflict?

Giving the photograph another glance, he debated how he was going to end Vicki. A knife? His hand around her throat, listening as she tried to breathe? Or maybe beat the bitch to death. She deserved to suffer for putting him through this last year.

He checked the time. The only flight coming in from

Denmark today had arrived two hours ago. Jefferies should be here soon. After spending almost ten hours flying, surely the man would come straight home.

Pablo walked through the extra bedroom. He'd decided that even if Jefferies told him what he wanted to know and didn't appear to recognize him, leaving him alive was too much of a risk. Or maybe he just liked killing.

The plastic tarp lay stretched out over the wood floors. He'd found some duct tape in the man's garage. He'd even borrowed a few of Jefferies's knives and had them set out on the one table in the room. He didn't know how easy or hard Jefferies was going to make it on himself.

Yesterday, he'd picked up a fifty-gallon drum at a hardware supply. He'd worked a case where a body had remained hidden for four years in a storage unit. He reached down into his pocket to make sure he still had Jefferies's key. He did.

Amazing how his time fighting crime made him a better criminal.

He'd been a good cop. Got a high from catching criminals and bringing their asses in. But the money sucked. He'd worked Homicide for a year, then moved over to Narcotics when he realized the financial benefits. He'd been doing his own thing when Rex approached him.

Those had been the good days. Rex paid him a nice salary to keep the cops off his ass, plus Pablo skimmed some off the top from the drug money Rex had rolling in. Stealing from him was addictive. Knowing he was smarter than one of L.A.'s biggest drug dealers gave him a sense of power. He almost wished he hadn't killed his father, so the old man would have known just how good Pablo was.

Pablo grabbed another scotch and went to wait in the dining room. He'd be able to see headlights pulling into the driveway from here.

He'd disconnected the garage door opener. The plan was to come up behind Jefferies when he walked in the front door. Then lead him into the bedroom so the fun could begin.

Leaning the chair back on two legs, he recalled Alison scolding him not to do that to her furniture. Her furniture? As if she'd paid for it. That was the first lesson he taught her. Nobody scolded him.

After that she'd become this scared mouse, walking on eggshells around him. He hated that side of her even more. It reminded him of the role he'd had to play with his dad. For seventeen years he'd been his dad's punching bag. In fact, it had been watching the cops trying to solve his dad's disappearance—the disappearance he'd caused by murdering the vicious bastard—that had gotten him into law enforcement. If he could best them at their own game, think how good of a cop he'd be.

Thirty minutes later, Pablo paced Jefferies's house. Where the hell was he?

Finally, headlights sliced through the dark house. Pablo moved behind the door. The sound of the engine rumbled outside. One minute. Two. The garage door wasn't working. Idiot.

Finally, the purr of the engine stopped. A car door

opened and shut. Footsteps slapped against the sidewalk. A shot of adrenaline fizzed through Pablo's veins.

The sound of keys jingling came next. The door
pushed open. Pablo moved in. He put his gun to the
man's temple. Jefferies, quicker than Pablo expected,
swung around. A suitcase came at Pablo.

The blow caught him right in the stomach. The
wheels of the suitcase bruised a few ribs. Air whooshed
out. Pain hit. Pablo slammed into the wall, but bounced
back. Jefferies shot for the door. Pissed, Pablo dove
across the entry room, grabbed the guy by the neck,
and slammed him into the wall. The crunching sound
of head versus wall was gratifying.

The guy hit the floor. Pablo feared he'd killed him
too soon. But no, he shot up. Pablo grabbed the guy
around the neck and pushed his gun to his temple.
"Fight me and I'll just make this harder on you."

CHAPTER
TWENTY-SIX

Vicki put on her robe and combed her hair before Juan picked up Bell for school. Looking into the mirror, she realized the doctor had been right, today she felt like a million bucks. When she kissed Bell goodbye, Bell insisted Vicki needed to kiss Juan, too.

"It's not like you haven't kissed him before." She made a cute face.

"She's right," Juan said, smelling freshly showered. The brush of his lips was quick but potent. His hand found her side, and his touch came soft yet warm against the curve of her waist. The second his lips pulled away, he dipped back in. This one lasted a breath longer. He tasted minty like toothpaste, with a hint of coffee, good coffee with cream.

When he left, she licked her lips and followed his suggestion to go back to bed. Closing her eyes, she thought about his kiss, about everything he'd done for them. She hugged her pillow and reminded herself that while she might not get forever, the here and now held promise.

She didn't wake up again until ten. The shower felt wonderful. In fact, *she* felt wonderful. She felt well. She'd barely combed her hair when she heard the doorbell ring.

Barefoot, wearing jean shorts and a pink I'M A GIRL T-shirt without a bra, she made her way to the door. Before she got there, her phone rang. Finding it on the coffee table, she checked the number.

It was Juan.

"Hi." She continued through the living room and peered at the door.

"Open the door. I have lunch."

"Lunch? Okay, you have officially gone too far." She opened the door.

"Never too far," he said.

Sweetie pranced in, followed by Juan with fast-food bags. The smell of burgers and fries reminded her she hadn't eaten. The sight of him smiling, looking way too official in his black Dockers and light blue button-down shirt, had her feeling underdressed.

He pressed his lips against hers. The kiss was no tongue, but all heat. He tasted like...

"Someone has been sneaking fries." She licked the salt and grease from her lips.

"Guilty as charged." He pressed his mouth to hers again. This time his tongue swept across her bottom lip. Gone was the taste of salt, but she savored a flavor that was...all Juan.

All want. All desire.

Sweetie barked. The kiss ended. Kneeling, she petted the dog. When she stood, she came up on her tiptoes and kissed him again. He pulled her against him, and she quickly became aware of her lack of bra. Her nipples tightened. Another tightness pulled low in her abdomen.

He continued kissing her as he slowly moved them toward the breakfast table. Setting the bag on the table, he pulled her closer.

"How are you feeling?" He ran his thumb over her wet lips.

"Good." She whispered the word against the pad of his finger and felt the damp desire pool between her legs.

"Not great?"

"Great," she said.

"Hungry?"

"Starving." She wasn't talking about food. But worried he might turn her down as he had last night, she reached deep for boldness, and grabbed for his belt buckle. She stared up into his dark eyes as she tugged the belt loose, slid it out, and tossed it across a chair.

His eyes brightened with a smile and heat.

"You sure—"

"Shh." She hooked her finger in his belt loop and gave him a tug. When his pelvis met hers, she felt the hardness behind his zipper.

Before she knew his intent, he scooped her up. As he caught her behind her knees, she looped her hands around his neck and shifted, wrapping her legs around his waist. Both of his hands cradled her butt. She tightened her legs around him.

His mouth stayed busy as he moved them to her bedroom. He gently placed her on the bed, then stood up and started unbuttoning his shirt. Below that, he wore a T-shirt. She watched him remove a shoulder holster with a gun and set it on her dresser. The gun should have made her nervous. It didn't.

He slipped the white tee up and over his head. His black hair fell back in place, looking only slightly mussed.

She stared at him shirtless, remembering seeing him like this when he'd been out jogging and wanting, aching to touch him.

He moved his hand to unbutton his pants. With a flick of a thumb, he released them, unzipped them. Then with a slow hand, he lowered them down his legs.

Her focus shifted to the huge bulge behind the blue fitted boxers. The empty ache between her legs became almost painful.

He grinned. "I guess I have to take your clothes off, too, huh?"

She started to reach down for her shirt.

"No. Let me." He eased in. Looking primitive, like an animal on the hunt, he moved toward her. With his knees on each side of her legs, hands bracketing her shoulders, he stared.

He didn't move. Or speak. Just devoured her with his eyes. She felt her nipples pressing against the cotton of her shirt. Then the backs of his hands brushed over her tightened nipples as he tugged it over her head.

She inhaled.

"No bra?"

She swallowed. "I wasn't expecting company."

He turned his hand over and took her left breast in his palm. He squeezed her nipple between his thumb and forefinger. She moaned.

"Beautiful," he said, staring at her as if hungry. Her nipples hardened even more, and she felt a line of pleasure trail straight down her abdomen to grow even stronger between her legs. She couldn't remember feeling herself go so wet so fast.

She wanted him. All of him. Inside her.

Reaching out, she caught the elastic waistband of his boxers.

He caught her hand. "No touching."

"Not fair." She brushed her other hand over his hard shaft behind the blue cotton.

He hissed and caught that hand, too. "You want that?" He glanced down. "You want it inside you?"

The boldness of his question brought heat to her cheeks.

"Do you?"

She swallowed. "Yes."

"Then you don't get to touch. Because if you touch, that's over."

"That's no fun." She tightened her thighs, the ache painful.

His smile was pure heat. "Oh, I'll make it fun."

He caught both her wrists and placed her hands over her head. "You keep your hands here." The sexy command sent sweet heat between her legs.

Releasing her wrists, he shifted his gaze to her breasts. "Did you know your lips are the same color as your nipples?"

She didn't answer. Her mind went to mush when he cupped both her breasts in his hands. Leaning forward, he took her right nipple into his mouth. He sucked her, hard, and when he released her, she lifted up, begging him not to quit.

But he sat up. The back of his hand slid down over her abdomen to the snap of her shorts. The touch, a mere caress, brought chills that were both cold and hot. He caught the button and released it. With a slowness that almost had her complaining, he lowered the zipper.

He pulled off her shorts, leaving her red panties on. After the shorts were tossed aside, he put one hand between her knees and, as if to savor every inch, he slid his hand up. The slow touch finally arrived at her thighs.

When he got to the V of her legs, he stopped.

"No," she muttered.

He grinned. "What do you want?"

When she didn't answer, he repeated, "What do you want? Tell me."

"Touch me," she said.

"Here?" He lifted his hand to her right breast and squeezed her nipple.

She moaned. Leaning in, he kissed her neck.

"Where do you want my lips?" He inched down. "Here?" He pulled the nipple into his mouth. "Or do you want them here?" He brushed his hand down her abdomen to the mound of her sex.

She moaned.

"Answer me."

"There." She lifted her hips.

"Here?" He tapped the entrance of her sex. The quick touch brought a gasp.

"Yes." She started to reach for him, then put her hands back over her head and resorted to begging. "Touch me. Please."

"Oh, I'm going to. But first I want to taste you." He kissed her abdomen. His tongue came out and left a trail of moisture down the top of her panties.

She let out a cry. "I'm ready." Without thinking, she reached out and tried to guide his hand between her legs.

"Wait," he said with more patience than she felt. "Just a little bit more."

"Seriously, I'm ready," she growled. "Get a condom."

He laughed. "Not yet." At least he touched her. His fingers slid under the elastic leg of her panties. He separated the folds of her sex. "Someone's wet."

She let out a low moan and nearly came, but he pulled his hand out.

"No." She gasped.

Gasped harder when she felt the sweep of her panties brushing down her legs. He caught her knees and pushed them apart. "Look at me. Watch me."

"I can't." She lifted her hips.

"Yes, you can. Look at me." His voice was deep. Entrancing. All sin.

She opened her eyes and lifted her head. His eyes, almost black, met hers. "Keep watching." He dipped his head down. His lips brushed against her. His tongue moved over her. She cried out. Her hips shot up. A finger entered her, and his tongue found her clitoris. Pleasure exploded.

Just when she could almost breathe, he slid another finger inside her, reached deep, and found a place that she was certain had never been touched. Pleasure that bordered on pain had her trembling.

She let out a sound, half moan, half cry. He moved on top of her. Then his mouth was on hers. He tasted like sex. Rolling her to the side, he pulled her against him. His arms held her tightly, her mind raced. Never had sex left her this... gone, weak, happy. She buried her face in his shoulder and tried to remember how to breathe.

It took several long seconds before she could open her eyes. When she did, he was staring at her. A smile widened his lips. His eyes were devil dark. Confident. "Have fun?"

"Yeah." Her face grew hot.

"Are you blushing?"

"No," she lied.

"Damn, you're precious." He pulled her closer. Her face landed on his shoulder. She felt his laughter against her cheek. The sound, so free, so honest, had her closing her eyes and savoring it.

She put a hand on his chest. "What about...?" She glanced down at the now bigger tent, pressing against her thigh. She could feel his hardness and his heat. The pulse of the sex had her wanting to give him as much as he'd given her. She imagined sucking him into her mouth. Taking it slow.

"I'm a little worried," he said.

She glanced down. "I don't think you've got any-thing—"

He laughed. "Oh, sweetheart. Not about that. I'm

worried I'm not going to last three seconds inside of you."

His grin was so sexy she wanted to laugh. And in that second she longed to hold on to the perfection of this moment, to how he made her feel beautiful, strong, happy. She wanted this to last. For them to last. Something about him...no, not something. *Everything.* Everything about him, from his ability to turn her to mush to the way he'd so easily won a scared five-year-old's trust. "That's okay. I'm two ahead of you anyway."

"Two?" He eased off the bed, his eyes locked on her.

Nodding, she watched him pull down his boxers. His sex, thick and proud, bounced out and reached for the ceiling. "Then let's go for three."

He found his pants on the floor and pulled a condom from his wallet.

She watched as he slid it on. The sweet ache started building between her legs again.

Easing onto the bed, he stretched out beside her. But he didn't instantly move on top of her. He touched her face. Her breasts. Finally, he slid his hand down between her legs. He knew how to touch. How to make a woman want. She was moving to the rhythm of his fingers when he pulled his hand away and moved on top of her. Spreading her legs, he found his place inside her.

He still took his time entering her. An inch at a time. Letting her body take him in. And she needed the time. Because there was a lot to take.

He set the pace. Slow at first. Then faster. Filling her, her muscles hugging his shaft. She wrapped her legs around his waist. He was right. He didn't last long, but it didn't matter. She came at the same time he did.

* * *

Juan didn't get back to the office until almost one. Not that he felt bad.

He felt...good. Walking-on-water good. When he moved past Mildred at her desk, he nodded.

"Hey. Stop," she said when he passed.

He swung around. "Yeah?"

She tilted her head and stared like a curious puppy. "You're smiling."

"Is that a crime?"

"No. How's that's precious little girl and her mom?"

"Good." He tried to rein in his smile. He couldn't.

"Dr. Murdock called and was looking for you. Said you had a lunch appointment with him."

"Shit." He'd forgotten his appointment with the precinct shrink. There went his smile. "I'll call him." His gut tensed. He'd had sex with Vicki and hadn't once thought of Angie. He knew she'd want him to move on, to be happy, but there was still something that felt wrong about it.

"I'm leaving early today," Mildred said. "I told Bell I had some books that belonged to my granddaughter that she's outgrown. I thought I'd drop them off at her house later. She told me she lives next door to you."

"Yeah," Juan said. "I'm picking her up from school later."

"Then I might see you." She stood and grabbed her

purse. "Ginger is taking over the desk. Warn Connor to be on his best behavior. She called him a dickhead. I think he slept with her and didn't call her back."

Juan frowned, even though he knew Connor was careful not to lead a woman on. Then for one second, he wondered if sleeping with Vicki didn't earn him the same title. Not that he planned to cut things off with her. But how far did he intend to let it go? The thought gave him pause.

"Juan?" Mildred said, as if she'd noticed he'd checked out.

"What?" Then he remembered. "Yeah, I'll tell Connor."

Juan walked into the office. Connor and Mark were both at their desks. He'd hoped they'd be out and wouldn't question his two-hour lunch.

"Heard anything from the morgue on Bates's body?" Juan asked Mark.

"No. Stone said he'd call when he had something."

Juan moved in. "Anything on that print they found on the car of Abby's shooter?"

"Nothing showed up on the Texas database. They're still running it in other states." Mark lifted his hands over his head and stretched. "My gut says he dumped the car and left the state."

"Yeah." Juan realized he should offer the print to Jody. He looked at Connor. "Mildred's leaving early. She asked me to tell you that Ginger is taking over the desk and you should lay low. She called you a dickhead."

Connor frowned. "I didn't even sleep with her. I flirted, that's all. We ran into each other in a bar and had a few drinks. Before the night was over, I knew she was looking for love, so I bowed out."

"Maybe that's the problem." Mark laughed and Juan joined in.

Connor glared over at Juan. "Enjoy my pain." Then he made a face. "Weren't you wearing a different shirt this morning?"

Juan looked down at his desk. Vicki had snagged his shirt and slipped it on, and she looked so good in it he'd told her to keep it and he went and grabbed a different one. "No."

"Yes, you were." Connor laughed. "Because Mildred mentioned we were dressed alike. You get lucky?"

"Stop." Juan heard Mark's chair turn toward him.

"Damn!" Mark said. "Good for you."

"I said stop." But Juan's smile reappeared.

A knock sounded on their open door. They all looked up at the redhead in the doorway. Her gaze shifted around the room, settling on Connor. Then her gaze moved to Juan.

"Someone's here to see you."

Juan noticed the tall man wearing jeans and a polo shirt standing behind Ginger. "Detective Acosta?" The man moved around the woman.

"That's me."

Ginger walked out. The man walked up to Juan's desk. "I'm Detective Sam Milbourn from LAPD."

CHAPTER
TWENTY-SEVEN

Crap. The cop looking for Vicki. Juan motioned to the chair in front of his desk, but had to work to keep his expression neutral. "How can I help you?"

"You called me." He lowered himself in the chair.

"Milbourn? Oh, yeah. A name came up in an investigation and I saw you had a bulletin out about a woman with the same name. A Vicki...Talbot?" He purposely got it wrong. Out of the corner of his eye, he saw Mark turn back to his desk, but the man wasn't an idiot. He'd probably figured out Juan was blowing smoke. He just hoped Milbourn wasn't in the smoke detection business.

"Trever. Vicki Trever."

"Right. I spoke with your partner. I explained our suspect was African American. He said the Trever you're looking for is white."

"Yes, but I was hoping to speak with the woman using the name. Maybe she knows my Trever."

"Wish I could help. I think I told your partner she disappeared."

"Did you get her address? I'm thinking Trever is hiding out around here. Maybe your suspect knows her."

"Like I told your partner, she gave false information. I ran her name hoping to find her. That's how I found your bulletin."

"What kind of case was she questioned in? Is she tied to a cold case?"

"Isn't that the Mitchel case?" Mark turned in his chair.

"Yeah," Juan replied. "A drug deal gone wrong. The buyer died on the scene. We thought the suspect in that case was the same one in an older case we're looking at. The first cop on the scene got the witness information. We tried to contact her and got shit."

"We were hoping to get a lucky break ourselves," Mark said. "Now we're suspicious she might even have been in on the drug deal. But from the officer's notes we know she was black. So definitely not the same chick."

Juan shifted the tension in his shoulders. Mark had his back. "If you get anything on a Trever that fits our description let us know. We'll do the same."

Milbourn frowned. "So you've got nothing that would help me locate this woman?"

"Not a damn thing," Connor added. "Frustrating as hell."

Juan leaned his elbows on his desk. His hands were sweating as he clasped them in front of him. Vicki thought other LAPD cops could be working with Valado and if so, Milbourn, Valado's ex-partner, would be in on it. The man sitting across from him could very well want Vicki dead. "This girl must be pretty important to bring you to Texas."

Milbourn's shoulders squared. "No, I'm...on vacation. Got family down here."

"In Anniston?" Connor grabbed a pen and tapped it against his desk. *Click. Click. Click.*

"No, uh, Red Clay." His voice came out tighter. "I touched base with my partner, he told me about your call. I thought why not drop by? Trever was my late partner's sister-in-law. She ran off with his kid."

"So a kidnapping," he said, wondering if Milbourn would correct him. When he didn't, Juan added, "Is the FBI on the case?" He knew they weren't.

The question appeared to put Milbourn on edge. "This is personal for me."

So he wouldn't even answer. Juan straightened the files on his desk, but never broke eye contact. "I get it."

"Yeah. I guess the drive over here was a waste of time." Milbourn's phone rang. He checked the screen, turned it off, then slid it back into his pocket.

"Sorry," Juan said. "If I get anything, I'll let you know."

"Yeah." Something about the way Milbourn said that one word had Juan worrying Milbourn wasn't buying the wrong-witness story. His footsteps echoed down the hall as he left.

Mark turned around and started typing on his keyboard. Connor focused on his computer screen.

Silence filled the office. The unnatural kind. The kind that waited. Waited for the other shoe to drop with a heavy dose of truth. "I owe you an explanation," Juan said.

"I figured you'd get around to it sooner or later." Mark turned in his chair.

"Me too." Connor pushed back from his desk and propped his feet up beside his keyboard.

"First, thank you." Juan knew he'd have done the same for them, but it didn't make it any less admirable.

"We're a team. Always," Mark said. "I trust that whenever I need to back either of you up, it's for a damn good reason. Until one of you proves me wrong, that's the way it'll be."

"I think that needs an amen," Connor said.

Juan told them about how he'd found out Vicki's real name. About calling the LAPD. About Pablo Valado faking his death. About calling Jody and her finding the logbook. And now looking into the murder of Marisol Willis.

"Do we have proof that Valado is alive?" Disbelief echoed in Connor's tone.

"Yeah, Vicki saw him," Juan stated with attitude.

Connor drummed his fingers on his desk. "Okay, we'll go with that."

Realizing he'd overreacted, Juan added, "There was some DNA found at Willis's murder. We think it could be Valado's. Jody's trying to get it rushed through the system, but you know how that is."

Mark turned around and started typing, but he tossed out another question. "So do you think the asswipe who was just here is dirty, too?"

"Yeah. It felt way off. I get wanting to help an old partner, but what he's not saying is that Valado was a suspect for his wife's hit-and-run death." Juan exhaled.

"I'm betting Milbourn doesn't have any family here. He seemed to pull that out of his ass."

"I smelled it, too," Connor added.

Juan started trying to put the pieces together. "I told Milbourn's partner that the witness was African American, so it couldn't be the same person. It doesn't even make sense that he'd come here to follow up."

"Unless he's desperate." Connor dropped his feet.

Juan ran a hand over his face. "Yeah. And if he is in on it, then I led him here."

"I don't think it's just you." Mark looked over his shoulder.

"What do you mean?" Juan asked.

"I checked Red Clay's bulletins. They've got your neighbor's picture up, saying she's a person of interest in a missing child case and might be in the area."

"Shit." Another dollar Juan owed Bell for the curse jar. As thoughts of Bell, innocent and afraid, whispered through his mind, it hit Juan that if Milbourn was here, Pablo could be as well. Was there any chance they knew where Vicki lived? Probably not. Or Milbourn wouldn't have come here. But doubt, fueled by fear, expanded Juan's rib cage. He stood and collected his gun.

"Why Red Clay?" Mark asked. "What's her connection there?"

"I don't know. But I'm picking up Bell early. I'll ask Vicki when I get there." He turned back. "I'm sending you Jody's contact info. Can you send her a copy of the fingerprint we got off the car the perp used in the Noel shooting?"

* * *

Pablo crushed the Coke can in his hand, imagining it was Sam Milbourn's neck, then slung it against the hotel wall. Why wasn't that bastard taking his calls? Pablo had called more than a dozen times last night. And at least that many since his plane had landed in Houston at six this morning. The calls went straight to voice mail, with the exception of one call. It rang a few times and then got disconnected. Had Sam turned off his phone?

He grabbed his phone and dialed the number again. "Answer or you're going to be sorry," Pablo muttered.

Killing Jefferies had been worth it. The man didn't know Vicki's exact location, but he gave Pablo her number with an area code around Red Clay, Texas. He even told Pablo about the saved message from the bitch warning Jefferies to be careful. Vicki suspected he'd killed Willis. Not that it mattered. Even if she told the cops all this, Sam would put up roadblocks. And there it was, a reason he needed Sam alive.

The line rang and when it didn't automatically go to voice mail, Pablo's hopes rose.

Turning around, he stared at the new laptop and clicked refresh to see if his tracker picked up the man's phone. He'd bought the laptop right after he'd left Jefferies's body at the storage unit. He'd found a tracking site and put in both Vicki's and Milbourn's phones. Most people didn't realize how easy it was to find someone through their phone. In fact, some spyware can get you within forty or fifty yards of a cell phone. Yeah, people could turn the location detector off, but most people didn't. He was counting on the fact that Sam was one of those idiots.

It had taken him almost three hours to drive to Red Clay from Houston. Unfortunately, a flight to any smaller town close to Red Clay would have required a ten-hour delay. He'd stopped twice at restaurants with Wi-Fi to see if either of them had turned on their phones. They hadn't.

He'd made a stop at a gun shop and bought a few weapons. A nice new Glock, a .38 Special for his ankle holster, and a knife. It was so much easier getting guns here than in California.

Funny how he felt naked without them.

Exhausted, not having slept in more than thirty-six hours, he'd gotten a hotel room. His plan had been to catch a few hours of rest while waiting for either Sam's or Vicki's phone to go online. He couldn't sleep. Not knowing that bitch was so close. Not fuming over Sam's disregard of his phone calls.

"Detective Milbourn," Sam finally answered.

"What the fuck?" Pablo seethed. "Why haven't you answered your damn phone?"

"This isn't your number and . . . my phone barely gets service here."

Could that be true? Sam wasn't answering because of poor service and he didn't recognize his number? "Where are you?" Pablo bit out.

"I'm in my car." Both Sam's vagueness and his tone set off more alarms.

"*Where* in your car?"

Sam's hesitation gave Pablo a shot of adrenaline that fueled his suspicions.

"I'm outside a restaurant in Red Clay. I haven't found anything yet."

Right then the Google map appeared on Pablo's screen, but he didn't know the area enough to know if the man lied without really checking the map.

"Why the fuck do I think you're lying?"

"Because you're paranoid," Sam said. "Why would I lie to you?"

"Because maybe you're thinking of stealing my money. Or you feel sorry for her."

"I don't want your dirty money. And I don't even know her." His voice again came out too high. A sign of a lie. "Why are you calling?"

"I got her number. She's somewhere around Anniston." Pablo kept looking at the screen, trying to see if Sam was where he said he was.

"Where did you get her number?"

Pablo stared at the Google map but couldn't figure out what town Sam was in. "From her piece-of-shit boyfriend. She's been calling him."

Sam gasped. "You killed him? Fuck!"

"I had to, he'd go to the police. Plus, Vicki told him I was alive. You're also right about her being in an abused women's program. He couldn't tell me which program or her location. But—"

"Damn it. I went to see Jefferies at his office. People will remember that."

"Don't worry, I hid his body." Pablo kept searching the map. "Exactly where are you?"

"I have to go. I'll call you later." Sam hung up. Furious, Pablo dropped down on the bed and pulled the computer closer to study the map. He finally got his bearings. That fucker had lied. He wasn't anywhere near Red Clay. He was in Anniston. Pablo caught a street name on the map and jotted it down.

Grabbing his keys and his laptop, he took off. There was a reason Sam was lying to him. And Pablo's gut said getting to the truth would lead him to Vicki.

* * *

Juan drove ten miles over the speed limit to reach Bell. He kept telling himself he was overreacting, but he needed to lay eyes on her and know she was fine. The more he thought about it, the more he realized that Milbourn showing up meant he was working with Valado. And the more he thought about that, the guiltier he felt for making that call. But maybe Mark was right. There had to be a reason Vicki's picture appeared in a Red Clay bulletin.

Either way, he'd been the one who led Milbourn to Anniston.

Parking in front of the school twenty minutes before Bell was due to get out, Juan gave the parking lot a check before leaving his car. Not seeing anything suspicious, he proceeded to the school office.

He didn't breathe until the office clerk said, "I'll get someone to bring her here."

Five minutes later, he walked to his car holding Bell's hand and listening to her tell him about her day. The girl looked up at him with so much trust, his chest tightened. He hoped like hell he hadn't put her in danger.

She climbed into her car seat in the back. He got behind the wheel and waited. "You buckled up?" He looked over his shoulder.

"Yes. Why am I playing hooky?"

"I figured your mom needed to see you, since she's been in the hospital."

She smiled. "She misses me when I'm at school."

"I know."

"Do you miss me, too?"

Her question almost hurt. He looked back at her and smiled. "Of course."

Her little face beamed.

As he drove off, his cell rang. He glanced at the number. Christina. Probably checking on Vicki. "Hey."

"Something weird happened." Her voice was too high-pitched.

"What?"

"I got a call from a manager at Finally Fit on Main. A cop came in with a picture of Nikki. He asked the receptionist if they'd seen her."

His hand clenched the steering wheel. "What did she tell him?"

"She gave him her address. He was a cop."

Juan's hand fisted around the steering wheel. "How long ago?"

"It just happened. What's going on, Juan?"

"Have to go. I'll call you later."

It'd take five minutes to get to Vicki's house. He looked back at Bell, who was distracted with pulling

a book out of her backpack, and then stomped on
the gas.

* * *

Vicki stared at her reflection in the bathroom mirror.
Juan should be here to deliver Bell soon, and the anx-
iousness she'd felt right after they'd had awesome sex
had grown.

Somehow, some way, she needed to get hold of her
runaway heart. Because she knew where it wanted to run.
To the hope, to the fantasy of forever. Where was her
cynical side that kept that dream at bay? Where was the
woman who kept her guard up with men? Where was
the woman who'd seen love as a weakness? A weakness
that had helped destroy her mom, that had killed Alison.

A weakness that could destroy her.

Was she feeling like this just because she was emotionally vulnerable right now? Had becoming a mother
awoken the more traditional dreams of happily ever after? Or was this gratitude for all he'd done?

Whatever it was, she needed to get it under control.

The doorbell rang. She hotfooted it to the dining
room window, hoping to see Juan's car.

Juan's car wasn't there, but an unfamiliar car was
parked in the street.

A knock sounded, loud and insistent.

Fear traveled down her spine. Her hands shook.

She went into the front bedroom, where she might be
able to see part of the porch.

Opening the blinds a sliver, she peered out.

She couldn't see the tall man's face, but she could see what he held. A smile widened her lips.

Flowers. Juan had sent flowers. Happiness filling her chest, she released the blinds and headed for the door.

* * *

Juan turned onto his street. A silver Honda sat in front of Vicki's house. Fuck!

He spotted a man standing at Vicki's door. Not Milbourn. He had darker hair. Pablo? He couldn't see the guy's face.

Juan's pulse raced. A glance in the rearview mirror brought up a dilemma. What should he do about Bell?

"Bell? Are you a big girl?" He hit his garage opener.

"Uh-huh," she said.

"I'm going to pull into the garage. I need to talk to your mom. Can you go in my house and take care of Sweetie for me?"

"Yes."

He parked in his garage. "We'll be right back. Stay in the house, okay?"

"Okay." She got out of the car.

When she disappeared inside, he slipped out the side door, grabbing his gun from his holster.

Finger on the trigger, he moved across the grass. He watched the man step around Bell's pink bike on the front porch. He heard Vicki's door open, and she let out a slight gasp.

Damn. He took off at a run. "Police! Don't move."

CHAPTER
TWENTY-EIGHT

Juan kept his finger on the trigger.

The man swung around. It wasn't Valado.

Vicki stood in the doorway, one hand pressed to her chest. In the other hand she held a huge vase of flowers. "What are you doing?"

"Who are you?" Juan asked the man.

The man's eyes widened in fear. "Ri-Richard Calder. I work for Yellow Rose Florist."

"Who sent the flowers?" Juan snapped.

"Aren't they from you?" Vicki asked.

"No." He focused on the man. "Who sent the flowers?" His gun inched closer.

"I . . . just deliver them. Isn't there a card?"

Vicki plucked the card from a plastic prong and opened it. "They're from Cal Phillips. Bell's friend's father."

Juan lowered his gun. "Sorry," he told the guy. "You can go."

He didn't need to be told twice. He bolted to his car.

"Come on." Juan holstered his gun.

"Where are we going?"

"My house."

"Where's Bell?"

"She's there. Let's move." He shut her door and nudged her forward, while looking down the street for cars.

They'd barely stepped into the garage when he heard an approaching vehicle. "Inside." He gave her a slight push. Almost closing the door, he peered out.

A black truck, one he recognized as belonging to a teen down the street, raced past.

"What happened?" Vicki held on to the vase of flowers as if they were her lifeline. A thought snuck in between his tiers of concern. He should have sent her flowers.

"Mama!" Bell called from the doorway entering the house. "I'm hungry."

"Let's go inside the house," Juan whispered, focusing on the problem at hand. Then he suddenly questioned if he should pile them in his car and get the hell out of town—or would Milbourn show up and see them? Perhaps recognize his car from the precinct?

He watched Vicki greet Bell. He hung back and called Mark to fill him in on what was happening.

"I'm on my way," Mark said.

Juan considered that. "No. Send someone else. Plainclothes. Milbourn saw you. Just have them here in case trouble starts, and if he leaves have them follow his ass. Valado could be here."

"Why follow him? Why don't we grab him now?" Mark asked.

"Without proof that Valado's alive or that Milbourn's involved, we've got nothing on him. And if Milbourn knows we've got Vicki and Bell, he could get an L.A. judge to order them returned to California. And we couldn't stop him."

"You're right," Mark said. "What's the plan?"

"Right now just send some backup in case Milbourn's not alone."

"You think Pablo's with him?" Mark asked.

"I don't know. But let's get Vicki somewhere safe and we'll figure it out."

"Okay, I'm sending someone now. Be careful." When Juan looked up, Vicki, still holding the flowers that should have been from him, stood in the doorway, worry etched in her expression. "Mark, I gotta go." He hung up.

"What's happening?" she asked.

He almost answered her, but Bell came and stood by her side. "Let's go inside the house," he said instead.

Vicki set the flowers on the coffee table. "Bell, watch TV. Juan and I need to have a talk." She picked up the remote and pointed it at the TV to turn it on.

"Hi, baby girl," Angie's voice spilled out.

Juan's chest tightened.

Vicki cut her gaze at him for one second, then found the other remote to turn off the DVD.

"Why can't I hear?" Bell asked.

"It's adult talk." Vicki gave Bell's shoulder a squeeze.

"Is he going to kiss you?" Bell smiled up.

"Watch TV," Vicki said.

Juan followed Vicki into the kitchen.

As stiff as a toy soldier, she faced him. "What's happening, Juan?"

"Detective Milbourn's in town."

Her chest lifted with a breath that came too fast. "Pablo's old partner?"

"Yes."

"Oh, God. He found us?" Fear welled up into her eyes.

"Christina called, said he showed up at the gym. He flashed his badge and someone gave him your address."

She cupped her mouth, tears filling her eyes. "How did he know we were here?"

A shot of acid burned Juan's stomach. "I called Los Angeles police, but—"

She stepped back. "You said you were helping us."

"I called when I first found your necklace. But I didn't tell them you—"

"I trusted you. How could you have done this?"

"I didn't... Vicki, you can trust me. I made up a story. But look, I don't think that's the only reason he's here. There's a bulletin with your picture on the Red Clay PD site. It's a town about forty miles from here. Do you have any connection there?"

"No. I..." Her eyes widened. "The flowers. Oh, God." She inhaled. "It was Alison's birthday. I sent flowers to her grave. I drove to Red Clay and I paid in cash. I didn't even sign the card. I didn't think Pablo would ever go to Alison's grave."

"He must've traced the flowers to that florist." He moved in and put his hands on her shoulders. "I didn't tell them you were here. I said it was a witness and I described someone who they'd know wasn't you. I was just trying—"

"It doesn't even matter. We have to leave." She turned.

He caught her. "It does matter. But right now you need to calm down. If you're scared, Bell will get scared."

She shook her head. "I need to get out of town. Out of Texas," she muttered.

"No. You're not running away this time. We are going to leave here. I just need to figure out a plan."

"You don't understand." Her voice became painfully low. "If Bell learns that her father's alive, she'll be terrified. I have to protect her." She swiped at a tear escaping from her lashes. "You saw what he did to her. I already failed on my promise to Mom to take care of Alison. I can't let Bell down. I can't."

"Look at me." He placed his hands on her shoulders again, could feel the fear vibrating off her. "I'm not letting anything happen. I've got the DEA in California and now my partners working this. I've already called Mark. We've got backup on the way now. Trust me."

She pulled in a deep breath. "You don't know what he's like. He's evil."

"He's not going—" His words were punctuated by the shrill ring of his doorbell.

"I'll get it," Bell called.

"No." Vicki and Juan tore out of the kitchen.

"Take her into the bedroom," he told Vicki.

As Vicki grabbed Bell and took off, Juan darted into

his dining room and peered out to see if a car was in his drive. There was one. But he recognized it and relaxed.

"It's okay," he called out.

He opened the door and motioned in Mildred, who held two bags.

Unfortunately, as she entered, he saw Detective Milbourn walking to Vicki's door. The man's phone rang and he pulled it out of his pocket. He answered the call, but then quickly dropped it back into his pocket.

"Shit," Juan muttered. *Was he alone?* He leaned to the left, but couldn't see the car that he must have parked on the street. Was Valado with him?

"What is it?" Mildred asked.

"Inside." Juan shut the door, fighting the urge to rush out, slam Milbourn against a wall, and demand answers. But his gut said that to ensure Vicki and Bell were safe, he needed to play this right.

* * *

"Mildred!" Bell barreled forward, arms open wide. The joy in her niece's voice was the polar opposite of what Vicki felt.

She watched the plump red-haired, grandmotherly woman embrace Bell.

"Hey, sweetheart," the woman said, patting Bell's back.

"Did you bring the books?" Bell asked expectantly. "Mom, she has some books that her granddaughter outgrew and said I could have."

"That's nice." Vicki's attempted smile felt like a deflated balloon.

"Hi, I'm Mildred," the woman said to Vicki.

"Can we go to my house? And bring Sweetie?" Bell glanced at Juan. "Please."

"No." From his tone and taut expression, Vicki's throat tightened.

"Why not?" Bell asked.

"We're staying here for a while." Vicki forced the words out.

"Oh." Bell looked at the bag Mildred held. "Can I see what you brought?"

"Sure." Mildred set the bag down, then looked from Juan to Vicki. She mouthed the words, *What's wrong?*

"Bell," Juan said, "why don't you go into my bedroom and spread everything out? We'll all come in and see what Mildred brought in a few seconds."

Bell tilted her head to the side as if she knew something was up.

"Go on," Vicki told Bell.

"More adult talk?" her niece asked.

Vicki picked up one of the bags and started for the bedroom. Bell followed. Vicki only stayed a second, then hurried back out to the living room.

Juan was talking to Mildred. But now he had his gun out. "It's too much to explain right now, but someone's outside Vicki's house and he can't know she's here."

"Milbourn's here?" Tiny pricks of fear crawled up Vicki's spine.

"Yes." Juan's shoulders tightened.

"We have to leave," Vicki said.

"Not now." He tapped his gun against his leg. "When

he goes." His gaze met hers. "We're safe. He doesn't know you're here."

Any semblance of safety shattered when the doorbell rang. "Shit!" Juan glanced at Mildred. "He probably saw you walk in. How good of a liar are you?"

She lifted a well-defined brow. "I've been known to tell a few tall tales."

"Good." The doorbell chimed again. "Act like this is your house. He's probably going to ask you about your neighbor. Say a woman lived there with a kid, but you haven't seen them in a week. Can you do that convincingly?"

"Piece of cake." The woman smiled with a bravado Vicki didn't share.

Juan touched her shoulder. "Go back in the bedroom." The doorbell chimed again. "I'll be behind the door in case he tries anything."

"You think...?"

"Go."

Pulse fluttering in her neck, she ran down the hall. Inside Juan's bedroom, she closed and locked the door. Bell, surrounded by books and puzzles, wore a Christmas-morning smile, but she took one look at Vicki and it disappeared.

"Why do you look scared?" Bell asked.

* * *

Pablo eased down the street where he'd last tracked Sam's phone. His soon-to-be-dead ex-partner answered the call, but hung up, then turned his phone off again.

Pablo stopped in front of a redbrick house. Suddenly the accuracy of the tracker's range of forty or fifty yards didn't feel so exact. Especially when the houses were so close together.

He studied the three houses. Sam had been here, visiting someone in one of these homes. Which one? Why? Was Vicki here?

If so, why was Sam keeping it from him? He had to be after Pablo's money. It couldn't be the logbook. Sam wasn't smart enough to open his own operation.

Right then he saw a pink bicycle on the porch of the white brick house next door. What was the chance that it was his kid's bike?

He almost pulled over, but a woman working in a flower bed across the street had turned and was studying him. Fucking great!

Driving off, he turned the corner and headed down the street parallel to the one he'd been on. The middle-income homes appeared abandoned. No doubt the owners mostly worked. He looked at the clock on his dashboard. It was a little early for schoolkids to be home. He passed six houses, believing one of these backed up the white brick house, then he parked between houses.

Before getting out, he looked left, then right. No one was around. He chose the house that didn't have a car parked in the driveway and moved to the side gate leading into the backyard. It was locked, but one good push got him inside. A dog barked next door.

Hurrying across to the back fence, he touched his Glock tucked into the side of his jeans, and glanced back to make sure he didn't see anyone in the house peering out the window. He didn't. The sound of someone's air-conditioner turning on filled the hot air.

A drop of sweat rolled down his brow. Hesitating, he peered through the fence slats to confirm he was at the right house. The white brick structure on the other side told him he was.

He hoisted himself up and over the fence. His feet landed with a thud. The nearby dog barked harder. He pulled out his gun, the weight of it feeling good in his palm.

Moving past a lawn chair, he took everything in. There were toy dishes on the side of the concrete patio. Was this Vicki's house? Was she home? The thought of being this close to her made his dick hard.

He peered in the living room window. On the sofa were a couple of stuffed animals and a blanket.

He went to the back door, turned the knob. Locked.

Afraid the sound of breaking the window might get the dog started again, he stuffed his gun back into the waistband of his jeans and pulled out his wallet. Before he'd become a cop, he'd gotten quite handy with credit-card entry. Some of the newer locks were designed better, but this one didn't look that new.

After only a couple of minutes, the lock gave. Gun back in his hand, he quietly stepped onto the wood floor. It creaked with his weight. He stopped and listened. Only the sound of the refrigerator making ice filled the house. The lack of noise told him no one was home. On the floor were a couple more toys. Beside them was a basket with some clothes in it.

He moved over to the basket. Picking up a woman's shirt, he mentally sized it up to Vicki's frame. It would fit her. Then he found a few kid-sized pink T-shirts.

This was their house, he felt it.

Why had Sam lied? Yup, he had to be trying to get the money for himself. A need to put a bullet right between that bastard's eyes bit hard.

Pablo let his gaze shift around the living room. And since Sam had been here, did that mean the money wasn't? He moved into the kitchen and opened the door leading out to the garage. A small Toyota was parked there.

A slight groaning sound had him turning around. Was someone home? Or just a water pipe creaking?

Light spilled out of a door left ajar down the hall. He went to the door and peered in, easing it open.

A feminine scent filled his nose as he scanned the empty bedroom. For sure it was her. He remembered her smell. Remembered wanting to fuck that smell. Adrenaline pumped through his body.

He moved to the bed. His gaze shifted, catching on the man's shirt hanging off the bedpost. So she had a man, did she? He was going to miss her.

A small suitcase sat open on the other side of the bed. Some clothes hangers lay scattered beside the luggage. He turned to the opened closet. It had a few clothes in it, but there were several more empty hangers left on the floor, as if someone had grabbed some things quickly and fled.

Fuck. Where was she? Did Sam have Vicki?

CHAPTER
TWENTY-NINE

Juan lowered his car visor. The setting sun beamed right into his eyes. Twisting his shoulders, he felt his gun pressing against a bruised rib. Probably the one Vicki had kicked. He wanted to pull the weapon out, but feared it would make Bell or even Vicki nervous.

Glancing in the rearview mirror, he saw Bell sleeping in her car seat with Sweetie asleep on the seat beside her. He reached under his shirt, lifted the gun out, and set it in the side pocket of the rented SUV Mark had picked up for them. He studied Vicki, seat back, eyes closed in slumber. The stress wrinkle between her brows had finally smoothed out.

It had been so tempting to send someone else to watch them while he went looking for Milbourn and possibly Pablo, but he couldn't imagine trusting their safety to someone else.

Besides, Vicki didn't trust that easy. Hell, she didn't

even trust him right now. His grip on the steering wheel tightened.

She'd been so upset about his call to LAPD that she'd barely spoken while they'd been at Mildred's, waiting for Mark to deliver a rental car. Since there was a slight chance Milbourn might suspect he was involved, Juan had left his vehicle behind.

Milbourn had driven off right after Mildred told him she hadn't seen her neighbor. She'd played her part perfectly. Juan owed her. Shortly after that, two plain-clothes officers parked in front of his house. But they'd been too late to follow Milbourn.

Juan had made quick work of grabbing the essentials at Vicki's house and they'd driven to Mildred's, where he'd decided the safest place to go was his and his brother's cabin on Piney Lakes. A hundred miles away from anything connected to Vicki's location in Anniston, it felt like it offered safety.

The drive on the quiet, curvy country road was sleep-inducing. How many trips up here as children had he and his brother spent sleeping the entire drive? His parents had bought the place when he'd been six, back before his dad had started really drinking and before the property shot up in value.

Right then the burner cell phone in his pocket rang. Another thing Mark had provided. The shrill sound shattered the silence. He answered it quickly, hoping it wouldn't wake up his sleeping passengers.

"Yeah?" He spoke in a low voice.

"Hey," Jody's chipper voice echoed across the line. "We got him."

"Got...him?" he asked, not wanting to say the man's name in case Bell was listening. He cut his eyes to the rearview mirror. She hadn't stirred. "Him?"

"Not him."

"You got the DNA back already?"

"Not that, either. I had one of my men go recheck the Willis crime scene, hoping we might find something the LAPD missed. We struck gold. The woman had a nanny cam. And you'll never guess who's on it."

"You sure it's him?"

"It's not the best image, but it was good enough that I just put out an APB on his ass. We're going to catch him. Oh, and that's not all. Can you handle some more good news?"

"Try me."

Vicki shifted in her seat and he glanced that way. Her gaze met his and she reached down to raise her seat.

He smiled at her. "What else you got?" he asked Jody.

"The print from the car that your partner sent. The one you think belongs to Noel's shooter? I got a match. It's from a Robert Duarte. U.S. Marshals picked him up about thirty minutes ago. I'm going to talk to him shortly. But get this: We learned he had ties to an Alexander Esparza. We don't know a hell of a lot about Mr. Esparza, except he had some drug issues about six years ago, but he had some fancy lawyer and got off. We've had him on our radar since then, but couldn't get shit on him. I think this is our Rex. The same guy who you thought was supplying the Guzman gang when you were undercover. And Esparza is mentioned in the logbook. I think you finally got your man. I know this has to feel good."

It did feel good. "Thank you," he said.

"We got someone looking into Milbourn now, but I told your partner if you run into him again, drag his ass in. We got enough to question him. I'll update you if I get anything."

"Yeah." He hung up.

Vicki peered in the backseat to check on Bell. "What is it?" she asked in a whisper.

His smile widened, but not knowing if Bell was awake, he chose his words wisely. "We got the proof you were hoping we'd get."

"On..." She mouthed the word *Pablo*. "That he's alive?" Her eyes widened.

He nodded.

Tears filled her gaze. "For real?"

"Yeah," he said.

She pressed a hand over her mouth. Then pulled it away and brushed a tear off her cheek. "I can't believe it."

"You can," he said.

She exhaled and it sounded like a pound of worry left her chest. "Have they got him in custody?"

"No. But Jody put out an all-points bulletin."

She leaned in closer. "In L.A. or here?"

"There for now. But—"

"What if he's already here?" Fear filled her eyes. "Isn't that what you think? Why we're—"

"We'll put one up here, too, just in case. And we don't know if he's here or if it's just Milbourn. That's why we're going to the cabin." He reached over and took her hand in his.

She looked down at their joined hands. When she glanced up, some of the fear had vanished. "I'm sorry."

"For what?" he asked.

"Everything, but mostly for...getting upset earlier about not trusting you. You've done so much and I know it seems like I don't appreciate it."

"You're worried. I get that."

The momentary silence was shattered when Bell let out a piercing scream. "Stop! Stop!" she pleaded.

His gaze shot to the rearview mirror. Bell fought against the restraints of her car seat. Her legs kicked, and her tiny hands punched into the air. Sweetie whined on the seat next to her.

"It's okay," Vicki said. "It's just a dream, baby." She unbuckled her seat belt and bolted over the console to get to the child.

Juan pulled over to the side of the road. He remembered Vicki telling him Bell sometimes had nightmares about what her father had done.

He curled his own hands into fists, fury curled inside his gut as he listened to the child's screams.

* * *

Holding Sweetie, Vicki watched Juan carry Bell up the cabin steps. Once on the porch, she gave the area a quick glance. Night claimed them. The darkness clung to the trees like a threat. Only a few lights showed in the distance. She hoped Juan was right about them being safe here.

It had taken Vicki fifteen minutes to get Bell to calm down. No doubt the crazy day and sensing Vicki's panic had stirred up the nightmare. They'd stopped off and gotten hamburgers and shakes. Then Bell fell back asleep.

Vicki, arms full of some of her things and a poodle, shut the door and put the dog down. Standing in the living room, Vicki glanced around. The fishing cabin, as Juan had described it, wasn't as rustic as she'd imagined it.

"I'll put her in one of the bedrooms," Juan said.

She nodded, taking in the granite countertops and a tile floor that looked like wood. The walls held posters of different kinds of fish. The sofa and chair were brown leather and huge. The kind you sank into and didn't want to leave.

Juan said the cabin had been left to his brother and him when his parents had passed. When more cabins started popping up and the lake became a little bit of a tourist area, they'd done some work on it and rented it out as an Airbnb. Luckily it was empty for the next week.

She set down a bag of snacks Juan had picked up when he'd gotten gas and leaned her baseball bat against the wall.

You know I have a gun, right? Juan had asked when she'd added the bat to the list of things to get from her place. She'd said it had belonged to her father and had sentimental value, which wasn't a complete lie. The fact that the sentiment had nothing to do with her dad shouldn't be important. The baseball bat was her security blanket.

Juan walked out. "Bell's awake and requesting your presence."

"Thanks." Vicki stepped into the bedroom and Bell held on to Sweetie like a teddy bear.

"Hey." Vicki sank into the mattress beside her niece.

The child looked up, sleepy and concerned. "Why did we come here?"

Vicki had known she would ask, but she hadn't come up with the best answer yet. "Uh, Juan wanted us to see his cabin."

"And that's all?" she asked.

"Yeah." God, she hated lying to a child.

"'Cause you're acting the same way you did when we left Phoenix and California. We're not leaving, are we?" Worry pulled at her thin voice.

"Not yet." Vicki pushed a strand of hair off her face.

"I don't want to leave. I love Sweetie and Juan. I know he's not your boyfriend, but you said he was a good guy. I like it here." A soft whimper left her lips.

The air in Vicki's chest thickened. "Honey, we're not—"

"And I like Mildred. And Suzie. I don't want to leave."

Vicki inhaled. "I'm not saying we're going. We'll have to see, okay?"

Bell's brown eyes glistened with tears. "Don't you like it here? Juan's nice. He likes you, even if you aren't his girlfriend. Don't you like him?"

"Yeah, I like him." *Too much.*

* * *

Juan came in with more of their things from the car just as Vicki stepped out of the bedroom.

"Do I need to grab some more stuff?"

"No. I've got it all. You have to be exhausted." He worried the stress might bring on another infection. He probably shouldn't have had sex with her, either.

"Did you want to put her in her pajamas? I got her clothes."

"Nah. She's asleep." Vicki looked around. "Who decorated this place?"

"Christina and . . . Angie. With directions from Ricky and me. No lace, no overabundance of throw pillows, no Norman Rockwell paintings."

"Norman Rockwell?" She looked up.

"He's an artist born in the late 1800s. Did nostalgic paintings of life, wholesome scenes. Family dinner stuff."

"I know who he is. My mom had some of his prints."

"So did my mom. She had them all over our house." He ran a hand over his face. "I think she thought if she hung enough of them on the walls, we'd become like the paintings."

Vicki lifted a brow. "I guess that's why my mom liked them, too." She yawned.

Juan moved in and pulled her against him. Damn, she felt good. "You okay?" He looked down at her.

"Yeah."

He gazed into her eyes. "Don't forget to take your antibiotic." He motioned to where he'd set out her pills on the counter.

She locked her hands around his neck. "Thank you for everything you're doing."

"You don't have to say thank you."

"I do. While my mama had many flaws, she insisted on manners."

"She did a good job," he said.

"I wouldn't go that far. In fact, most of my parenting skills come from doing the opposite of what she did."

"Sorry." His body responded to her closeness, but he told his libido to take a hike. She needed rest.

She pulled away. "Can I get a glass of water?"

"You don't have to ask. Actually, sit down and I'll get it for you."

"I can—"

"Sit," he said.

She did as he told her and he set the water and bag that contained her pills in front of her. He went to pull out her pills and her phone spilled out too.

He looked at it. "You took the batteries out of it like I asked, right?"

"Yeah. They're in the bag, but no one has this number except Joanne Butler."

"Just to be safe. Cell phones are traceable by anyone. I left mine at home. I'm using a burner right now."

She took the pill, then stood up and moved to the bag with the snacks. "It claims I need to take it with food."

She pulled out a pack of the mini powdered donuts he'd picked up at the service station when he'd gotten gas, opened it, and ate one. Moving to stand in front of her, he brushed some white sugar off her bottom lip. She set the donut package down and looked up. "Is it really going to be over?"

"Yeah."

"Has the DNA come back?"

"Not yet."

"Then how do they know he's alive?" The worry crease between her brows deepened.

"One of Jody's men went back to the scene and found Willis had a nanny cam."

Tears filled Vicki's eyes. "She was so nice. She didn't deserve this."

"I know." He put his hands on her shoulders. She leaned her head on his chest. They stood like that for over a minute. Her gentle weight felt good against him. Crazy how good someone leaning against you could make you feel stronger, more solid, grounded.

He moved his hands down to her waist and she inched closer to him. He started swaying side to side. The only sound echoing in the cabin was of their feet sliding on the tile. Even the appliances seemed to hold their breath. His hand eased up and down her spine.

"Are we dancing?" A hint of humor laced her words.

"You like to dance?" He peered down at her.

"I like this. But I suck at dancing," she said.

He smiled. "I doubt that."

She set her chin on his chest and looked up at him. Her hazel eyes held the slightest smile. The wrinkle between her brows had smoothed out again. Dipping his head down, he pressed his mouth against hers.

He let himself savor the moment, the sweetness of powdered donuts, the softness of her mouth. As he was about to pull away, she deepened the kiss.

When it ended, he brushed a finger over her lips. "You know, I don't think...You should rest tonight. In fact, if you'd prefer you have the master, I can sleep on the sofa. Or you can sleep with Bell." He paused. "I mean, I don't know how sleeping arrangements are handled with children."

Vicki's front teeth pressed into her bottom lip. "To be honest, I haven't dealt with it yet. Wait, I take that back. When Alison and Bell lived with me and Dan..." She stopped talking. "It wasn't an issue. This shouldn't be, either."

"Good," he said, but thinking about her sleeping with another man didn't feel that good. He pushed that thought away. "This morning was amazing." He swiped her bottom lip, still damp from their kiss, with his thumb.

"I know." Her smile reached her eyes, then she shifted her gaze to the table.

He saw the silk flowers there and remembered the arrangement she'd gotten earlier. He glanced back at Vicki and the confession just slipped out. "I should have sent you flowers today instead of Suzie's dad."

"No. You didn't—"

"Yeah," he said, not liking the jealousy he heard in his voice. "I don't like the way he looks at you."

She chuckled. "You know I've never...I've hardly spoken with him."

"I know." His hand lowered to the small of her back. "I'm...rusty at the whole relationship thing."

"Me too." She chuckled. "Maybe I should've sent you flowers. I think the score was three to one." No sooner than the words left her lips, her face blushed and he could tell she wished she hadn't said that. He liked her mix of shyness and brazenness. He liked her.

He laughed. "As it should be." He felt blood start to pump south. "I'm happy you moved next door."

"So am I." She brushed his bangs off his forehead. "But seriously? I've turned your life upside down."

"Yeah, but it needed turning."

She kissed him. While his tongue slipped inside her mouth, her hand slipped under his shirt. The brush of her soft palm moving over his abdomen had him hardening. When it ended, he asked, "You sure you shouldn't just rest?"

"I'm sure," she said seductively.

"Then you want to move to the bedroom?"

She nodded. They left the living room. He shut and locked the door. Her hazel gaze looked up at him with desire.

He grinned. "You're going to have to keep from screaming this time."

"I did not scream." She moved toward him, her hips swaying.

He laughed. "You did."

He caught her and pulled her close. She started unfastening his shirt. Her touch, easing down a button at a time, had him holding his breath.

When he lost his outer shirt, he pulled off his shoulder holster and gun and set them aside. Then he tugged his T-shirt up, slow and easy, for her pleasure.

She moved in and slid her hands down his chest

again. Palms soft as silk brushed down his stomach, but stopped at the waist of his jeans. He kicked off his shoes. She kissed his chest as he loosened his belt and unzipped his pants.

She took a tiny step back and her smile came off as sexy, sweet, and so soul-spinning that the world as he knew it spiraled out of control. His life was changing. Right now, right here... with her.

He caught the hem of her shirt, pulled it up and off. Her bra, the same pink as her shirt, was almost too pretty to take off. Almost. Reaching behind her, he released the hooks without a hitch.

The sexy fabric slipped to the floor. Her breasts were soft globes with dark rose-colored tips. Globes that fit perfectly in his palms.

"Damn, you're pretty." He unsnapped her shorts and added them to the pile of clothes at their feet.

He eased her closer to the bed.

When the backs of her knees came against the mattress, she fell back. Leaning up on her elbows, she stared, bold and brazen, at the bulge behind his boxers.

He ran his thumb under the elastic of his underwear. "You think I could lose these?"

She nodded and her cheeks blushed again.

His body, already primed and pumped, begged for release. "Only if you remove yours."

She reached down, lifted her hips, and slid off her panties. He got harder at the peek of moist pink skin between her legs.

"Your turn." Her words came out breathless.

He pushed the cotton down his legs. Hard and ready, he stepped out of the clothing and crawled into the bed. She slipped her hand down between their bodies and fisted his sex.

A moan escaped his lips. "I don't know how much of that I can handle."

"Then I guess you'll have a hard time with this, too." She pushed him on his back and eased down the mattress. He watched as her lips came around his shaft and took him deeper. His sex throbbed. He let her take him inside her mouth once more before he pulled away. "I want to be inside you." He got out of bed and rolled on a condom.

Back in bed, he slipped his hand between her legs and found her wet and ready. As eager as he was to find release, once he pressed himself inside her, he wanted to savor the feeling.

Slow and easy. In and out. Deep, then shallow. Gentle moves. Staring into her eyes, he entered her harder with each stroke. Her breathing came quicker. Her eyes closed. When she came, she bent her head back and a sweet sound of pleasure spilled out. He pressed his mouth against hers and caught the sound.

When she finished, he grinned. "Told you, you screamed."

She blushed again. He laughed. He pulled her closer, then sank into her again. "Damn this is good. Come again," he growled. "Come on. Do it, Angie." His orgasm hit. He went to pull her against him, but she stiffened. "You okay?"

"Yeah."

"I didn't hurt you, did I?"

"No."

The words *I love you* climbed up from that soft place in his chest and sat on the tip of his tongue. Then, unexpectedly, an image of Angie filled his mind and the words dissolved. How, he wondered, could he feel so goddamned wonderful and guilty at the same time?

* * *

He'd called her Angie. That hurt. It could've been just a slip of the tongue. It could've been...But the sex had been...more intimate, more...Juan had made love to her. Now she couldn't help but wonder if in his mind he'd made love to her or his late wife?

Stepping from the shower, she donned a nightshirt and walked back into the bedroom. The patio doors were open. She moved over and saw Juan standing there, staring out. He'd slipped on a pair of sweats but was shirtless. When she noticed the tightness of his shoulders, fear hit.

"Is someone out there?" she asked, hugging herself.

He turned around. "No. It's fine. I just stepped out." His gaze met her eyes. "Your worry wrinkle is back."

She reached up and ran a finger over the center of her forehead.

"It's safe here." He reached for her, slipped his arm around her shoulder. "I'm not going to let him hurt you. Trust me, okay?"

She looked up at him. "I do," she said. And it was

mostly true. She trusted him with her life. It was her heart she worried about.

Not that she could be angry about it. She'd gone into this knowing he still loved his wife. He was helping her. They were attracted to each other. They were adults. She just needed to remember that this wasn't a happily-ever-after fairy tale.

In fact, when it was over, she'd be going back to Los Angeles. Connecting with her old clients. Restarting her business. Resuming her life. She just needed to enjoy this for what it was. Respect. Attraction. And good sex.

She needed to protect her heart. And Bell's, she thought. She wasn't the only one falling for Juan.

Her lingering thought of returning to California and restarting her business reminded her of who wouldn't be there. Marisol. "I'm going to check on Bell."

* * *

Juan watched Vicki walk back inside, leaving him alone on the balcony. Was he just imagining something was wrong with her because of what he was feeling?

He ran a hand down his face. His fingers still smelled like her. He looked up at the sky. The stars were bright, and a breeze shifted in the trees. How many times had he come to the cabin since Angie had died and stood in this very spot and talked to her like she was still here? He glanced back inside. He'd made love to Angie in that same bed.

Right then, his phone, left in the kitchen, rang. As

he moved to answer it, he noted the time on the bedside clock. Eleven-thirty. Who would be calling...?

He checked the number before answering. Jody's number stared back at him. "Hey... what's up?"

"I'm afraid this call isn't going to be good," she said.

CHAPTER THIRTY

Juan stood in the kitchen, hating every word Jody spilled.

"Shit," he muttered when she stopped talking.

Right then he heard footsteps behind him. He turned.

"What is it?" Vicki asked.

The look in her eyes had his stomach clenching. This was going to hurt her.

"Okay," Jody's voice carried through the line. "I'll call you if we learn anything else."

"Yeah." He hung up.

"What is it?" Vicki repeated.

He motioned to the sofa.

"What? It wasn't Pablo on the tape? They don't believe me anymore?" She dropped down. The couch sighed with her weight. She gazed at him and clenched her hands in her lap.

"It's not that." He sat beside her and considered how to tell her, but realized there was no good way. "Jody's men weren't able to contact Dan Jefferies. So she sent them to his house. His car was there but no one answered. They went around back and found a window had been broken."

Her eyes went round, then she shook her head. "No. He...he could still be in Denmark. He could have taken an Uber to the airport. He did that sometimes."

He reached for her hand. "His luggage was there. And they found some smears on his floor that they think are blood."

She gasped. "Please, no!"

He squeezed her hand. "I'm sorry."

Her eyes closed. Tears still leaked out. "It's my fault. First Marisol and now Dan." She drew in a shaky breath.

"Hey." He touched her face. "Look at me. This is not your fault."

"Yes, it is. He wouldn't have gone after them if not for me."

"I get that, but you didn't have anything to do with what he did. You can't be responsible for what some monster did."

And just like that, his own words echoed inside him. How many times had he heard those same words from Dr. Murdock?

Now, for the first time, he believed them. "Look at me," he told Vicki. "Don't start blaming yourself. I did that. I took the blame for Angie's and the baby's deaths. Right now, knowing you are about to do the same thing makes me realize how wrong I was. How wrong you'll be to take that on. Don't do it."

He held her and let her cry. It took almost twenty minutes before she stopped. But she didn't move and neither did he. It was another ten minutes before he heard Bell call out. "Mama?"

"Right here." Vicki jumped up and brushed the tears off her cheeks. "What's wrong, baby?"

"I need to use the bathroom."

Vicki disappeared down the hall. In a few minutes, she walked back in. "She's a little nervous. I'm going to sleep with her."

Standing, he went to Vicki and pulled her closer. "You okay now?"

She nodded. He knew she was lying, but he didn't know what to say to make her feel better. As he watched her move back into the bedroom where Bell was, he hoped it didn't take her three years to shed the guilt.

Sweetie came up to him and barked.

"You gotta potty, too, huh?"

She danced from side to side. He found her leash and his gun. Right then his phone dinged with a text. He grabbed his phone and stepped outside.

It was from Jody again. He read it. More bad news.

She'd talked to Noel's shooter. He claimed he didn't know Esparza, but when asked about Pablo Valado, he admitted knowing him and even gave the alias the man had been using.

Jody had checked flight records and found the man had flown to Texas this morning.

Fuck. He dropped his phone back in his pocket.

Knowing for sure the man was in Texas sent a shot of adrenaline to his gut.

* * *

A noise out on the bedroom patio had Juan jackknifing out of bed. Fear shot pain through his veins. He snatched his gun off the bedside table and went to the sliding glass doors. The second he pulled back the curtain, he saw a raccoon haul ass across the railing.

Breathing too fast, Juan glanced at his phone on the bedside table. It was three. He hadn't slept a wink.

He remembered how devastated Vicki was hearing the news about Jefferies. Was she sleeping or, like him, wide awake worrying?

He walked out of the bedroom. From the hall, he could see a light on in the other bedroom. He eased the door open. The lamp on Vicki's side of the room was on. She had her back to him, so he couldn't see if she was asleep or awake. Silently, he moved into the room.

Her eyes were closed. She lay so close to Bell, he couldn't tell where one ended and the other began. In fact, Vicki's arm rested across Bell as if to protect her. That had him remembering how the child had screamed in her nightmare on the drive up here. Damn, if the need to protect her didn't swell in his chest as well.

The golden hue from the bedside light made them look like a painting. A Norman Rockwell painting. Even when they were asleep, the love between these two was apparent.

Juan's chest grew tighter. Part of him wanted to crawl

into the bed, become a part of the picture, to be a part of a family and love. Then he remembered he'd had a family. Almost had one. Closing his eyes, he envisioned Angie, her stomach round with his daughter.

He left and walked back into his bedroom. He stared at the pile of clothes on the floor. The guilt from when he and Vicki made love returned and had his lungs feeling as if they might explode.

"Damn it!" He stood up, grabbed a blanket, a pillow, and his gun, and went to sleep on the sofa.

* * *

At six-thirty Saturday morning, Pablo sat in the hotel's restaurant, his computer on, nursing a cup of coffee and a foul mood. Neither Sam's nor Vicki's phones had come online. But fuck, he was losing patience. Fury burned his stomach, while lack of sleep burned his eyes.

He was half tempted to go back to California and kill Sam's wife and child. Right now, killing someone would feel good.

The waitress moved in and set a plate down. He looked down. "What the hell? I didn't order scrambled eggs."

The waitress smiled. *Smiled.* "Oops, sorry."

"Sorry? I fucking told you I wanted my eggs sunny-side up."

"I-I'll get you a new plate." Her frown tightened, and she reached for his plate.

"Hurry, and I'm not fucking paying for it. And refill my coffee. It's cold."

Scowling while still smiling at him the way only a Southern woman could, she backed away.

He'd been about to ask for her manager, but something on his screen flickered. He pulled it closer. "Finally!"

Vicki's phone was on. "Where are you?" He held his breath, waiting for a location to pop up.

Finally, a Google map came up. He studied it. Where the hell was Piney Lakes, Texas? Then again, it didn't matter. All that mattered was she was there. And he'd be there soon enough.

* * *

Vicki woke up at almost eight that morning. The emotion in her chest felt too heavy. Part of her wanted to close her eyes, go back to sleep and forget.

"You finally awake?" Bell asked, stuffing her things back in her backpack.

"Almost," Vicki said. She'd been aware that Bell had been awake for a couple of hours.

"Did you see the book about bugs that Mildred gave me?" Bell held up a book.

Vicki gave her niece a forced smile. "No. I didn't see it."

"You want me to read it to you?"

"Let me wake up and we'll do it later. Okay?"

Bell nodded, looked at the book, then frowned. "I remembered something."

"What?" Vicki asked, worried it was about Bell's father.

"About me having a dream in the car. Do you think Juan thinks I'm a baby for waking up and crying?"

Vicki's heart suddenly felt swollen, and each beat made it feel more bruised. The child had no idea how brave she was, considering all that had happened. "No. He understands it was just a nightmare."

She reached over and took Bell's hand in hers. "You know I love you, right?"

"Uh-huh. Do you think Juan loves me, too?"

Damn. "Why wouldn't he?" she said, again aware this was going to hurt Bell when things ended. Vicki kissed her. "I'm going to go see if I can find some coffee to make."

* * *

"Wake up," Bell said in a singsong voice.

"Bell!" Vicki, sitting at the kitchen table, scolded when she saw the girl kneeling beside the sofa next to Juan. "I told you to play silently and let him sleep."

"He opened his eyes before I said anything." Her little-girl whine came with an extended lower lip.

"She's right. I was awake." Juan sat up and ran a hand through his sleep-mussed hair. His dark eyes met hers and she remembered crying on his shoulder last night about Dan. Dan, who was probably dead. She recalled Juan telling her she couldn't harbor the guilt. His words had helped more than he knew. But with that relief came another memory and a pang of regret. She remembered him calling her Angie when they'd made love.

A mix of emotions pulled apart the happiness and the hope she'd clung to the last few days. She looked away from him and at Bell, who stared at the floor as if Vicki had hurt her feelings.

"I'm sorry," Vicki said to Bell.

Juan touched Bell's shoulder. "It's all good, isn't it?"

Nodding, Bell asked, "You want me to read to you? It's about a girl who hates bugs. I know all the words but a few."

Juan smiled. "Do you hate bugs?"

"A little. You want me to read it to you?"

"Let me make some coffee and then you can read it to me." He ruffled Bell's hair, and the sweet gesture sent an ache to her chest.

Vicki watched as he stood, giving Bell his back, and bent down to pull a gun out from under the cushion. No doubt he thought seeing the gun might scare Bell. He was right. It scared Vicki. Seeing it reminded her that they were still in danger.

With the weapon against his bare abdomen, he walked into the kitchen and put it in a cabinet, high above Bell's reach.

Turning, he sniffed the air and looked around. "You made coffee?"

"Yeah. I found it in the cupboard."

He faced her. Her gaze went to his bare chest. Then, so as not to stare, she glanced at the table. "I hope you don't mind, I plugged in your computer."

"Of course not."

She stood, poured him a cup of coffee, doused it with cream she'd found in the fridge, and held it out to him.

"Thank you." He took the cup but continued to

study her as if trying to read her emotions. "You sleep okay?"

"Yeah. Why don't you get dressed and I'll get the donuts out."

"Okay." He reached up and ran his finger between her brows as if pointing out her worry line. The touch doubled the lump of achy pain in her chest. The kind that usually came when someone you loved touched you when you were angry.

She reminded herself of two things: One, she didn't love Juan. She couldn't. And she'd keep telling herself that for as long as it took to believe it. Two, she couldn't be mad at him. Who knew what would've happened if he hadn't been here these last few days?

"You sure you're okay?" His words came out as a whisper that brushed against her sore heart.

"Fine." She stepped back.

* * *

Five minutes later, they were all at the table eating donuts. Juan had downed six mini powdered donuts and was still hungry. Vicki hadn't finished two. She sipped coffee without talking. Bell never stopped talking, about Sweetie, about bugs, and asking him about all the different fish on the posters on the wall. He tried listening, but he found himself watching Vicki and worrying. Her silence bothered him. Was she feeling bad again? Or was the niggling thought that she was upset at him right?

"Did you take your antibiotic?" he asked.

"Yeah."

Juan stood, grabbed the coffeepot, and refilled their cups.

"Are you ready for me to finish reading the book?" Bell asked while dusting off the sugar from her fingers.

"Let him drink his coffee," Vicki said.

"But he said—"

"Bell, let him drink his coffee." Impatience rang in her voice.

"Okay." Bell scooted off the chair and moved back into the living room. "I'm going to draw a picture of a bug for Mildred."

"That's good," Vicki answered.

"Mom?" Bell called two seconds later.

"What, hon?"

"What's the date today? I'm signing and dating this picture like a real artist."

"September tenth," Vicki answered.

"Shit," Juan said. "No."

"You owe me a dollar," Bell said.

He ignored Bell and snatched his phone up to see the date, praying Vicki was wrong.

She wasn't.

Guilt filled his lungs. Yesterday, he'd had sex for the first time. He'd had sex twice. Yesterday of all days. On his and Angie's anniversary. "Shit."

"Ooh," Bell said.

"Bell, stop." Vicki's gaze cut to him. "What is it?"

"Nothing!" He got up and walked out of the cabin.

He stood out on the porch, the sun burning in his eyes, guilt burning his chest.

The door behind him opened.

"Juan?" Vicki said.

"Yeah."

"You okay?"

"Fine." He didn't look back.

Her hand came to rest on his arm. "What's wrong?"

"Nothing. I just need a minute." His tone wasn't angry but impatient, and he instantly regretted his words.

"Sorry," she said.

He turned around. The hurt he'd heard in her apology showed in her eyes. "No, I'm sorry. I just..." He ran both hands through his hair.

"I know Bell's a lot to handle in the morning." Frustration filled her voice.

When he realized she thought he was upset with Bell, he felt even guiltier. "No. It's not her. I just...realized that yesterday was Angie's and my anniversary. And instead of honoring that day, I..."

"Slept with me," she finished for him, her voice flat.

He nodded. "I'm sorry. Look, this isn't about you. It's..."

"You're right. It's nothing to do with me." She walked back inside so fast that he felt the wake of her departure.

He stood there, hands gripping the porch railing, and realized how bad that sounded. He wanted to explain, but how could he when it didn't make sense to him? He wanted Vicki, he cared about her. He had every right to move on, yet it didn't change the fact that he felt guilty.

Walking back into the cabin, he still wasn't sure what

to say, but he couldn't leave the tension in the air like this.

Bell wasn't in the living room. Vicki sat at the kitchen table, looking at the computer.

He sat down beside her. "I'm sorry. I didn't mean to sound...angry. I'm not. I just—"

She looked up. "You don't have to explain."

"I think I do." He worked hard to sound patient.

"No. You don't. I get it."

"What do you think you get?" he asked.

Silence hung in the kitchen for at least a minute before she answered. "You love your wife."

He couldn't deny that. "That doesn't—"

"Stop. You don't have to explain. I get what this is, Juan." She drew in a sharp breath.

"What do you mean?"

"This thing between us. It's not...serious."

"Wait. I didn't say—"

"Stop worrying, Juan." She stood and opened the fridge.

His mind raced for the right words.

"We need to go to the store for some food," she said.

She continued to stare in the fridge. He was unsure what felt colder, the appliance or her.

"Vicki, can we please talk? Come sit down." He motioned to the empty chair where she'd been sitting.

Right then, his gaze shifted to the computer. He read the words across the top of the screen: *Apartments in Los Angeles: Let us help you find the perfect place.*

He read it again. "What are you...?"

She looked back. He motioned to the laptop. "What's this?"

"Just looking."

Emotions reeling, he stood up. "You're moving back to Los Angeles?"

"When it's safe." She blinked. "It's...it's where I can make the most money."

"So...you can just walk away from this?" He motioned between them. "From us?"

Her eyes tightened. Her lips thinned. "There is no us, Juan. You made that clear."

"I never said..." He stood up and went to her.

She held out her hands and shook her head. "Yes, you did."

"No. Look, I know it sounded bad, but—"

"You called me her name." Her words came out gnarled with hurt and anguish.

"What?"

"When we made love. You called me Angie!"

"Fuck. I'm sorry. It wasn't...It's not like—"

"I feel like I'm the other woman. And I refuse to be the other woman."

A noise echoed from the front porch. The squeak of the screen door opening sounded too loud. Damn, he hadn't even shut the door.

Juan shot across the room and grabbed his gun.

CHAPTER
THIRTY-ONE

Finger on the trigger, he swung for the door. When he saw his brother and sister-in-law, his breath caught, and he immediately lowered his gun.

"Hi?" Ricky's eyes widened.

If he had any doubt whether his conversation with Vicki had been overheard, it vanished when his sister-in-law said, "I think this might be a bad time. We should go." She gave her husband's arm a tug.

"No," Juan said, and then, "Yeah, probably." Juan's mind spun.

His nephews' voices sounded from the porch. They walked in, each holding a handle of a big ice chest, and dropped it on the living room floor.

"Hi, Tío," Ricky Jr. said.

Bell, with Sweetie barking and dancing on her leash, ran out of the bedroom. "I think she needs to go...

potty." Her eyes went round when she spotted Juan's family.

Juan glanced back at Vicki. She blushed as if embarrassed. Hell, he felt it, too. His gaze shifted to Bell.

Had they been talking loud enough for the kid to hear? "Bell, this is my brother and his family. Why don't we take Sweetie out front for a minute." When he headed to the door, he motioned for Ricky to follow him.

* * *

Pablo had sat in his car in the parking lot of Lakeside Shores, palming his gun. She was here. Somewhere. Vicki's phone had come on, then gone off before his program narrowed down the exact location. But it appeared she was on the northwest side of what looked more like a fishing or weekend getaway place than a full-time residence. He got out of his car.

Only a few minutes into the walk, he remembered why he hated Texas. The sun beat down on him and the air felt thicker than syrup. If not for the heat, he hated this place for the damn bugs. He swatted at an insect buzzing close to his ear.

He'd done a quick Internet search of the area. The two-mile area contained about a dozen or so cabins. His mind raced trying to gather a plan, but there were just too many unknowns. Was Vicki alone? With his daughter? Or was the owner of the man's shirt he'd found in her bedroom with her?

The good news was the cabins appeared to be two-

or three-acre lots, so no close neighbors to hear any screams. And he definitely planned on making her scream. The graveled road forked. Left or right? He managed to get the Google map pulled up on his phone.

The map was useless. It didn't show the two roads.

He stared out to see if he could spot a cabin down either road. He couldn't. But if it was set back in the woods, he wouldn't be able to spot it from here. Taking the right fork, he walked down the road.

Five minutes into the walk, he heard footsteps. He ducked into the woods and pulled out his knife. Some brush blocked most of his view, but not so much that he didn't notice that the person coming toward him was a woman. Was it her?

In the distance, he heard kids yelling and a dog barking. He stayed hidden. As the woman moved forward, he saw she was older than Vicki.

He crouched down behind a clump of pine trees. About a dozen bloodthirsty mosquitoes circled him, looking for a meal. Not until the woman turned the bend did he stand up. As he moved back to the road, thorny vines clung to his jeans and one found its way under the hem to prick his ankle. "Fuck!"

He stomped out of the brush and started back down the road. The lane curved and he spotted a cabin up ahead.

Was that it? Was the bitch there? He moved that way.

* * *

Juan walked outside. Bell followed the boys to the side of the cabin.

Juan turned and faced his brother and sister-in-law. "I should have let you know I was here. I'm sorry, but—"

"We can leave," Christina said.

Juan glanced back at Bell. She and the boys were hanging together while Sweetie danced on her leash.

"Or we could stay," Ricky offered. "Maybe be a buffer to whatever you guys were arguing about."

"I think we should go. It sounded personal." She cut him a disapproving look.

Juan raked a hand over his face and realized having them here was bad for several reasons. The top one being they were hiding out from a murderer. "I hate to—"

"Ricky, let's just go," Christina cut in.

Juan's phone, tucked in his pocket, rang. Juan pulled it out. Mark's number flashed across the screen.

"I'll call you right back." Frustration rang in Juan's voice.

"No! It's important!" Mark's reply came with tension.

"What is it?"

"Your phone's been ringing off the hook."

"My cell?"

"And your desk phone. I had a few hours and decided to come to the office. I finally answered it. It was that cop, Milbourn. He said he needed to talk to you about Vicki Trever. I informed him you didn't have any other info. He still insisted on speaking to you. I told him you were out of town. He asked if you were in Piney Lakes, Texas."

"What? How does—"

"He said Valado is there now. Something about him tracing her phone."

"No. She took the battery out."

"Look, what matters is I believe him."

"Fuck!" He turned to grab Bell, but she wasn't there. "Where's Bell?"

Christina shifted closer. "When we stepped out, I told the boys they could go to the playground. I'll bet she went with them."

"Shit!" Every muscle in his body clenched. Acid rose in his throat as his mind replayed Bell's cries from her dreams.

Mark continued, "I called the Piney Lakes police. They're on the way. Connor and I are driving there now."

Juan hung up.

"Bell?" he called.

Right then Sweetie came running up the trail. She didn't have a leash attached. He looked back at the cabin. He had two people to protect, but one was a hell of a lot more vulnerable.

He took off at a dead run to find Bell.

* * *

No one had been in the last cabin. He had broken the window and gone in. Between the air conditioner being off and stale air, he knew he had the wrong place. He studied the Google map again. "Fuck!" He should have taken the left on the road.

He took off. About fifty yards down the right road he spotted another cabin. Concerning him were the two cars parked out front. Hand on his gun, he eased up to the porch. He moved to the window.

A smile pulled at his lips when he saw her, alone in the kitchen. Her back was to him, but he recognized her hourglass shape. Need churned in his gut.

There was no sign of his daughter.

Could he be lucky enough to have found her alone? Or was someone in another room he couldn't see in?

He spotted a small patio to the left of the house. Taking the steps silently, he moved around the cabin. There was a set of sliding glass doors. The curtain was pulled back just enough. He peered inside the empty room and gave the door a push—locked. Holding his breath, he listened to see if he heard anyone talking. Nothing. He moved around the side and peered into another bedroom, also empty. He took off back to the front, moved up the porch, pressed against the wall, took out his gun, and looked inside again.

A smile pulled at his lips when he saw her at the kitchen window looking out. He pulled out his Glock, twisted the doorknob, and smiled when it turned. The bitch was making it easy for him.

The door squeaked as he moved inside. She turned. Her expression froze. The fear in her eyes sent a thrill to his dick. He bolted forward.

She screamed. He saw her gaze shift to a baseball bat that leaned against the wall. She dove, he caught her and yanked her in front of him. His gaze and gun stayed on the hall in case anyone rushed out.

"Shut up," he ground out. Then he slammed her head into the wall.

She went limp and fell to the floor. She must have been faking it, because she rolled and put a foot right into his face. He felt his lip bust. The coppery taste of his blood filled his mouth.

"Fuck you!" he seethed, grabbing her by the ankle. She kicked his arm with her other foot and broke his hold. Her next kick caught him in the gut.

While he gasped for air, she managed to get free and to the door. Had her hand on the knob. He lunged at her, caught her by the legs and slung her around. Losing her balance, she came down and hit her head on the edge of the coffee table. The loud clunk told him she'd hit hard. He snatched her up, turned her over. She squirmed, trying to flip side to side, like a fish about to die. He grabbed a fistful of hair and slammed her face on the floor.

She went still. He yanked out the zip ties he'd stuffed in his pocket. Grabbed her hands and pulled them together.

She started twisting again. He went to tighten the ties. Before he got them pulled all the way, she rolled over and kicked his chest. Damn, she was a fighter. She was halfway to her feet, but unsteady as if dizzy. Blood dripped from her head. He dove at her, pinning her to the floor. Putting his hand around her throat, he squeezed. Squeezed hard.

She kicked, fought to get free, but he had her. She was his now. Not to kill. Not yet.

When he saw her eyes start to roll back in her head, he loosened his grip on her throat. She gasped for air.

"Where's my money and book?" He felt the knife

heavy in his pocket and decided right then that slicing her throat was the way he'd finish her. But only after she told him what he needed to know, and after he'd had his fun.

"Tell me or I'm going to hurt you bad."

* * *

Juan cut the corner and saw Bell and the boys standing by the swings. Sweetie's leash was tied to a tree.

Bell was safe, but what about Vicki?

"What's wrong?" Ricky asked, gasping for air as he stopped beside him.

Juan looked up. He saw his elderly neighbor sitting on his porch waving at him. He knew Mr. Buxton had shotguns. Right then, Christina, pulling in air, stopped beside him.

"Go!" Juan pointed to Mr. Buxton. "Take Bell and the boys. Stay in Mr. Buxton's cabin. He's got guns. Use them if you have to, but don't let anyone else in!"

"What the hell is it?" Ricky asked.

"Just do it!" Juan took off. Thinking he'd make it faster through the woods, he darted off the path.

He was only halfway there when he heard Vicki scream.

He pushed himself faster, jumping over brush, plowing through his fear that he was going to be too late.

More screams turned his abs rock hard.

As he approached the cabin, he saw the door was ajar.

He slowed down and took the stairs silently. His gut

burned and air became locked in his lungs. He leaned over and looked through the window. Vicki lay on the floor, and Pablo was on his knees straddling her. He had a gun in his hands and a knife lay on the floor beside him.

"Tell me where my money is or I'm going to get that pretty little daughter of mine and hurt her again!"

With fury and disgust aimed at the man, Juan bolted through the door.

Pablo must have heard him, because he turned, pointing his gun at Juan. A shot rang out.

Juan dove to the side. The bullet missed, but his hand slammed against the coffee table, dislodging his gun from his grip.

The next second passed in a whirl.

Juan lunged forward, wrestling Pablo's gun away. The sound of his weapon hitting the floor offered little relief when the man's fist plunged into Juan's gut.

Air whooshed out of his mouth. The man slammed on top of him. Juan blocked Pablo's punches and landed a fist in the man's mouth and his teeth cut into Juan's knuckles. Then a glint of something metal in Pablo's hand caught Juan's eyes. A knife. Coming right at Juan's face.

He managed to grab Pablo's arm with both hands, stopping the blade from sinking into his eye.

With his other hand, Pablo grasped Juan around his throat. The tightened grip blocked Juan's air. To prevent Pablo from choking him, he'd have to let go of the man's forearm, risk being stabbed.

He was still weighing his options when a cracking sound echoed above him. Pablo slumped to the floor.

Juan sucked air. Vicki wavered, her ankles still bound, but she stood over him. Baseball bat in her hands, she had tears and blood streaming down her face.

Jumping to his feet, he kicked Pablo's gun and knife across the room. *Thump. Thump. Thump.* His heart slammed against his ribs.

Vicki's knees gave, and he caught her. "How badly are you hurt?" *Thump. Thump. Thump.* He sat her on the coffee table, then bolted for his gun. His gaze flipped from Vicki to the unconscious man.

Blood gushing sounded in his ears with every throb of his heart. "Are you shot or stabbed?" he repeated.

She didn't answer.

Eyes on Valado. Then eyes on her, he grabbed the knife from the floor, and cut the ties around Vicki's ankles.

"Answer me!" Standing, he positioned himself so he could see Valado and her at the same time. He parted her hair where blood had pooled, feeling her tremble. The gash didn't look like a bullet wound. But she had blood all over. *Thump. Thump. Thump.* "Vicki, are you shot or stabbed?"

He reached to lift her top when she shook her head. "Bell?" Her voice came out raw and raspy. Breathless. As if she were waking up from a nightmare and realizing it wasn't a dream, her eyes cut to Valado.

He did the same. He needed to secure the perp. He needed her out of here.

"Bell's fine. Can you walk?"

She nodded.

He pulled her up. "Go! Police are on their way."

His gun remained pointed on Valado. One move. One sound. One blink of an eye and Juan would shoot him.

Footsteps pounded onto the porch. The oxygen in the air went missing. When no one screamed police, Juan swung his weapon to the door. Milbourn, gun drawn, stormed in the doorway.

Adrenaline tightened Juan's finger on the trigger. "Drop it!" he ordered, all his attention on the new threat.

Milbourn lowered his weapon. Then in a flash, he raised it. Juan shoved Vicki down before a gun exploded. But it hadn't been Milbourn's.

Juan swung his gun on Valado at the same second another pop sounded.

The man was now sitting up. Blood squirted out from a hole in his forehead. His eyes remained open, unmoving. Empty. His upper body wavered, then dropped to the floor with a dead thud. The hem of his jeans on his left leg was raised and showed an empty holster.

Juan turned to Milbourn now collapsed against the wall. His gun dropped and clanked against the tile floor. His knees gave and he slid down the wall.

"Where are you hit?" Juan asked.

Milbourn looked down at his right thigh, where blood gushed through a hole in his jeans. When blood pooled on the floor, Juan knew the bullet had hit the femoral artery. He yanked off his belt and fit it around the man's upper thigh. He pulled it tight. Then tighter.

Milbourn screamed.

"We gotta stop the bleeding," Juan told him.

Vicki came and sat down beside Milbourn. He looked at her. "I tried...to stop him. I gave your sister the book, told her to give it to the police if he didn't...didn't leave her alone. But when she took his money, he..."

"What money?" Vicki asked, her voice scratchy and raw. Juan saw the bruising around her throat. Saw the blood oozing from her lips. The thought of how close he came to losing her sent acid burning a path to his gut.

Milbourn closed his eyes. "He stole it from the drug..." He took in a deep breath. "After you were found in Phoenix, I had the PI leave so you could escape. But I..." He let out a moan. "I should've never sent him, but Pablo threatened..."

Juan grabbed his phone and dialed 911, spitting out the address, asking for an ambulance and cops. "Are you at Lakeside Shores?" the operator asked.

"Yes."

"Cops and an emergency crew should be arriving now. Is everyone okay?"

"No. Tell them to hurry."

"Stop." Vicki's voice brought Juan's gaze up. She reached for Milbourn's hands as he loosened the belt.

Juan dropped to his knees and retightened the belt. "Loosen it and you'll die."

Milbourn reached for the belt again. "I've screwed up. I don't want my wife and daughter...They don't deserve..."

Vicki caught his wrist. "Look at me. My mom screwed up. She screwed up over and over again. But the thing that's the hardest to forgive her for is drinking herself to death."

Juan heard someone call out. "Police! Come out with your hands up."

"Stop!" another officer yelled.

"Juan!" Ricky's voice echoed outside.

Juan bolted up. "Don't shoot him!" he screamed. Ricky rushed inside, fire in his eyes and a shotgun in his hands.

Juan's heart felt too big for his chest. He snatched the shotgun away and yanked him away from the door. "That was stupid."

"You'd have done the same thing."

Juan couldn't deny it. He called out, "All's clear. I'm Detective Juan Acosta, I called 911. We're unarmed. You can come in." He looked at Milbourn. His chin slumped forward to his chest. Blood still oozed from his leg. "We need a medical team in here now."

CHAPTER
THIRTY-TWO

Juan watched as medics lifted Milbourn onto a stretcher. Seconds later, with sirens blaring, the ambulance sped off. A second one pulled in almost immediately, and they loaded Vicki in it.

Juan crawled into the back with her and gave her hand a squeeze. "I'll be up there as soon as I talk to the police."

"No. Check on Bell."

"I'll do that before I come up."

She nodded.

Juan sent his brother to go check on Bell first. He made short work of explaining things to the police, but assured them he'd be available for questions later if they needed him. Then, as promised, he took off to see Bell, who was with Christina and his nephews at Mr. Buxton's cabin.

He found Mr. Buxton sitting on the front porch, a shotgun beside him.

"Thank you," Juan said.

"And here you acted like you didn't want me to have my guns here."

"I take it back." Juan pumped the man's hand and walked inside. Ricky and the boys sat at the kitchen table lining up dominos. Ricky looked up when Juan walked in. Christina sat on the sofa with a teary-eyed Bell in her lap. Sweetie lay beside them.

When the child saw him, she scrambled out of Christina's arms and ran right into his. He picked her up. She put her hands on Juan's cheeks.

"Where's my mama?" Her young voice shook. "Why wouldn't they let me go back there?"

Juan realized he didn't know what to tell the child, but he offered out something. "She fell and hit her head and she's at a doctor getting stitches."

"Can I go see her?"

"She wants you to stay with Christina and take care of Sweetie. You are going to go back to Anniston to her house, and we'll pick you up as soon as we can."

"No, I stay with you." She leaned in. "I don't know them."

"But you can trust them. Christina is really nice and I need to get your mom. So you have to go with them. Can you be a big girl for me? Please, Bell."

Bell pouted, but nodded. "I was scared. When I saw you run away."

"I know, but you don't have to be scared anymore. I promise."

She rested her head on his shoulder. "I love you."

Juan closed his eyes and savored the sweetness of those words. "I love you, too." And saying it made his eyes sting.

The child lifted her head and sniffled. "Did she really fall?"

"What?" Juan asked.

"My other mom used to say she fell, but really my dad pushed her. I saw it."

A knot formed in the middle of his sternum. "Bell, I'd never push your mom."

"I know you wouldn't. You're a good guy. But there are bad guys, too. My daddy was one." Tears rolled down her cheeks. "He hurt her and me, too."

"I know, but I won't let anyone hurt Vicki or you ever again." And somehow, damn it, he vowed to keep his word.

A few minutes later, when he set Bell down, she went to the table to watch his nephews knock down all the dominos they'd lined up.

Christina, emotion in her expression, looked at him. "That's so sad."

"I know," he said.

"She really does love you."

"It's mutual," he said.

"And her mother?"

"I love them both," he said, and damn if that didn't feel good. He glanced at his sister-in-law. "But I screwed up and I don't know how I'm going to unscrew it."

"I know, I heard." She made a face.

"Yeah. But I swear I wasn't thinking about...That

was just a mistake. But I did…Angie's and my anniversary was yesterday and I forgot it, and when I remembered I felt guilty. And Vicki knew it. I didn't know what to say. How can I explain to her that I want her in my life but I feel guilty for wanting it?"

Christina put a hand on his arm. "Do you know about different stages of grief?"

"Anger and shit."

"Guilt is part of it, too. I know, when my sister died, I blamed myself for not helping her. So what's happening to you is normal. The fact that you admitted loving Vicki says you're moving past that stage."

He exhaled. "I don't even understand, because like I said, I love them. The other night I woke up, and Bell and her were sleeping together and the lamp in the bedroom was on. They looked like a Norman Rockwell painting. And I wanted to be in that painting."

Tears filled Christina's eyes again. "Tell her that," his sister-in-law said. "That's exactly what she needs to hear. And while you're at it, teach your brother to say stuff like that."

Juan looked at Ricky playing with the kids. "He'd die for you or his boys," Juan said.

"I know. Both of you are good guys. And you deserve to be happy. So go convince that kid's mom to give you another shot."

* * *

The doctors had given Vicki a sedative to help relax her. The only way they'd let her leave the hospital was if

Juan promised to stay with her. It was an easy promise to make.

It was almost six when they left the hospital. Right before she got into the car, she asked, "How did he find us?"

"I don't know. Milbourn said something about a phone, but that doesn't make sense." He got behind the wheel.

"We're picking up Bell on the way, right?" she asked.

"Yeah."

She leaned back against the headrest and in less than five minutes, she'd fallen asleep. He'd wanted to use the drive to talk, but he could tell she needed the rest.

She woke up when he pulled into his brother's driveway. She looked at him. "Should I come in?"

"No. I'll get her."

Bell was asleep when he picked her up. By the time he got back to his house, she'd woken up, but Vicki was out again. He woke Vicki up, walked her in, and took her straight to his bed.

Bell joined her on the bed. She hugged her mom, and asked if it hurt to get stitches. Then she looked at her mom's black eyes and frowned. "You fell hard."

"I know, but I'm fine." After that conversation ended, Bell announced she was hungry. Vicki pushed her covers off as if to get up.

"No," Juan said. "I can do it."

"Yeah, you sleep, Mama." Bell tucked her hand in his. She looked up when they got to the living room. "You won't make me eat vegetables."

He smiled. Later, he'd have to let Bell know that her mom's rules were to be followed, but not tonight.

After they both ate some cereal—without the healthy kind mixed in—he walked her back to bed. She crawled in and scooted over beside her sleeping mom. "You can sleep here." She patted the mattress. The sight of them together, in his house, in his bed, in his life turned the air he breathed sweeter.

As hard as it was, he answered, "No, I'll sleep on the sofa."

"But Mama's asleep and I don't want to be alone while I go to sleep. Can you just stay until I fall asleep? Please?"

"Okay." He stretched out beside her, and nothing had felt so right. When Bell's eyes closed, he wanted nothing more than to just stay right there, claim his place with them. But he couldn't risk Vicki waking up and thinking he'd overstepped his boundaries.

* * *

"You're a sleepyhead," Bell's voice came at his ear.

He opened one eye and grinned. "Am not." He grabbed her and pulled her onto the sofa. Her laugh filled his heart with warmth. When he looked up, Vicki was standing a few feet from his sofa, smiling down at him.

"Good morning," he said. Her smile had to be a good sign, didn't it? Oh, he knew they needed to talk. But he cherished her smile.

Sweetie jumped up on the sofa. Juan sat up.

"Can I let her out back?" Bell asked, climbing off the sofa.

Juan nodded and Bell and Sweetie ran out the door.

"I was going to head home," Vicki said. "So I told her she could wake you up."

"Home?" He dropped his hands on his knees, suddenly nervous.

"I think you've taken care of me too long."

"It doesn't feel that way to me." He stood up. He ached to kiss her but held back, unsure if she'd welcome his affection. "How are you feeling?"

"Sore. But okay." She blinked. "Did you hear anything about Milbourn last night?"

"I checked in with the Piney Lakes police and they said he was doing well."

"How much trouble is he going to be in?"

"I don't know, but before I left for the hospital I spoke with Jody. She said if he cooperates and is willing to testify about who Valado was working with, she'd try to get him a deal."

She nodded. "That's good."

He studied her, wanting to read her, but he couldn't. "Did you take your pills this morning?"

"Not yet. I think they're still in—"

"In the suitcase in my car. Let me get it." He took off toward the garage.

He came back in with the suitcase and Bell's backpack. When he went to set the backpack down, he realized it was open and all her things fell out.

Setting down the suitcase, he picked up the fallen items and saw what was under a book. "Shit," he muttered and held up a cell phone as he stood up.

Vicki stared at it. "That's my old phone. What's Bell doing with it? I threw it in the garbage."

Juan ran a hand over his face. "She had it when you were in the hospital. I forgot all about it. She said you told her it was broken, but it still worked for games."

Vicki blinked. "Is that...how he found us?"

"I bet so," he said. "I should have remembered—"

"No, I should've gotten rid of it better."

"It doesn't matter now, does it?" he asked.

"Right," she said.

He opened the side pocket where he'd stowed her antibiotics. "How about I make us some coffee?"

"I can just..."

"Please?" When he saw her slow nod, he took off to the kitchen. She moved to the back window and watched Bell.

Coffee scents filled the house, and they both sat down at the kitchen table. He turned his cup one way and then the other, steam rising from the mug. He finally looked up. "I want to apologize again for calling you Angie and for getting upset about the anniversary. I want you to know that I'm—"

"Juan, you don't have to explain."

"Yes, I do." He put his hand on hers. She didn't move her hand, but he swore he felt her flinch. And that made his insides quake.

"Juan, everything has happened so fast."

"It doesn't feel fast. It feels right." He ran his thumb over the top of her knuckles. "I don't want to lose you, Vicki. I'm ready—"

"Juan, I had no right to get so upset. I didn't go into this relationship blind."

"Well, I did," he said. "I didn't know I was going to

fall in love with you and Bell. But I wouldn't change a thing. And I want this. I want you and Bell in my life."

"But we..."

He remembered Christina saying he needed to tell her about... "At the cabin, I saw you and Bell in bed. The light was on and it was like looking at a Norman Rockwell painting. I wanted to crawl in that bed with you two. To put myself in the painting. I want us to be a family, Vicki. I know you're scared of trusting someone because of what your mom put you through and then what your sister went through, but even Bell knows I'm one of the good guys."

She put a finger to his lips. Was she about to say no? Tell him again that she needed to think about her career?

He moved her hand. "I get that your career would do better in California. So, I'll go with you."

She gasped. "No."

"Because you can't trust me? Vicki, I—"

"Nooo. Because I'm staying in Texas."

"Here?" Hope made him breathless. "With me?"

"Yes. You're right. I'm scared, but you're my... Rockwell painting, too. Bell loves you. She loves your dog. Your friends."

"And you? Who do you love?"

She smiles. "Sweetie, of course. And you. Your friends aren't bad, either." She turned her hand over and laced her fingers with his. "I still think we should take it slow, but..."

"Is this slow enough?" He stood, pulled her up, and without hurrying he kissed her.

The back door opened, and Bell and Sweetie came rushing in. "You know, you two kiss a lot not to be boyfriend and girlfriend."

Juan laughed and picked her up. "Do you think your mom will be my girlfriend if I ask her?"

Bell's eyes widened. "I think so." She looked at Vicki. "Will you be his girlfriend, Mom?"

"Yes, I think I will."

Bell laughed. "And then...then are you going to get married?"

"Bell," Vicki said.

"But girlfriends and boyfriends get married."

"She's right." Juan looked from Bell to Vicki, the air filling his chest felt new, fresh. This was happiness.

Bell wiggled in his arms. "And if you get married, that will make you my daddy? My real daddy? And then Sweetie is mine, too." Excitement widened her big brown eyes.

Vicki cleared her throat in a warning.

Juan just laughed, then looked from Vicki to the precious little girl. "I'd love to be your daddy."

She squealed and hugged him again. Vicki moved in and it became a group hug. One with a whole lot of love. One that could've appeared in a Rockwell painting.

EPILOGUE

One month later

Vicki, cell phone to her ear, stood outside on the patio of Juan's brother's home. "Did the key work?" she asked Joanne Butler. When Vicki had gone to put away her important papers Juan had packed, she'd found she had two keys tucked away in the envelope: the key to the safety deposit box and the key to the storage unit where she'd left her mom's things. She recalled she'd given it to Alison to store some of her belongings when she'd left Pablo, and Alison had paid for the unit for a couple more years.

"Yes, it...worked. To be clear...everything in there is a donation? You're sure?" Joanne appeared to be choosing her words carefully. The caution in the woman's voice told Vicki that she and Juan had been right. Alison really had taken Pablo's money.

"Yes. Everything." Vicki smiled.

Vicki looked over to the hot tub, where Bell and Juan's nephews splashed and played. Sweetie ran around and barked as if she wanted to jump in. The dog had become Bell's loyal companion.

"You know it'll be put to good use," Joanne said.

"I know." Vicki sighed.

"I did find a box that had some old photos. I set them aside in case you wanted them. I can mail them to you."

"That would be great." Something about being in a good place in her life had Vicki feeling a little forgiving of her mom's flaws. Maybe Alison was right. There were a few memories she could salvage and call good. "Thank you. For everything."

"You're welcome," Joanne said.

After they hung up, Vicki glanced out. Sitting at the patio table were Juan, Ricky, and Christina. The smell of the burgers sizzling on the grill flavored the air. It had been only six weeks, and yet she felt like a member of their family. Bell already called Juan's nephews her cousins, and it was Uncle Ricky and Aunt Christina. Of course, Juan became Daddy almost immediately. Vicki looked down at the ring on her finger.

Two nights ago, he'd surprised her. Her idea of slow and Juan's were a little different. Not that she was complaining.

Juan glanced up and smiled. Vicki's heart swelled with how perfect the scene was before her. Like Juan had said, a Rockwell painting.

Juan stood and walked over.

"Who was that?"

"Joanne Butler."

Curiosity lit up his eyes. "What did she say?"

"Just that the donation was appreciated."

"So...?"

"Yeah," she said.

"Good." He wrapped his arm around her waist.

"Thank you," she said.

He lifted a brow, grinned, and got a playful twinkle in his brown eyes. "For making you scream last night?"

She bumped him with her shoulder. "For this." She waved a hand out. "For sharing your family. Your friends. Your life." She paused. "And for last night."

He laughed and kissed her.

When Connor Pierce agrees to help FBI agent Bree Ryan with her search for her sister's killers, he knows better than to get personally involved. But as the investigation grows more dangerous, so does the attraction between them, putting their lives and their hearts on the line.

Don't miss Connor and Bree's story in *Don't Look Back*, the next gripping thriller in the Texas Justice series!

Available Summer 2020

About the Author

Christie Craig is the *New York Times* bestselling author of thirty-nine books. She is an Alabama native, a motivational speaker, and a writing teacher who currently hangs her hat in Texas. When she's not writing romance, she's traveling, sipping wine, or penning bestselling young adult novels as C. C. Hunter.

You can learn more at:
    Christie-Craig.com
    Twitter @Christie_Craig
    Facebook.com/ChristieCraigBooks

Keep reading for the bonus novella

HOT TARGET

by April Hunt!

Rachel Kline came to Vegas to find her missing friend. Next thing she knows, she is swept up in a police raid and being bailed out of jail by the irresistibly sexy, infuriatingly cocky Alpha op who rescued her a year ago. Lewis Callahan has always had a soft spot for Rachel and is more than happy to hang up his cowboy hat to help her out. But with targets on their backs and killers on their tails, it's one high-risk game they're playing. And it's not just their hearts that are on the line...

FOREVER

PROLOGUE

Sandy Oaks Medical Research Facility
Eighteen months ago

The ants occupying Rachel Kline's hospital bed won the battle against her sanity. Whipping off the heavy faux-knitted blanket, she dropped to her hands and knees and searched for the offending little creatures.

"You've got to be in here somewhere, you little bastards." Seeing only the white starched linen, she tugged at the corners, thinking they'd sought refuge between the plastic covered mattress and metal bed frame.

"Well, well, well. Isn't that a pretty sight. Gotta say that this view is even better than the one outside." The low, slow drawl she'd grown accustomed to during the last month brought a sigh to her lips.

"I wouldn't know. I haven't been outside in a week."

Rachel abandoned her quest for the insects and flipped around, making sure her pajama bottoms covered her backside.

Logan, by comparison, made her feel frumpy. Tall, broad shouldered, and with a penchant for wearing inappropriate or lame-joke T-shirts, the man was always put together and never without a grin on his face—or his cowboy hat on his head. A few months ago, he would've been the exact kind of guy who'd catch her attention.

Now she forced herself to admire from an emotional distance. "Why is it that every time I turn around, you're there?"

Logan's mischievous smirk blossomed as he set a brown paper bag on the nearby table. "If I didn't know how much you love my visits, sweetheart, my feelings would've been hurt just now. It's a good thing you're one of my favorite redheads."

"Can you go visit the other one today instead of me? Maybe if you're keeping Penny company, she'll be less likely to make surprise drop-ins too." Rachel slid out of the bed.

She hated being bitchy. She loved Penny like a sister and owed her, Logan, and his team *everything*, including her life. But she could sense the looming darkness that came at least once a week, and she'd rather not have an audience.

Unable to hold off anymore, Rachel scratched her tingling arms until red marks popped up over her skin. Logan's gray eyes immediately latched on to the move, forcing her to stop.

He was right. With nothing much to do in Sandy Oaks, the government-run medical research facility she'd called home for the last month, she looked forward to his visits. But over the last two weeks, he'd formed a habit of popping up on her worst days. She'd first thought it a coincidence, but second-guessed it now.

She second-guessed a lot of things—especially herself.

And that was usually when Logan magically appeared.

"Seriously, Logan, can we not do this today?" Rachel fought against a sudden rush of woe-is-me. "I don't have the energy."

He leaned his jean-covered rear end against the table and never once took his eyes off her. "Rough morning?"

"Rough everything." Her skin itched again, the ant-like sensation slithering its way down the back of her neck. Rachel shifted on her feet uncomfortably, trying to keep her involuntary jerks to a minimum.

Two days before her next dose of meds, her body waged war on itself, almost like clockwork. The doctors kept telling her that the frequency would lessen, but she was still waiting for that time to come, anxious to get back to feeling like herself.

"Why aren't you going?"

"Because you want me to." Logan moved to the reclining chair across from where she stood and leaned back, getting comfortable. "It's been a month, Rachel."

Rachel clenched her teeth until her jaw ached. "I'm fully aware how long it's been."

"Then why aren't you cutting yourself some slack?"

"Would you be taking it easy on yourself if the shoe were on the other foot?"

He wouldn't answer, but it didn't stop him from glowering from a distance.

Four months ago, starry-eyed and eager to change the world, Rachel had traveled with a local NGO determined to bring education to rural Honduran children. Instead of her feeding the minds of youths, Diego Fuentes had fed her his latest drug cocktail. Kidnapped from her assigned village and experimented on as if she were a guinea pig, she'd prayed for death more times than she could count.

Even now, a month after her release, drug withdrawal hijacked her body. Her schedule revolved around medications and tests, not to mention therapy—all because of a drug that had been forced upon her. And that all revolved around the *physical* fallout of her imprisonment in Honduras. It didn't touch the untold horrors that flashed through her mind in dark, enclosed places.

When Logan helped free Rachel from the Fuentes compound, he might have saved her life, but he'd also helped her exchange one prison for another.

CHAPTER ONE

Present day

No windows. No open doors. No way to prevent the walls from closing in. Rachel Kline shut her eyes and battled a looming panic attack.

In through the nose. Out through the mouth. Hold. And repeat.

The relaxation technique she'd learned in Dr. Hamilton's office failed miserably, taken down by the severe stench blend of vomit and urine invading her nose. She gagged, barely fighting off a second gag as she shifted on the cold metal seat.

Rachel's pink Converse slid into a gooey substance puddled on the floor. That summed up the last five hours—one big, inexplicable glutinous mess that had started with a Nevada-bound flight and ended in a cliché.

A Las Vegas jail cell.

Despite tight quarters, mysterious substances, and glares from her holding cell acquaintances, she'd do it all over again if it meant helping her friend.

"Are the accommodations not lofty enough for you, princess?" came the smoke-ravaged voice that had become like nails on a chalkboard during the last hour. "You want me to talk to the manager? Maybe they didn't realize that they had royalty right under their noses. Go ahead and tell them again that you don't belong here. I'm sure they'll listen this time."

The older woman's chortle elicited a few snickers from the others. No fewer than twelve pairs of eyes watched the exchange, waiting for one of them to say or do something to offend the other, and take part in a wrestling match. Rachel didn't plan on doing either.

She summoned the blank, dead stare that came all too easily and locked her eyes on the other woman. "You really like hearing yourself talk, don't you?"

Rachel's insulter jumped to stilettoed feet. Her red-stained lips pulled into a snarl, and she pointed her spindly, needle-tracked arm at Rachel accusingly. "You think you're too good for the likes of us? Is that it, bitch? You think your shit smells like fucking roses?"

"I never said that, or anything close to it." After a three-month imprisonment by the drug world's Dr. Frankenstein, Rachel related better to the women in this holding cell than she did to her own family.

She *got* them. She understood them on the most basic level, including understanding how living in a drug-hazed cloud of no responsibilities, no inhibitions, and no regret made life pretty darn easy. *Hard* happened after the cloud disappeared and the guilt swept into its place.

Hard happened when you hadn't been there for your friend when she needed you.

The woman stepped closer, her movement jerky. "Squeaky-clean, wholesome princesses don't get swept up in brothel raids, and you got tossed in the back of the van just like the rest of us."

"I told you once, and I'll tell you again, I was looking for my *friend*."

"We're all looking for a friend, honey. It's why we do what we do and who we do it for. Maybe that's where your friend is... Did you ever think of that? Maybe she performed her duties so well that the higher-ups took notice. Or maybe she couldn't hack it and she's already *gone*."

Rachel lurched to her feet, her earlier panic forgotten as she stood nearly nose to nose with the other woman. "She's not *gone*."

"Tone down the bickering." A middle-aged guard appeared on the other side of the bars. His chunky fingers fumbled with his massive key ring until he slid open the door. "Rachel Kline. Let's go."

Rachel faced off against the other woman's condescending glare, careful not to so much as bat an eye despite her heartbeat pounding in her ears.

"Don't make me set the damn hose on the two of you," the guard warned. "Dammit, Stella. Back the fuck off. I don't get paid enough to deal with your shit."

With a quirk of her red-stained lips, the other woman

took a small step back, wiggling her fingers. "See you around town, princess."

Rachel hoped to hell not.

At a hurried clip, she followed Officer Marrow down the long corridor and toward out-processing to collect her belongings. Not that she'd had much. After listening to Carly's voice mail that morning, she'd barely managed to grab her driver's license, much less anything else.

"One wallet. Six hard candies. And a buck seventy-five." The out-processing officer crammed her things into the divot beneath the glass divider along with pen and paper. "Signature on the dotted line."

"Did anyone find a small black backpack? I think I must've dropped it at the...uh...place." Rachel signed for her items and slid the roster back into the hole.

"There was a whole lot of shit confiscated at that raid site, but no bag."

That wasn't what she wanted to hear, and she couldn't give a list of its contents because she didn't know what was inside. Carly had left that bit of information out.

"I'm going to give you a bit of advice, hon. *Go home*," Officer Tooley suggested. Except for the fact that she was decked out in the desert uniform of the Las Vegas Metropolitan Police Department, the silver-haired officer could've easily passed for Sophie Hansen, the woman who'd practically raised her and Penny from the time they'd reached double digits. "A girl like you doesn't belong in cesspools like we raided tonight."

"We're in agreement there, believe me. But I can't leave until I know my friend's okay."

The older woman flashed Rachel a sympathetic look. "I hope for her sake, and yours, that you find her and she's not someplace worse."

Rachel hoped that too.

Carly's not being at the brothel would've been comforting if she hadn't said in her last message that she'd be there—and that if she wasn't, something was wrong.

"If I'm not there, you need to get the contents of the black bag to the authorities," Carly had instructed. "And you need to be careful, Rach. He'll do anything to make sure that doesn't happen."

Carly hadn't clarified who *he* was, or what was inside the bag. She'd hung up, and Rachel's every attempt to get in touch with her had failed.

For the usually stoic, independent woman to admit that level of desperation, things had to be *bad*. Thanks to what they'd both been subjected to in Honduras, bad for them was pure hell on earth for others.

Stepping into the waiting room, Rachel looked around for the recipient of her one and only phone call. An eclectic array of people sat in the green plastic chairs, including a few handcuffed to the armrests, but no Charlie. And the pink-haired Alpha operative wasn't someone who could be easily missed.

After a second scan, she opted to check outside. Warm desert air washed over her, a blessing after the putrid stench of the holding cell. Rachel savored the clean scent and leaned heavily on the front railing. Her hands trembled, her body showing its relief at no longer being trapped in close confines. The more violently they shook, the tighter she clutched the banister.

"If it isn't the redheaded jailbird finally taking flight. Took you long enough to make an appearance, darlin'. I started to think you chiseled your way out instead of taking the easy route." The familiar deep voice caressed Rachel like silk.

Keeping her back toward its owner, Rachel tried in vain to compose herself. Counting to a hundred and performing thirty minutes of meditative yoga wouldn't do a damn thing when it came to Logan Callahan's presence.

She mentally braced for impact and turned toward the flirty Texan.

Over six feet of solid muscle and southern charm, Logan leaned casually against the red brick of the police station. Worn blue jeans encased muscled thighs, and a red plaid button-up shirt, its cuffs rolled to his elbows, revealed strong, corded arms.

And his hands...

Rachel nearly drooled there on the walkway as his fingers massaged the brim of the black Stetson in his hands. Personal experience had taught her that those hands had more talent than most people had in their entire bodies—and not because he was an Alpha sniper badass.

For one blissful night, she'd experienced what it was like to be on the receiving end of those hands—and afterward, she'd woken to reality. It was hard to believe she'd slunk out of Logan's bed a mere twelve hours ago—well, technically it had been *her* bed.

"Cat got your tongue?" Logan's mouth lifted at the corners.

Gray and gleaming with mischief, Logan's eyes never strayed from her face, but tingles erupted over every inch of her body. The same thing had happened last night, and, if she was honest with herself, every time they were within an eyeball's glance of each other.

Rachel crossed her arms over her chest like a shield. "Charlie was my one phone call."

Logan flipped his hat and propped it back on top of his mop of wavy blond hair. "She's on assignment."

"She didn't say anything about an assignment when I called."

"Guess Stone must've assigned it to her afterward."

"What about Penny?" Rachel challenged.

"Battling a serious case of morning, noon, and night sickness compliments of the little Ortega that's taken residence in her uterus. And before you start running down the Alpha roster, I'm *it*, darlin'. I'm without assignment and happened to be in town scoping out the Mil-Tech convention for the boss man. Keep up this line of questioning and you'll have me thinking that you don't want me here."

She didn't.

She needed structure. She needed order. She needed to keep her head on straight if she was going to find Carly before it was too late. None of that would happen in Logan's presence, and it had nothing to do with his abilities because, as with everyone else associated with Alpha, with him failure wasn't an option.

The deficiency lay entirely with her.

"Do you want to tell me why you came all the way out here to take a walk on the wild side? Pennsylvania has jails that you could've visited without wasting your frequent-flier miles." Logan's tone remained light, but there wasn't a doubt in Rachel's mind that he knew the significance of her setting foot on a plane.

Confined spaces sent her heart into her throat. An entire plane ride trying to swallow around an organ? Not a pleasant experience. "I told Charlie—"

"That Carly was in trouble, but you were pretty vague as to what kind. Are we talking relationship issues, work problems, or a combination of the two?"

"It's not something that you'd understand."

Something flashed in his eyes, there and gone so fast Rachel didn't catch it. Logan's usual wide, easygoing smile tightened. *False bravado.* She'd perfected that technique too, so Penny and the others would stop worrying over her.

Sometimes it worked. Sometimes it didn't.

Logan pushed himself off the wall and closed the six-foot distance between them. Stopping less than a foot away, close enough for her to see the slight tic in his jaw muscle, he drilled her with a fixed stare. "You'd be surprised at both the depth of my understanding, darlin', and my observational skills. You came all the way out here to help Carly, yet you're the only one I bailed out of the clinker."

"There was no bail exchanged because I was never charged. And don't act like I owe you some huge favor. I called Charlie nearly *two hours* ago. I think the wait makes up for you having to cut your vacation short."

Logan cocked up a single dark-blond eyebrow. "It may have been a matter of wrong place at the wrong time, but you were at a freakin' brothel moments before the place was raided. Or did I get that fact wrong?"

Rachel's cheeks heated. Earlier nausea long forgotten, she pierced him with her best eat-shit-and-set-yourself-on-fire glare. "If you have something to say, cowboy, say it and stop dancing around the question we both know you want to ask. Actually, on second thought, *don't*. Because it's none of your damn business."

She turned away. After one step Logan gently snatched her elbow and whirled her back. Taken off guard, she didn't have time to put on the brakes. Her chest collided with his, and then he held her captive.

"It *is* my business, darlin'." Logan's voice was deceptively calm.

"The last time I checked, I was responsible for my own actions. If I want to kill over a year of sobriety with a trip into the lower dregs of Vegas society and a good ol' brothel visit, then that's what I'm damn well going to do. So you, Logan Callahan, can kiss my—"

"I'm going to kiss you quiet if you don't stop talking for one damn minute!" Logan trapped her face between his palms. "I know you weren't at that house looking for a magic carpet ride."

Rachel grasped her anger with both metaphorical hands. "You do, do you? And how exactly do you know that?"

Logan smirked, his lips widening as her annoyance grew. "Take that burr out from beneath your saddle and stop searching for a reason to be pissed off at me."

"I don't have to look too hard."

"You didn't seem angry when my mouth was kissing

the hell out of you last night—or this morning. Did I snore afterward? Or maybe it was me hogging the covers that had you running out the door without so much as an 'I'll see you later.'"

"I don't have time for this conversation—or your ego. Because like you said, Carly wasn't in that jail cell with me, which means she's still out there somewhere."

Logan looked as if he wanted to say something, his gaze momentarily dropping to her mouth before he gave a slight nod. "What did Carly say during her phone call?"

"It was actually a series of messages scattered throughout the week, but it was the one she left last night that has me worried. Something has her scared of her own shadow, Logan, and *that's* why I went to that hellhole. She said she was in big trouble and the only way to get out of it was stashed back at that house."

"What was it?" Logan asked, all business.

"I don't know. She didn't say, and the police raided the place before I walked the length of the first room. This is my fault. I should've checked my voice mails sooner. I should've taken her calls. I should've listened to them before this morning, and I didn't."

"How were you to know that something was wrong?"

"Four phone calls in a day, Logan. I usually hear from her once a week, twice if she had a rough day at work. I didn't listen to her messages until hours later. To an addict in the midst of a crisis, *one minute* could mean the difference between life and death...but *hours*?" Rachel's voice cracked. She averted her gaze, guilt clawing apart her insides. "Some way to repay someone for quite literally saving your life."

Carly had done that and more.

If not for her going against Diego Fuentes and leading Rachel, Penny, and the other women to safety, their bodies would've been buried beneath the tons of steel and concrete that made up the Fuentes compound.

Logan cupped her cheek, and on reflex she tilted into his touch, butterflies fluttering around in her stomach.

The flirting jokester, the man quick to whip off a snappy retort or flash an audacious wink, was gone, and in his place was a much more stoic version. Logan's gray eyes softened, the slight wrinkles around them more evident with the downward tilt of his mouth.

"Rachel." His calloused thumb caressed her cheek.

His gaze darted around her face as if he didn't know exactly where to focus his attention. She wanted him to kiss her, to touch his mouth to hers and leave her incapable of speech—or thought. His gaze flickered to her mouth, and for a brief moment she thought she'd get her wish—until those same eyes dropped to her chest.

"Get down!" Logan's body lurched, his arms wrapping tightly around her as he knocked her square off her feet and onto the hard ground.

CHAPTER TWO

Midlunge, a whip of air zipped over Logan's right ear, the bullet causing it barely missing the top of Rachel's head. He rounded his shoulders and cushioned their fall to the hard gravel.

One moment he'd been contemplating the best way to extract that all-telling sorrow pooling in Rachel's pretty green eyes, and in the next his sniper training had locked on to the red dot flashing on her chest. Conditioned to respond, his reflexes pushed him into action.

Arms locked around Rachel, Logan rolled their entwined bodies log style across the unforgiving ground, not stopping until a big black pickup was between them and the sniper's trajectory.

"Why did you—?" Rachel's question stopped as a second shot slammed into the ground, two inches from the truck's front. Her eyes widened into twin green saucers. "Is someone *shooting* at us?"

"They're sure as hell not inviting us to dinner."

She leveled a glare at him. "This isn't the time to crack jokes."

"Sorry. Reflex." He slipped his weight off her, gently ducking her head below the truck's handle. "And no, they're not shooting at us. They're shooting at *you*. I thought you had a shining, sweet disposition. How in the hell did you manage to make mortal enemies out of someone after being in the clinker for only a few hours?"

"Again with the jokes."

"I'm not joking, sweetheart. Even Stone hasn't had people taking shots at him within hours of setting foot into a town."

Logan let the sharp look she threw his way roll off his back. She didn't like his inopportune humor, and he wasn't fond of waking alone. It hadn't mattered that he'd expected it. It *burned*.

It burned because the person slinking away had been *Rachel*.

Another shot plowed into the ground, three inches closer and off to the right. *The sniper changed position.* "When we're in the clear, we're talking about why Carly needs you to buy her ticket to freedom. But right now, we need to get the hell out of here."

"I vote for going back into the police station—or getting the dozens of officers that are inside to come out. Isn't this the kind of situation that warrants reinforcements?"

"Most definitely, but unless you have your cell on you, it's not going to work."

"Why?"

He gestured to the shattered technology four feet away. "Because those half-dozen jagged pieces is what's left of my phone. Guess they didn't factor bullet dodging when they durability tested that model."

"So we're making a run for the building?"

"That's probably the worst thing we can do." Logan dropped to his stomach, trying to get a visual on this dickwad from beneath the truck carriage, but the asshole's perch was too high.

He returned to a crouching position and instantly had five and a half feet of pissed-off redhead fisting his shirt front. "Explain to me how being surrounded by a roof, four walls, and a lot of armed law enforcement is a bad idea? It sounds pretty damn safe to me."

Logan gently peeled her fingers away, and when all ten digits were freed, he clasped her hands in his. After a year and a half of longing for Rachel from a metaphorical distance, last night he'd finally gotten a small glimmer of what having her in his life would be like. It would be one thing if he fucked up his chances with her himself, but he wasn't about to let a faceless bastard take them away.

"I need you to listen to me, darlin'," Logan directed calmly. "We can't risk this asshole waiting us out, because if he's had the slightest bit of sniper training, that's what he's prepared to do. He's stationary right now, which means we have to make sure we're not."

Rachel went ashen, but otherwise stayed calm as she flicked her gaze to the truck providing them cover. "And I'm guessing we can't jump in the truck and hot-wire the damn thing for a mobile getaway?"

"You guessed right. He'd have a clear shot angled downward. We'd be two sitting ducks."

"We can't go inside. We can't get in a car. What exactly *can* we do?" Rachel's breaths quickened.

Logan surveyed their surroundings, soaking in the sights of the Las Vegas strip. The simple two-story police station stood out in a sea of oversize casinos and swanky hotels. Despite the eleven o'clock hour, people littered the sidewalks, their shoulders brushing against one another's as they headed to their destinations—or to nowhere in particular.

On the left, ten yards separated him and Rachel from a large group of tourists. They stood beneath a traffic light, waiting to cross to the other side of Las Vegas Boulevard.

Logan threaded his fingers through hers. Shifting his weight over his booted feet, he mentally plotted the best route. "We can get lost in the crowd."

"Are you freakin' crazy?" Rachel hissed. She looked at the traffic light as if it were a million miles away. "Someone's waiting to take a shot at us and your grand idea is to step out into the open?"

"Not into the open…into a hell of a lot of foot traffic. Crowds are instant camouflage. He's not going to take a shot unless we give him one, and that's not something I'm planning on doing." He tugged her close and tucked a loose auburn curl behind her ear. "You have to trust that I know what I'm talking about…and if there's anything I know without a shadow of a doubt, it's what goes through a sniper's head before he's about to make a hit."

Rachel didn't look comforted. Back to biting her

lower lip, she stared him dead in the eye, a thousand unspoken questions lying in wait.

Logan understood her unease. A job description revolving around death didn't make for lighthearted conversation, and when people realized you made a living putting bullets into people's heads, they usually looked at you differently, even those who claimed to care about you.

Logan had learned his lesson about opening up years ago, and it was why he didn't talk about his time in the Marine Corps.

Rachel's fingers tightened around his, and her free hand wrapped around his wrist. "Okay. I'm ready when you are."

Her unfiltered trust in him nearly made him puff out his chest.

He took a deep breath and dragged his head back into the game. "When I say go, you haul ass. When you think you're going as fast as you can, go *faster*—and zigzag. Do *not* go in a straight line. And whatever you do, don't look back at me. Just know I'll be right on your pretty six."

"*Back* at you? Why are you going to be behind me?" Rachel's concern had him brushing a soft kiss over her cheek.

"You got this, darlin'. *We* got this." He purposefully didn't answer, eyeing the stoplight and silently counting down with the digital number. The instant the flashing palm lit green, Logan nudged Rachel into the open— and he followed close behind.

After three steps, three more shots zipped their way, too damn close to his right heel. Careful to keep his body between her and the line of fire, he dodged left and right, following Rachel as she quickly implanted them in the center of the moving crowd.

He couldn't have done better himself.

They followed the flow of foot traffic, never traveling in a straight line. Logan snatched a red ball cap off the head of a passing teen and tugged it over Rachel's auburn waves, and the second they stepped onto the sidewalk, he snatched himself a blue one.

A tingle warmed the back of Logan's neck, and not in a good way. He interlocked their fingers and picked up their pace. Tourists littered the walkways, some slowing their steps to take in the sights. In front of them, an older couple stopped abruptly for a photo with a window display. Logan guided Rachel to the right, barely avoiding a collision.

That damn tingle intensified.

"We need to get off the street." Logan scanned their surroundings before ushering Rachel through a neon-flashing door. "In here."

They stepped off the street and into a small gilded foyer. A statue of Elvis, in all his life-size, sequined glory, stood sentinel on an elaborate mini stage while the low, drawling tones of the man himself crooned about love from an overhead surround-sound system.

"No...freakin'...way." Rachel's whispered surprise directed Logan's gaze to the center of the room, where a sparkling, sequined aisle led up to a grandiose altar.

Decorated with green vines and musical note cut-outs, the arch stood as the room's focal point—and canopied the older couple standing beneath.

"Welcome to the Fools Rush In Chapel of Love!" Decked out in garish bell-bottoms and jaw-encompassing sideburns much like Stationary Elvis, the man stepped forward. He gestured to his teased-wig-wearing female counterpart. "Priscilla and I love bringing young couples together in the holiest of matrimony."

Logan couldn't censor his laugh. It erupted from his throat, earning him a pointy elbow in his side. He rubbed the sore spot, still not able to wipe the grin from his face. "What the hell was that for?"

"An Elvis chapel? This is your idea of a good place to disappear?" Rachel hissed.

She shifted to drill him with another jab, but he looped his arm around her waist and pulled her close enough that she couldn't do any real damage. "I figured we'd kill two birds with one stone. How does that saying go? When in Rome?"

Rachel's green glare could've punctured solid steel.

"Not the right time?" He smirked, guiding Rachel deeper into the room...and away from any windows. He turned toward Elvis and gestured to the banner hanging on the wall. "Do any of your themed wedding packages include a wardrobe?"

"*All* of them do." Priscilla clapped her hands excitedly, the gold bangle bracelets on her arm jingling. "We've got an extensive collection. Pick an Elvis-and-Priscilla era and we have multiple choices—from the fifties straight through to the seventies. You won't find a selection like ours anywhere else in Vegas."

"Logan," Rachel groaned beside him.

He pulled few bills from his wallet, flashing her a side

wink. "Looks like my bride-to-be is having a change of heart, but I'll pay you for two changes of clothes, minus the I-dos... and the use of your phone."

Elvis blinked, glancing at his wife. Both were obviously confused, and a whole lot less perky realizing they weren't about to land customers. "You don't want a wedding?"

"Our evening's pretty booked solid, so we're going to have to pass on it for tonight."

Priscilla eventually broke into a small smile, taking Rachel's hand. "Earl, you're on young stud patrol. I'm going to take this one into the back and get her glamorized. Between studying online tutorials and my new jasmine-scented maximum-hold hair spray, there won't be a bouffant higher this side of 1976. You just leave everything to Edith."

Rachel's eyes went wide. "Oh, no. I don't need the full treatment. Really. Truly."

"Nonsense, honey. If we're not providing you the wedding of an era, the least we can do is glam you up to the nines. Heck, we'll amp it up to the high teens."

Rachel's head spun around, her lips mouthing a silent *Help me* moments before Edith ushered her through a gold-beaded curtain. Instead of intervening, Logan waved. "Have fun, darlin'. Can't wait to show you around town after your makeover."

Grinning over Rachel's still-heard polite refusals of hospitality, Logan turned back to Elvis-Earl. "The King went through a Hawaiian-shirt phase, right? You got anything like that lying around?"

* * *

Rachel blinked repetitively, hoping harder each time that the last six hours had been nothing more than a nightmare. But no luck. Despite her having talked the older Priscilla down a few hair inches, her auburn waves had been tamed by at least a half can of extra-hold hair spray.

Edith clapped her hands gleefully as Rachel warily eyed her reflection. "You look like you stepped straight out of a Bond movie. I couldn't be any happier—unless you let me exchange those sneakers for some hot pink go-go boots. The heel on them is to die for. It'll give you the height you need to be able to look your fella in the eye."

Dying was what might happen if Rachel wore them. She could count the times she'd worn anything with a heel higher than a tennis shoe on one—or *no*—hands. With her horrible luck, she'd be in a mad dash for her life and would trip over her own two feet.

"We're going to be doing a lot of walking, and I'm not exactly the most graceful person." Rachel smiled. "But thank you, Edith, for everything you've done for literal strangers straight off the street. This means a lot."

"Oh, it's nothing." Edith's cheeks pinked as she waved off the thank-you. "And as for being a stranger, you became friends the second you walked through the door. We should be thanking *you* and your special man for making the night of an old, bored couple. Earl and I like to talk big about being a Vegas wedding destination, but truth is, we haven't had one here in about a month—and from what I understand, it was annulled two weeks later."

"And here we stroll in and burst your bubble." Reaching out, Rachel squeezed the older woman's hand. "You have my promise that if I ever decide to take that big leap into holy matrimony, the only place I'll even consider having it is here."

"Oh, hush now, but thank you, hon." Edith smiled bashfully, glimpsing at her watch. "Oh my. That handsome man of yours probably thinks that I've kidnapped you."

Rachel folded her clothes and stuffed them into the souvenir bag Edith gave her before following the sweet woman to their back office.

"Earl and I will be out front if you need us." Edith smiled, closing the door after her.

Rachel tried soaking in the sight of the elaborately decorated office, but the man standing with his back to her held her attention hostage. Talking on an honest-to-God landline phone, and wearing board shorts and a blue-and-yellow Hawaiian shirt decorated with smiling pineapples, Logan still looked delicious—and lethal.

Rachel studied him, wondering which version of Logan was closest to the real one. In Honduras she'd seen the badass commando, hell-bent on finishing the job. But even during missions, he kept things light and his teammates' eyes rolling with his witty banter and humor—as he'd done during Penny's party.

But when everyone left? When it had been only the two of them?

Intense Logan appeared, and instead of ignoring, or hiding, or running—all things she'd gotten good at in the last year and a half—she'd practically lured him into her bed. Something about Logan Callahan defied all her inhibitions, and she couldn't wrap her head around why that was. The more she tried, the more the answer evaded her.

His usual smile nowhere to be seen, Logan's stern focus sharpened the chiseled angles of his face. Even his eyes, usually full of mirth and humor, narrowed in concentration as he listened to the person on the other end of the old rotary phone.

He looked...grim. And that was never a good sign.

"Is everything okay?" Rachel cleared her throat, announcing her presence.

Logan's attention snapped to her. He held her gaze a few agonizing moments before dropping down the length of her bare legs. She self-consciously tugged on the short hem of the dress and mentally cursed the unforgiving polyester fabric.

Logan dragged his eyes away with a bit of difficulty that nearly pulled a smile to her face. "Fuckin'-A, Char. I only understand half of what you say during a normal conversation, much less when you go off on a rant. Stifle the British curses and dumb down what you just said."

"That's Charlie?" Rachel's ears perked and she stepped deeper into the office, stretching her hand out for the phone. "I want to talk to her."

Logan looked physically pained. "You're killing me here, babe. You know that?"

"I recently did my CPR recertification, so I can bring you back—*if* you give me the phone."

She held his stare and refused to blink. No way did she think she could wear him down, but he relented, handing her the receiver with a sigh. "Fucking killing me," he murmured.

"Fancy hearing from you, Charlie, you know, considering you're on assignment and all." Rachel spoke into the phone, but watched Logan's faint wince. "Or maybe it wasn't a long one? It ended ahead of schedule? Or maybe it wasn't far away?"

"Which of those options would make you want to flog me less?" Charlie's melodic English accent normally put Rachel at ease—but not tonight.

"None of them."

The female Alpha operative cursed. "Okay. Fine. I wasn't on an assignment. But instead of seeing it as me feeding you to the wolves—er, wolf—think of what could've happened if I hadn't dialed Logan. If you'd been out there alone, waiting for my arse to first roll into town, we wouldn't be having this conversation. So really, you should be thanking me. And you're welcome."

Rachel raised her brows, and even though Charlie couldn't see through the phone, it was as if she sensed her doubt.

Charlie chuckled. "*One* day, you'll thank me, and when that day comes, I'll take your appreciation in the form of slushy alcoholic drinks."

"Uh-huh."

Charlie was right—at least about Logan being the reason why she was still breathing. But it didn't negate the fact that the operative's motives *at the time* had had nothing to do with survival and everything to do with Rachel's drunken admission that Logan Callahan pushed all her hot buttons.

"We need to have a long talk about your underlying Cupid complex," Rachel warned her meddling friend.

"Will do, but in order for that conversation to happen, you need to do whatever Logan says." At her prolonged pause, Charlie added, "I'm dead bloody serious, Rach."

"I'll listen—as long as it has nothing to do with leaving Vegas without Carly."

As she said the words, she locked gazes with Logan, making sure he understood that she meant every word.

He leaned against Earl and Edith's desk, folding his arms across his chest. He didn't look happy, his jaw flexing wildly as if he was clenching his teeth. But he didn't argue.

On the other end of the phone line, Charlie sighed. "I already broke that news to Logan because I knew that was going to be your response. It's the Kline stubborn gene rearing its head. He was deluding himself into thinking he could talk some sense into you."

"And the reason he's glaring at me as if he's swallowed a cup of rusty nails is because you cleared him of that notion?"

"Only regular rusty nails? That's actually an improvement. Every curse that came out of his mouth earlier sounded like those nails were doused in gasoline and set on fire." Charlie's husky laugh brought a grin to Rachel's face. "He doesn't like the idea of you sticking around, and he's going to gripe about it in true Alpha-male fashion, but he gets it."

"Could've fooled me."

As if hearing both sides of their conversation, Logan

lifted a single questioning eyebrow. Rachel looked away and tried to collect her thoughts—something that didn't happen easily when she stared at him too long.

"I don't have my cell," Rachel informed Charlie. "I must have dropped it during the commotion at the raid. What if Carly tries to contact me? How are we going to find her?"

"That's why you and Logan are about to go phone shopping. We'll link the new phone to your old number, and when she contacts you, I'll ping her location. You just have to keep her on the line long enough for me to lock on to a decent radius."

That sounded too easy—and hopeful. Rachel's stomach twisted into a knot as she worried about the worst-case scenario. "And what if she can't call? When she left that last message, she was really scared about something."

"We're going to remain hopeful, okay?" Charlie gentled her voice. "But in the meantime, I'll be working the brothel angle."

Rachel snorted, pinching the bridge of her nose as her head throbbed. "Good luck getting any of them to talk. They're not exactly a forthcoming bunch."

"That's why I'm letting surveillance talk *for* me. I'm putting traces on your little jailbird friends, backtracking their movement prior to the raid, and following the ones that are slowly being released. As soon as I get a hit, I'll give you and Logan a heads-up."

"*Stella,*" Rachel blurted the name of the bleach blonde who'd gotten in her face.

Computer keys clacked on the other line. "Stella."

"I don't know her last name, or even if that's her real first name, but it's what the others called her. She didn't hide the fact that she didn't like me asking questions, or that I didn't belong. If she knew *I* wasn't supposed to be there…"

"Maybe she'd have recognized Carly too. I'll make that a starting point."

Guilty desperation clawed away at Rachel's insides. "Charlie, I know Stone doesn't approve of some of your fact-finding methods, but—"

Charlie chuckled. Rachel pictured the other woman's face lighting up with a mischievous smirk. "Don't you worry about the big growly boss man. Penny's keeping Stone preoccupied by practicing her mother-smothering skills. I don't even think she's allowed him to push a button on the telly remote, much less settle in front of a computer. But that's what he gets for acting like a big baby because of a little flesh wound."

Rachel shook her head, amused at the level of teasing among the operatives. During their latest mission, in Miami, Alpha's leader had gotten a little more than a flesh wound. A few surgeries on his shoulder and a torturous round of physical therapy and he was still a bear to be around.

"Do me a favor," Charlie added. "Be careful out there, and I know Logan can be a narcissistic pain in the ass, but he knows what he's doing. Listen to him. And make sure you check in with me when you get to a safe location. Hopefully I'll have some more information for you."

Rachel listened to the dial tone for a few seconds before returning the phone to its cradle and facing Logan.

His intense stare nearly backed her up a step, but she stopped herself. There was no better time to jump out of her comfort zone than that moment.

Masking the slight tremble of her hands, Rachel propped her palms on her hips. "You're not going to try talking me into going back to Pennsylvania?"

"Would it do me any good, or would I be wasting my breath?" Logan asked pointedly.

"I think we both know the answer to that question."

He released a noncommittal grunt. "Yeah, we do."

"So...cell phones? Are we really going to be able to get anything this late at night? It's nearing midnight."

"This is Vegas." Logan rubbed his palm over his face, looking tired. "There's a twenty-four-hour shop a few blocks down. Once we have a communication channel set with Charlie, we'll find someplace to lie low until she gets us the information we need to track down Carly."

Rachel narrowed her eyes on him in a fixed stare. "Lying low sounds an awful lot like waiting and doing nothing."

"How has not waiting worked out for you so far, darlin'?" Logan pushed off the desk and closed the distance between them. He stopped when the front of his shirt brushed against her dress, making the postage-stamp-size office feel ten times smaller. Cupping her chin between his fingers, he directed her gaze to his. "We're going to find Carly. I promise you that much. But I'm not dragging you around this city with a target on your back and no damned idea where we're headed."

"So what do we do between lying low and planning

our next move?" Rachel regretted the question the instant Logan's gray eyes darkened.

"We're going to figure out who the fuck you pissed off enough that they sent a goddamned sniper to wait you out at the police station. And then we're having a talk—a nice long, answer-revealing conversation about everything that's been going on in that pretty little head of yours for the last twenty-four hours. And you best believe I'm not taking *nothing* for an answer."

Registering his determined expression, Rachel swallowed the lump that had formed in her throat. "Maybe I'm not ready to talk, Logan," she whispered.

"Didn't ask if you were, sweetheart. Just warning you that it's going to happen, so you best get ready."

The office door flew open, crashing against the wall. Logan blocked Rachel from the new arrival, spinning toward the threat, his gun raised.

"Oh my." Edith's mouth dropped open. Her face paled as she glanced nervously from the handgun to their faces, only regaining a bit of color when Logan tucked his weapon back into the holster beneath his shirt. "I wanted to let you know that we have some not-very-hospitable company out front, and they're not looking for a wedding package either."

CHAPTER THREE

A low shout from the front room drew their attention. Edith's eyes shifted nervously down the hall. Logan, holding a finger to his lips, slunk out of the office and edged his way to the golden curtains.

In the middle of the foyer, a large-shouldered thug pinned Earl's throat against the wall with a beefy forearm, making the older man's face turn multiple shades of purple. Off to the side, a second goon pointed a Colt at his head.

Too many people. Too many ways this entire situation could go FUBAR—fucked up beyond all recognition.

Logan glanced over his shoulder to a worried Edith and Rachel. "Lock yourselves in the office and don't come out until you hear me on the other side of it."

Rachel wrapped a protective arm around the older

woman, but looked hesitant to leave. "What are you going to do?"

"Take out the garbage. Go." Logan waited until Rachel's concerned eyes disappeared behind the office door, and then he easily slipped into Alpha mode. Forcing his face blank, he cracked his neck and pushed through the curtain. "Hey, Uncle E. You didn't tell me what you wanted me to do with those ukuleles."

Thug Two whipped his Colt at Logan.

He lifted his hands in mock surrender and skidded to a stop. "Hey. Whoa. What's...?"

Maintaining his grip on Earl's throat, the slenderer of the two men growled, "Who the fuck are you?"

"I-I-I'm the nephew." Logan amped up the airhead routine, bouncing his eyes around the room before settling them on Earl. "Shit, Unc. You said you paid those gambling debts. Aunt Pris is going to shit kittens when she finds out you freakin' lied to her, man."

"How long have you been here?" Thug One demanded.

"A hell of a lot longer than I'd like. I was supposed to go out with a smokin'-hot card clerk from over at the Luxor, but I got roped into doing inventory—and by roped, I mean guilted into doing it."

"You see a couple come strolling through here?"

"Through here?" Logan snorted, slowing lowering his hands. "Nah. This place hasn't seen any action in over a month—which is why Uncle E needs to chill on the spending spree. Look, I don't know how much he owes this time, but we'll make a payment by the end of the week. Let him go. Christ, you're going to give him a heart attack or something, and we definitely don't have enough money to pay off you guys *and* medical bills."

The Colt's owner bored his calculating glare into Logan.

Logan glimpsed an image of his past self deep in the recesses of the guy's gaze, one from eight years ago who'd earned the title Crack Shot: The Man Who Doesn't Miss.

That Logan had closed himself to everything except his orders, wind direction, resistance, and speed. He'd executed the job flawlessly, no questions asked or second-guesses allowed. Forget a conscience. That shit got turned off on an assignment because survival meant forgetting that your job description was *killer*.

There wasn't a doubt in Logan's mind. The man aiming a gun at his head was the bastard sniper who'd taken those shots at Rachel outside the police station.

White-hot fury burned its way through Logan's veins. At his sides his fists clenched until his knuckles popped. It took everything in him not to whip out and disarm the asshole, and then beat him senseless.

The guy had nearly taken Rachel out of his life when she'd just walked into it—even if it had only been for twelve hours. As soon as the shit-storm hovering over their heads—and Carly's—dissipated, Logan would be remedying her lack of presence.

Rachel just didn't know it yet.

Logan ripped his gaze away from the sniper before he registered Logan as a kindred spirit, and played it cool. He fidgeted on purpose, shifting his weight from leg to leg. "Seriously, man. We'll get a payment to you by the end of the week. Hell, we'll come up with something in two days. I swear."

The thug working up Earl released his hold with a curse. The older man clutched his throat, gasping as he doubled over.

Thug One barked an order to his friend, "Let's get the fuck out of here."

"I think we should make *sure* they don't know anything." Logan's admirer studied him carefully.

"You don't get paid to fucking *think*. Every second we stay here with our thumbs up our asses, they're getting further away."

Logan held his breath as the two men stalked toward the exit as if they hadn't nearly strangled a man for information. At the door, the sniper threw back an unnerving glare and followed his buddy back onto the street.

Logan quickly reached Earl, who was finally returning to a normal color. "Are you okay?"

"What—?" Earl gasped.

"Don't try to talk. Your throat's going to be sore for a while. I'm sorry about all of this. I really am." Logan guided him into the back of the chapel, where he knocked on the office door. "Rachel. It's me."

The door flung open. Rachel's pale complexion rivaled Earl's still-tomato-red one. "Is everything okay? What happened?"

"They're gone for now. Pretty sure I just met friends of your friends." Logan released Earl as Edith rushed to her husband, helping ease him into a chair. Regret gnawed at his insides. "I'm sorry for not putting an immediate stop to that, but if I had, there'd be no telling what those guys would've done to you two once Rachel and I left. They needed to think they'd sniffed the wrong trail."

Earl cleared his throat, wincing. "Don't worry about me, son. I've taken on bigger bullies in my heyday."

"I'm so sorry for bringing this to your doorstep. They have my friend and I can't..." Rachel's voice trembled as she apologized to the older couple.

"Oh, honey. Don't apologize," Edith gushed. "Earl's right. We've handled a lot worse. I'm just worried about you two. Those guys obviously meant business."

Logan cradled the back of Rachel's head and drew her against his chest. Her body trembled against his, and unlike the last time he'd held her this close, it wasn't from desire. What had started as a desperate need to protect her eighteen months ago had morphed into something else without his even knowing.

He still wanted to protect Rachel more than he wanted to take his next breath.

He also wanted *her*—and she wouldn't make it easy.

Hell, both their pasts wouldn't make a relationship between them a walk in the park, but the more time he spent with her, the more he realized it was worth the risk.

"So do we." Logan gently tilted Rachel's face up to his. Tears welled in her eyes, nearly gutting him, but nothing had fallen. She'd latched on to that internal strength of which he'd grown proud. "You hear me, darlin'? We're not giving up. I promised you that we'd get Carly out of this and I meant every damn word. You believe me?"

She nodded, easing from his embrace. Logan wanted to haul her back, but to make good on his promise, they needed to keep moving.

He turned to the older couple. "Do you guys have a rear exit to this place?"

"Of course." Edith led them through a back storeroom, where Logan swapped out his pineapple shirt for a black one on which the Thug Squad hadn't laid eyes, and to a fire exit. "It lets you out in the alley. Go left and you hit the street parallel to the Boulevard. There's an electronics store about a block down. They're not the friendliest of sorts, and I'm pretty sure they do some shady deals in the back room, but they'll do in a pinch."

Rachel wrapped the older woman in a firm hug before doing the same to Earl. "I don't know to thank you both."

Edith patted her back, smiling. "Thank us by coming back when you're ready and letting us give the two of you the wedding of your dreams—on the house."

Rachel's cheeks reddened. "Oh, no. We're not—"

Edith flashed a wink. "Honey, take it from a woman who tried running away from a man with a mission. All you're doing by denying the inevitable is wasting time that can be put to better—and a lot more fun—use."

Logan kept his grin to its minimum. He slipped into the alley, making sure it was all clear before easing back into the chapel. "We got to make tracks. The more distance we put between us and here, the better off everyone will be."

With one last round of thank-yous, Logan's hand found Rachel's—the ease with which they linked only fueled his determination for them to have that talk later—and they stepped back out into the dry Vegas heat.

Compared to the tourist hustle of Las Vegas Boulevard, the street running parallel could've served as the filming location for a postapocalyptic movie. A small group of barely legal-looking kids braved the mostly deserted sidewalks, lost and out of place as they hovered over their cell phones, Googling their position. Locals, perched outside rundown pawn shops and cash-quick storefronts, eyed them warily as they walked the street.

Sparky's Electronics sat a block and a half from the chapel's rear exit, nestled between two gentlemen's clubs. The main entrance chimed as they entered, causing the two older men standing at the counter to look their way.

"We're closed." Crag faced and glowering, the clerk behind the counter jiggled the toothpick dangling from his mouth.

"Really?" Logan kept his voice light. "The window brags that you're open round the clock."

"Needs updating."

"I see. Here's a little something to stay open a few extra minutes." Logan tossed a couple hundred-dollar bills in front of him. "We want a pair of those phones you have in the case, and we'll do the rest."

The clerk grumbled, but grabbed the money and dug out two boxes, then dropped them in front of Logan. "I'm keeping the change as an inconvenience fee."

"Suit yourself." Logan yanked the phones out of their boxes. He booted them up and went directly to the carrier's server screen and activated them. Once finished, he stuffed one into his cargo shorts and handed the second to Rachel. "We'll set these up further when we get to where we're going. I want this on you at all times, and make sure you put it somewhere it's always within easy reach."

"And where exactly would that happen to be?" Rachel challenged.

Logan couldn't tell if she'd meant it to sound like a dare, but that's how he took it. Having temporarily forgotten about their wardrobe change, he scooted his attention down her legs and up to where the dress cupped her breasts, revealing a tantalizing amount of cleavage.

"Seems like you've got a perfect spot." Logan expected a smack, or at least a muttered curse. Instead she sent her pretty green eyes on a dramatic roll and stuffed the phone into one cup of her bra—her pink, lacy, and somewhat sheer bra.

"Good enough for you?" Rachel pulled her mouth up into a sexy half smirk.

His mouth went dry. Now they both had a small bulge beneath their clothes, except his made it a hell of a lot more difficult to run.

He cleared his throat, wincing at the razor-like pain, and channeled his go-to method for covering discomfort. "Let me know when you need help getting that back out. I'd be more than honored to lend you my services."

Rachel snorted. "Of course you would."

"I'd do that and a hell of a lot more for you, gorgeous."

Fuck-a-rump—that was the truth. He'd do anything to keep her safe and happy, or make her life even a little less shit-tastic. Keeping both an emotional and a physical distance from her *should* be the first step in making sure that happened, but he couldn't do it. Even after their secret sniper had jogged a few unpleasant memories.

Because when he peered into Rachel's emerald-green eyes, he didn't see the million pieces of his blown-apart soul.

He saw hope—and healing.

He saw *them*.

* * *

Logan's broad shoulders tensed. His mouth, usually twisted into a permanent half smirk, tightened. He looked less like the carefree Alpha operative and more like a tiger prepped to pounce. A woman could get whiplash trying to figure out which Logan she was walking with.

"Why are you looking at me like that, darlin'?" Logan, with one hand on the small of her back, didn't even glance her way as he ushered her forward.

"Just trying to figure out the inner workings of Logan Callahan," she replied honestly.

Logan guffawed. "Don't waste the energy. A good many specialists have tried and failed. I'm a black hole."

Rachel didn't like the adamancy in his statement—or his case-closed tone. Before she could dig deeper, Logan muttered a curse. He gripped her elbow and spun her around, gently pushing her back against the nearest building.

"What was..."—Rachel's protest died on her lips as Logan crowded into her personal space as though such a thing didn't exist—"that?"

Guiding her head to the side with a touch of his finger, he trailed his mouth along her jaw. From her chin to her ear, the faint caress caused an eruption of goose bumps and made her heart thump wildly—but this time, it wasn't a need for space that created the breathing difficulties. What Penny called the *quirky* aftereffects of her abduction ceased to exist around Logan.

Rachel tightened her fingers into his shirt and brought him closer. For close to a year and a half, she'd fought both her fears and her addiction to Freedom, and now that she considered herself strong enough to stand on her own, she had a new one.

Logan.

Logan Callahan, six and a half feet of brazen, sultry Texas man, was her current drug of choice. One addiction for another.

Unable to wrap her head around its meaning, Rachel shifted to pull away.

"Do *not* move." Logan propped an arm alongside her head and banded the other tightly around her waist.

Two men stepped out of a pawn shop ten yards away. Logan's body immediately tensed, then tightened more as they approached.

The slenderer of the two barely spared them a glance as he glared at his friend. "No way in hell am I going down with you when the boss finds out that you fucked up. You're supposed to be some kind of hotshot and you fucking *miss*?"

"I'll remedy the situation." Cold and unemotional, the bulkier man didn't look the least bit frazzled.

"Yeah, you damn well better remedy it, because the boss pays good money for your services. He's not going to tolerate any fuck-ups."

As the two men rounded the corner and moved out of sight, Rachel released the breath she hadn't known she'd been holding. "That was a little too close for my comfort...especially since I'm guessing those are the men from the chapel."

"Two and the same. You didn't recognize either one of them? Maybe they'd made use of the brothel earlier tonight?"

"No. That doesn't mean they weren't *there*, but I didn't have any run-ins with either one of them. And trust me, I would've remembered—especially the bigger one. He gives me the willies."

"Then we still have to figure out how they know you." Logan threaded his fingers through hers and led the way down the street. After carefully checking the intersection where their two new friends had gone, he hustled her onward at a fast clip.

They passed no fewer than ten pawn shops and a dozen little chapels, each bragging about exclusive packages.

Rachel pumped her legs, working hard to keep up

with Logan's fast pace. "I get that you want to be surrounded by a roof and four walls, but do you have a particular destination in mind?"

"Ideally, I'd like to get back to the conference hotel where there's practically an entire fucking army of cops and former military, but I want to get you the hell off the street, so I'll take what I can get."

"You were really here for a conference?"

He tossed her a small smirk. "Mil-Tech, where grown-ass boys come to talk about guns and shit. It was supposed to be a working vacation—my first in two years. And then your sweet self blew that out of the water with a single phone call."

Rachel mulled that over a second when the realization struck her. If they weren't hustling at a pace to put a professional speed walker to shame, she would've skewered him with her best teacher's glare. "You already had plans to head off to Vegas after we...*Are you serious*? You have an issue with me ducking out on you this morning when you were going to do the same thing to me? Talk about double freaking standard."

"Not even close to the same thing."

Rachel mentally berated herself for feeling guilty for leaving without so much as a note. "How do you figure?"

"Because before I left, I planned on waking you with my mouth between your legs and once you came, sliding into your delicious body until we both blew our tops. Slinking out on tiptoe hadn't even come across my mind."

Heat rushed to her cheeks. He sounded dead serious. "Must be nice not to have a self-conscious or unsure bone in your body."

Logan glanced her way.

Crap. She hadn't realized she'd said that aloud.

Logan brushed his thumb along the back of her hand. "During our sit-down conversation, we're tacking on a reply to that comment. Hope you're not prone to developing bedsores, sweetheart, because this chat is getting longer by the minute."

Rachel clamped her mouth shut, growing more and more uncertain about how she was going to survive this mega, all-revealing conversation.

Logan came to a sudden stop. Ten yards ahead, their two new friends stood outside a strip club, talking with the guy manning the door. The shorter of the two flashed what looked to be a picture—probably of her. The bouncer shook his head.

"Fuckin'-A," Logan murmured. "I owe Penny an apology. I've always thought that *she* was the Kline most likely to piss someone off enough that they'd put a hit out on her."

"Technically she's an Ortega now."

"Semantics." Logan took the next right, steering them closer to the Vegas strip.

They stepped onto the Boulevard and were immediately swept up by a large wedding party. Rachel clung to Logan's hand as they went with the flow of pedestrian traffic.

"We're not making it to the Bellagio. This way." Logan's arm wrapped around her waist and they stepped off to the side, nearly face-planting into a window to avoid getting trampled.

This time, Rachel eyed the sign on the business door before they stepped through.

FANTASTICAL SUITES: THE BEST FANTASY HOTEL IN VEGAS.

CHAPTER FOUR

Logan peeked out the Stranded Beach Suite window and onto the street below. Despite its nearing one o'clock in the morning, the Boulevard moved along at its normal fast clip, tourists and vacationers oblivious to the things happening around them.

He wasn't one of them.

Quiet and contemplative, Rachel aimed her silent scrutiny at him the second they'd reached their hotel room. He did the same thing when plotting his next move. Right now, he'd pay big bucks to know what was happening inside Rachel's head.

Satisfied they hadn't been tailed to the hotel, Logan faced her. Six feet away and standing next to the banana-leaf-covered king bed, Rachel crossed her slender arms over her chest and studied him, her expression a blank slate—*guarded*—and he couldn't blame her.

He hadn't been back from his first deployment more than a week before learning that wearing your emotions on your sleeve made people damn uncomfortable. Those who didn't run straight for the hills often wanted to fix you. And so he'd perfected that same technique. The blank mask, or better yet, the fake one, was always the easier option.

So far, his gran had been the only one to see the raunchy T-shirts and shit-eating grin for what they were—additional camouflage. But something about the way Rachel looked at him... Maybe she saw through it too, probably because she had her own.

He'd seen it on more than one occasion, in the checklists, worn and overused, that she hid in her pockets, and in the quick, frequent smiles that didn't quite reach her eyes. And between errands and exercising and tutoring children at the youth center, he'd be hard-pressed to recollect a time when she'd sat for longer than a ten-minute stretch.

Having already made contact with Charlie, and with nothing to do but wait until they got news, Logan leaned his ass against the wall and struck a pose similar to Rachel's.

"Want to take a dip while we wait?" Logan taunted, gesturing to the already-filled hot tub.

Tucked into the corner and encased in a faux rock facade, the Jacuzzi looked more like a pond than anything man-made. Lily pads floated on the bubbling surface. Electric bamboo torches had replaced modern lamps, casting a golden glow throughout their Stranded-themed room.

"I'll take your silence as a no. Good. Then since we're relatively safe here in our own little oasis, we can fill in the blanks. Let's start with Carly's messages."

Rachel blinked, barely withholding her surprise. "That's where you want me to start?"

"Don't you worry your pretty little head, darlin', we'll backtrack to all the rest, but I need to wrap my head around what exactly we're dealing with on the Carly front. In case you didn't pick up on it, you pissed someone off."

"Maybe I'm an intimidating person."

Logan slowly eyed her slender frame. "Depends on what kind of intimidation we're talking about. And before you fly off the handle, yes, I know you're not helpless. Training with Charlie and Penny has definitely given you some nice moves, but you're not an operative."

"I'm not exactly a kindergarten teacher either. At least not anymore."

Rachel lost the stiffness in her spine, her shoulders dropping as if weighted with the mass of the globe. Logan pushed off the wall and gently guided her to the edge of the bed. "Sit before you keel the hell over."

Once she settled, he dragged the desk chair over and sat directly in front of her. "Now, let's hear it. Start with Carly's phone calls, and why she sent you to a freakin' brothel."

Rachel glanced at her hands, folded in her lap. "Carly called me a few times since Tuesday, but I never seemed to be able to catch it. I kept meaning to call her back, but it was a crazy week with preparing for Penny's birthday party. Days went by without me realizing."

"But she left messages?"

"And she sounded like her normal self and just said she was checking in and to call her back when I got the chance. Last night, she called again, but I was…" Rachel glanced down to her restless hands.

Logan slid his over her fingers, giving them a firm squeeze. "You didn't answer that call either because you were with me."

She gave him a faint nod.

He wanted to kick himself in the ass, or hell, between the legs.

He'd stayed after the party had broken up, offering his cleaning services. And as they'd put her apartment back to rights, they'd bantered back and forth. The more he teased, the pinker her cheeks had become, and he loved knowing he was one of the few people who could get a rise out of her. Eventually she'd dared him to put his lips where his flirts were, and so he'd kissed the ever-lovin' hell out of her.

"Your phone rang," Logan realized. "When we were… in the kitchen."

And they'd ignored it in favor of stripping off their clothes.

He brushed his thumb over the back of her hand. "I'm so damn sorry, darlin'."

Tears brimmed in Rachel's eyes. "It wasn't something either of us could've realized. She'd sounded fine in all of her other messages, gushing about her new boyfriend. Her last voicemail was a complete one-eighty. It wasn't the calm, steady Carly. She was scared out of her mind, and really thought that what-

ever she'd hidden at that brothel was her only way
out."

"And you're sure she wasn't—"

"High?" Rachel finished bluntly. "No. She's been
doing so well, probably even better than me."

"I know you don't like to think about it, babe, but a
lot can happen in a short period of time to—"

"Derail an addict?" Rachel pulled her hand from
his, shooting him a hard glare. "Trust me, Logan, I'm
aware. But thanks to Freedom and Diego Fuentes, I
also know how a person behaves when they're flying as
high as a Chinese kite. That wasn't Carly. It was *fear*—
pure and simple."

Logan hated the surge of pain in Rachel's eyes as she
realized what he was about to say. "I want to help Carly
too, and I want to believe that wherever she is, she's okay.
But you also need to prepare yourself for the alternative.
Healthy Carly wouldn't be hanging out at sex dens filled
with drugs, or put you at risk. And that's what she did,
darlin'. The second she asked you to collect this magi-
cal black bag, she put a target on your head—a big one.
We may not know what's in it, but her friends obviously
do, and they're willing to hire a professional to make sure
you can't do anything with it."

"I know." The first tear slipped down Rachel's cheek,
quickly followed by a second. This time, Logan couldn't
simply hold a hand. He sat next to her and pulled her
into his arms. She went willingly, her tears soaking his
shirt in seconds. "I *know* all of this, Logan. I do. But
I have to believe she's okay because if she's not...it's
totally on me. *I'm the reason she fell.*"

"The hell you are." Logan tugged her chin up, demanding her attention. "Does it suck that you didn't intercept her phone call? *Yes.* But the blame isn't on you."

"So you're saying it's *Carly's* fault?" Rachel's eyes narrowed.

"No," he said, treading carefully, knowing he'd stepped into an active minefield. Pre-Rachel, he'd would've crossed it without a care in the world, knowing that the end result justified the means. But now, holding her in his arms, her damaged heart might as well be his. "I'm saying it's the fault of Fuentes and his entire damn drug emporium. It's the fault of the drug pushers on every street corner, all over the globe. It's the fault of assholes who make money off of people's hard times. But it sure as fuck isn't yours...*or* Carly's. Neither of you asked for this to happen. It happened *to* you."

"I may not have been the one to put the drug in my veins, but I became an addict all the same. Addiction doesn't discriminate between voluntary and forced."

"You're right. It doesn't. What matters is how you handle it, and you did so gracefully."

"So gracefully that the school system turned down my job application," Rachel said dryly. "Although I can't really blame them. I don't know how I would feel about a drug addict teaching my child."

"So you keep at them. You show them everything you have to offer, and eventually they'll realize that you have a hell of a lot to give those kids. But you don't give up. That's not you."

And it wasn't.

Since the day he'd first laid eyes on her eighteen months ago, he'd recognized her for what she was—a fighter. Her recovery had been a hard one, difficult to watch, much less experience firsthand. He'd visited her in the hospital, witnessed her struggle to remain upbeat, and so he'd irritated her.

He'd flirted unabashedly.

He'd carried on inane conversations, bringing up topics he knew would get her blood boiling.

And he'd done it to show her that she still had a hell of a lot of fight in her.

"If it looks like I handled everything so well, it's because I had Penny's support, and Charlie's, and *yours*...and everyone else's at Alpha." Rachel wiped the dampness off her cheeks. "Carly didn't have that backup. *I* was her backup. I should've made myself more available. I was her friend, and I let her down."

Logan hated seeing her beat herself up. Palming her cheek, he ran his thumb over her jaw. "Sweetheart, you're trying to heal too."

"I'm fine." Rachel's brightening green eyes belied her words.

They both knew she hid more than she admitted aloud.

He gentled his voice. "There's no reason to put on an act for me. It's just the two of us here."

"I'm not putting on an—"

"You're trying to con a con man, darlin'."

She pushed his hand away and got to her feet. "You know what? You're right. I *am* putting up a front. I smile and laugh. Because if I don't, people I care about worry while others look at me like I'm going to raid their medicine cabinets the second their backs are turned. But pretending is so..."

"Exhausting."

Rachel's gaze snapped to his. "Exactly."

Logan didn't talk about his time in the Marine Corps. *To anyone.* And for all the reasons Rachel pointed out. Truth made people twitch. But he couldn't watch her pretend anymore. He couldn't let her think she was alone.

"I get the need to pretend everything smells like sunshine and roses." At her shocked expression, he added, "I laugh. I joke—sometimes in excess. I wear raunchy shirts that have my gran praying for my everlasting soul. Because if I don't, what people see would scare the shit out of them. People get a little antsy around a grumpy guy who can shoot a fly off a horse's ass at twenty-five hundred yards—go figure. Add in having the highest kill count for the shortest length of deployment and antsy turns to scared shitless."

"You're not joking now, and you weren't last night— at least not when we were together," Rachel pointed out, her voice soft.

"And look what happened. You ran for the hills."

By laying his cards out there for her to read, he'd handed her an invitation to turn tail and run—again. Standing, he paced the length of the room, fully aware of her gaze locked on him.

Sliding his fingers through his hair, he released a heavy breath. "I could try and blame it on emotional exhaustion and always having to keep a game face on, but that's not what it is when I'm around you, Rachel. I drop the act because I savor being with you, and being *me*. It feels *right*. Last night was no exception, or at least I thought so before I woke up and realized you were gone."

"I left because—"

"Of Carly's message. I know, but can you tell me without a doubt that you wouldn't have tried ducking out regardless?" At her silence, he let out a humorless laugh. "Thought so. Damn, it was like reliving the past."

Fuck.

Rachel, all too observant, cocked her head to the side. "Considering that was our first time together, I'm guessing you mean someone else?"

"My fiancée."

Rachel's mouth fell open before she could catch herself. "You were engaged?"

"Yep. And no, no one at Alpha knows." Suddenly exhausted by the entire damn conversation, Logan rubbed his face and turned toward Rachel. There was no sense in keeping it bottled up anymore, and part of him didn't want to. In order to give whatever they had together a chance, he needed it all out.

He leaned against the edge of the table, distancing himself so he could think. "After I came home from my first tour of duty, I proposed to my high school sweetheart. I was barely twenty, old enough to die for my country but not old enough to have a beer. As soon I passed my qualifiers, I went into sniper training, and then, before long, another tour. We kept pushing the wedding off. Now I realize it was a blessing in disguise. We had no business thinking about marriage."

"Just because you were young?" Rachel's voice held no judgment.

"No, because after every tour, I came home different. At first Ann tried ignoring it, but she eventually demanded reasons for my change."

"People change over time, Logan. It's the natural progression of things."

"It is, but it was more than the passing of a few years. I was a *Marine*...a Marine *sniper*." Logan clarified, "Every aspect of my deployment revolved around death. But I finally told her about the things I'd both seen and done. I purged it all. And when I woke up the next morning, it was to an empty apartment and her ring sitting on top of my rucksack."

Logan braved a glance at Rachel, both shocked and awed at the tears in her eyes. "Why are you crying, darlin'?"

Her chin trembled. "Because you bared your soul to her and she let it lie there out in the open, unprotected. You deserve so much more than that."

"I'm finally believing that...but it's taken awhile."

Realization dawned in her eyes. "The smiles. The jokes. The raunchy T-shirts..."

"All camouflage."

Logan's feet remained glued to the floor as Rachel slowly walked to him. With every step his throat dried more, so that by the time she stopped in front of him, his tongue stuck to the roof of his mouth.

As she looked at him through her silk lashes, a pool of emotions swam in her gorgeous green eyes, ratcheting up his heart rate until the sound of each pump thumped in his ears.

Rachel tentatively touched his arm, making him realize he'd bunched his hands into fists. "I didn't run out on you because you made me nervous. At least not in the way you think."

Logan's hands itched to touch her, and he did. Looping an arm around her waist, he slowly guided her against him. His body tingled where they touched, the sensation intensifying when she slid a hand around the back of his neck and into his hair.

There it was again...that sense of rightness he'd never felt with anyone. "Maybe you *should* be running in the other direction. You would if you knew what was good for you."

"I *do* know what's good for me...and it just so happens that it's a moody former Marine sniper who can pull off both a yellow pineapple shirt and one that claims him to be an Orgasm Donor."

A small smile tilted Rachel's lips. As he cupped her cheek, Logan caressed the curve of her mouth with his thumb. "You like my shirt, do you, darlin'?"

"You said you didn't want to pretend with me, Logan, and I feel the same way about you. You *do* make me nervous. Without a doubt. But it has nothing to do with what you shared with me and everything to do with how alive and powerful you make me feel."

"You don't need me to make you feel powerful. You're strong all on your own."

Rachel smiled, her gaze flicking down to his mouth and back. "And *that's* exactly what I mean."

Lifting to her toes, she brushed her mouth against his. Swept away on first contact, Logan shifted his grip and invited her to deepen the kiss. And she did. She gave him so much more than he could ever hope to give her.

Logan had once vowed to never again leave himself vulnerable.

But with Rachel, he felt anything but.

He felt powerful.

CHAPTER FIVE

Uncertainty didn't stop Rachel from approaching Logan, or kissing the hell out of him. For once she ignored that self-conscious, unsure voice in the back of her head and followed that warm tug in the center of her chest straight into Logan's arms—as she had the previous night.

Her heart throbbed, aching from his story and, more importantly, the emotion his words conjured. And she understood it. She understood *him*.

Maybe that was why this felt so damn right.

Muffled by the window, the honking cars and roaring engines became background music to the sway of their bodies. Rachel couldn't touch Logan enough. She ran her fingers through his hair, holding him close in case he dared pull away. His hands, in return, anchored her firmly against his body, his calloused fingers kneading her hips.

Everyone else treated her like fine china, but not Logan. It was a heady feeling for someone who'd felt trapped for the last year and a half.

Logan's mouth pulled away, making her groan in protest. Panting as heavily as her, he gifted her with a crooked grin. "You need to make sure this is what you want, darlin'. I'm not going to pretend to know what's happening between us, but going this route isn't going to make it any clearer."

"Maybe not, but it makes me certain of a few other things." At the inquisitive lift of his eyebrow, she added, "That I don't want you to stop touching me. That I don't feel like damaged goods when you're kissing me. And that when you're holding me, I feel like the person I was before I went to Honduras."

"You took the words right out of my mouth." He gently caressed her mouth in a featherlight kiss. "We'll figure all of this out—including us. And we'll do it together."

Rachel agreed in a soft whisper, "Sounds good to me."

Logan gave a slow glance around the room. As his attention returned to her, a coy smirk lifted the corner of his mouth. "On a scale of one to ten, how much do you trust me?"

Rachel barely contained a chuckle. "Is that a trick question?"

"Close your eyes and don't peek."

"For how long?" Rachel didn't mask the wariness in her voice as she watched him carefully.

"Until I tell you to open them."

Getting that kind of order from anyone else, Rachel

wouldn't have agreed. But this was *Logan*. She closed her eyes and sensed a small puff of air in front of her. "Did you check to see if I was peeking?"

Logan chuckled. "I know you Kline women are allergic to surprises, so yeah."

He kept her guessing as to what he was doing, because he didn't stay in any one spot. He walked back and forth across the room, either dropping a kiss to the back of her neck or caressing her bottom each time.

Off to the far left, something purred to life, filling the room with the sound of bubbling water and the faint scent of coconut. The unmistakable sound of a lowering zipper made her catch her breath.

Logan's clothes.

Seconds later, water gently sloshed as if being disturbed. "Am I allowed to open my eyes now?"

Logan's voice dropped to a masculine purr. "Go ahead, gorgeous."

Rachel blinked, adjusting her vision to the newly dimmed light. Logan had turned off the main brights and found the switches that operated the wall-mounted tiki torches. It resulted in a romantic glow, both on the hot tub and on the man lounging inside.

Shadows darkened the planes of Logan's face, and slick and dotted with water droplets, his bare chest looked oh-so-touchable. Her gaze dropped to his clothes on the floor.

Shirt. Pants. *Boxers.*

"Got pretty comfortable, didn't you?" Rachel teased, thankful for the dimness masking her warm cheeks.

"It would be a hell of a lot more comfy if you were

in here with me." Logan's stare heated her to her core. Arms propped on the ledge of the faux hot spring, he crooked a long figure in her direction. "Lose the clothes. I want to see Rachel—not Priscilla."

Rachel's heart skipped a beat. He'd seen her naked before, but this time felt different. She reached around to her back, found the zipper, and lowered it until all that held the dress in place was her hands. Watching Logan as the dress dropped to the ground with a weighty thunk, she caught the firm bob of his Adam's apple.

"Goddamn, darlin'. You're gorgeous." Logan's hands gripped the edge of the tub as if he was trying not to reach out. "Now the rest."

A sudden sense of rightness washed over her, and before Rachel realized, she'd unhooked her bra, letting it fall to the heap along with her dress, and next were her panties. "Better?"

"Come here." Logan's eyes glittered, feasting on her body as she carefully made her way to the small steps leading into the hot tub. At the final step, Logan wrapped his hand around hers and supported her descent into the warm water. The second she was within arm's length, he eased her onto his lap.

Her legs parted automatically, making room for his waist. "I'm here."

"Damn straight you are." Skin on skin. Body against body. Trapped between them, his rock-hard erection pushed into their stomachs. "I wanted to take my time with you."

"And now you don't?"

A heady combo of mischief and desire burned in his

eyes. His hands, slow and steady, ran up her torso, gently cupping her breasts. "Now I want to be inside of you."

Lowering his mouth to her left breast, he placed an open-mouthed kiss over her nipple. The bud instantly tightened, sending a zap of heat straight to her core. Rachel squirmed. "I think I like that idea better."

"I love the way your body reacts to me," Logan brushed his thumbs across both aching nipples. "Always so hot and primed."

"No different than yours." To demonstrate her point, she rolled her hips. Her lower stomach brushed softly against his erection.

His chuckle ended on a groan as she rolled a second time, shifting her weight on his lap until she brushed him from root to tip. "Maybe a *little* different."

Rachel ran her hands up his arms and over his shoulders. Threading her fingers into the back of his hair, she firmed her grip and heard him hiss as she lowered her mouth to his. That's all they needed to stoke the fire. On a deep groan, Logan slipped into her mouth and devoured her like a man who hadn't eaten in months.

Every slow glide of their tongues zapped a new electrical current through her body. When he thrust, she parried, occasionally sliding back far enough to nibble on his bottom lip. The cat-and-mouse play turned the kiss hotter, their touches more brazen.

His hand kneaded her hip in an attempt to hold her still while its coworker ran its fingers along the sensitive flesh of her inner leg. Rachel opened her thighs wider. "Touch me, Logan. Please."

"Where?" Logan circled his fingers over her mound, not quite touching her where she needed him the most. "Here?"

Rachel whimpered, swiveling her hips in an attempt to get him where she wanted him. "I don't need all this foreplay, cowboy. I'm more than ready."

Logan kept his touch slow and purposeful as he teased her opening. His slid his fingers through her wetness, avoiding the hot throbbing button of her clit. "How about here?"

"Please." Panting, Rachel pushed her mound closer to his exploring hand.

"Good things come to those who wait, darlin'."

"I don't want to wait anymore." In a burst of need, she reached between them and palmed his cock.

Logan groaned. "No damn fair."

"More than fair." Rachel grinned as his length twitched in her hand. Her tease worked.

On a low growl, Logan plunged two fingers into her body. She gasped, one hand gripping his shoulder to keep herself upright as he pumped. At every three or four thrusts, his thumb brushed against her clit. Her body quivered, tightened in preparation for a big finish, but she didn't want to come without him. Exerting more pressure with her hand, she pumped his throbbing cock in what became a delicious give-and-take.

"Fuck. Stop." Logan caught her wrist, halting her movements. "I'm one pump away from blowing and no way am I doing it in a damn hot tub when I could be coming inside of you."

* * *

Logan couldn't grab the condom fast enough. He needed Rachel more than his next breath—or hell, his Stetson, which was currently lying somewhere in a police station parking lot.

Unwilling to tear his eyes away from her glittering green gaze, he felt around the edge of the tub until he grabbed the foil packet. Fingers wet and slick, he ripped into the package. The condom blasted from the wrapper, hitting him square in the face before plopping into the water.

Shock froze him a split second, followed by the stinging pain. "Holy hell."

Rachel's soft giggle slowly turned to full-blown laughter. "Did the condom just hit you in the eye?"

"And now I'm freakin' blind!" Blinking furiously, Logan willed the tears to dry up and his eyes to focus, but the harder he tried, the more his frustration built.

"Stop and let me see." Chuckling, Rachel's hand slid over his face, soft and gentle as she cupped his cheek and tilted his head up.

Her oval face slowly came into view. Her cheeks, pink from the warmth of the hot tub, were arched high in a beautiful smile. And her hair, hanging in damp auburn waves, fell in soft ringlets off her bare shoulders.

She took his breath away.

"You're so fucking gorgeous, darlin'."

"Says the man who can't see," Rachel teased, her smile widening.

"I can see just fine now." His eye still stung like a son

of a bitch, but hell if that would stop him from being with her. He anchored an arm around her waist, holding her close, and searched the bottom of the hot tub for the offending rubber. "Where's that damn—aha!"

He plucked it out of the water only to have Rachel take it from his fingers. "Maybe I should do the honors this time...to make sure everyone keeps their eyes in their sockets."

Logan's chuckle was cut off by a long groan as she rolled the condom onto his length. He'd made a damn fool of himself, but his dick sure hadn't softened. Sliding his hand back between her legs, he realized it hadn't dampened her arousal any either.

"Where were we before I got blindsided?" Logan pushed his hips into her hand.

"Right about"—Rachel hovered over him before sinking onto his cock in one drop of her hips—"here."

"That's what I'm talking about." Gripping her thighs, he eased her into a slow rocking motion that made them both groan. They fit perfectly. Like a dream. And unlike last time, he wasn't about to let her slink away after.

It wasn't long before her muscles tightened around him like a vise. His cock throbbed, pulsing. His balls ached with an impending release. Sliding his hand between their bodies, he brushed his fingers against her clit.

Rachel erupted in a powerful cry, her trembling body conjuring his own release. They picked up the pace, thrusting and gliding through the pleasure until the fierce waves gentled.

Logan brushed a series of kisses over Rachel's bare

shoulder, smiling with the knowledge that she sounded as winded as him. "I hope you realize that I'm not letting you sneak away this time."

"If I tried, I'd probably slip on the water and fall on my rear end." Rachel chuckled nervously.

Logan didn't want any miscommunication. He trapped her chin between his fingers and held her attention hostage. "After this is all over, after we find Carly and make sure she's safe, I want to see how far we can go with this."

Drawing her bottom lip between her teeth, Rachel whispered, "This?"

"*Us.* You and me. I'm not hiding anything anymore, Rachel. I've wanted this…*you*…for a long time, and I'm hoping that's what you want too." Logan's chest felt heavy and light all at the same damn time. He kissed Rachel again, unable to stop touching her. As he shifted their bodies closer, his cell rang.

"Fuck." Logan groaned. "I got to—"

"Go. Get it."

He missed Rachel's body the second she lifted off him, but he hustled out of the water, catching a glimpse of her bare ass as she followed him and grabbed two towels from the bathroom. He reached the phone at the same time that she covered her gorgeous body.

"What have you got for us?" Logan asked in lieu of a greeting.

"About damn time you answered. Busy getting a massage or something, cowboy?" Charlie huffed on the other end.

"Or something." Logan chuckled. "Update me."

"Interesting little tidbit about Rachel's cell mates... they've all been released."

Logan put the phone on speaker and nodded Rachel over. "They've *all* been released?"

"Every single one of them, from those who'd been charged with drug possession to prostitution. No bond hearing. No little chitchats in the judge's chambers. The charges were simply dropped as if they never existed, which means—"

"They have a guardian angel who happens to be pretty high on the food chain," Logan finished.

"Or who has control over someone who is. I've been trying to tie the brothel to a property, but it hasn't been easy. Instead of a name, it's linked to a line of dummy corporations. I'll be able to narrow it down eventually, but Carly's not going to have that kind of time."

"But your gut's whispering a specific name, isn't it?" Rachel asked.

"It is," Charlie admitted. "I don't have the proof yet, but I'll go back to my original hair color if Dean Carson isn't involved in some way. And by *some way*, I mean with his grimy convict paws all over it."

Logan dwelled on Charlie's hunch. "Why does that name sound familiar?"

"He's the owner of that new casino that opened on the strip, Sinful Players, along with a few others, a handful of nightclubs, and a couple of apartment complexes. And according to Carly's tax records, she's not only employed at Sinful Players, but she lives in one of the employee suites."

"Is this news to you?" Logan glanced to Rachel's

shocked expression, disappointed that she'd slipped back into her dress.

Rachel's brow furrowed. "I knew she changed apartments because of issues with noisy neighbors, but I didn't know she'd moved into a hotel, or that her public relations position was with one of the casinos."

Rachel's mouth opened and closed before she nibbled on her lower lip, deep in thought. "Carly's new boyfriend's name is Dean."

Logan didn't like the sudden change of direction— for all their sakes. "Would you recognize him if you saw a picture?"

Rachel nodded. "She sent me one of them at some kind of charity event last month."

"Charlie?"

"Already texting you," Charlie announced.

Five seconds later, Logan's cell pinged with the new notification. He brought the image up on the screen and slid it toward Rachel. "Look familiar?"

"That's him. I don't remember Carly ever telling me his last name, but that's definitely the new boyfriend."

Logan's gut twitched. "So Carly's new boyfriend isn't only her landlord and her boss, but probably the owner of the drug brothel."

"This entire situation's getting worse by the second," Rachel admitted worriedly.

"Yeah, babe, it is." Logan grabbed his shorts and tugged them on. "Do me a solid, Charlie, and get a set of wheels delivered to our hotel. And we're going to need two sets of undercover duds—one for sleuthing and one for a swanky night out."

Charlie's silence spoke volumes.

"You got something to say, Sparks?"

"Am I on speakerphone still?"

Logan locked eyes with Rachel. Her frown dipped lower as she addressed Charlie. "You don't need to waste your breath. There's no way I'm staying behind."

Charlie's voice softened. "Hon, I know you've come a long way, and Carson may not be Fuentes, but he hasn't gotten where he is in Vegas's underground by being a pussycat."

"Which is why Logan's here. We have no idea what kind of shape Carly's going to be in, and that means that I need to be there too."

"Rachel can handle it," Logan added. He spoke to Charlie, but his eyes never left the woman standing next to him. Rachel stared him dead in the eye, gifting him a small smile of appreciation.

On the other line of the phone, Charlie sighed. "Fine, but know that your ball sack's on the line. Penny's gone downright feral. Any payback against the male persuasion she can dish out, she will."

"And what exactly did the male species do now?"

"Made morning sickness an actual thing."

Logan grinned, imagining the fiery redhead on the warpath. "Tell her all payback should be aimed at her husband. He's the one that helped her create that little dictator in residence."

Charlie belted out a laugh. "Don't think she hasn't. I'll email the two of you what I have on the den and the casino, and I'll keep working on uncovering more links. If Carson owns one hole-in-the-ground business,

chances are that he owns a hell of a lot more. Be careful.
Let us know if you need anything."

"Our night-on-the-town packages?" Logan wanted
to make sure the pink-haired operative didn't forget
their undercover gear.

"Everything will be there within the half hour," Charlie promised. "And I'm also going to help Stone formu-
late some kind of backup, because as capable as you
are, Dean Carson's underground network is nothing to
sneeze at."

"Sounds good, Char, thanks."

Charlie disconnected the call. Logan tried wrapping
his head around all the information. If Carly really had
gotten mixed up with Dean Carson, chances were high
that they would need more than two pairs of hands.

CHAPTER SIX

After two hours of lying low, Rachel inspected her new and improved hair from left to right, angling her head to look at it from different vantage points. Maybe she'd taken the undercover thing a degree too far, but nothing could be done about it now.

About seven inches of wavy auburn hair currently lay on top of an empty Sweet Mahogany Clairol box, leaving Rachel with a stylishly shagged and shoulder-length cut. The style lightened her head by a good few pounds, or at least that's how it felt.

Adding to the drastic transformation was Charlie's *sleuthing* outfit.

The black leather pants clung to her legs like a second skin, making them look miles longer than reality, and the dark, curve-hugging tank left little to the imagination. If this was the operative's idea of low-key,

Rachel dreaded seeing what she'd chosen for their appearance at Sinful Players.

"Here's goes nothing." Unable to procrastinate any further, Rachel tucked her burner cell into her cleavage and opened the door.

One step and she collided with a rock-solid chest. She bounced back, off balance and arms flailing. Logan quickly settled her back on her feet—and against him.

"I realize I'm known for making the ladies swoon, but that has to be a new record. I don't even think you had the chance to lay eyes on me," Logan's deep voice teased.

"Guess you're growing more potent."

Rachel braved a glance up, and holy hotness. Dressed in a Henley, its sleeves rolled up to his elbows, and dark jeans, Logan epitomized masculine perfection. Him in any outfit—cowboy attire, camo, or a glittery ballerina costume—put women aged sixteen years to eighty at risk of drowning in a puddle of their own drool.

Logan's gaze traveled down the length of her body, lingering on her legs before traveling back up in a lazy stroll. As his gray eyes darkened, his grip on her hips tightened. "You look fucking incredible, darlin'. I don't know whether to thank Charlie or strangle her. Keeping my head on straight is going to be one hell of a challenge."

Rachel rolled her eyes at the exaggeration. Nothing took Logan's attention away from a mission, but the compliment still conjured a little stomach flutter.

"You cut your hair." Logan tucked a strand of now-dark-brown hair behind her ear. The lock stubbornly bounced back into position along her cheek.

"Uh. Yeah. I may have gotten a little carried away." Any concern about her self-imposed new haircut was melted away by the heated look in his eyes. "You like it?"

His fingers slipped into the shortened strands, brushing her cheek in the process. "I love it. I mean, I loved the long locks too, but this suits you. It's spunky. Edgy."

She cocked a dark eyebrow, fighting not to laugh. "I don't think I've ever been called edgy. Maybe before Honduras, but definitely not since."

Rachel quieted. But unlike at other times, mentioning her time in captivity didn't paralyze her. Steady and sure, her heart continued at a slow trot, and each breath eased in and out through her lungs without so much as a quick catch.

A slow smile spread on Logan's lips. "Maybe your edginess was in hibernation, waiting until you were ready to take another whirl."

Rachel brushed her hand over Logan's stubbled jaw and into his own freshly trimmed hair. "Or maybe the right person needed to come along and coax it out."

"I like the sound of that too." Logan slowly eased her into a soft kiss.

Resting her palm on his chest, she melted against him, hating the eventual break in contact. As much as she'd like to stand there and kiss him all night, they were saddled with a time constraint. Two o'clock in the morning didn't mean much in Sin City, but it could mean everything to Carly.

"We're going to have to push pause and continue this later," Rachel teased, hearing Logan groan.

"You're right. Let's go bring Carly home where she belongs." Palming the small of her back, he grabbed the bag holding their casino clothes and guided her downstairs to where a black SUV sat out front. He held her door open, his eyes ogling her legs as she slid into the passenger seat. "Remind me never to get on Charlie's bad side."

"Why's that?" Rachel grinned, already knowing where his mind had gone.

"Because I hate to think about what she would've dressed you in if I had pissed her off." Logan dropped a kiss on her mouth before coming around to the driver's side.

His stride remained easy, but there wasn't a doubt that he was aware of everything happening around them, from the gathering tourist group on the right side of the sidewalk to the group of twentysomething men about to break out into a scuffle. Everyone at Alpha Security did it—including Charlie. They watched without staring and catalogued everything without writing it down. Having spent so much time at Alpha, even Rachel was more aware of her surroundings.

Logan pulled their SUV into traffic, jumping out in front of a cab.

Rachel turned her attention to the street slowly passing them by. They'd gone over their plan a few dozen times, and with each one she'd grown more anxious and formed more questions.

Logan's hand slid over her knee.

"You okay?" He alternated glances between her and the traffic in front of them, concern tilting his mouth into a frown. "I can turn around and drop you off back at the room...do this on my own."

"No. I was just thinking." Rachel's heart warmed at his concern, and knew that she would've felt different about the suggestion a few short days ago. But with Logan it wasn't about a lack of faith in her abilities or her coping mechanisms. He simply wanted to protect her in general, not because she wasn't strong enough to deal.

"About?"

"I think the reason Carly told me the location of the bag was because she knew she wasn't going be at the brothel when I got there," Rachel admitted painfully. "She'd run out of options, and that worries me, Logan. She'd never put someone in danger if she thought there was another choice."

Logan nodded, face grim. "I think you're probably right. But I also think she called you because she knew if anyone could find a way out of a shit-storm, it would be you. We'll find that damn bag and get whatever's inside to the proper authorities...and then we'll bring her home. Trust me?"

Rachel covered his hand with hers, this time giving him the reassuring squeeze. "I trust you more than anything or anyone."

And she did.

Logan nodded, and his throat worked overtime as he swallowed an unspoken emotion. There wasn't a single reappearance of his crooked smirk the rest of their drive to the Vegas suburb where the raid had taken place. Twenty minutes later, Logan pulled the SUV to the side of the road, a few houses from the shut-down brothel.

Wooden planks boarded up the broken windows, and yellow police tape covered the front door. The place would have looked far from inviting even without questionable people loitering around the block.

Logan's jaw hardened as he glared at the nondescript brick house. "What the hell were you thinking going into a place like that alone?"

"It's really not as bad as it looks," Rachel lied. The falsehood earned her Logan's sharp glare. "Okay, so it's pretty bad."

"The raid was a goddamn blessing," Logan growled.

"I would've wished it happened a few minutes later... like after I'd gotten my hands on Carly's little black bag. At least then maybe I'd have deserved getting shot at."

"No one deserves getting shot at. On second thought, some people do, but you're definitely not one of them."

They climbed out of the SUV and headed down the sidewalk. Off in the distance a dog barked. On the left a light post buzzed and flickered before blinking out.

Guiding her with a light hand on the elbow, Logan used his other to pull his gun free. "Let's go around the rear. And stay behind me."

The back steps creaked as they climbed onto the rickety porch. Logan yanked the police tape away and leaned his shoulder against the door itself. It gave way easily, and Rachel flicked on her flashlight.

No one had bothered to clean the place up after the raid. Trash and party remnants littered the floor and counters. A small creature scurried away from her flashlight beam. Rachel tried not thinking about it as she swept the light across the room, finally finding the intake vent along the far wall. "Right there. She said it was the largest vent just outside the kitchen."

Rachel dropped to the ground and pulled out the small screwdriver they'd brought with them while Logan watched their backs. It didn't take much effort. With one screw out, the grate collapsed onto the floor. She aimed the light inside and peered around. "I don't see anything. It's just one big hole that goes to the basement."

"Feel around the inside of the walls."

Rachel threw him a glare. "You want me to blindly stick my hand inside a dark crevice and feel around?"

Even in the dim light, she saw him grin. "You wanted to come along."

Rachel ignored his chuckle and shoved her hand into the dark abyss of the air vent. She felt around, reaching up until her fingers bumped into something soft. She worked at the edges and pulled it free.

A small wave of relief hit her as she shone the light on a small black bag. She tore into it, pulling out its only content. A flash drive. "Someone took shots at me because of a freaking piece of plastic and metal."

"Makes me wonder what's on that piece of plastic and metal." Logan helped her get to her feet. "We need to download whatever's on that drive and send it off to Charlie. Something tells me that whatever it is, Carson's not going to want too many pairs of eyes on it— especially ones belonging to law enforcement."

* * *

Logan locked his eyes on the woman on the computer screen in front of him and not the one grunting in the back seat of the SUV. At least until a softly muttered curse pulled his attention to the rearview mirror.

Rachel, visible from the waist up, shifted in the back seat, tugging on the leather pants still trapping her legs. Her perfectly cupped breasts threatened to spill from her bra.

"Having a problem back there, darlin'? Need an extra pair of hands?" he teased.

Her eyes found his in the mirror, and her threatening smirk matched his. She gave one sharp final tug and pulled herself free. "Tell Charlie that I love her, but she's never picking out my clothes ever again. Changing outfits shouldn't have me breaking out into a sweat."

"Did it do the job? Because really, that's all that matters at this point." Charlie's voice filled the truck. The Alpha operative had been working her technical magic with the information they'd sent her from the flash drive.

"If their job was chafing me? Then yes. They did it to perfection."

Charlie snorted as she worked from the other side of the computer screen. "You didn't get caught snooping in a crime scene, so they worked."

"Sweatpants would've worked just as well."

"But your legs wouldn't have looked killer doing it."

Logan chuckled, enjoying the banter. "The woman does have a point."

Rachel grunted at him before slipping a sleek red dress over her head. A sharp contrast to the black leather, the evening gown encased her body like a soft glove. But the plunging neckline made her bra a no-go. Realizing she had to take it off, Rachel mumbled another string of PG-rated curses.

"So what do we have, Char?" Logan yanked his attention back to their immediate task.

"My decryption software is just about done and..." Charlie tapped a few more keys before letting out a long, low whistle. "Bloody hell. If Carson believed you had this, it's no surprise he's sent someone to snuff you out."

Rachel climbed over the middle console and into the passenger seat. "It's incriminating?"

"It's more than incriminating, and not only to Carson, but to a long list of business associates. He's kept a running log of transactions between him and a bevy of well-knowns."

"You're talking what? Celebrities or something?"

"Not just celebrities, but businessmen and high-ranking government officials—local, state, and federal. And if I'm seeing all this correctly, and I am, his charge for keeping them supplied with all the best drugs is *favors*. Pulled strings. Contacts. Information on this little piece of plastic is enough for the DA to dish out at least two dozen arrest warrants—and that's a conservative number and only what I can see straight off the top. And let me tell you, some of the people on this list aren't the type to go down easily. If they get wind of its existence, Carson's in for a world of hurt."

Logan and Rachel exchanged glances, but it was Rachel who spoke. "Carly must've found it, and either got caught with it, or tried brokering some kind of freedom."

"But not before contacting you and putting it in what she thought of as a safe place." Logan nodded. He turned back to Charlie on the laptop screen. "Make sure this information gets to the proper authorities. Rachel and I are going to check out Carly's apartment at the hotel, and then have a look around the casino... see if anything catches our eyes."

Charlie nodded, her face grim. "Trapped animals rarely just lie down and roll over. Be careful."

Logan cocked up an eyebrow. "An animal analogy, Charlie? Am I rubbing off of you?"

The pink-haired operative snorted. "As if, cowboy. Backup's already en route, but you still need to watch your arses."

They ended their video call and, after making sure they were sufficiently dressed for an appearance at Sinful Players, drove around the corner to where the casino's valet stood sentry at the main doors.

Logan handed the SUV keys to the attendant along with an unmistakable wad of cash.

"To make sure he puts it in the spot nearest to the side exit," Logan explained when Rachel flashed him a questioning look.

Dean Carson had spared no expense when designing his latest hotel and casino. Laid out in an extravagant design, marble-tiled floors covered the main lobby, and in the grand foyer, a two-story fountain trickled into an indoor lagoon. Light from suspended chandeliers bounced off the colored glass artwork that hung from the vaulted ceilings. The effect was a staggering display of colored rainbows throughout the hall.

At close to four in the morning, the place was going strong, with only a few stragglers looking as if they were about to call it a night. Nearly everyone else looked upbeat and lively, as if they had a few more good hours in them.

Draping a hand over Rachel's lower hip, Logan guided her through to the hotel's grand entryway and to the rotunda of elevators that would take them to the sixteenth floor. The second the elevator doors closed them in, he spun her around and dropped a scorching kiss to her mouth. Getting lost in the feel of her lips on his didn't take any acting.

He slid his hand across her hip and over her ass. Rachel moaned against his mouth, slipping her palms beneath the hem of his shirt and quickly finding the path of hair that bisected his eight-pack abs and disappeared beneath the waist of his pants.

They'd wanted to create a diversion for anyone watching on security cams, but the joke was all on him. He could barely remember his name, much less what they were about to do.

"Keep traveling south, darlin', and you're going to have your hands full." Logan nipped her bottom lip.

Rachel chuckled, dipping her fingertips into the band of his suit pants. "Did you mean that to sound so dirty?"

"You're killing me here, sweetheart," Logan groaned against her mouth. As the elevator came to a stop, his arm banded tighter around her waist. "Ready to maul me out in the open?"

"Let's go for the Oscar." Rachel wrapped her arms

around his shoulders and locked her legs around his waist. She fixed her mouth to his a second before the elevator doors opened, spilling them into the hall.

Groping what they couldn't kiss, they stalked the sixteenth-floor corridor in a flurry of heated kisses and overloud groans. Logan pushed her back against the wall, kicking an empty room service cart for good measure.

In his eight years in the Marines and his five with Alpha, Logan had never once bypassed security cams by tangling limbs with a sexy redhead-turned-brunette. But he wasn't complaining. Only problem was that their hallway show was supposed to distract Carson's goons from realizing the room they were entering wasn't their own, but it was also distracting Logan.

Logan palmed Rachel's ass, kissing her as if he needed the contact to breathe. He spun, gently pinning her to the door of 1605 as he searched his pocket for their access card. "You're too damn good at this distraction thing."

"Thank you." Slightly out of breath from their kisses, she pulled the credit card from his jacket's inner pocket and placed it in his hand. "I'm more than a little disturbed that a little piece of plastic is all it takes to get in one of these rooms."

"It also takes a little finesse." He inserted the card in the crack of the door and jimmied it into the locking mechanism. In less than two seconds the door clicked open. Logan dropped her to her feet and took the lead position. "Stay behind me until we're sure the room's safe."

A typical size by hotel standards, the room was

devoid of generic hotel furnishings. Framed, expensive artwork hung on the walls. An overstuffed sofa and armchair created a cozy sitting area in front of the double-wide window, and the king-size bed overflowed with decorative pillows.

And someone had destroyed it all.

"Either Carly's allergic to the hotel cleaning service or someone destroyed this place after their last visit." Logan double-checked the bathroom, making sure they were alone.

Rachel picked up a broken picture frame and stared at the image until tears welled in her eyes. Logan came up next to her, sensing the regret tightening her body as he gazed at the two smiling faces in the photo.

Rachel and Carly.

After their imprisonment in Honduras, neither of them had had it easy. People nodded as if they understood the challenges even the smallest task took, but they didn't. Hell, even Logan didn't understand it all, no matter how he tried.

But Carlotta had.

Logan had thanked God every day that Carlotta and Rachel had been able to lean on each other through the rough patches. Helping Carly now was one small way he could thank her for being there for Rachel.

"I want to stop Carson, but I want to find Carly even more, Logan. I owe it to her." Rachel returned the picture to its upright position.

Logan brushed an errant lock of brown hair off her cheek. "This isn't your fault, darlin'."

"No. But I sure as hell didn't make it any better. I can't

believe Carly would've known about Carson's dealings and stuck around. The last time we spoke, she'd never been so resolved to stay clean and out of trouble."

Logan took her hand and squeezed. "Maybe he hid it all from her. We already know the bastard's resourceful. He could've kept her in the dark about his little side businesses and by the time she'd realized, he'd gotten her mixed up in something. It doesn't mean she went down a bad road willingly."

Hope glittered in her eyes, and Logan would do anything to keep it there.

"Let's keep looking around. If we're lucky, we'll find something that may give us a clue as to where she might be. But we need to hustle before our adoring audience realizes that we didn't go into our own room."

"And if we don't find anything?"

"Then we head down to the casino. Maybe we'll get lucky and run into one of your old roommates, but I'm not making any bets on it. I'm also making sure Charlie has that backup at the ready—to be on the safe side."

"I thought everyone's on assignment. And even if they aren't, it'll take too long for them to get here. Who's Charlie calling in to help?"

"Nice thing about having a boss that's as badass as they come is getting to draw on his connections. Stone will hook us up."

CHAPTER SEVEN

Rachel wanted to hunt down Dean Carson, grab him by the collar of his thousand-dollar suit, and demand answers *and* her friend. Instead Logan guided her into the posh, overindulgent casino that drew the affluent Vegas community like a bear to a honey hive.

Excitement buzzed through the casino floor. Charlie's choice of undercover outfits fit in well with the high-priced dresses and suits. Even the waitresses and casino attendants were dressed to impress, their "uniforms" probably having cost more than one of Rachel's old teacher paychecks.

A busty brunette hostess sashayed up to a blackjack table with a tray of drinks, sliding her ample hips in between a pair of businessmen. The older of the two smiled at her and cupped her ass with his hand.

Rachel's stomach rolled. "Some of these waitresses must know *something*."

Logan ran his hand in a soothing caress up and down her back. "They might, but they're also employees of a known criminal. Chances are that even if they do know something, they'll be too scared to say anything. And if they're close to him on the hierarchy, they could rat us out to Carson in the hope of getting on the man's good side. It's not a chance I'm willing to take. Yet."

Rachel hated that he was right. If they drew Carson's attention, finding Carly would be next to impossible.

She sank against Logan's side as they walked deeper into the room. People littered every square inch of the casino, one not distinguishable from the next—except for the security.

Dressed in dark suits and ear comms, the gorilla-size men strategically positioned themselves every six feet. Neither the men nor the awkward bulges beneath their jackets were exactly subtle.

"Why does casino security need to be outfitted like they're ready to step onto a battlefield?" Rachel murmured.

"Noticed that, did you?" Logan chuckled dryly. "You're hanging out at Alpha too much. But yeah, they'd set off a metal detector by getting within fifty feet of one. Let's try not to do anything that puts us in their crosshairs."

Logan spun her into his arms, chest to chest, and dropped his gaze to her mouth. On reflex, her tongue flicked out, wetting her bottom lip. "Looking at me like that isn't going to keep us off their radar," she said.

"Darlin', me not touching you is a surefire way to draw attention, because every male in this room, bulky security included, is going to wonder what the hell's wrong with me." He brushed his thumb over her jaw, concern glimmering in his eyes. "I just want to make sure you're okay."

"I'm searching for my missing friend who just so happens to have a crime boss boyfriend known for dabbling in every branch of illegal activity that's out there. How do you think I am?"

"I'm not going to let anything happen to you."

"It's not me I'm worried about." She braced her palm on his chest and watched his gray eyes darken. "So if we're not questioning the employees, what are we going to do? Play a few games of roulette?"

"Something like that."

No one paid them any attention as they worked the room, bypassing the crowds of people sitting on red leather chairs in front of high-end slot machines. Every game appeared to have high stakes.

Logan's arm firmed around her waist as they approached a blackjack table. "We'll have a good view of the room from here. I'll try my luck with you as my charm while you inconspicuously look for your friends. If you see any of them, or if you lay eyes on Carly, you let me know. Hopefully Stone's backup will make an appearance soon."

Logan entered the next game and Rachel stayed on his arm, casually glancing around in between giving him encouraging kisses on the cheek. Waitresses in butt cheek–revealing minidresses strutted the room, some carrying trays filled with drinks while others appeared to be patron eye candy.

Rachel scanned every woman who walked by, and with each one, her frustration grew. All these people and not a single one looked familiar—until her gaze traveled over two young coeds trying to cash out at the counter and the blonde standing next to them.

The last time she'd seen Stella had been in the Las Vegas holding cell, and she had been far from put together. Rachel almost didn't recognize her. Her makeup was now artfully applied and flawless, her sequined dress molded to her stick-thin figure like a second skin.

Rachel took another hard look to be certain it was her. The put-together Stella picked that moment to look her way, snagging her gaze. Recognition blazed in Stella's eyes from across the room.

"We have a big problem." Heart thundering in her chest, Rachel sidled close to Logan. "The blonde over there is the head honcho of the brothel and I'm pretty sure she made me."

Logan's gaze was focused on two slowly approaching brutes. "I think we've *both* been made."

"Sir, we're going to have to ask you to come with us." A pair of Carson's goons stopped behind Logan's shoulder.

Logan threw on a grin, playing with his newly acquired tokens. "Sorry, fellas, but I'm not done exhausting my monetary funds. Give me a few seconds to sweeten the pot a little bit and then I'm all yours."

"Coming with us wasn't a request," the taller of the brutes announced. "The house has rules about counting cards and working against the dealers."

The patrons seated around the table gawked eagerly as the tension escalated.

Logan took a menacing step closer to the first guard. "I was doing no such thing."

"Then you won't mind coming with us and clearing it up with the boss."

Logan's gaze shifted between the two men before he glanced around them. At least four nearby guards looked on alert. "Actually, I do mind. As you can see, I'm entertaining a lady friend."

The second guard leered at Rachel, making her skin crawl. "She looks more than capable of entertaining herself."

They wanted to separate them.

The guard closest to Logan stepped forward, putting them nearly nose to nose. He lowered his voice for only their ears. "We can do this one of two ways, buddy. But only one of them ensures that your lady friend remains unscathed. And in case you're dense, it's coming with us without a damn argument."

Logan's body stiffened, prepping to go on an offensive that wouldn't work.

Rachel squeezed his arm before he did something to make the situation worse. "It's okay, baby. I'll be perfectly fine here until you get his all cleared up."

"I'm not leaving you here." Logan glared at the two guards.

"Logan," Rachel murmured, brushing her lips over his cheek. "We don't have a choice."

"You have your cell. Call Stone—"

"My fingers are practically dialing already." She

pulled him into a kiss and said louder, for surrounding ears, "I'll have a special prize for you later. Hurry back, baby."

Rachel watched as Logan followed his two new friends through the casino, and rescued her cell phone from her cleavage. She'd barely finished typing head-quarters' number when someone yanked the phone from her hands.

"If it isn't the snooty princess someplace else she doesn't belong." Stella's ruby-red lips jerked into a cat-that-ate-the-canary smile as she stomped on Rachel's phone with a daggerlike heel. "Are you going to tell me that you being here is a coincidence? Again?"

Rachel lifted her chin and met the other woman's glare. "No. I'm still looking for my friend, and I think you know exactly where she is."

"I don't make a habit of stalking the boss's playthings. There's too damn many of them to keep track of."

Rachel couldn't call the other woman out for lying, because, sadly, she didn't think Stella was making up Carson's fondness for women.

"Since I'm such a sucker for a happy ending, why don't I take you to the boss and you can ask him about your friend yourself?" Stella's red-tipped fingers dug into Rachel's arm like claws.

"As soon as my boyfriend comes back, we'll do that."

Stella's smirk poured ice into Rachel's veins. "Oh, honey. He's not going to be coming back. The boss has other plans for him, although they're not as pleasant as what he has in store for you."

Rachel stepped back, running into a brick wall. Even if the oversize goon behind her hadn't had manacles for hands, there'd have been no way Rachel could outrun the gun Stella pulled from her purse.

* * *

Logan's skin itched with the need to bust into action, and Carson's two goons divesting him of his gun didn't dampen the desire one bit. He needed to ditch the assholes and get back to Rachel. Whatever the hell had been tipped into motion wouldn't end well if he didn't do something, and soon.

With one thug in front and one on his rear, Logan let himself be led into the casino's inner sanctum. Above his head florescent lights flickered ominously, giving everything, including the walls, a sickly ashen color. It was a new building, but the damn place could've been the backdrop for a horror movie.

"Have to tell you guys, I'm not impressed with your tour. I thought it would be more...lively," Logan quipped dryly.

"Probably a good thing for you that it's not." The goon in front pushed through an exit door.

Hot, humid Vegas air hit Logan in the face as they stepped into a darkened alley. Oblivious to their presence, a homeless man with his cart piled high with personal treasures trudged toward the main street. And on their right, pissing against the building, another man wobbled unsteadily on his feet.

"Hey, asshole. This isn't a fucking public bathroom,"

Goon One growled. "Take your limp dick and get the hell out of here."

The leather jacket–clad guy ignored the directive, taking his time zipping his pants.

Carson's thug pulled out his gun and stepped toward the wall pisser. "Hey, fuckhead. Didn't you hear me? *Get lost.*"

Less than an inch away from contact, the interloper's arms whipped out, reacting much too fast for someone who'd been slinging back a few drinks. Carson's goon folded like a pretzel, the stranger's fist meeting his nose with a sick crunch.

The thug stumbled into Logan on his way to the ground, giving Logan the chance to divest him of his gun. He pistol-whipped Carson's remaining goon, not stopping to watch him hit the ground before spinning back around.

Logan and the wall pisser aimed their guns at each other.

Fully prepared to do whatever it took to get back to Rachel, Logan tightened his fingers around the butt of the Glock. "You'd be doing us both a favor if you dropped the damn gun, turned around, and walked the hell away."

"Not until you do."

"That's not going to happen."

"Then that's going to be a problem," a second voice announced.

Sans shopping cart, the homeless man had sneaked up behind Logan, looking no longer homeless—or helpless—with a silver Magnum aimed at Logan's head.

He didn't need to be a mathematician to know his odds sucked ass. "I really don't care what your beef is with these guys. I'll leave you to hash it out with them. But I need to get back in that casino and I need to do it right the fuck now. Nothing against you nice gentlemen, but I'm prepared to do anything to make that happen."

The dark-haired wall pisser stepped closer, not missing the subtle change in Logan's grip. "Those are the words of a desperate man."

Fuck yeah he was desperate, more so with each damn second he remained in this damn alley.

Grinning, the stranger slowly lowered his gun. "Stone said there'd be no telling what you'd do if we didn't get our asses here quick. I guess he knows you pretty damn well, huh? You look a split second away from tearing Carson's casino to its foundation."

Carson.

Stone.

Everything clicked.

"You're the backup." Logan pocketed the thug's gun and searched the now-unconscious guy for the one that had been taken from him. Finding it, he slid it back into its holster. "You guys sure know how to make an entrance."

"Wasn't on purpose. We improvised when the three of you came bursting out that door." The nonhomeless man thrust out his hand. "Cade Wright. And the ugly bastard with the ability to pee on command is Knox Steele. I'm Washington, D.C. Special Crimes and he's... What the hell are you going by these days?"

"*Complicated,*" Steele answered with a faint smirk.

Logan cocked an eyebrow as he shook Wright's hand. "Well, speaking from one *complicated* guy to another, thank you. You guys are a long way from D.C., but I'm not complaining."

"Me either," Wright chuckled. "I no sooner told Steele tonight that I expected a little bit more action for the Mil-Tech convention being in Vegas, and voila...we got a call."

Steele threw his friend a challenging look. "I've offered you a life of action and head busting but you keep turning me the hell down."

Wright shook his head, obviously having heard this before. "It's not the right time, man."

"When the hell are you going to realize that she's not a little girl anymore?" Something unspoken shifted between the two friends.

"When I'm *dead.*"

Logan interrupted the little spat. "Not that I don't appreciate you guys being here, but I need to get to my lady before that fuckwad Carson puts his grimy hands on her."

"Sorry." Steele sent his buddy one final glare before turning back to Logan. "He's a stubborn jackass, has been since we were kids. We're here to help however we can. How do you want to go about this?"

Logan's cell rang from inside the first goon's pocket.

"They get there?" Charlie asked the second he pulled it free and answered.

"Cavalry's here. We're about to go inside and get Rachel."

"Do *not* make a move right now," Charlie warned.

Logan's hand froze on the exit door. "And what the hell is that supposed to mean?"

"It means I cracked through the surveillance cameras located around the casino and Rachel was escorted off the main floor by a small entourage."

"So where is she now?"

"I don't bloody know because the only feeds I've been able to find are those from the public areas of the hotel and casino. But I can tell you that she hasn't left the building. The only car traffic that's happened in the last half hour has been flowing *into* the lower-level parking garage."

"So if she's still inside, why am I not going back in there to get her?"

Charlie muttered a slew of British curses before speaking to him as though he were a toddler. "Because, *Logan*, they know what your ugly mug looks like. The second you step through those doors, they'll be on you before you can do a complete two-step."

"So what would you have us do, Charlie? I'm not leaving her in there to fend for herself." Logan's frustration was escalating by the second.

"I'm about to tell you, Callahan, so stifle it and listen before I put my boot through this phone and kick your bloody arse," Charlie threatened. "For a corrupt bastard, Carson has a pretty sophisticated security setup. It's practically impossible to dig my way through, but if I had a Hide-and-Seek it would be a different story."

"What the fuck's a Hide-and-Seek?"

"Our golden all-access ticket to everything Sinful Players, but you need to go see a friend of mine over at the convention hall. I'll text you his room number. You find Cache, tell him what you need and that it's for me, and he'll hook you up."

"And it'll help us find Rachel."

"As easy as a bloody Marauder's Map."

"Send me the info. I'm bringing Rachel home where she belongs."

"To Pennsylvania?"

"To *me*."

CHAPTER EIGHT

Rachel willed her heart to ease up on its vicious pounding, but she wasn't any more successful now than she had been when Carson's goons first shoved a sack over her head. It swirled as if stuck in a typhoon, unable to concentrate on the murmured voices surrounding her.

"Move, bitch." Something sharp poked her back. Her leg buckled, sending her crashing knees-first onto a hard floor. On her left a hand gripped the top of the hood—and her hair—and hauled her back to her feet.

Rachel swallowed a cry.

"Don't like it rough, hon?" Stella's smoke-addled voice taunted near her ear. "Maybe you shouldn't have stuck your nose where it didn't belong."

"Said like a woman who doesn't have any friends... which is so surprising considering you have such a sparkling personality," Rachel fired back.

Someone ripped away the hood, and with it a clump of Rachel's hair. She bit her lip to keep from crying out, refusing to make a sound as Stella pushed her face within an inch of hers. "And what did that friendship cost you, sweetheart? You were so busy worrying about that bitch friend of yours and now you're *both* in for a world of hurt."

Stella shoved Rachel into an open elevator. At this point her lungs usually seized, but now, without a hood over her eyes, she soaked in her surroundings and tried figuring out their location.

Oversize and cold, the elevator's wide walls and sparse interior identified its commercial use. Stumbling onto well-meaning tourists wouldn't be likely.

Rachel wiggled her hands, wincing as plastic ties bit into her wrists. She'd survived Honduras. She'd beaten the hell out of Fuentes and his drugs. She was well on her way to conquering the world of love and romance.

She could sure as hell beat this too—with or without being saved by Logan Callahan.

Stella's sharp nails dug into her arm as she yanked her from the elevator and into another corridor. "Let's go, princess."

Above their heads, pipes of different colors ran north and south, and the tiled floor gave way to cement. Eerie music spilled into the hall, slowing Rachel's steps until she received another rough shove.

"Don't look so worried. You're about to get what you've been asking for." Grinning, Stella swiped a badge in front of an electronic pad and pushed open an unmarked door.

A startling burst of colored strobe lights had Rachel blinking her eyes into focus. Bodies occupied the room, all in varying stages of dress—and undress—as they moved in some semblance of a dance. No one glanced their way as they entered, too busy partaking in the elaborate buffet of drugs laid out on a massive, bar-size cherry countertop.

White powder. Injectables. Pills.

Rachel's stomach twisted into a knot, but not from a desire to get her hands on any of it.

That amount of drugs could ruin a lot of people's lives.

Rachel immediately recognized Dean Carson. Sitting regally in a plush, high-backed chair, the dark-haired *businessman* looked like a king on his throne. An unconscious woman lay at his feet, her head of dark hair draped over his lap in a tangled mess.

"Am I supposed to believe that this little scrap of a thing is the one who's been making a nuisance of herself around my town?" Carson's cold black eyes tracked Rachel as Stella shoved her closer.

"One and the same." Stella sneered.

"For a former schoolteacher, you've proven to be very evasive, Miss Kline."

Rachel failed to mask her surprise.

"Did you think I didn't know all about you?" Carson asked, smugly. "I've heard every fantastical detail about your time with Carly in Honduras, about how you saved her, how you believed in her when she didn't believe in herself. But she never told me how *crafty* you were. You eluded my men for hours, literally dodged a bullet fired by one of the best assassins in the business. If I didn't know any better, I'd say you were less a guardian angel and more like a cat with nine lives."

"Maybe your men aren't as skilled as you think they are," Rachel quipped dryly, summoning Logan's nerve-induced wit.

A smile slithered onto Carson's face, turning Rachel's stomach. "I employ nothing but the best. I demand respect, loyalty, and obedience—all of which your friend lacked."

"There doesn't get anyone more loyal than Carlotta."

"I think you really believe that, because I'm not being overdramatic when I say that most people wouldn't risk their lives poking their noses into my business, no matter what—or who—was on the line."

"I'm not most people." Rachel glared, refusing to back down. "And I'm not leaving without her."

Carson's smile widened. "You may think differently when you realize the great disservice Carly did you by getting you involved. You see, she took something that didn't belong to her, and then she did a foolish thing by hiding it."

"Seems to me that if you want it that bad, it was smart of her to hide it from you."

"I can see why you and Carly befriended one another—both beautiful, both stubborn. But I haven't gotten to where I am today because I'm stupid. I know she told you where the flash drive is, and if you really are here to save your friend, you'll tell me where it is."

The woman propped against his leg groaned. Her hair obscured the majority of her face, all except one black-and-blue cheek and swollen-shut eye. Rachel didn't need to see the rest to recognize Carly.

"You bastard!" Rachel lurched forward and received a sharp yank on her hair, pulling her back straight into a severe stomach punch courtesy of one of Carson's goons. "What did you do to her?"

"I did what needed to be done when someone threatens me, and then thinks they can just up and leave." Carson entwined his hand in Carly's hair and stretched her neck to a harsh angle. Carly, barely conscious, whimpered. "She needed a little reminder that her life is *mine*. Now I know she won't forget it."

"Her life is *hers*," Rachel spit.

Chuckling, Carson stood. Carly spilled onto the ground. "You really shouldn't fill her head with silly notions that aren't true. Look at her. Does she look like a woman who's capable of standing on her own two feet?"

Held by two goons, Rachel stood helpless as Carson stalked toward her. Stopping a few inches away, he trailed a finger down her cheek, the sensation coating her throat with bile. "It's sad—one drug whore trying to give another false hope. *You can change. You control your life.* Bullshit. You know what controls your life?" Carson jerked her chin toward the table of drugs. "*That.* You may not be putting it into your body, but it still controls some part of you. And if I control the drugs, I control you."

Rachel couldn't deny it. Drugs didn't call to her anymore, but Honduras had changed her in a fundamental way, and for a damn long time. Dressing rooms made her break into a cold sweat, and bedroom windows remained open at all times, a chilly scenario during a Pennsylvania winter. And as Logan had pointed out earlier, fake smiles had become her talent.

Every single one of those quirks belonged to a *past* Rachel.

Riding a rush of determination, Rachel ripped her chin from Carson's hold, spitting in his face. "No. *I* control me. As a matter of fact, you couldn't be any less in control. You're right. I *did* have the flash drive, but I don't anymore. It's only a matter of time before hell rains down on you in the form of the entire Las Vegas Metropolitan Police Department—and that's the best-case scenario for you. Because God help you if my friends get to you first."

Pain exploded behind Rachel's eyes as his fist slammed into her jaw. A kaleidoscope of colors swept across her vision, but shadows crept close behind. Starting in the periphery, they slowly overtook everything until her world plummeted into darkness.

* * *

Logan, Knox, and Cade reached the Mil-Tech hotel in record time, and once they got to the venue, the two friends slipped away to their room to prep and grab a few toys.

At nearly five in the morning and packed up for the day, the convention center stood eerily empty. Logan followed Charlie's texted instructions and hightailed it to the central elevators to find room 1202. Once there, he rapped on the door, and after five seconds, he did it again.

"I didn't order room service," came a scratchy, nervous voice.

"Not room service." Logan leaned toward the small peephole, knowing someone watched him from the other side. "I'm looking for Cache. I'm a friend of Charlie."

"Charlie?"

"British pixie with a mostly-bad attitude and fondness for making grown men cry?"

The door opened as wide as the privacy lock allowed. A blue eye covered by thick-framed black glasses peered through the slit. "You forgot to mention ill-tempered."

"Figured that was lumped in with the bad attitude." Logan chuckled. He didn't want to scare the shit out of the kid, but this whole damn process needed to move ten times faster. "She sent me here to grab a Hide-and-Seek . . . said you were the person to hook me up."

The kid muttered something under his breath before slamming the door closed. A second later, it opened again, and a pale, spindly arm ushered Logan inside.

Cache—which Logan doubted was his real name—paced the room. "You're sure she said Hide-and-Seek? It's not exactly used for commercial purposes."

"I guess it's what she needs for *this* purpose. She said you owed her."

Cache sighed, pinching the bridge of his nose. "I knew that favor was going to come back and bite me on the ass. Hold on."

He rummaged through a black duffel before producing a quarter-sized metallic disk. He handed it to Logan, looking as if he wanted to change his mind and take it back.

"This is it?" Logan asked, unsure.

Cache nodded. "All you need to do is find a breaker box and attach this to both the black and red cables."

Logan waited for a more in-depth explanation. "Just pull and attach?"

"Unless you wanted to get electrocuted, first you'd shut down the box." Cache snorted, taking the Hide-and-Seek back and showing him the small hub on each side. "Once the power's off, you detach the red wire from its post, remove some of the protective sheath, and then wind it one full rotation around the HAS hub. Then you do the same with the black wire and attach it to the other side. Once everything's wound tight, you flick the power back on, and voila. Whoever has access to the HAS has access—and control—of all digital signatures that are linked—like alarms, electronic door locks. It's like a digital skeleton key."

"Huh. Isn't this a neat little toy." Logan stuffed the Hidey thing in his pocket. The move made Cache wince. "Any breaker box?"

"Any one."

"Thanks, man. I mean it." Logan turned to leave.

"Do I w-want to know what you're going to d-do with it?" Cache stuttered.

"Depends."

"On?"

"If you want plausible deniability."

"Oh, hell." Cache waved him off, suddenly looking eager to be rid of him. "Go. And tell Charlotte that we're finally even."

Logan nodded and made his way back to the lobby, where he met Knox and Cade, each with an oversize duffel slung over his shoulder. "We set?"

Steele patted his bag as if it were a newborn. "We have what we need and then some to make sure we get your girl back where she belongs."

"Good. Because I'm not accepting any other outcome."

CHAPTER NINE

Logan stood in the alley behind the casino, grinding his molars tighter with each passing second. Sending the D.C. cop to put the Hide-and-Seek in place played with his control issues, but getting spotted before they located Rachel wasn't a scenario that he could allow to happen.

No damn cowboy antics tonight, not with her life on the line.

"Everything's in place. We're ready to start seeking," Cade announced into Logan's ear via the comm-piece.

Logan waited by the exit door, one hand on the handle, ready to move the second he got the all clear. "Tell me you got a lock on it, Charlie."

"Give me ten seconds to make a feed loop and reroute it back through the casino's signal. That way, you'll be ghosts walking. They won't see you coming until they stumble on you face-to-face." Charlie's smooth, British determination calmed Logan the tiniest bit.

A grin lifted Knox Steele's mouth. "Giving them a fake video feed and a false sense of security. Impressive as hell, sweetheart."

"You're handsome *and* smart, so I'll forgive you for calling me sweetheart. How are you not already wearing a ball and chain, Steele?"

Knox chuckled. "How do you know I'm handsome— or not involved with someone?"

"Because Stone's incapable of having ugly friends, and the latter was a good hunch. Warning, though, even the hardest of asses eventually fall." A few seconds later, Charlie gave them the all clear. "You guys are good to go. I'll navigate you around the goon squad as best as I can, but you still have to keep alert for any surprises."

"I don't care if I have to decommission an entire army of Carson's men. I'm getting Rachel—and Carly—the hell out of here." Logan rushed through the back door with Knox on his heels. Cade met them at the first corridor. "Be our eyes, Char? Where to?"

"She's still not on camera," Charlie informed him, "but we didn't expect them to have visual proof that they're kidnapping innocent women. My best hunch is that they're going to be keeping her far away from the business as they can physically get."

"Sublevels." Knox nodded. "Places as big as this have them so they don't disturb the daily guests. Kind of like an underground little world. The question is, Which direction do we need to go?"

Charlie let out a triumphant shout. "North."

Logan walked, not even questioning her judgment.

Steele and Wright followed, and it was Wright who questioned. "Does someone want to explain to me exactly how we know to go north? I recall failing middle school geography, but I think there are three other directions."

Charlie's singsong voice hinted at the smart comment about to come. "Logan, did your new friend question my judgment?"

Logan chuckled. "He doesn't know you like I do, darlin'. Humor him."

She sighed. "Fine. Take all the fun out of this. I say north, Detective Wright, because I see a few hotel guests lingering where they shouldn't be, and them, along with a bevy of thick-necked goons escorting them, disappearing through the same lone door."

"And beyond the door?" Steele asked.

"Nothing. I'm blind. So let's use our deductive reasoning, boys. Shall we?"

Cade snorted a laugh. "Don't question the English lady—duly noted."

"That's what I tell Navy all the time, but trying to get it through his thick, bald head is like trying to squeeze a watermelon through a cheese grater."

Logan smirked, thankful for a little glimmer of humor in this fucked-up situation, because the closer they got to the north end of the building, the more security there was to avoid.

They played it carefully, Charlie instructing them as she watched the live—*real*—feed. Escorted by security, couples decked out in their finest evening wear disappeared behind an unmarked door. A minute or so later the guard would reemerge and leave the way he'd come, only to bring another couple.

People went in, but not many came out.

A muffled shriek turned Logan around to the sight of Knox Steele, one hand over the mouth of a busty bleach blonde and his other clutching a key card that looked a hell of a lot like the one the guards used to get into the mystery room.

Knox slapped the card into Logan's hand. "Look what I found sneaking around the corner. And she's practically giving us a personal invitation."

Logan recognized her immediately. Anger toward the woman who'd played a part in separating him and Rachel burned through his veins. "Stella, right? You've missed your jail cell at LVMPD so much that you committed a kidnapping to get back there? Let's get you topside and hand you over to your friends in tan. And this time, they won't be so eager to let you out of their sight."

She struggled in Knox's hold, her muffled rambling difficult to translate. Logan nodded to the security operative to carefully relinquish his hold on her mouth. "What was that?"

"What the hell is wrong with you people?" Stella hissed. "It's like none of you have any damn sense of self-preservation. First the brunette, now the damn redhead. You'll never get through that door without being detected. The second you stride in without an escort, they'll shoot you."

Logan stroked his chin. "Then I guess we need an escort."

His meaning registered and her eyes widened. "Your little girlfriend has been a thorn in my side ever since she strutted into my damn house. No way in hell am I risking my ass for hers. I'm not the self-sacrificing type."

"You help us, and I'll make sure our police friends know it. Maybe helping us shut down Carson will put you in their good graces."

Stella glowered, but contemplated silently before rolling her eyes. "Whatever. I'll do it, but I hope that bitch is worth it. Because if Carson doesn't shoot you, the hired gun he has on retainer will."

"That *woman* is worth everything." And a hell of a lot more.

Logan wasn't looking a gift horse in the mouth. For some reason Rachel had given him a chance, and he wasn't letting it slip by without grabbing it—and her—with both hands.

And his heart.

All the drama and hurt in his life had been nothing compared to the idea of losing her. He wasn't letting that happen.

"You sure about this, man?" Wright asked, his concern evident. "You'd basically be going in there blind."

"As sure as I am about anything." Logan licked his palm and slicked his hair back away from his face in his best sleazeball impression and then slid his gun into the band of his pants.

They couldn't storm into the room, guns blazing.

They didn't know the layout or the number of civilians present. And hell, half Carson's goon squad could be stationed just on the other side of the door. An all-out breach wasn't smart, so they had to opt for the complete opposite: quiet and unobtrusive.

It went against every fiber of Logan's being, but he needed to bring down Carson, ensure Rachel and Carly's safety, and avoid getting his ass shot in the process. If he stormed the room like a commando, one if not more of those things would be compromised, and he wasn't willing to risk its being Rachel's safety.

"Here. Put these on." Wright tossed him a thick pair of black-framed glasses. "If they work for Clark Kent…"

"Later, you're going to have to explain to me why you have a pair of glasses in your pocket." Logan chuckled and slipped on the frames before taking Stella's arm from Steele. "You make one wrong move in there, twitch, or grimace, and I can guaran-damn-tee that God himself won't be able to help you."

"This is your funeral, buddy. You better not make it mine too," Stella grumbled, buzzing them through the door.

The phrase "drug den" didn't come close to describing the level of debauchery in the room. Naked bodies swayed to the pounding music. Those not dancing had taken entertaining to an entirely different level. One woman, head thrown back in pleasure, lay sprawled naked on a table as people snorted white powder off her body.

The thought of Rachel's being subjected to any of this shit made Logan see red.

"Where would Rachel be?"

"My guess would be with the boss, and if that's the case, then she's already fucked up."

"*Where's* your boss?" Logan growled.

Stella tipped her chin toward the far corner.

Logan located Dean Carson immediately, deep in conversation with the eerily silent man from the chapel. His gaze shifted to the ratty mattress pushed against the far wall. One woman, her hands bound and chin dropped to her chest, hovered over an unconscious brunette—*Rachel and Carly*.

Nausea gripped Logan's stomach like a damn fist.

"Charlie," he murmured into his comm, "you need to get LVMPD here like you did me—ASAP. And make sure paramedics are joining the party."

Charlie sucked in a breath. "Bloody hell. Rachel or Carly?"

"Rachel's sitting upright for now, but from a distance Carly's doesn't look too good."

"All right. I'm on it."

Charlie immediately started coordinating a bigger strike than Logan could do alone or with the help of his new D.C. friends. There were too many unknown factors. Too many ways for everything to go straight to hell. And as much as he wanted Rachel safe and in his arms, he wouldn't risk her life by going off half-cocked.

But God help anyone who got in his way.

* * *

Rachel didn't move, afraid too much jostling would worsen Carly's injuries. Cradling her friend's head in her lap, she counted each shallow breath and watched the time increase in between chest rise and falls.

Carly had been through a lot. Her left cheekbone, blackened and asymmetrical, was probably broken if not shattered entirely. The eye on that same side was puffy and swollen shut. One arm, cradled against her chest, hung slightly lower than the other, and with every faint move, Carly moaned.

Rachel pushed a strand of hair off her friend's cheek and brushed a kiss over her cool forehead. "I'm so sorry, Carly. I'm going to get you out of here. I don't know how, but I am. And then you're coming back to Pennsylvania with me."

"Ra-Rach." Carly groaned, sucking in a sharp breath.

"Sh. Don't try and talk if it hurts." Her gaze skidded over to the drug buffet, and even though it killed her to ask, she did. "Carly, have you...Did he—"

"No," Carly whispered. "No drugs. Just...b-beat me to hell. Did y-you g-get it?"

Rachel smiled wanly. "Yeah, we got it. Don't worry. Soon he's not going to be able to hurt you or anyone else again."

Carson's familiar growl pulled Rachel's attention across the room to where the bastard spoke in hushed tones to the two men Rachel recognized from the Elvis chapel. None of the three men looked happy, which meant things might be looking up for Rachel and Carly.

"Darlin'," a familiar voice drawled.

Rachel's head snapped to her left. Sitting in a plush chair, legs crossed and looking completely at ease, was a sexily nerdy Logan. She rubbed her eyes, thinking she'd somehow dreamed him up while still awake.

"Are you okay?" Logan murmured, his gray eyes crashing into hers. Worry lines wrinkled his face as he looked to Carly and back up to her. "Carly?"

"I'm fine, but Carly..." Rachel swallowed down the emotion. "I don't know what he did to her before I got here, but she's not in good shape. Her breathing's getting really shallow."

Logan scanned their surroundings. "We're getting some reinforcements in place, and once everything's set to go, we're shutting this the hell down and getting you and Carly medical attention."

A commotion broke out across the room. A door burst open, and smoke spilled into the room as people shouted and scrambled in all directions. Armed figures stormed inside, barking orders and fanning out.

Cops.

Backup.

"Let's go." Fingers bit into Rachel's shoulder, making her cry out and release her hold on Carly.

Carson was dragging her toward a second exit when a small explosion erupted. More smoke filled the room, accompanied by a series of harsh flashes of light. Rachel coughed, unable to see Logan through the haze. Carson resumed hauling her backward. She dug her feet into the concrete, trying to slow him down as she screamed Logan's name.

Carson pushed a gun to her head. "Scream one more time and it'll be the last thing you do, bitch. Now move your fucking feet."

Rachel hesitantly obeyed, realizing that he was leading them to another service elevator. It lurched into movement, going up and up. The doors slid open, and he dragged her onto an open rooftop.

The sun momentarily blinded her. She blinked against the harsh rays, taken off guard by the wall of heat slamming down on them. The last time she'd been outside, it had been full dark. The city below them was uncharacteristically quiet—except for the steady roar of the black chopper hovering a few dozen feet above the rooftop.

"Looks like our ride's already here," Carson gloated.

"You're not going to get away with this. It's already over, Carson. The cops are on to all your sordid little backhanded deals."

"I don't need to get away with it. I just need to get away. Your boyfriend's a little preoccupied downstairs and will be until after we're long gone. He didn't come for you. He's—"

"Right the fuck here, asshole." Logan's voice sounded like music to Rachel's ears.

Carson spun them around, and there stood Logan. Two armed men Rachel didn't recognize flanked him— and all had guns aimed in their direction.

"Take a step closer to the helo or clutch that gun any tighter and you're going to get a firsthand demonstration of how not distracted I am," Logan threatened, his voice low.

With his eyes trained on the man holding her hostage, Rachel had never seen Logan look so deadly, as if he wanted the other man to move so he could fire off a shot.

"Goddamn hero types." Carson burrowed his gun deeper against Rachel's temple. "You move, Captain America, and your girlfriend's brains get splattered all over the damn rooftop. I don't care who the hell you think you are, you aren't faster than a bullet."

"If anyone's brains are getting splattered, it's yours."

"You think I don't know how to use this gun?" Carson screamed. Spittle flew out in all directions. Eyes wild and frantic, the man who'd earlier tried baiting her with his eerie calm disappeared, replaced by someone a lot more unhinged.

"No. I know that my reflexes are a hell of a lot faster than yours. Seriously, Carson, there's no place for you to go. You think the cops flooding the place are here for a damn stroll? You're *done*—along with anyone who's ever dirtied themselves by getting into bed with you. If you don't come along quietly, how long do you give it before one of your business associates considers you a liability? Because my guess is that it's not going to take long."

Behind her, Carson's body tensed. The gun against Rachel's head shifted. Rachel didn't think. Summoning the countless hours spent watching Logan and the others train, she twisted and dropped to the ground. A crisp series of pops followed, and suddenly she wasn't alone on the ground.

Carson dropped beside her, blood blossoming on his arm and knee.

His gun lay only inches away, forgotten as he howled in pain. Rachel picked it up, gripping it with shaky hands as she tried lifting it toward the bastard who'd hurt her friend.

"Darlin'." Logan's voice barely shimmied its way into the rush of images flashing through her head. Hands raised, he stalked toward her with determined steps. "Sweetheart, you need to give me that gun."

"He hurt her, Logan." Tears streamed down Rachel's cheeks, dripping off her chin and onto the ground. "She found out who he was and she tried leaving him... and then he hurt her so that she couldn't. Who does that to another person?"

"A really bad one." Logan reached her and dropped down to his haunches. His hand settled over hers, lowering the gun and expertly sliding it out of her tingling hands. With his other he cupped her cheek and tipped her eyes up to his. "But he's not going to hurt anyone else ever again. I promise."

"And Carly..."

"Paramedics are with her and already doing their magic."

Logan pulled her into his lap at the first soft sob. She clutched the front of his shirt until her fingers ached. By the time the sobs finally dissipated, his shirt was soaked through, and another set of paramedics had arrived for a still-howling Carson.

"I'm one big, hot mess," Rachel hiccupped.

"Yeah, but you're a damn sexy hot mess," Logan teased, brushing her hair back. "And you're *my* hot mess."

Rachel's throat went dry as she prayed he meant

it and feared that he did at the same time. Lowering his head, Logan brushed a ghost of a kiss over her lips. "Baby, we've both got a handful of issues to work through, but the nice part in this entire fucked-up situation is that we don't have to do it alone anymore. We'll help each other heal. That's what you do for me, Rachel Kline. You mend things inside me that I didn't even know were broken."

Rachel wrapped her arms around his neck, pulling him closer. "I feel the same way. I'm done running away from everything, Logan. Now I'm running *toward* it...toward *you*."

Logan grinned. "I like the sound of where this is going. Tell me you love me as much as I love you and there's no getting rid of me."

"Good—because I *do* love you. And I can't wait to see where this goes."

"I already know." Logan dropped a kiss onto her nose.

"Care to share it with me?"

"Eventually."

EPILOGUE

Las Vegas, Nevada
Fools Rush In Chapel
Six months later

Prehistoric butterflies danced an Irish jig in Rachel's stomach, and had since she'd woken up that morning. Any concern over being back in Sin City for the first time since the ordeal with Carson had quickly vanished as a new flurry of concerns swooped in.

"No! Stop! *Don't put that in your mouth!* Violet Mae, put that down *right now*!" A shrill, childish giggle immediately followed Elle's soft scolding.

Behind Rachel a swatch of pink toddled as fast as her little legs would carry her, white rose petals clenched in her fist. Elle scooped up her daughter, barely managing to pry the flowers from her hand before she tried eating them again.

"And here I thought breastfeeding was a key component to getting back to prepregnancy weight, when in reality all I needed to do was give birth to Trey's little spawn," Elle joked, tickling the one-year-old's stomach. The room filled with childish squeals, making them all laugh.

Penny rubbed her swollen belly, looking every bit eight months pregnant. "I'd volunteer to birth an entire horde of little Ortegas if it meant seeing my feet again. Or hell, putting on my shoes without using one of those long-stick shoe horns would be fantastic."

Charlie tossed Penny her hand-wrapped bouquet of white and yellow daisies and winked. "You're already scheduled for an eviction, so stop being so dramatic."

"Says the woman who disappears when she turns sideways—and it's called an induction, not an eviction."

"So you're kicking that little person out with drugs instead of a note on the door. Same diff." The pink-haired operative slid Rachel a small smirk. "You look absolutely gorgeous, love. Logan's going to lose his marbles when he sees you walking down the aisle."

"Everyone ready? We need to get this show on the road." A familiar gasp made Rachel smile. "Oh. My. Heavens."

Rachel turned toward the older woman she now called friend and twirled. "What do you think, Edith? Is Charlie right? Is Logan going to lose his marbles?"

She clapped her hands. "He's going to lose something, honey, that's for sure. You couldn't look more beautiful even if I dressed you myself."

Charlie mumbled something under her breath about

a go-go wedding dress and Penny elbowed her in the side, shutting her up. The operative chuckled and everyone grabbed their bouquets.

Ever since Logan had proposed, a second into the New Year, Rachel had known exactly where they needed to say their I-dos. Luckily, Earl and Edith had been eagerly up for it. The older couple had gone all out. Elvis still occupied every nook and crevice of the small chapel, but the girls had helped place the flowers. Even the life-size Elvis mannequin held a bouquet of gerbera daisies and wore a black suit jacket instead of his sequined jumper.

Rachel shot a quick glance around the back room. "Aren't we missing someone?"

"Here! I'm here!" Carly sprinted down the hall as if she weren't wearing heels, skidding to a stop. "Sorry I'm late. I got—"

"Roughed up by a chicken?" Charlie teased, plucking a pink feather from Carly's slightly unkempt hair. "You may want to fix the lips, love. And if you have your cell phone on you, I suggest you tell ol' lover boy Chase he may want to make use of his handkerchief."

"I don't know what you're talking about," Carly said innocently before not-so-discreetly firing off a text.

Edith hustled through the gilded curtain, and while she barked orders, getting everyone into position, Stone stepped through the canopy.

The Alpha leader looked at a loss for words as he pulled her into a gentle hug. "You're breathtaking, Rachel. Logan's a damn lucky man."

She squeezed him back. "I think I'm the lucky one."

From around Stone's broad shoulders, the girls lifted their eyebrows. Ever since she'd returned from Vegas months ago, there'd been something different about the usually broody Alpha head, and bets had been laid down from a secret love to divine intervention.

Stone offered Rachel his uninjured arm. "We should probably move this along. Your guy's about to crawl out of his skin out there—in a good way."

The music began, summoning the procession. Elle stepped through first, gently nudging her daughter in front of her and coaxing her into tossing the flower petals. Carly came next, tears in her eyes as she kissed Rachel on the cheek before following. And then Penny and Charlie, the maid and matron of honor.

"You're up next, Charlie." Rachel dropped her gaze to the new addition to the operative's jewelry collection, a gorgeous sapphire ring that she now wore on her left hand.

"But at least I put up a good fight...unlike some of you girls, who fell at the drop of a crooked smirk. It's embarrassing. I'm the only one with any kind of self-control," Charlie teased, squeezing her hand before disappearing.

Rachel held her breath as the music changed, signaling Stone to guide her through the gold curtain. She found Logan instantly. Standing beneath a music-note archway with Earl at the ready, he watched her slowly walk the aisle. As she reached the halfway point, he left his position and eased her out of Stone's arms with a slow kiss.

Rachel giggled as their friends whistled and cat-called. Little Violet, not knowing what was happening, clapped enthusiastically.

"You're supposed to wait until I get to the altar, and I'm pretty sure we have to recite a few vows before you kiss the bride," Rachel teased.

"Darlin', we waited long enough for this. I'm not waiting a second longer than I have to." With a mischievous smirk, Logan swept her legs out from beneath her, giving his boss a wink. "Thanks for giving the bride away, man."

Stone chuckled. "My pleasure."

Logan hustled back to the altar before putting her back on her feet. "Sorry about that, Earl. I'm just anxious to make this beautiful lady mine before she comes to her senses and changes her mind."

"Not going to happen, cowboy." Rachel looked up into Logan's smiling face.

"Why? Because you know I'll keep bringing you back?"

"No, because I'm already yours. This is only a formality."

As Logan cupped her cheek, the usually tough Texan peered down at her with glittering gray eyes. "And I'm already yours, darlin'. Forever and always."

Acknowledgments

Authors may start off writing for themselves, but it very quickly changes and becomes about the readers. We couldn't do what we love if it weren't for your loyal support and eagerness to fall in love time and time again. So if you read for personal enjoyment, or to share your love of romance with the world via your blog, thank you so much for taking the time to fall into our worlds.

My family never ceases to amaze me, always laying the foundation of support, and never once complaining about those weeks in which we order pizza one more time than is considered 'healthy.'

To Madeleine Colavita, and the entire Forever team. You're incredible to work with and I'll be forever grateful to you for helping me bring men like Logan into the world.

My agent, Sarah E. Younger, your unwavering support and solidarity has no boundaries, and I'm so incredibly grateful that you chose me from your inbox all those years ago. There aren't enough words to describe how incredible you are.

To my #girlswritenight crew, Tif, Annie, Sidney, and Rachel. You know how to give a good pants-kicking, and I don't know how I'd ever write or plot a book without you.

And to my Alpha Security heroes and heroines—you jumped into my head and demanded to be heard, and I've loved every single second of this wild ride.

About the Author

April Hunt blames her incurable chocolate addiction on growing up in rural Pennsylvania, way too close to America's chocolate capital, Hershey. She now lives in Virginia with her college sweetheart husband, two young children, and a cat who thinks she's a human-dog hybrid. On those rare occasions she's not donning the cape of her children's personal chauffeur, April's either planning, plotting, or writing about her next alpha hero and the woman he never knew he needed, but now can't live without.

You can learn more at:
   AprilHuntBooks.com
   Twitter @AprilHuntBooks
   Facebook.com/AprilHuntBooks

DON'T MISS A MOMENT OF HEART-STOPPING SUSPENSE WITH APRIL HUNT'S ALPHA SECURITY SERIES!

THE ALPHA SECURITY SERIES

Looking for more romantic suspense?

LETHAL REDEMPTION
by April Hunt

Top FBI profiler Grace Steele was just a girl when she escaped the Order of the New Dawn, and she swore never to return. But when Steele Ops needs her help extracting a young woman from the secretive cult's clutches, she's all in...even though the mission requires posing as an engaged couple with the man who broke her heart nine years ago. Includes a bonus novel by Piper J. Drake!

FOREVER STRONG
by Piper J. Drake

Ying Yue Jiang believed her kidnapping was a case of wrong place, wrong time, but she soon realizes that she has become a pawn in a dangerous game. When the handsome and mysterious Azubuike Anyanwu is hired to protect her, he discovers a traitor in her father's organization. As both tensions and attractions grow more intense, Ying Yue and Azubuike will have to test their allegiances and trust in each other in order to stay alive.

Discover bonus content and more on read-forever.com.

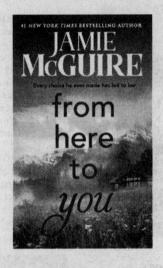

FROM HERE TO YOU
by Jamie McGuire

When Darby Dixon learns that she is pregnant on the morning of her wedding, she realizes that marrying her abusive fiancé would be the worst decision of her life, so she flees to the small town of Colorado Springs...and into the arms of Marine Scott "Trex" Trexler. Trex knows Darby is the woman he's been waiting for his whole life, so when her ex starts making threats, he'll do anything it takes to protect her and her unborn child.

TWISTED TRUTHS
by Rebecca Zanetti

Noni Yuka is desperate. Her infant niece has been kidnapped, and the only person who can save her is the private detective who once broke her heart. "A pure adrenaline rush."–*RT Book Reviews*

DON'T BREATHE A WORD
by Christie Craig

When special agent Juan Acosta meets his gorgeous neighbor, he knows she's hiding something. As he gets closer to the mysterious woman and her daughter, his investigation uncovers dark secrets that will put them all in danger. Includes a bonus story by April Hunt!